Camouflage

Camouflage

A Novel

C. C. Avram

Writers Club Press
San Jose New York Lincoln Shanghai

Camouflage

All Rights Reserved © 2000 by C. C. Avram

No part of this book may be reproduced or transmitted in any form or by any means, graphic, electronic, or mechanical, including photocopying, recording, taping, or by any information storage or retrieval system, without the permission in writing from the publisher.

Published by Writers Club Press
an imprint of iUniverse.com, Inc.

For information address:
iUniverse.com, Inc.
620 North 48th Street
Suite 201
Lincoln, NE 68504-3467
www.iuniverse.com

ISBN: 0-595-00523-3

Printed in the United States of America

Acknowledgements

To all the inspirational people in my life who have knowingly and unknowingly contributed to Camouflage—thank you. Special and grateful acknowledgement is made to my son and to MVP for their never-ending encouragement and support; to ita Anderson for understanding my vision and translating it into a wonderful work of art and to Janis Holmberg for her editorial contribution.

Camouflage

Chapter One

July 1999, NEW YORK, 65th Street at Central Park

Her eyes flew open, possibly from a sudden noise or a dream, but she knew it was neither. Wide awake and unable to go back to sleep, the young woman lay motionless for a few minutes before swinging her legs over the side of the bed.

"Oh, bloody hell!" she muttered, looking regretfully at the clock. It was only 5:00 a.m. Staring into the darkness she felt panicked, and moment by moment the feeling of dread grew more intense. It was an unwavering feeling, a dark, foreboding omen. An urgent call to action in her psyche. She was convinced—no, she was certain that something was wrong.

Switching on the bedside lamp, Helen Stern rummaged through the side table, retrieving a black leotard. Abandoning her nightshirt, she pulled the spandex, in one deft movement, over her hips. Padding to the bathroom, she splashed water over her face, brushed her teeth, hooked a terrycloth robe around her neck, laced her sneakers and headed to the kitchen to fill her squeezy bottle with iced water. "*Damn,*" she cursed under her breath as though the walls could hear. "*I can't take much excitement this morning.*" Flipping the switch on the electric treadmill, Helen pressed the speed dial until she was running at full speed. Forty-five minutes later, dripping wet but somewhat calmed, she was ready to take her shower. Under the steady stream of the hot water more of the dreaded feeling was washing away.

Used to rigorous emotional control, Helen had already steeled herself against the inevitable, so by the time she was striding down East Sixty-Fifth, she was resigned to facing any disaster head on. Helen Stern always projected an image of confidence and success and today was no exception. Fashionably dressed in a chocolate brown mid-calf skirt and matching Safari jacket, her tiny waist was cinched with a yellow crocodile belt. Around her shoulder a brown and tan silk scarf flapped in the gentle breeze. Matching T-strapped shoes and a bag slung diagonally across her torso completed the attire. Helen moved quickly and purposefully through the crowd. Her mind kept intruding on her morning walk. *Maybe I should turn back and wait.* Yet, as she deliberated she found herself hastening her pace to the office. What good would being cloistered away from bad news do? Sooner or later it would catch up with her. And indeed, with a gazillion projects to do before her final demarche, Helen Stern could afford to waste no time.

Raising her eyes to the gods as though to receive approval, protection, and the strength too see her clandestine plan through, Helen instead saw, with a new clarity, the mammoth Jacobson Industries building gleaming into the Manhattan skyline. *My final triumph,* she sighed. If there was any pleasure to be derived from this uncertain period of her life, a period plagued by a state of internal chaos, this glass building, climbing sixty-five stories into the sky, was it. The very edifice would soon catapult her to unprecedented fame. It was a thought that pleased her very much and calmed the tsunami that had been rising in her.

"Charlie, Charlie. Stop, this minute. Now!" A frantic voice was screaming, and immediately Helen came to a standstill. Turning in the direction of the turmoil, she saw a little boy heading at full speed toward her, chasing a ball bouncing into the busy street. Instinctively she jumped in front of the tyke as he ran head-on into her long legs.

Bending down, she hoisted the two-year-old before he could slip away and found herself squeezing him dearly to her chest.

"My ball, my ball," the kid squirmed, trying to wiggle out of her hold.

"Oh, thank you. Thank you so much." A young, slightly chubby mother, now out of breath lunged forward to retrieve her son. "I should have been watching more carefully. Thanks again, Miss…"

"Stern." Helen offered, reluctantly handing over the little boy. *You should better protect your child.*

"What's his name?" Helen stared at the kid suppressing her rising emotions. *A mother's duty is to protect her child. A mother's duty is to protect her child.* The mantra chimed in her mind.

"Charlie. And he is very hyperactive. Thank the lovely lady, Charlie," the mother admonished lovingly as the child tried to hide his face against her shoulder. Tenderly the woman kissed the top of her son's head, and Charlie looked up, a broad smile on his face.

"Tah you," the tyke said shyly, clutching his mom's hand as she put him down onto the sidewalk. Helen watched as mother and son retreated, relief and joy spreading over their faces. *Oh, she lamented, I should have had a mother to protect me. I should have experienced the gaiety of childhood. I should have been loved.* A deep cloud was quickly descending on her and Helen hurriedly turned away from the disturbing memories, hastening her way to the office.

For the rest of her morning walk, Helen was unusually affected by ordinary events of life. Mothers taking their children to bus stops, joggers running their faithful dogs, and lovers kissing good-bye at crosswalks all seemed to burn a sense of loss into her consciousness. Even the homeless, wrapped in dirty clothes, ensconced in their sidewalk homes engaged her mind. "To be so lucky," she sighed, dropping a twenty-dollar bill into a cup on the sidewalk.

"God bless you, Miss," mumbled a dirty head poking out from under a tattered blanket. "Life sure is hard today ma'am, but it's worth living, ain't it ma'am, as long as there's hope."

Hope! Incredible! How could a home on the sidewalk of New York leave anyone with hope? As hideous as his life looked, even the homeless man seemed more peaceful and content than she had ever been. At least, he was able to sleep soundly on his concrete bed while she, soon to be Mistress of the Jacobson Empire with everything to live for, was restless, unsettled, and hopeless.

"Was it wise to halt her plans before there was no turning back?" Helen's mind questioned, but something deep in her soul would not let her. She wanted, no! she *needed* this victory. *Please,* her rational self kept arguing, *isn't it time to ride off into the sunset and leave the past behind, where it belongs? No! Her irrational self answered that there is no future without a past.* Try as she did, Helen's mind kept drifting to the one man, who after so many years of carefully orchestrating the demise of her mother, was causing her to doubt her motives. *Why damn you? Why now when I'm so close?* In all the years of consciously encasing her heart in ice, no one had penetrated its cold exterior. Now here he was, chiseling away, chipping bit by bit at her anchor of hate, and in the process warming the cockles of her soul, rapidly thawing the ice that had encased her heart for so many years. If only she weren't so jaded. If only she could believe in love and the goodness of the human spirit. If only she weren't so scared of being heartlessly abandoned again, maybe....*Stop it, Damn it!* Helen ordered her mind. *Why bother. People always disappoint.* But there was no stopping the flood of memories detailing their incredible night together.

As their bodies had united, expanding between the contradiction of the lightness and darkness of passion, every fiber, every muscle, every nerve of her being had been consumed. Responding to the uncontrollable, unbearable desire, momentarily Helen had forgotten the past. The pain…

"Don't ever leave me," Helen had murmured, her eyes pleading.

"I'll never leave you. Never! I love you, Helen," he'd whispered, concerned by the bewildered look in her eyes.

He loves me. He loves me. Her mind had screamed as the words resonated in her brain. Warm, comforting words that had spun a cocoon around her numb heart, caressing and exciting her with each echo.

Looking back, even to this day, Helen still blamed the tasty Irish coffee and the brandy they had been drinking for her impaired judgment. Regardless, never did she regret, for a moment, their togetherness, except perhaps the realization that they could never be together because she couldn't let go of the past.

"Are you nuts, lady?" A taxi screeched to a halt and Helen jumped backwards at the sound of the blaring horn, landing safely on the sidewalk, her reverie interrupted by the commotion of car after car squealing to an abrupt stop. "You have a death wish or something? You crazy *chica*. *Stupida*. You coulda cause a bad accident." The taxi driver pointed at her angrily. "*Vaya*. Go on now." He waved her across the street. As he wound up his window, he was still pointing and shaking his head, lapsing into his native language.

"Thank you," she mouthed hurriedly crossing the street.

"Christ! What on earth the matter with you, lass?" she remonstrated loudly. "Bloody daydreaming again." But worse than the trip down memory lane was that she had no idea how long she'd been lost in thought.

Entering her office, Helen threw her bag inside a cabinet, composed herself, made coffee, and shuffled through the papers on the massive oak desk. Restless and still perturbed over her premonition, her near death escape, and general malaise, she rose to look out the window. Pressing her face firmly against the window, she peered down onto the busy street below. From her fiftieth-floor office, the people bustling around looked like ants.

Suddenly her mind began racing—again. As a child, daydreaming was her only friend. Today, she treated her alto ego with much respect. Many people thought it was a schizophrenic habit, but she didn't give a damn. She and her muse had made it this far and she hadn't hacked anyone to death…yet. "Well hi there," Helen welcomed her intrusive mind. For some reason, she always felt obliged to answer any questions her muse posed, no matter how ridiculous. They had often had dragged down, brawling disagreements.

"*You know, Helen. You're insatiable. Happiness, huh? You want happiness. What is it really? Shouldn't you be happy watching the sunrise, observing the bustle of Manhattan, sipping that delectable cup of coffee in your hand, being at the top of your game? What else do you want from this illusion called life?*" "How about some more happiness?" her mind answered, "and some peace. What about peace, eh? I need some peace."

Tears, for the second time that morning, welled in Helen's eyes as she realized how alone and unhappy she had been most of her life. Had she purposely chosen a life of loneliness because she wouldn't forgive, or was she lonely because she hadn't been loved? Helen knew the answer. It was her obsession with vindication and retribution that had caused her loneliness. *You haven't always been lonely. You were happy once*, she thought as the tears fell. She and Maya had been happier than happy. They had shared great times together. Today she would give anything to be back in the cozy kitchen in Hampstead, but alas....Helen shifted her position from the window to the silk sofa near the floor–to–ceiling glass wall. If only she could sink into its softness and bury herself away from this turmoil that kept rearing its ugly head. Hampstead! The thought cemented. She could always go home. Indeed, she could go home, and that's just what she would do.

Suddenly with that resolve, Helen perked up and was ready to face the morn. At that very moment she walked over to the phone to book a flight home. Back to the cozy kitchen in Hampstead and to Maya. Now that her plans were near completion, it was time to make peace with Maya. Before she could move, a pealing and persistently ringing phone spurred Helen into action. By the time she registered that it was ringing on her desk, it had already chimed four times. She sprang forward to grab the line.

"Hello. Hello," she heard the click as she picked up. "Ah hell…" Helen banged the desk and then the phone back into its cradle. She hated the stupid nostalgia that had caused her to miss the call. *What a bunch of hogwash her mind was conjuring up. Maya was no better than her mother was. There was no home to go to and she should get used to that. Her longing had been nothing more than a case of cold feet at her impending triumph. Even brain damage from overwork would be an acceptable explanation. Better yet, an acute attack of PMS would do fine, but loneliness….naah.* Helen felt her body go cold as another explanation seeped into her consciousness. Could she be experiencing the duality of good and evil? Maya had always warned her that evil could overtake good in a moment of anger. *Evil! Helen spat.* No way would she buy that. Evil was far different from retribution, and this silent war she waged against Andrea Jacobson-Preston was definitely one of retribution. "Yes, yes, yes," she stomped her feet angrily. "*Retribution is my right and I want it. What mother has done to me is loathsome, monstrous, appalling and cowardly. I will triumph and I deserve it.* In less than a week she, Helen Stern would…

The phone summoned her attention again. This time she grabbed it on the second ring.

"Oh no, no, no, no. Please no!" she wailed at the caller.

Chapter Two

The Hamptons, Long Island Nineteen Years Earlier

Not much fanfare had accompanied Helen's arrival to New York except, perhaps, that she was almost run over by a car. It seemed, from that day forward, young Stern was to retain a penchant for moving vehicles! A visit to Andrea's Central Park apartment, the last address Helen had for her mother, yielded a stern, "Mrs. Preston rarely stays here anymore." A hefty bribe and a heart-stopping smile to the liveried doorman got Helen the information she needed. Stepping into the street, expecting the cars to stop for pedestrians as they often did in England, Helen soon found out how dangerous such habits could be. Mimicking fellow cab seekers, she backed up to the sidewalk waving a slender arm around foolishly until a yellow cab lurched to a stop. Another wad of dollars got her to the Hamptons.

Looking through the rear window as the car sped away, the New York skyline, though impressive, left her cold. It was far too new a city for her taste. Glass buildings. Huge skyscrapers. Littered sidewalks. Not her style. She preferred the thousand-year-old stone buildings etched with history that were prevalent in her own homeland. The buzz of the venerable city, however, was undeniable, a lot like London and to a great extent more enticing.

"It has to be the next house," the driver informed Helen an hour or so later, as he approached a massive gated property. "The house we just passed was 664.

"Then let me out here," Helen instructed, giving the driver a generous tip. Hoisting her duffel bag over her shoulder, she walked the short distance to 666 Baldwin Street, Preston Estates—a property spanning an entire block. How appropriate, Helen mused, that Andrea Jacobson's house number was the alleged mark of the devil. Strolling casually past the tall wrought-iron gates, she observed a uniformed chauffeur waiting patiently for a tall, elegant man who was walking briskly toward him. The two exchanged dutiful greetings as the handsome chap slid into the rear of a Rolls Royce. Moments later the heavy iron gates silently opened, and the Silver Shadow glided down the driveway. Before the gates closed, Helen slipped inside and hid behind a large elm tree.

A wide cobblestone driveway wound itself up to a front door that could hardly be seen from where she stood. On either side of the walkway, gas lamps that lit the path at night still glowed. Helen waited until she was sure no one was approaching before creeping quietly to the back of the house. An Olympic-sized swimming pool, cobble-stoned inlaid, was girdled by thick shrubbery that created a natural fence for the pool. Dancing clovers and buttercups overhung the blue water as they dipped and twirled to the music of the wind. A well-tended rose-garden, hedges and garlands stretched as far as the eyes could see and offered a respite for the overburdened mind. Helen nestled into the tree swing, spiraling higher and higher into the air with each effort. She felt an eerie kind of peace and was immediately transported to the childhood memory of belonging to a happy home, the one she'd dreamed of night after night. Lingering on the wooden swing, dangling from the now bare apple tree, Helen lost track of time. It was in a beautiful garden not unlike this very garden that Andrea had betrayed her. Hurriedly she jumped down from the swing and made her way back to the pool area. The pain had surfaced with a vengeance.

To the right of the house was a five-car garage. Two of them were open, boasting very chic, expensive cars. Helen tried to imagine what extravagance lay behind the doors that were closed. Why would a family have five cars? She supposed all the servants had their own luxury car. What utter and distasteful profligacy.

"*Well, old girl, all your pain, at least economically, has been worth it, 'cause missy, you've hit paydirt here.*" The discovery, though inconsequential to Helen emotionally, still caused her to do a jig and dance on the cobblestone. Andrea had a lot to lose....a lot. "*Impressive indeed, My dear Miss Stern. And to think one day very soon, this will all be yours.*"

Fifteen minutes later, with absolutely bolstered composure, Helen chuckled, making her way up the driveway. "*Let the game begin,*" she said aloud, moments later ringing the doorbell of the massive door. An old white-haired matron, whose cold, penetrating, wise eyes suggested she was used to doing battle, opened the door.

"Yes?" Her tone was sharp. She seemed surprised that someone was on the premises unannounced.

"The gate was open," Helen offered, no hint of an apology for her intrusion.

"What do you want, young lady?"

"I'm looking for Andrea Jacobson-Preston, please."

"And who may I say is calling?" The woman eyed the luggage on the step.

"Her daughter. She'll know." Helen smiled wickedly, no joy reaching her lips.

"Her daughter? What nonsense is this?" Melissa looked quizzically at the woman in front of her. No resemblance to Andrea whatsoever.

"Nonsense? I assure you I am not, and have never been about nonsense."

"Do you have a name, child? This sort of scam happens more frequently than you imagine to wealthy people. Who put you up to this?" Melissa wondered which of Andrea's past lovers was in cahoots with this waif, but there was something. Dressed in washed-out blue jeans, ripped to shreds at the knee, and a skimpy white shirt showing her belly-button, the girl's façade was certainly not like anyone Andrea would know, much less a daughter.

"I'm Helen. No one put me up to this. I *am* Andrea's daughter." The girl was impatient with the inquisition.

"Helen who? You mean you have enough notoriety to have just one name?" Melissa snapped, noting the British accent.

"Helen Stern."

"Stern?" Melissa looked up sharply. Stern?"

"That's what I said. Getting a little deaf, are you?"

"And a smartass too, eh?" Melissa said knowingly. "Come in. I'll send for Mrs. Preston." Her voice was strong and authoritative.

Helen moved trance-like into a very tasteful hallway, one that unquestionably showed proper breeding. A domed ceiling, made entirely of beveled glass, supported a Waterford Crystal chandelier which in turn sparkled in the morning sun, its light kissing the highly polished black and white checkerboard foyer. In the center of the room on an ornate, round, pedestal table stood a crystal vase filled with an exquisite kaleidoscope of fragrant flowers. Double staircases spiraled dramatically from each side of the foyer, ending at an archway that framed massive French doors.

While she waited, Helen wandered down the hall toward a heavy wooden door and peeked inside. It was a library. A very masculine room, expensively laid out for intellectual pursuits. Andrea husband's study, no doubt. On a massive cherry desk flanked by a deep red, dimpled, high-backed leather chair, a matching red leather sofa, a plaid fatois, and a cherry side table were several golfing trophies and a porcelain frame that held a picture of Andrea and a little boy.

On cherry-paneled floor-to-ceiling bookcases leaned a decorative ladder ready to be climbed to reach the highest shelves, some twenty feet up. Several leather-bound books boasted the name Dr. Scott

Preston—Andrea's husband. A psychiatrist. How fitting. For Andrea to abandon her child suggested a certain madness indeed. Around him, Helen resolved to be very careful. Psychiatrists had eagle eyes and clever ways of prying information out of people. She had to be very careful and diligent in concealing her true motives for coming to Preston Estates.

At the other end of the room French double doors stood open. The room beyond them was probably the most exquisite, certainly the prettiest room she'd ever been in. Stark white, two entire walls were floor-to ceiling glass windows, boasting beyond them the radiant colors of the rose garden and the vibrant green shrubs that grew thick against the fence. A tall weeping willow was bending and bowing, no doubt, to the queen, for this had to be the study of Andrea Jacobson-Preston. The light oak furniture was a dramatic contrast to the deep cherry of the library. Silken drapes caressed the walls before flowing gracefully into a heap atop the highly polished blanched wooden floor. A muted oyster-colored silk sofa was the commanding piece of furniture in what could have been an intimate setting for lovers. In front of the couch was a marble fireplace, its mantle laden with *objets d' art*. On the desk were two pictures: one, she guessed, was Andrea's husband and their son, and the other was a photo of a stunning teenage girl in an antique silver frame. Helen leaned closer to look at the picture and with a start realized it was herself. Suddenly the room was very hot and beads of perspiration were forming on her upper lip. Helen passed a hand over her face and sat on the edge of the desk to steady herself. Why would Andrea have a picture of her in open view? Wasn't she trying to conceal that she had a child years ago?

The obvious hubbub in the foyer alerted Helen that she was trespassing. She made her way back to the entranceway. A tall, slender, elegant woman, even from the back, was urgently speaking to the white-haired women who'd opened the door.

"Where is she?"

"Probably nosing around." Melissa answered. "She seemed the type."

"Hello, Mother," Helen said quietly. Andrea, hearing the unmistakable voice, froze for a split second before turning in the direction of the voice she had longed to hear for so long.

"Hello, Mother." Helen repeated. "I'm home."

"Oh my God! Oh my God, it's really you. Helen, oh my dearest Helen." Andrea rushed to embrace her child, holding her so close that breathing was difficult. "I knew you would come," she whispered, obvious moisture clinging to her lashes. "I knew you would come home."

Just then a five-year-old boy who had bounced up the stairs only moments before was again descending, this time sliding down the banister.

"Mommie, Mommie." He grabbed Andrea by the leg. "Is this my sister? Melissa said I have a sister." He looked suspiciously at the woman standing next to his mother.

Helen Stern, five-feet eight inches tall, an inch taller than Andrea Jacobson-Preston, looked affectionately at the little boy.

"Hello there," she smiled. "What's your name?"

"You have a funny accent," the child snapped, "and I can't tell you my name if you're a stranger. Mommie says I can't talk to strangers."

Considering they were half-brother and sister, they didn't resemble each other one bit. Helen's jet-black hair, cropped close to her head, matched her fiery, angry black eyes, a perfect contrasted to her brother's dusty brown coloring and tiger-striped eyes, a fact that proved him to be Andrea's child. Her attire of little more than casual torn jeans, a shirt, and scuffed pointed boots, a style of the young and reckless rather than a sign of poverty, was also quite a departure from the young boy's preppy, clean-scrubbed look. Unlike her mother and brother's *café au lait* complexion, Helen was a wonderful chestnut color.

"She's not a stranger, Reggie. She is your sister." Andrea hoisted the child onto her hip. "This is Helen, from England. Helen, meet my son and your brother, Reginald."

Melissa watched the scene, her eyes narrowing with concern.

So even after her four-year disappearance, Helen's arrival in the Hamptons had been expected. And as planned, within weeks she had assimilated into the Jacobson-Preston family, acting as a big sister to Reginald and trying to endear herself, without much success, to Melissa, the family's old guardian.

"Good morning, Melissa." Helen was cordial, helping herself to breakfast.

"What so good about it?" Melissa barked. In the wizened face of the old matron were etched years of devotion to Andrea. An observant look would have shown that though old, Melissa was a woman who missed nothing, a woman whose physical frailty was not replicated in the razor-sharp brain that worked like a perpetual wheel. Helen had gleaned this fact from the very moment that Melissa had opened the door to her.

With her stepfather, Scott, Helen had exercised a similar caution and to Andrea she was polite and distant. Allowing herself to be drawn into a warm relationship would come when she was ready and according to plan. In time. Her future plans required absolute trust from her mother, but she was not yet ready. Andrea, it seemed, was pleased that her long-lost daughter had finally come home and was eager to do everything in her power to make Helen feel welcome. Frankly, Helen was delighted to play the role of the "prodigal daughter," or so it would seem to anyone observing what appeared to be a model family.

Chapter Three

Jacobson Industries, (JI) Madison Avenue, 1989, Eight Years before.

Helen took the left bank of elevators to her fiftieth-floor office. Walking at lightning speed down the corridor, her shoe heels resounded against the marble floor.

"Good morning." She smiled enthusiastically at the staff who greeted her with deference. The entire fiftieth floor was now occupied by Wakefield, and as Helen glanced around, she had a renewed appreciation for her hardworking and dedicated staff who had helped her chart the course of success. Yes, indeed, in just seven short years she had accomplished a lot and there was no question she had made it in New York. Now she was well on her way to living her dream.

Born in Surrey, England, Helen had had more than a curious beginning. But more curious to her was getting used to American culture. Had she not lived in London, or shopped at Harrods with its constant barrage of tourists, she surely would have had total culture shock, especially after her first Thanksgiving on Madison Avenue. But it was really the day after Thanksgiving that even after seven years was a vivid and living memory. In fact, she could still hear her mother's voice:

"*Today we must go shopping,*" Andrea had announced after breakfast. "Scott?"

"I'm not crazy," Scott announced, voicing NO repeatedly at Andrea's insistence.

"I'll go with you, Mommie," Reginald had piped up.

"Oh thank you, darling," she'd ruffled the top of his head. "What'd you think about helping Dad and David get the car ready for our little trip. You would be good company, and a big help to them today. You know, son, Dad's not as good a help with cars as you are. I'm sure there are lots of things David needs your help with, like helping him carry his tools, and looking under the car! Maybe Helen and I should go alone so we can hurry back to help you guys. We'll bring you something wonderful."

"Sounds swell to me, Mom." Reginald had already been unconcerned about his diplomatic rebuff.

Helen loved anything to do with shopping, so not much coaxing was needed for her to jump at the idea. But she hadn't been prepared for the crowd in Manhattan at that time of year! Never had she seen so many people of so many nationalities all perfectly content to be elbow-to-elbow. Barely able to move under the pressure of the sheer mass of people, she reflected on the wisdom of Peter, the chauffeur. The driver, who had dropped them off on Madison Avenue, had been content to wait for them in front of the Plaza Hotel where they were to meet later. Despite the crowd, Helen's excitement wasn't dampened, although she'd often taken refuge in the private rooms of Saks and the like—rooms reserved for the rich and the richer. She had loved every minute of the excitement of shopping. After leaving Andrea and setting a time and place to meet up again, Helen ducked into Cole Haan, Bloomingdale's, Ralph Lauren, and the numerous specialty stores along the Avenue. It hadn't been long before she was laden with colorful bags bearing the insignia of these stores. After all, she had to look like a shopper! Her serious shopping was to be delivered. When she'd met up with her mother, Helen noticed, to her surprise, that Andrea had only a bag or two.

"Mom, I thought you were in the shopping mood. This was your idea," she'd said.

"I have a confession to make. I hate shopping, but when I come out on this day I really feel a part of the New York crowd. Sometimes you can live in New York like a hermit, especially if you hate publicity as I do. On this day, not even the paparazzi are brave enough to risk their lives for a celebrity picture. On this day," she had repeated triumphantly, "most celebs feel free to be lost in the crowd. But look," she'd held up a couple of bags, "I've bought a few things."

Indeed, there was no reason for Andrea Jacobson to ever leave her home to shop. The everyday household management, like the stocking of cupboards or the replacement of worn-out towels, was attended to by the family's old guard, Melissa, who made sure such trivia would never be a concern to Andrea. Jacques, her personal designer, saw to heir wardrobe. Locking arms, Helen and her mother, sharing a moment of intimacy, or so Andrea thought, had stepped into the halted traffic.

Roasting chestnuts! Yumm! The Salvation Army charity collectors dressed in their black outfits were ringing their bells to reggae Christmas music! From the swaying bodies to the lilting music, this was a Kodak moment. Even the hot dog stands were adorned with their Christmas decorations. The horse-drawn buggies, their plumes all festive, the miles and miles of wonderful window decorations, even the floor-to-ceiling Henri Bendel Department Store Christmas tree that dominated the center of the store for four floors, was truly exciting. For a girl whose country's Christmas celebrations were legendary throughout the world, this excitement and overwhelming feeling of freedom could only be experienced in New York. Never had she forgotten that day. For her it had stood as a sign of excess and possibilities. The "possibilities", from the look of things, that had become her reality.

Finally reaching her office suite, Helen hung her scarf on the brass coat hanger outside her door.

"You're late this morning, Miss Stern." Ruth Walters looked at her watch. Rarely did she arrive in the office earlier than her boss, unless Helen had an outside appointment. And there were none on her schedule.

"Good morning, Mrs. Walters." Helen handed her coat to her assistant. "I had a spur-of-the-moment breakfast meeting. What's my schedule like today?"

Mrs. Walters checked the appointment book.

"Human Resources is sending over three people for you to look at and then you have a two o'clock with Ms. Kreiza."

"Kreiza?"

"She is the designer who just took her company public. You wanted her recommendation on good CPAs and attorneys who might handle our business."

"Right. Everything sounds fine," Helen nodded her acceptance, retreating to her office. Mrs. Walters always felt impressed as she watched the long legs of her boss stride confidently and purposefully away. That girl had the longest and most curvaceous legs she had ever seen! Such a class act.

As Executive Vice-President of the ever-growing Wakefield, formed when she'd graduated from Columbia, Helen was convinced that Andrea Jacobson had only created the company to appease her guilt for abandoning her at birth. But today, Helen was responsible for its increasingly favorable position in the eyes of the JI's Board of Directors, and although still privately held, there was talk of taking the company public and bringing it under the fold of JI. To Andrea's credit, Helen had to admit she'd allowed her to develop the corporation with little interference in its operations.

With only a few staff members needed to round out the Wakefield team, she was hoping these candidates might prove to be her last interviews for sometime. So far, she had personally hired all of the forty-five people who now worked in her division, making sure to check their backgrounds thoroughly. Helen believed in a lean and mean organization, and even though many would consider the amount of work suitable for twice the number of staff, she taught them to gain more with less, and everyone was handsomely paid. It was important to

Helen that none of her employees had been previously employed by any division of JI and that there was something in their past she could use, if necessary, to control their behavior. This was essential should she ever need their unprecedented loyalty.

"I'll take some coffee, Mrs. Walters," Helen buzzed on the intercom, looking around her office with satisfaction. It was magnificently appointed and she deserved it—and more. The more, she knew, was simply a matter of time.

Pulling the duetts to cover the glass portal, Helen sat behind her desk, awaiting her coffee. Being idle was not a good position for her mind as it would drift without encouragement, sometimes just floating around in space trying desperately to envision life with real parents. Andrea Jacobson-Preston. Who would ever have thought she would be her mother!

In America, much had changed in Helen's life for the better. After all, she had gone from being an almost destitute runaway to becoming a top player in *the* New York circle. Where else would one be allowed, on the strength of her drive alone, to succeed? Surely not England. Bound by its set standards and rigid class system, perhaps classism in England was, in the final analysis, really no different from racism in America. Helen had even learned how to be politically correct. And she'd made it just as Frank, or was it Liza, would always sing, "*If You Can Make It There...*" Indeed, New York was the only place in the world to test one's ability to succeed.

Unlike her mother, who craved privacy, Helen loved publicity and adoration. Before she ran away to Jamaica, she was used to being treated royally, or at least gingerly because of her 'powers". And as much as she was smoldering about Andrea's disavowal, she loved claiming status as her daughter. And boy, had it opened numerous doors and drawn countless unsolicited suitors! To her mother's chagrin, she had rejected at least ten offers of marriage. For some reason, Andrea thought Harrington, the son of an investment banker, was a good choice for a husband. Ridiculous. Marriage was of *no* interest to Helen; to be the most powerful woman on Wall Street was, and she'd be damned if she would claim that status because she was a trophy wife. So far, she'd done well on her own and had made all the right moves for her career. Once she'd secured her position as a dutiful and grateful daughter, it would be time to change history. Best of all, she no longer had to practice fortune-telling like some gypsy half-breed.

"Oh," Mrs. Walters poked her head around the door, coffee in hand. "Yesterday, we got an invitation to your class reunion at Columbia on June 8th. How shall I respond?"

"Answer yes, Mrs. Walters. Yes, of course." Helen had something to prove. She would show those clods who was most likely to succeed, especially Drake Lambert. Taking a sip of the steaming black coffee, Helen hoisted her legs on top of her desk and rocked back in her swivel chair. She wondered what Drake was doing with his life now. She hoped a lot better than he'd done at Columbia.

At Andrea's insistence, Helen had enrolled at Brown University, earning her BA in International Business. Even as a bit of a loner, Helen Stern was slated for stardom. After Brown, she enrolled in Columbia for a joint Business/Law degree in International affairs. Her success was not only made easy by her high GPA, but by the fact that her mother was Andrea Jacobson-Preston, capable of donating a new building to the school.

Helen delved into college life, much of it uneventful until she met Drake Lambert, a reputed Southern blue blood. From his behavior, one would most likely assume his father to be grand master in the Ku Klux Klan. But what Helen had gathered made far more sense: he was actually not from good stock at all.

"Ever seen a coon so uppity in your life? 'Cause she went to school in Switzerland and her mother, because of affirmative action mind you, owns half of the world, doesn't elevate her to be in *our* company."

It was obvious his comments were meant for her, as he'd deliberately raised his voice just as she'd passed the table where he was seated in the library. Still today, Helen felt the rage of his comment as though it was just yesterday. Suddenly she had been consumed by an inferno, fueled by her "powers" that as Maya had said, proved uncontrollable under such anger. She had risen from her chair forcing herself to remain calm as she'd approached Drake.

"You weren't speaking to me by any chance, were you?" She'd glared at him, a madness flashing behind her black irises.

"And if I was?"

"Then, my friend, you should pick your opponents better. You should know about the 'Ancient Art of War.'"

Inside her dorm room, Helen had dropped her backpack to the floor and kicked the door shut with tremendous force. She had never understood, and still today didn't understand the intolerance of Americans for people who were different. Why had Drake called her a coon? She had done absolutely nothing to incite this spite. What was wrong with her foreign education, anyway? For God's sake, she was a foreigner! In her state of anguish, she had been glad that Lisa, her roommate, was not going to be there. They'd planned an all-nighter in the library, but Helen, too upset to continue her studies, had returned to the dorm. She hated the damn room to boot; the barren cubbyhole of no more than a single bed, too short for her anyway, boasted a chest of drawers, an unsightly pegboard and little else.

Helen had paced—long angry steps, but still she was unable to forget Drake Lambert's snide comment. Incensed and filled with a hatred that had seized her in its unyielding grip, she had desperately wished she could call Maya for guidance, but she couldn't. Finally, her anger won, and before going to bed, she had removed a chest that she'd kept concealed in her trunk. Retrieving the talisman inside, she'd placed it on her bedside table and fixed her gaze on a single spot. When she was in a hypnotic state, she willed herself to bring Drake Lambert's face into focus. It seemed she sat there for hours.

The following morning she'd heard from Lisa that "Snaky Drake" had been taken to the hospital in the middle of the night with severe abdominal pain. Rumors had it he was in the Intensive Care Unit fighting for his life.

"Helen," Lisa had cried at Helen's nonplused attitude. "He could die! And if he does, oh my God, you'll regret making light of this."

"I can't imagine that I would," Helen's face had been unmoved. "I abhor bad behavior and in my world such behavior gets its just desserts. Besides, in my understanding of the continuity of life, death is just another incarnated state-more pleasant, too, I hear. My dear Lisa," she hastened at the alarm on Lisa's face, "everything in life has an opposite. Love, hate. Good, evil. Don't you agree?"

Yes, indeed, she looked forward to going to her class reunion. It was the first year she had accepted the invitation.

Jane Kreiza's Office, Later That Day.

"So, how did you get into the fashion business to begin with?" Jane asked.

Helen looked the woman up and down. She wondered if she was trustworthy or even a nice person. For a successful woman, Jane was clearly unpretentious.

"Quite a fluke, really," Helen said, wondering how much of the story she would tell her. "Well…I…"

"Well…" Jane coaxed, clearing her throat urging Helen to continue.

"Well," Helen finally said. "I was a teenage model. After college I studied with Jacques St. Pierre in England and then Madam Jovier in France. As you can see, I learned fashion management backwards."

"What difference does that make? It seems to me you have done a marvelous job with Wakefield," Jane said supportively. "When I see women aspire to be all that they can be, I feel very proud. We women must stick together and forge a change for all, don't you think?" She scrutinized Helen through a cloud of smoke. This was a strange woman, Jane concluded, but she liked her for some reason.

"Yes, women should," Helen offered solemnly.

"Unfortunately," Jane continued, "the attorney I have to recommend to take your company public is a man. A very arrogant man who fortunately has everything to be an ass about. He's the best in the industry. His name is Anton DePaul." She handed Helen a card for the law firm of Bingham, Lewis, Viking & Gould.

Chapter Four

In her years as division head of the Wakefield companies, Helen had unquestionably proven herself sharp, capable, ambitious, and a great leader. Above all, her fashion instincts were impeccable and honed more and more each day. Wakefield's office productivity and its contribution to the bottom line of Jacobson Industries were becoming legendary. Likewise, her increasing responsibilities obviously reflected the confidence Andrea had in her. Her official role, in reality, was more important than her title as Executive Vice-President of the burgeoning Wakefield, but Helen knew it was only a matter of time before she had *carte blanche* throughout Jacobson's Industry. She was as certain of that fact as she was that one day she would become President and Chief Executive Officer of the entire Jacobson dynasty. In fact, she was banking on this.

The concept of the Wakefield Company, if not its name which she hated, was her brainchild while at Columbia. The fashion design market had been the next logical step for JI that had purchased a textile plant in Asia. The initial plan, as Helen saw it, was to back upstart designers who had artistic tendencies but no cash. Not only would this strategy garner the most innovative young designers while increasing the use of the textile plants, but also labor cost in the U.S. could be controlled. This elite group she would name "The Fashion Think Tank of America." What the hell. Everyone deserves a little respect.

Many of the designers eager to have their work represented never bothered to scrutinize the contracts they signed. Naturally, Helen used her legal training and savvy to make sure the artists belonged to her well after their fame came. To maintain the image they wanted to convey, as well as to control the excessive costs of supermodels, Wakefield Company also set up its own modeling agency. As a novice in the world of fashion, Wakefield focused mainly on appealing to mid-range female executives who were as bored with couture as with the high prices they levied. The untapped marketplace of disgruntled middle America was where Helen wanted to play for awhile. From her surveys, she gathered that these women wanted to stop wearing ties and pin-striped suits and had no interest in reflecting the feminist androgyny of their parents. These were the women who would welcome the new, fresh fashion. So predicted, so it was.

Wakefield Company buzzed with success. The young brainpower sitting behind the circular conference table sipping sparkling water and chewing on carrots were the best and brightest in their field of expertise. Everyone in the company looked forward to the weekly meeting where ideas bounced off the walls until the room was in a frenzied pitch from excitement.

"How are we doing?" Helen asked at the weekly Monday morning staff meeting. Chance, the VP of Marketing, smiled.

"Things are definitely on track, but we sure could use an increase in advertising budget."

"So what's new?" someone from design piped up.

Chance ignored the comment. "So far we have captured 20 percent of the marketshare for the eighteen-to thirty-five-year-olds. With a great campaign, which requires money," Chance emphasized, "there is no reason we can't gain upwards of 45 or 50 percent. No one has challenged our theory yet, but with this kind of success, competition is not far behind, I can guarantee it."

"What figure are you projecting to capture the increased marketshare?" Helen spoke directly to Chance.

"I would say 2 million."

"And what is our budget?"

"Half a mil."

"So," she looked around the room at her staff of forty-eight. "Who's got chips out there to cash in? Even if I could get a few hundred thousand, or most unlikely a million, we'd only be at 50 per cent of our projected need. I want to know what we can get for free, whom we know in publicity at major fashion magazines, who owes us a favor, or who just simply hates our designers? We also need to know who we can buy for cheap."

"I know this girl who's to die for. She'd be perfect as our signature model. She'd be hot," Chance offered.

"Who?" Helen was interested in the idea of an icon.

"Her name is Franchesca. She is a paradox, really, because she can be ultra feminine on one hand and undefinable on the other. She is a struggling model from Brazil who needs a break. Franchesca could represent anything: black, white, olive, male, female, whatever. Honestly, she is the perfect model and would work for little or nothing. She is having a rough time finding work because she has a bad rep at other agencies. They say she drinks and pops pills too much. From what I know, she's off the sauce so this could be our lucky day. She might need a baby sitter for awhile, but if we can get her to do this, she would be perfect. I guarantee sales would skyrocket. Every woman under twenty-five will want to look like Franchesca." Chance's smile was one meant to instill confidence in her recommendation.

"Guarantee! That's a strong word. Get in touch with her," Helen said, turning to the group for more suggestions.

"I know someone at *W* and Macmillan Publishing," Ralston McNamara, the flamboyant designer from Chicago, said. And so it went on for an hour. And call in their chips they did.

And it was not very long before Franchesca, the exquisite, exotic, and sensual being, was becoming a household name. Freelancers and well-known photographers alike were clamoring to get a shot of the new beauty whose image—they were convinced—would make them famous. In front of the camera, Franchesca sizzled. Sad indeed were the agencies who dismissed her without trying to rehabilitate her. Indeed, Franchesca Rivera was the ultimate model—beguiling yet distant, exotic yet common, driven yet relaxed, sophisticated yet urchin-like, tough yet soft. Indeed, a photographer's dream. And to her audience she was like the Mona Lisa, who no matter where you stood, she looked back just at you. Franchesca, to Chance's delight, was America's new darling.

Franchescaitis overtook New York. With lightning speed, billboards, bus shelters, and store windows spread her image as a Wakefield icon throughout the country. With the success of the Franchesca line, the company was at 35 percent of market share, and best of all, Franchesca was a Wakefield exclusive. Jacobson Industries was packing a lethal punch in the fashion industry. Suddenly every designer wanted to rent a Wakefield model. The prices for renting were hefty, but it did not stop them from calling. They would pay anything, too, for they wanted the obscure yet feminine look Wakefield had popularized. Unfortunately they had to settle for great models, but they weren't Franchesca, for she had an exclusive contract with Wakefield. So from the fashion division, a modeling spin-off began to earn the company not only a significant income, but a reputation to rival. Every new and upcoming model wanted to have Wakefield Modeling Agency on her resume. Helen Stern was creating enemies.

Under the burgeoning Wakefield fashions, Helen was exhausted. With the success of the modeling agency, she was forced to hire a Senior VP of Talent. Tristy Saddler had a background in modeling and fashion as long as one's arm, and brought many contacts for publicity. Her immaculate sense of style, coupled with her finishing-school touch, made her a natural for fine-tuning the beautiful, yet green, models into superstars.

In 1994, Helen Stern was the new savvy businesswoman in town. She had turned a challenge into a gold mine. No question, she had succeeded with every challenge posed by Andrea Jacobson-Preston.

Chapter Five

To Chance, Helen Stern was drop-dead beautiful. The jet eyes that gazed steadily from behind perfectly arched, yet unplucked eyebrows, were observant and indeed conversant. A gleam and a slight mischief always seemed to dance behind the piercing eyes, but it was the flash of fire that would make anyone who was even remotely sensitive feel uneasy. To the expert eye it would have been obvious that Helen Stern had a "gift." To the unsuspecting eyes, however, if Helen Stern felt anything but sincerity, the camouflage was never allowed to slip. No one had the ability to read her true persona. Yet, as distant as she kept her inner sanctuary, one had to admit she never appeared packaged or distant. In fact, just the opposite was true. Very few people could describe Helen as insincere. Even the slightest doubt would soon be forgotten as the charming British accent, interspersed at will with fluent German, Italian or French, calmed even the most suspicious. Helen, who was somewhat of an enigma to her staff, was not only exotic and elegant, but became the talk of the party crowd around the city.

In New York, it was uncommon to have one black woman among the jet set of commerce, much less two. And worse, they were women whose beauty threatened even the most securely married woman no matter what their origin or social status. In the department of beauty, Helen and her mother, Andrea, possessed an exquisite and unusual charm.

The black women were often termed exotic and mysterious. "Damn them!" Andrea would toss the paper every time a reporter referred to them as exotic. "Exotic!" she would hiss, "connotes a plumed bird, or a rare breed of marsupials, but it does not connote cultural diversity. Damn idiots these Americans!"

"What do you think?" Helen turned slowly as though on a rotating pedestal. Her voice, with its lilt, always in Chance's opinion seemed to caress her words. Often enough, that velvet voice would turn to ice whenever necessary. "It's our new work couture line," Helen announced.

Dressed in a chartreuse and navy Wakefield suit with a simplicity that characterized all their designs, Helen, with her flawless figure, elevated the outfit to a new level of sophistication. Around her small waist she sported a Chanel navy and gold chain belt, on her lapel was a ruby and gold Cartier tiger, matching midnight navy pumps, and sheer classic navy stockings completed the attire.

"*Oy Vey*," Chance gasped. She knew what battles lay ahead. "I thought this type of fashion was off limits to us?" Chance raised her eyebrows, waiting for the caustic words to fall from Helen's lips.

"It is. But so what?" Her tone was surprisingly calm. "We are making money hand over fist, who would dare to deny us anything? Who do you think would push the envelope, Chance? We can just about do what we want, and I want couture."

Chance shook her head. She hated to see what would happen if these two stubborn women clashed. *The War of the Roses* would be tame in comparison to the combat between Helen Stern and Andrea Preston. Dare she say this might be World War III?

"Do you play chess, Chance?" Helen observed the woman in front of her intensely.

"No, I'm afraid not," Chance answered, feeling flustered and uneasy in Helen's presence. It was the eyes that bore through her.

"Then you should learn. You'd be amazed to see how the very same strategies in chess apply in the world of business and to life in general. How do you expect to win if you don't know how to play the game?" the voice demanded.

"But chess is only a game."

"And in a game it's easier to lose than it is in life, isn't it? Learn to play Chess, Chance. A missed opportunity in business can have very serious consequences, Chance, especially if the player is a novice. Never underestimate the strategic power of the pawn, my friend. Never! Success in Wakefield is our pawn in this game we play. Once we have locked in our position, we can go in for the win."

Chapter Six

Chance

Dashing through the airport at high speed, trying to balance her luggage on tipping wheels, Chance riffled through her purse to find her passport. Christ! Knowing her, she had forgotten it on the table. With great relief, she located it in the side pocket of her Fendi purse.

The line waiting for the international Northwest flight, thank God, was manageable. "Good day, Miss. We just have a few questions to ask, if you don't mind. This will speed up the line."

"Thank you. I don't mind at all," she glanced at her watch. Thirty minutes before flight time. She hoped the gate was close.

"Did you pack you luggage yourself, receive any gifts from anyone, leave your luggage unattended?" the baggage handler was firing questions one after the other. Academic to say the least.

By the time the whole ordeal was done, Chance, wishing she'd left her mother's house immediately after dropping off Pookie, had to run at full speed to the gate, luggage and all. Thank goodness, coming down the aisle toward her was an empty transport vehicle.

"Could you help me?" Chance waved down the buggy driver, discreetly handing him a twenty-dollar bill. "I have ten minutes to get to my gate, and I'll never be able to do it with this luggage."

"It's against regulations, ma'am, but why don't you just limp over here to this cart?" He winked at her.

"Thanks." She beamed a smile.

To the world, this tall, gracious woman was the epitome of class. Today, although casually suited in a navy blazer, navy and gray Hermès scarf, gray riding leggings, striped navy and white oxford shirt, and matching Cole Haans, there was no way to miss the meritocracy. Working in the fashion industry had a way of making one totally cognizant of one's outward attire. In public, Chance always looked as though she'd walked off the cover of *Elle*, which amounted to a daily routine when one worked at the Wakefield Company. But, on her days off, Chance relished being comfortable in jeans, oversized shirts and baggy dresses. Today, as any other in the past decade, no one would remotely suspect any poor white blood running through her veins. Far removed was she from the trailer park in Boston.

"Thanks again." Chance hopped off the trolley at gate twelve of Concourse F, remembering to limp a bit.

Chance hurriedly explained her position to the flight attendant, who was just getting ready to close the door.

"I'll hold the flight for you, madam, while I process your papers." The attendant was gracious.

"I really appreciate this. Thank you, Ms. Sterling," Chance said, looking up from the badge on the attendant's lapel, flashing her a charming and grateful smile. Fortunately, when she arrived on board with her kit and caboodle, there was an empty row and she didn't have to disturb passengers already tightly belted. Looking around, she espied her assistant seated a few rows away in economy class. Jackie was rolling her eyes in disbelief. Chance shrugged her shoulders.

"A glass of Dom, ma'am?"

"Yes. Thank you." Chance accepted the glass of bubbly. Normally drinking was a no-no, but today, she needed a sedative. Taking a sip of the sparkling liquid, savoring the tingling taste, appreciating its smoothness, Chance wondered why people had to be excessive. Why not take the pleasure of spirit, rather than the awful byproduct of its excess. The smell of the alcohol evoked in full force, a past she'd rather forget. Chance was lost in thought, re-living her journey through life thus far.

Up to this very morning, she had been hesitant about getting on another plane. Though traveling, which had been such an intrigue back then, was the deciding factor for taking the position at Wakefield, it had gotten old fast. Not even the numerous frequent flyer miles, the extravagant expense account, or the glamour and celebrity status of her clients were enough to get her excited about going on this wonderful, all-expense-paid vacation—a reward to the top producers at Wakefield.

"We can't just throw away a free trip," Chance's assistant exclaimed. "We've worked for this. We are the best of the best and that's why we are being rewarded. And, don't you forget how long it has been since we've had a vacation. Do you know how many dates I've turned down over the past three years? For goodness sakes, I'm looking forward to finding an Italian paramour!"

Chance felt a twinge of guilt. Depriving her faithful assistant such an opportunity after so many years of hard work was not a thought she relished, and Jackie was a devoted assistant. Not only had she worked relentlessly for the success of Wakefield, but in Helen's eyes Jackie could do no wrong. She was a woman at the top of her game and wanted nothing more than to be the best administrative assistant in New York.

It wasn't that Chance didn't appreciate the exotic vacation. After all, she was the one with the most markers to call in. Yet for her, the ultimate vacation would have been an uninterrupted week in her beautiful condo. If that seem too drastic, then she could always use the time to furnish her place with more than a bed, a couple of pots and some linen. In the three years Chance had worked for the incomparable Helen Stern, the thought of time for shopping, much less time for a vacation had never crossed her mind.

Previously Senior Merchandising Vice President for DKNY, Chance had worked her way to the top of the fashion industry quite successfully, if not conventionally. Her ability was legendary in the profession, and everyone, at some point or the other, had tried to lure her away. Until Helen Stern, no one had succeeded. Chance was not sure why she had even considered Helen's offer. True, the salary and profit-sharing plan were double what she had, and the offer, if goals were met, to be a preferred stock holder when the company went public was attractive. But there was more to it than that. There was....something ineffable, in her gut. Looking back, she clearly saw it was Helen's ability to merge with her mind-set and the promise of full control for worldwide marketing.

The risk of going to a start-up firm was not lost on her, and though the deep pockets and tremendous success of JI made her feel secure, in her heart she'd have accepted the job regardless. It had been time to show the world just what Chance Livingston, poor and trashy, was made of. The position to head up a team of fashion wannabees next in command to Helen Stern had afforded her more creative freedom than she ever imagined. The goal of making Wakefield a viable profit center was a challenge for them both, but Helen Stern, with little previous experience in either fashion management or the workplace, proved to be as hard a task master and worker as everyone else on the team. Some people, Chance concluded, were just born to lead.

Several people in the growing organization had crashed and burned under the stress of the work demands. If anyone had thought of asking for vacation, it was understood that they would become an outcast, barred from the privilege of the inner circle. As much as it was their right by law, Chance knew that breaking the momentum of the team was an unforgivable crime in Helen's mind. No one was ever outwardly fired for asking, but because they became *persona non grata* they eventually felt pushed out and resigned. "I cannot abide this interruption of work. I must have only the best around me. Chance, this is a competitive industry and only the fittest will survive. I have no patience with lack of excellence," Helen often reminded her. Helen Stern never appreciated that people got tired, had families, or just needed to be in a different environment momentarily. By the time the team had been perfected Wakefield had the best and most dedicated team in place, and they were poised to win. Chance liked Helen, but at times she could not abide her haughty, down on Americans attitude. She had on many occasions, when Helen was in a particularly slanderous mood, felt like telling her to take her dead ass back to crumpling old England. Even after two hundred years it hadn't dawned on the Brits that they weren't ruling the world. Frankly, Chance had never seen anyone quite as driven as Helen Stern. It was rumored that only her mother was capable of such focused and laserscopic attention to details, but most admitted that Helen was even worse. Today she respected Helen's titanic vision and unwavering commitment, acknowledging with admiration that whatever drove her had worked marvelously.

And by jove, (her Brit emulation), they had done it! The high voltage project that had sapped the energy of even Helen Stern was completed. Before they brought the project to the marketplace, however, Helen had given the entire core team of fifteen the three-week vacation of a lifetime. They could all go to Italy, or for those needing time away from their team members, any place of their choice. Chance knew that this vacation was to be savored, for what was to come would be brutal. She only wished she could spend it at home.

So that morning, reluctantly packing for the trip to Italy, the only decision still causing Chance a bit of stress was what to do with Pookie. Pookie, Chance's finicky Siamese, queen in her own home, had all the comforts in her custom cat domicile, and detested the thought of being sheltered in a kennel. She was packing up Pookie's backpack when abruptly she'd stopped, sat on the side of the bed and welcomed copious tears that had been boiling inside her for years.

Too busy building her career and blotting out the past, Chance had not dated much. Her fear of people finding out about her past kept her from mingling too closely. Consequently, she was a loner who'd learned to clamp down her emotions and to live without feeling too much.

In need of a pep talk, Chance was about to ring her only sibling, Christy, with whom she was very close, when the phone rang. The C to the fourth-degree family they were called, because everyone's name in the family of four began with the letter C. Christy, three years Chance's junior, was a successful Wall Street attorney. She too, much to their parents' chagrin, was busy building a career with little concern about getting hitched. For children of alcoholics they had turned out, at least on the surface, remarkably well. Nothing like running away and poverty to give a person the survival instinct. Looking at the clock, realizing it was the time her mother usually called, she blurted as she answered the phone. "Now listen to me, Mom, I just put an ad in the *Wall Street Journal* for a mate, and I promise a child will come nine months later. At least I'm trying eh!"

"I see Mom's been coming on heavy again. She has actually given me a rest," Christy's soothing voice echoed.

"Live before you, die before you," Chance echoed their childhood phrase for coincidences. "I was just about to dial your number when the phone rang.

"Yeah? What were you gonna call about?"

"I have a slight change of plans. Remember the trip I was telling you about? I will be going to Italy after all. I'm hoping you'll take Pookie."

"I can't, Sis. You'll have to find another house sitter. I have to be at a conference in Geneva just about the same time you'll be in Italy. I was just calling to tell you to take that trip after all. Wasn't planning on going, but I had to take this guy's place who's working a humongous merger deal. Too bad because he is rather dashing and I would relish being in the office alone with him while the others are gone. Why don't you call Mother dear about the kitty and let's plan to spend the weekend together in Europe? Why not catch a flight over to Geneva and come to the banquet with me on Saturday? Lots of high-powered attorneys to choose from. Isn't it time?"

"Attorneys! Boring. Remember, I like my guys on the edge of danger. You know, the mountain climbers, race-car drivers, gods of thunder and lightning. High risk, it's in my blood. How could you forget so soon?"

There was still some pain left in her sister's voice, Christy thought. It had been eight-and-a-half years since her sister's fiancé had been killed in a car accident. As far as Christy was concerned, she had not grieved appropriately, throwing herself first into school and then into work. No wonder the pain still lingered. "Wait. I have a better idea. Why don't I come over to Italy, and we'll go to the film festival there. I'm tired of attorneys."

"That sounds awesome. In fact, that sounds superb. Let's talk when we get to Europe, and let me get off this phone so I can call and beg Mom to take my fur ball."

Chance was proud of the little brownstone she and Christy had purchased for their parents. Four years before, the children had insisted on their parents' sobriety and had them moved to New York. "No Dad, Mom," Chance has said sternly, "we'll not change our minds. Tell me what use is there being in the same environment when you're trying to change? This is what you both need."

Reluctantly Mr. and Mrs. Stevenson had agreed. It had been rough on the entire family; all those nights at ALANON and Alcoholics Anonymous, but they'd survived. Now the Stevensons had been sober for three years. If there was one thing the girls could say about their parents, no matter how dysfunctional they were, they loved each other and in their own sick way they loved the children they had brought into the world. Now, everyone had a new life. That her parents had now taken an interest in their children was something Chance resented, but tried to hide. Too much emotional challenge might send them spiraling back to the abyss of drunkenness. Anyway, she consoled herself, who said walking on the dark side of life cannot yield successful kids.

"Anything else for you?" The flight attendant interrupted her reverie.
"Yes. How long is the flight?"
"To Paris, six hours and then an hour to Italy." She looked quizzically at Chance.

Chapter Seven

Chance loved Milan. And the Italians, it seemed, from their constant "I love *Americano* and *bellisima, bellisima*," felt the same about her. And through the week in Italy, Chance had never regretted taking the trip or for that matter her chic wardrobe. What in heavens name would she have done with tacky clothes in *Milano*? If Italy was this magnificent then Paris, being the fashion capital of the world, must be awesome, she thought, for Milan was truly top notch. A Gothic city, the Eternal City they called it, with its tremendous price tags and the lavishly decorated boutiques huddled together in intimate groups, was breathtaking. Its ambiance was as welcoming to patrons as was the hospitality and friendship of the storekeepers. The simplicity of the Italian people seemed a contradiction, for the flavor of Milan was one of sophisticated understatement. The busy streets with separate lanes for commercial traffic, if one could call them that, were narrow and cobble-stoned. Bustling, refined, and upbeat were words she would use to describe the city.

"*Buena noche*," Valentino always greeted her with his toothless smile every evening as she arrived for dinner at Trendili, her favorite restaurant. She'd made friends with four old men who were always playing cards at the same table.

The day before the gala event, Chance waited for her sister to arrive from Geneva. Christy, who had traveled extensively with her Wall Street firm, knew how to navigate in Europe. She arrived at the hotel, *Casa Svizzera*, at almost exactly the time she was expected. Because the hotel was adjacent to the Galleria, they spent a part of the day shopping before strolling, arms linked, through the Duomo, Milan's legendary cathedral. Then it was over to the Via della Spiga district to Montenapo where they spent the rest of the afternoon. Chance had never seen hand-made linen of the quality she saw in the little boutiques, nor such wonderful leather bags and shoes. Christy took delight in being her sister's tour guide.

"Too bad we don't have time to take in a performance at *La Scala*. You would just love it! The acoustics are tremendous. One day we should bring Mom and Dad here. Let's stop at the *Museo Teatrale* and buy them a memento. We can peek in the theater while we are there. With gilded grandeur it is magnificent and awe-inspiring. That will remind us that we have conquered the world, Sis. You and me together. Maybe next time we can catch an opera."

That evening they dined in grand style, playing their exalted status to the hilt. The girls had *osso buco* with *risotto alla milanese* in the garden of the *Boeucc* and downed two bottles of Taittingers, a luxury they only allowed themselves on special occasions. They had vowed never to tempt their predisposition. Chance and Christy were quite happy when they made their way back to *Camparine Café*.

"Who would ever believe we were the daughters of two of Boston's noted alcoholics?" Christy's laugh resounded.

"Not so loud," Chance whispered in a slurred voice.

"Ah, who gives a shit. No one knows us."

It was against the girls' rules to drink too much, but somehow they felt they had something to celebrate—overcoming the challenges of life.

The following evening the women spent hours dressing for the "ball."

"Wait a minute, you need some more blush and a little more eyeliner," Christy said.

"No, thanks. I feel really natural tonight."

"As you please," Christy said, heading into the bathroom.

The contrast of the women was stunning. Chance was tall and big-boned with dark, straight shoulder-length hair cut in a page boy style.

Christy was only five feet, three inches with a mop of unruly red hair that constantly strayed into her eyes. Beautiful though they were, if one looked closer, their sunken cheeks gave away their fragility from too many years of neglect. When Christy alighted from the bedroom she was in a pale yellow, back-less chiffon dress with matching shoes and purse. The yellow contrasted only slightly with her wan complexion, but was vibrant against her bright red hair. Sometimes Chance felt if there was any giveaway of their past, it was their pale complexion. It wasn't porcelain, it wasn't milky, just plain pale, almost a look of malnutrition.

The Livingston girls, forced to fend for themselves most of the time, had been scrawny kids. Their diet of whatever they could buy with the money left over after their parents' alcohol binge did not leave them with much hope for pearly white teeth or a healthy, robust complexion. Tonight, even with the slight pallor, her sister looked breathtaking. Chance, though her plain black dress was elegant in comparison to her sister's chic attire, felt like the evil stepsister. Deciding after a quick glance in the mirror that she wouldn't receive the award for the worst dressed, but that indeed Christy was right about an image enhancement, Chance sharpened her look by adding a bit of color to her cheeks and a touch of Lancôme *Fire Red* to her lips. Tonight would have been perfect to test out one of those glamorous, to-die-for slinky, colorful frou-frou fashions Helen swore would turn a woman into a tiger.

"I think women are tired of black," Helen often argued for her proposed new line. "What America needs is some glamour and some femininity. Women are tired of being staunch. What's wrong with sexy anyway? I truly feel femininity is needed after the feminist era."

And, as though a testament to Helen's philosophy, when she arrived at the event, her sister and many of the attendees were superbly attired in all the colors of Joseph's robe. There were fashion models and glamour girls everywhere. Some of them on an obvious mission. She knew for a fact that a majority were there only to look around for husband number four. Likewise, there were many guys who came to shop for the next trophy wife, and still others who could be slain in less than one minute by a pretty face. Men such as Jason Biddel, who even though he knew of the beauties' purpose, always fell for their packaged wit and charm. Most women said he hardly cared about them as people as long as they looked good on his arm. Consequently, he changed wives every six years. Thank goodness he had more money than most and gracefully accepted the price of his fantasy. Those alimony bills had to be fortune in themselves. Chance looked around the room. There were lots of New York faces, but there were many people she had never seen before. One day, she would write a book, and get notoriously rich by calling it *The One-Minute Guide to Spouse Shopping.*

With an event full of drop-dead model types, there was no reason for the darkly handsome man across the room to have noticed her. He was strikingly good-looking, and exuded confidence. She wondered idly who he was. Was he on parade as a potential rich husband, or maybe a movie mogul and therefore the giver of a film contract? Or was he simply looking for a quick affair that would cost him little more than an expensive piece of jewelry, a sizable gift that the soon-to-be indigent companion could hock for real cash so that he could thereby salve his conscience? If so, then why her?

Standing around in a-step-above-black-tie affair in her elegant but plain black dress didn't help matters much. Thank God she could hide behind the power of the champagne glass. Chance flashed a bold smile, acting more confident than she actually felt. Deliberately moving out of his view, she felt the twinge, then the light perspiration and finally the slightly quickening pulse of nerves or severe attraction. Damn! Fancy coming to Italy to feel the embers of beginning passion. It had been a long time. She wondered what Mr. Sensual's high-risk problem would turn out to be.

Hell, there goes her power-lounging, carefree vacation. Her overseas medicine for the inevitable postpartum plunge. She had counted on this time to regain her sanity and replenish her energy, especially since she was keenly aware of the high-gear projects ahead of her, and now this love attack. Approaching a group of people, chatting gaily with her sister, Chance almost succeeded in distracting herself from the good-looking man across the room.

"Fun party, eh, glad I came," her sister whispered, grabbing yet another glass of free-flowing Crystal from the waiter, before turning back to bachelor number one for more drunken conversation. Now Chance was really ready to go home. She didn't like Christy drinking herself to this state. Best bubbly or not, as soon as she returned from the ladies' room she was taking her sister home. No need tempting genetic fate.

"Radical, original, unflattering to an admirer, very attractive in women. Shows an enormous amount of self esteem." The voice was caressing the hairs on her neck. "Would you like to join me tomorrow for a party in my honor?" The man was dangerously close. So close that she had to distance herself before turning to face him. Even after he'd stopped speaking, the deep, baritone voice still pierced her consciousness, and his unwavering stare unnerved her even more.

"Nice way of telling a girl she is a misfit. Who exactly would I be joining?" Chance studied the face now several inches away from her own. "Someone important I guess, if there is a party in his honor."

There was a look of surprise, and then a nonchalant recovery. "I am Victor Innes Palmer," he said, incredulous she did not know who he was. "You can call me VIP for short. And you?"

She smiled. "I like that. V.I.P is always an important acronym, even if the bearer only gains notoriety from the initials. I am Chance."

"Yes indeed, I would say that's a most appropriate name. I am honored." He brushed his lips lightly against the back of her outstretched hand. An electric spark started in the hand he held and traveled all the way to her toes. "Well?" he prompted.

"Well, what?"

"Will you join me?" He took out a pen and pad and began writing.

She was about to answer when their short conversation was punctuated by flashing bulbs, and what appeared from nowhere to be a slew of reporters. Victor Innes Palmer turned to face the camera, obviously comfortable with his importance. Maybe he was important after all. Before putting on the ritz, he reached over and stuffed a crumpled piece of paper in Chance's hand. She waited until the frenzied group had moved over to an impromptu press conference before she uncrumpled the paper.

Tomorrow night, I want to continue our CHANCE meeting at Capolinea in the Navigli district. Eight sharp. I hate waiting.

VIP.

How on earth could he be so important and she hadn't heard of him? It was definitely time to go.

In the cab home, Chance related the story to Christy.

"Humm VIP, VIP. Can't say I've heard of him. But he surely is handsome."

"Should I meet him or ditch the note?"

"Ditch! Are you crazy? There has never been anything better for the soul than a holiday romance. You never have to see him again if you don't want. If I had nothing to do tomorrow, I would be begging to come along or I would definitely try to make you feel guilty about being such a traitor. Fortunately, I accepted a date with Emille tomorrow. Now who did you say he was again? VIP? Some pretentious initials, eh? Wait a minute. Did you say VIP? as in VIP? I swear I've heard of him before, but frankly I can't recall. Anyway, let's just have some fun. His initials VIP are probably the only important things about him, and he staged the whole scene today. Maybe he's a famous magician."

Chance rolled her eyes at her sister's drunken irrationality. "Maybe," she answered, "but how is one to find out unless she investigates?"

Chapter Eight

NEW YORK

Helen couldn't stand waiting. She paced up and down her office impatiently awaiting her mother's arrival. Somehow Andrea always pre-empted her importance. No matter how she wheeled and dealed, shone with brilliance, made the most complicated business decisions seem as routine as brushing one's teeth, she always felt a novice in the presence of her mother. And needless to say, there was always something not quite right. The last detail that only Andrea could see in an otherwise perfect plan would be pointed out. She must remind Chance to safeguard against such future oversights, but she knew it wouldn't matter. Andrea would find something. The door opened and her mother, never announced, breezed in, the power of her position exuded in every step. At Sixty she looked forty-five—tall, slender, and immaculately dressed in a Vera Wang suit. My God, Helen thought, even the air stood still for her entry. The only fault she could find with the woman's attire was that she wasn't wearing a Wakefield design. Damn her to hell! She should be showing her support for the line. It made Helen completely aware that Andrea did not take the Wakefield project seriously.

Likewise she had never kidded herself that it was her superior management skills that earned her the right to manage the company. It was more than obvious that it was Andrea's way of vanquishing her guilt. The tremendous success of Wakefield was a great surprise to Andrea, for

Helen was convinced that her mother had never expected her to create a profit center for the company, much less a part of the business generating cash.

"Good-afternoon, dear. Sorry I'm late. Had lunch with Scott, and he couldn't stop talking about this new offer to head the Psychology Department at Harvard General. I'm sure he's not even considering it really, but it's such a boost to his ego, and it's always nice to know someone appreciates you. I was being a dutiful wife." She reached over and pecked her daughter's cheek. Helen winced. Here she was about to embark on the biggest discussion of her career at JI, and Andrea was out stroking her husband's bloated ego instead of being on time. She seemed to always put everyone and everything before her own flesh and blood.

"That's wonderful, Mom. I didn't mind at all," she lied. "What will you have?" She opened the enclosed cabinet. "Brandy?" *What you really need is cyanide, Helen thought.*

Helen's office was spacious and appointed to grandeur. The muted oyster walls were accented with panels of silk wallpaper, one entire wall boasting a beveled glass panel. It was a lot more fashionable than Andrea would have chosen, but she had to admit it was tastefully done. Helen, too, was proud of her sanctuary and the personal triumph she felt of having the only decor that departed from the traditional furnishings at JI. In her mind, it meant that she had won a little battle, even if she alone was privy to the fight. Yes, everything was wonderful at JI. Her only complaint was not being on the sixty-fifth floor; the entire floor that was reserved for Andrea and her entourage. One day soon all that would change.

"Water, *avec* gas, preferably *Perrier*," Andrea said, glancing at her name on a bound document.

"Twist?" *What you need is cyanide.*

Andrea nodded, picked up the report off the glass coffee table, flopped down on the exquisite silk sofa then rested her bag on one of the oak armchairs nearby. She kicked off her shoe on a priceless, eighteenth-century, handmade Persian rug and tucked her feet under her.

"What do we have here?" Looks rather important."

"It's what we are here to talk about, Mother, but please allow me the opportunity for a formal presentation."

"Formal, eh. Great, let's hear it."

Helen did not hesitate. "The revenue generated from Wakefield is quite significant. I think we can both agree that it is a viable venture. In that light, I have a few concerns. First, I really feel that a name change is in order. We need something with much more *oomph* and certainly a name more tied to JI. Secondly, as you know, we have gained significant market share in the eighteen to thirty-five age group. Our name is synonymous with quality at a good price and with fashion that is on the cutting edge. I want to expand our market beyond working women and early teens. Working women often have a different taste from women of leisure and even if they didn't, they cannot comfortably afford couture. I want to move up market, couture, to women who have gained money, power, and status as an extension of their husbands or through family legacy. This is an untapped market for us, and I think there is a lot of money to be made if we can keep our fresh look in the couture market. Our surveys show that we are getting lots of calls from these types of women asking us to do custom clothes for them. I guess our look is so revolutionary that they are very interested. Why, mother, would we turn our backs on this lucrative market?"

"You know how I feel about couture, Helen. We've discussed this umpteen times, even before this venture started when I told you to carve out a niche and stick with it. The working woman is your niche. Couture is off limits. Tell me, how do I explain to my dear friends that I am going into cut-throat competition with them?"

"Mother, the couture market is big. Huge! If it's not us it will be someone else who copies our idea. Wakefield's fashion will be sort of a couture hybrid anyway." Helen's eyebrows drew together in displeasure.

"I'll have to think on that. I can't give you an answer right now. I'm sorry, darling," Andrea looked at her watch. I have to take a conference call. Let's talk later. I'll ring you."

"Now, Mother." Helen voice was sharp and Andrea head snapped back. "I want to talk about it now." Helen clenched her teeth. "About the name change. What do you think of the Helen Companies? It would conjure up a good image in our clients' minds. The old becomes the young kind of stuff. You know what I mean," she said sheepishly.

Andrea laughed aloud at the inference, but she was concerned about Helen's tone. "You're calling me old. But I get what you mean. The pass the baton deal. I actually think it's a good idea. "Now what else, and do hurry, will you?"

"We need an increase in our advertising budget."

"Ahuh."

"It's to help with the transformation from Wakefield. Additionally we need an increase in 'Generations' advertising budget."

"Really? What do you have in mind for this new transformation?" It was meant to be a question, but it came out more like a sarcastic statement. Even this ticked Helen off.

"I haven't quite put all the details down yet, so I would rather wait to outline the exact plans." Helen was careful not to sound defensive.

"Good. Then it can wait. I have to run." Andrea got up and walked towards the door. "By the way," she paused, "don't forget the party for Jacques' new line that we have to attend tonight. And try not to mention anything about our conversation, will you? Who is your date?"

"I actually don't have one."

"How about inviting Harrington? Are things okay between you two?"

"Mom, things are as fine as they are going to be. I am going alone."

"See you later then." Andrea left the office somewhat awed. Helen was quite a surprise. She wouldn't admit to her how much the success of Wakefield, having become the cash cow of the JI, had helped some of the bruised and battered operations in other parts of the company. The barbarians of Wall Street with their mergers and acquisitions had affected JI more than Andrea cared to admit to anyone.

Andrea was still in a pensive mood when she arrived at her office. She should have a talk with Helen. It was time.

"The call came in, Bingham, Lewis, Viking & Gould. It sounded urgent," Janice, Andrea's assistant, informed her. "Shall I ring the number?" Janice's tone was questioning and implied a familiarity. But there was no one in the world who protected Andrea more except perhaps Melissa.

"No, Jan, not just now. Call Scott for me, would you? Remind him that it's Reggie's birthday next Wednesday and also about the party at Jacques' tonight."

Inside the plush office, Andrea paced slightly. Things must be worse than she thought. Today Andrea's mammoth enterprise was a lot less stable than she would have liked. The move to Asia had been, in hindsight, a bad decision. It had caused financial erosion to JI, and with the hostile Asian climate of the eighties, it had created angst among customers both here and abroad. Now she was faced with the prospect of downsizing her American holdings. Many would prefer she dumped the foreign investments, but she was not about to make that decision until she heard the latest figures. She had leveraged a lot on the expansion. Her corporation was primed for a hostile takeover; and the barbarians were hounding at her heels. She poured a glass of Chivas and then dialed the CFO's office.

"Barry, this is Andrea. Would you come up to my office, please?"

"Be there in a minute."

Moments later Barry Whithouse entered the sprawling office carrying a stack of computer printouts.

"I would ask what's the verdict," Andrea said casually, "but I just had an urgent call from the law firm Bingham, Lewis, Viking & Gould. I guess that answers all my questions. Barry, give it to me straight."

Barry sat down at the intimate conference table and spread out the computer printouts. He was a tall, wiry man with horn-rimmed glasses and graying hair at his temples. Squinty, black eyes peered over his glasses. There was absolutely nothing in Barry's physical appearance that alluded to his powerful position at Jacobson Industry or the steel-trap mind that rivaled a computer. What Barry didn't have in looks he made up for in brains. His deep blue suit and striped silk tie, however, hinted he was a successful man. Not only had Barry made it in the world of high finance and was the top brass Chief Financial Officer at JI, but his slight stature was an advantage when he went to war. He sat behind the table and looked at Andrea squarely.

"We got a letter this morning by registered mail from Bingham, et al." Barry removed his glasses and passed a hand over his tired eyes. "It informs us that they are representing a hostile takeover against us. It doesn't, however, say who is trying to sink us. All I can say is thank God for Wakefield because without their revenues our company would not be in a position to fight a hostile takeover. If we have to wage this fight, we could suffer irreparable damage. As I see it, we'd have to lay off six thousand workers by the end of the year, maybe sooner. Everyone is doing it: AMEX, IBM and Kodak. The real problem is, JI is made up largely of young, energetic people, so early retirement offers will be minimal." Barry's slow, measured speech always irritated Andrea, and today she had very little patience.

"I don't want to do that, Barry. What other options do we have?" Andrea's tone was only fractions short of a snap.

"Dumping our overseas assets."

"Out of the question? Wakefield needs the textile factory."

Barry was unperturbed by Andrea's impatience. He had worked with her for over twenty years and there was nothing she could do to ruffle his feathers.

"Maybe it's wise to transfer ownership of the textile plant to the Wakefield umbrella. It might be wise also to put Wakefield in Helen's name alone while we iron out the wrinkles with JI. After all, Wakefield is still a privately held company. When we lay out the Initial Public Offering (IPO) plans of Wakefield to the board, I'm sure they will be excited enough to go along with the transfer of the plant. A hint that we will take Wakefield public will make everyone hold onto their JI stocks, maybe even buy more, for this move will restore their confidence in our bail out plans. We can hide the growing assets of the textile factory for now if we transfer the company under the Wakefield umbrella."

"Wonderful. Barry, you are a genius!" Andrea acquiesced to his analysis and logic, always noting that he was a brilliant man.

"What's your agenda like tomorrow? I'd like to schedule a meeting with Helen. I would also like you to take a more detailed look at a proposal she has for expansion. After you've looked it over, I'll meet with you. What did you say the earnings of Wakefield were?"

"350 million."

"Wow. That's my daughter," Andrea beamed. "What do we have to do to get rid of the blood hounds, Barry?" Andrea fixed her eyes on him.

"That, I don't know just yet," he answered honestly.

Helen's Office

Helen slumped in the chair after pouring herself a spiked coffee, her dander flaring to allergic proportions. Her spiel about Generation X and their differing taste from their parents, the entire crux of her argument was still unheard. She'd spent hours preparing her document and it was brilliant, too; how little black dresses of the eighties had given rise to styles that were vivid and vibrant—a recapture of femininity if you will. How colors were far more interesting and styles were fluid, sexy and feline. How superwomen like her mother had clearly been replaced by women who knew the power of their femininity. All to no avail.

She hated Andrea. Not one day had gone by that she hadn't plotted revenge against her mother. From day one, everything she did was strategically planned to make her ultimate win more gratifying and Andrea's fall from grace more devastating. After all, it was the reason she came to America. Sure, Andrea had tried hard to make up for abandoning her, but it wasn't enough. She had to pay for the life and the pain she'd been forced to endure. Helen sipped the alcohol-laced drink and smiled. Today, Andrea's slight raised Helen's blood pressure significant notches. This was not one of those times when her resolve for revenge was weakened by a dose of Andrea's disarming behavior. She felt justified today in her quest. Looking for comfort, Helen allowed her mind to travel fast backwards down the dusty road of memory lane to the large kitchen in Hampstead.

She could actually smell the cinnamon. As a child, Helen loved that kitchen more than anywhere else in the big, rambling house. The kitchen, decorated as a social room, was a meeting place for all occasions. If she was not hovering around Maya on an overstuffed chair by the fire, she was begging Cookie to help with dinner or to be taught how to prepare an exotic dish.

"Child, you are an absolute nuisance," Cookie would always reprimand her. "Why do you need to learn to prepare Beef Wellington? You are going to grow up and marry a prince. You'll never have to cook."

"Nothing like being independent. What if I marry a pauper?"

"Out! Out of my kitchen," Cookie would pronounce after losing yet another argument with a mere child.

But one night in particular stood out vividly in Helen's mind. It was the night before Christmas and the house had been decorated in grand style for the festive season when numerous guests would be entertained at Christmas and on Boxing Day. The smell of baked ham and scrumptious cookies filled the air. Little Helen Stern had rubbed her hands together in anticipation, as it was about the time Nan would let her have her very own Santa cookie. That night everyone stood in the drawing room trimming the tree, peering from time to time out the windows at the soft snow falling.

"Look at how the branches have turned into icicles." Lizzy, Helen's nanny, lifted the wee girl to peer out of the window. The child was somewhat torn; for her this was the happiest and saddest time of the year. A time when she missed a father most of all. Maya saw the flicker of sadness on Helen's face as she hung the final decorations on the freshly cut pine tree.

"Who wants to hang the angel?" Maya asked, knowing Helen would be up the ladder before anyone could say boo.

"I will, I will," the little chestnut-colored girl shouted, already on the ladder, arms outstretched. When the Christmas tree was finished and finally lit in ceremonious tradition, Maya led the way to the kitchen.

"Time to bake the puddings," her voice echoed.

Baking plum pudding was a routine Maya handled herself.

"I wanna help," announced eight-year-old Helen, skipping and bouncing in delight toward the cozy kitchen. With its open hearth glowing yellow and floral pillows strewn casually on the enveloping sofa, the bright kitchen was not only a functional meal preparation enclave, but a place where much company hovered around chatting and playing games. Many little ones who refused to miss the excitement had fallen asleep on the cozy rugs and chairs.

"Wash those hands then," Maya reminded.

Cookie would then help Helen up the stool to lather her hands under the kitchen sink. Together they measured and poured, separated and folded, added spirits and boiled water for plum pudding. Nan would make at least six big puddings and a little one just for Helen.

"For a pretty urchin," Nan handed Helen her own pudding dish to pour batter.

"Thanks, Nan," Helen looked up at the older woman, a funny look on her face. "Why don't I call you Mummy like all the other kids call their moms? The kids at school want to know why you are Nan and why your skin color is different from mine." It was the moment Maya had been dreading. She'd hoped the time when Helen would question her heritage would not come this soon. Most parents didn't have to face such life-altering questions this early. For even the most dreaded question, discussing the birds and the bees, could wait a little longer. The thought of talking about sex didn't make Maya panic as much as telling a little girl about her strange beginnings.

"There's nothing to a name. I called my mother Mimi. I'm not sure why, really, that's just the way it was. But in your case, Helen, I am Nan, because I am not your real mother. Your mother was from a different country altogether. Where she came from, all the people were brown. She couldn't afford to take you with her when she left, but I can tell you she loved you so much. When she left she asked me to take care of you. She wanted you to have every opportunity the world had to offer."

"Was I a bad girl?"

"Oh, honey, no. How could anyone so precious be bad?"

"Well, why didn't she leave me something to remember her by? A favorite blanket or a Blinky." Helen was thinking of her dog-eared, pot-bellied teddy that accompanied her to bed every night. Over the years he had gotten raggedy as he had to be washed every time she had an accident. She never meant to wet him up in her sleep, but Blinky should have gotten her up to go to the bathroom! After all, she was just a kid.

"I think because she was too old to have a blanket or a Blinky."

"Uh huh. Well, it's hard to listen to those kids at school." Helen looked pleadingly at Maya.

"Sometimes, duckie, it's best to make lemonade when life gives you lemons. Just think of all that sugar at the bottom of the glass and all the yummy pulps floating on top."

"But we only drink lemonade in the summer. What do I do in the winter?" Helen said innocently. The child was far too wise for her age.

"Then you can always find something special and wonderful for that time of the year. You tell those kids they shouldn't be so nosy. And you," she tucked the little chin, "just know that you are loved, very loved." She continued to pinch the little nose and tickle a rib. "Who loves you, who loves you," the tickle was harder. Helen was now rolling around on the floor with her Nan. Maya would have preferred the answer, just because I'm Nan and that's that, but instead Helen said, "I know you love me, Nan, but I want a mummy like everyone else."

Ah, well. Maya thought of her next diversionary tactic as she lifted the sad little girl onto the counter stool.

"How about a lick?" Maya held up the spoon from the left-over batter of Christmas pudding.

That did the trick. Helen loved the deep brown batter with lots and lots of raisins. Somehow it always seems to make booboos better. Her pixy face, now covered in the sweet, sticky mixture, was a sight Maya would always cherish. She wiped the little nose, mouth and hands and shooed her off to the nanny. "Don't forget to brush," she sang after her, relieved that the first trial of what were to be many more intense questions was over.

Helen's fourteenth birthday party arrived. Maya had said it was going to be a special treat, and Helen had come from boarding school in Geneva for the party. Over the years, she had learned to distrust special treats because for Maya, they were somehow related to telling fortunes and giving spiritual advice to the multitude of people who came to visit them.

She was only six years old when she started learning the benefits of her spiritual "gift". For a while, she enjoyed the attention and the control it brought her, but now she was tired of being forced to look into the dark lives of people. Having to give grown people advice was a drag. After all, what could she tell them that they wouldn't already know if they cared to listen to their own psyche? Tonight was to be her initiation as a Master Teacher.

The party was already a bore to Helen. There were hundreds of people in attendance. She wondered what would happen at her sixteenth! Helen was just creeping up the stairs when the doorbell rang. When she opened the door, an incredibly beautiful woman was standing there. My-My, she thought. I sure would love to look like that when I grow up.

She must have stared for awhile, because the woman moved closer to the entrance and cleared her throat.

"Oh, pardon me. Please come in." Helen was sure she was a model or a movie star, but instead it turned out to be one of Maya's old school buddies. Helen felt tranced. Something strange was happening to her. The connection she felt to the stranger at the door was disturbing. So much so that she followed the woman around all night. And when they had talked in the garden, Helen found herself wishing desperately that somehow she was her mother. She felt a deep loss when her feelings were unsupported. That very night she made up her mind to do everything in her powers to find her parents. When she found her mother, she'd give her the lovely butterfly broach Andrea Jacobson-Preston had given her.

After the party had ended, Helen's thoughts drifted again and again to the statuesque woman. She really wanted a mom like Andrea Jacobson-Preston and a dad like the man in the painting Andrea had given her. A strange picture to have given a child, she thought, but the diamond and sapphire broach had made up for that. She would cherish that butterfly broach, not because she knew it had to be very expensive, but instinctively she knew it would make her mother happy. Totally forlorn and unhappy, Helen had sobbed herself to sleep.

As if the obsession that followed wasn't enough, Helen had gone back to school and fallen in love for the first time. Looking desperately for a love that was different from Maya's, she practically made a fool of herself over Geraud.

The international boarding school, *La Briton,* was the ultimate cosmopolitan world. Kids from all over the world were sent to learn to be critical thinkers and well-mannered ladies and gentlemen. Geraud was new that semester, and boy was he ever handsome, handsome with a capital "H". Yet, unlike his looks suggested, he was sensitive and kind. For her he'd been a great comfort, and their budding friendship offered her a level of security that allowed her to unshelve secrets, expose thoughts and feel her pain. But most importantly, he was chestnut as she was. Just transferred from the French school in Geneva, Geraud, too, it seemed, welcomed her friendship.

"Where are you from?" She handed him her books to carry.

"France."

"Any you?"

"I'm English, but my mother was from Jamaica."

Geraud told her his mother was French and his father was a politician of high rank from the *Côte d' Ivoire*. To have married a foreign woman had caused, it seemed, quite a controversy among his people, and he finally relocated his family to France. Geraud, like Helen, was a bit of a loner. Childhood traumas create kids who are insecure and mature beyond their years. Neither of them had ever associated with a bunch of teens who knew nothing but shopping and boy-talk. Both displaced in one way or another, they had something in common.

With her highly developed sixth sense, it was often rumored that Helen was a witch, a statement she vehemently denied. Chanting and accepting one's special gift did not qualify a person as a witch, she'd argue stubbornly. After all, this was not the sixteenth century! And Geraud's devotion to music had gotten him labeled a weirdo. So, Helen, in her isolation and infinite wisdom, convinced herself that Geraud and she were destined to be together. Apart from the hairless, be-pimpled Spaniard, Raul, they were the only members of the outcast club. But Geraud was not weird. He was just smart. Too smart to converse idly with adolescent tomfoolery. He had a mission, and it seemed he had the discipline to accomplish it. Best of all, in Helen's mind, he was a master at the piano, an instrument which she had avowed to master herself. In addition to their love (in her mind; they hadn't even kissed), they shared their ardor of music. Although she was quite good at the piano, she was mesmerized that at sixteen Geraud was already a well-recognized maestro and destined to be a virtuoso. Often there was no separation between Geraud and his piano. He practiced every free moment he had. Helen would sit and listen to him, a look of longing punctuating her beautiful, young face. It was a new feeling for her. On occasions when she was overly moved by his work, she would join him at the piano. He hadn't realized she was so good a pianist.

Helen's emotions followed him wherever he went with his music, for when Geraud played, his hands, body and mind became one with the instrument, and she could not help but be drawn into the spirit of the work. When he had played the *Dance of the Flowers* from the *Nutcracker* especially for her, she had fallen hopelessly in love with him. Loving Geraud had made her forget the pain and the intense obsession of trying to find her parents. How she longed for him to touch her, caress her, and take her to the mountain top she'd often heard so much about, but Geraud had not even so much as kissed her.

The following semester he started dating Simone Alexis, a native of Gabon.

Helen felt mortally wounded. There was nothing to look forward to with Geraud out of her life. Whatever was wrong with her that made everyone want to leave her? Helen had wailed herself into a tizzy. Then it came to her. She could visit with Andrea Jacobson-Preston, the woman from her fourteenth birthday party. A change of scenery would certainly do her good. It was now the only thing she had to look forward to after Geraud's rejection. And Helen was quite ready for anything other than being a fortuneteller. What she needed was some quiet time to sort out her life.

And then she'd read the article that tore her life apart. Running away from her lucrative career as a young fashion model was yet another reason to blame Andrea. For four years she'd lived in Jamaica in the shadow of her mother, searching and digging for anything she could use against her. If only that woman knew how her betrayal had altered the course of Helen's destiny and the stone she'd created where her daughter's heart used to be, she would perhaps understand her bitterness.

"Miss Stern, are you there? Miss Stern? Miss Stern!"

Helen was jarred back to reality as Mrs. Walters voice got more fervent.

"I'm here, Mrs. Walters. Just had on my headphones for a minute."

"Mr. Harrington Baldwin is holding on line four."

"Tell him I'm not here."

Ah, she shrugged off the memories. She was doing exactly what should be done. Even if Andrea was her biological mother whose shame and guilt of leaving her infant child was giving her this opportunity at Wakefield, she would never be able to feel grateful to her. It was too little, too late. And because she wanted couture she would get couture.

Chapter Nine

Jacques St. Pierre's Soirée

The limo pulled up to the curb of Seventy-Ninth and Park. Helen gathered her taffeta skirt and stepped gracefully out of the car, the chauffeur offering her a steadying hand for assistance. As many times as he had seen Miss Stern, he could never keep his eyes off her legs, and tonight was no exception. For the past twenty years he had worked for celebrities *and* the rich and famous. He had seen beautiful women, driven them for nose jobs, face lifts, tummy tucks, and divorces. He knew more than he should about their private lives and yes, he was discreet, but he had never seen a woman as captivating as Helen Stern. It was more than her beauty that intrigued him. It was that she was untouchable and mysterious. This was one socialite he knew nothing about; she was very much like her mother in that regard.

The doorman ushered her into the private elevator, he too, ogling her mile-long legs. He twisted the old-fashioned brass door latch, and the mahogany-paneled elevator lunged upward, opening again in the foyer of St. Pierre's penthouse. On the table inside the foyer was a gold monogrammed guest book and a platinum Cartier fountain pen resting in a Waterford inkwell, waiting for the next dignitary to scribble a unique presence. The huge, marble table was adorned with long-stemmed white roses and purple orchids. Votive candles trimmed the circular marble ledges that exposed an incredible view of the Hudson River adding an elegant and romantic touch to the ambiance. Just inside the doorway the party buzzed as men and women bustled around in elegant St. Pierre's attire. A mixture of expensive perfume and cologne permeated the air.

"*Cherie, bonsior,*" the host himself greeted her. "*Vous etes seul?*"

"I'm afraid so. Understandable, though, as I work so much. Who has time for love and romance? Alas, it forces one to go to social engagements alone. Harrington sends his apologies." Helen failed to tell him she had all but told Harrington to bugger off, even as persistent as Harrington could be. A trait of the wealthy who have a hard time hearing No. She knew her mother would have loved to see her with Harrington, and that was the more reason to spurn him.

"My dear, you force me to repeat an awful cliché. All that work…"

"Got it." She stopped him, a faint smile glossing her ruby lips. She loved Jacques. If it weren't for Jacques, she didn't know where she would be today. Probably an addict on the streets of London. Too bad she had skipped out on him back then, but she was glad he hadn't held it against her. Interning with Jacques had been a pivotal and invaluable experience. Not only that she had most enjoyed getting to know him, but also it was such a wonderful time. She thought back to their practical jokes and scrumptious meals.

Immediately following graduation, Helen had taken a three-week trip back to England. Still angry with Maya, she'd never bothered to visit her childhood home at Rollan Hills. Much of her time in England had been spent at her mother's designer, Jacques St. Pierre's agency, doing a fashion internship and learning the inside workings of the fashion industry. In her opinion, Jacques was an awesome designer, one of the very best in the industry. His vision of beauty translated itself into unique and exotic designs, and the tastefulness of his opulent establishment reiterated his talent. The private rooms for each patron were individually decorated with hand-painted wallpaper and fabrics, and boasted themes of the head patron's homeland. Thus a French patron would feel at home with the Eiffel tower looming in the distance of a French scene on the wallpaper. Helen's favorite spot was the Greek patron's room that overlooked the Acropolis while Yanni's music was piped into the sound proof room. Picking up the last of the discarded garments, she had headed into Jacques' office suite.

Jacques had been sprawled out, exhausted, on the sofa in his office. The elegant office with its Edwardian architecture and furnishing was a soothing place to be after a hectic day. A glass-enclosed gym hidden behind the heavy drapes complete with sauna, massage table and a Jacuzzi welcomed the weary body or the charming philanderer, and Jacques was still very much the consummate playboy. It was a long day of "if anything could go wrong it would," but Helen felt energized.

"What a trying day this was," Helen announced as she flopped down beside Jacques. "I'm glad it's over. It surely felt like Murphy's law was at work today," Helen sighed, stretching her legs out before her.

"*Oui*. That it was." Jacques had pulled the ascot from around his neck.

"You know what Murphy's law is?"

Jacques nodded wearily.

"So then, do you know about O'Brian's?" Helen had said, smiling.

"From the look of things, tomorrow could live up to his law."

"I have not heard of this one. What does it say?"

"It says that Murphy was an optimist."

They had both laughed uncontrollably before Helen finally composed herself and said. "You *Monsieur*, could do with café. I promise this coffee will cure all this laughter, for it is so old. I made it this morning!"

"Thanks, but no thanks," Jacques had made a face. "But, *ma chérie*, on a serious note, I am very impressed with your fashion aptitude. You are getting very good at this and you handled yourself very well today, *ma belle*. Why not stay with me for a while longer and learn all there is to know about design?"

"Thank you, Jacques." She had touched his hand lightly at the kind offer. "I just wish I could, but I've already made arrangements to travel to Paris to work with Madame Jouvier. It's such a swell opportunity. Do you think I should cancel?"

"No! No! No! It is an opportunity of a lifetime." Jacques had been impressed with Helen's take charge and go get it attitude. He told her she was destined for success.

"I must confess, though, that I chose to do my internship in the fashion industry because of you. Mother couldn't have been more pleased with my choice. She really respects you, Jacques."

"And I her." His voice had been a little sad.

Helen had looked up sharply at the tone of his voice. Could he still be in love with Andrea? She'd continued the conversation, giving no clue as to her thoughts.

"We think the next logical arena for JI is the fashion industry, especially with JI owning the Asian textile factories."

"I suppose your mother would catch…err, how do you say this.…"

"Flack."

"Yes. Flack about moving production to Asia. But by God, the cost of American labor makes doing business at a competitive price impossible." Jacques shook his head.

"That it is. And let me tell you, they are lawsuit happy. Big billboards of unscrupulous barristers advertising their services. You have never seen anything like it," Helen agreed, distressed.

"Of course I have and apartment there but I try to spend as little time in the country as possible. Too awesome for me." Jacques switched the subject abruptly. "How about changing the venue? All this chatter is making me hungry. Supper?"

"That sounds wonderful. And I agree with you about the awesomeness of New York, but in my opinion that's what makes it so exciting." Helen's delight about her new home had been obvious. "America is such a hard country to fathom as there is really no 'American Culture.' Not like in England, France, Japan or Africa. That's why it's so easy to succeed there if one wants to. Look at me!"

"My dear," he had chuckled, "I wouldn't exactly say you are typical or even a good example of the underprivileged."

"I suppose you're right, but you know you had a hand in my success, Jacques." She had touched his arm. "I don't think I ever really thanked you for preventing me from being on welfare. "The dole," she offered in explanation, "was going to have to be my next means of support if I didn't find work. Please let me show my appreciation by treating you to supper. That is, of course, if you can deal with a new woman's attitude and permit me to pay."

"Why, Miss Stern, I would be honored."

Later at the Savoy, when they had been seated in a dimly-lit private room near a window, it seemed to Helen that Jacques had grown more handsome. The graying hair at his temples gave him a very distinguished look and made his naturally jet hair more intense in places. A waiter appeared discreetly from time to time, awaiting a signal of readiness.

"*Ma chère,*" Jacques eyes had twinkled, "it is wonderful that you chose to come back to England. I am so happy to have you. Now," he'd smiled beguilingly, "tell me all the news about your mama."

It seemed that Andrea still cast a love spell on Jacques.

"Mama is *très bien*. She sends her love and an invitation for you to visit next fall for our grand opening of the new enterprise that I will manage. I can't tell you much about it, so please don't ask. Company confidentiality, you know."

"It's funny, but I had dinner at this very restaurant with your mother many years ago when she had just signed the Hanoi deal. We actually sat right over there." He pointed to a spot two tables away.

"Now it seems rather strange to be again sitting with her daughter. You couldn't have been more than twelve or thirteen. To think you were a young lady who I didn't even know existed! Now here you are, all grown and self-confident, and ready to make your mark on the world. But my dear, why did you not tell me when you modeled for me that you were Andrea's daughter?"

"That was, indeed, a regret. But it took me so by surprise when you said you were once in love with Mother and, to be frank, it was a bad period for us. I had just found out she was my real mother. I must say how glad I am thought that our resemblance seemed to have sparked an unconscious desire for you to help me. I really owe you a lot."

"Helen, my dear," he had patted her hand, "I am glad things have worked out for you. Sometimes life is so complex and unpredictable. To think destiny delivered you to my door steps!" He had shook his head in disbelief. "I am truly happy for you and Andrea and will always be there for you both."

She had been sure then that Jacques was still in love with her mother, and it made her tense and angry. Everyone was in love with Andrea. The Andrea whose love for her own daughter did not prevent her from abandoning the child.

"Ah, it is true. Things don't really change do they, Jacques? They just go in circles. But isn't that the real meaning of life—to pass our destiny on to our offspring and to those whose lives we touch? Otherwise what purpose can there be? But it's good to grow up and be able to fully appreciate people. Now that I'm twenty-something, can drink legally, can try to run an empire on my own, you no longer seem so old to me. I think life is planned that way."

"What do you mean?"

"That time stand still just long enough so the young can catch up to the old, if not for eternity, for a brief moment. Do you know what I mean?"

"Yes," he had said quietly. "At some point every experience in life becomes known to all. I call that point the intersecting point of life."

"That it is," she had replied. "What do you say you take me dancing. I want to show off my new American moves." Her voice hinted of familiarity. "After all, I think we are at that intersecting point."

"Ah, here comes your mother now." Jacques', wonderful voice brought her back to the present. He moved toward the door as though pulled by a magnet. He had all but forgotten his conversation with Helen.

Andrea moved confidently into the room, her arm intertwined in Scott's. A floor-length cape that showed off her legs to advantage covered the black satin and organza Valentino under-dress, which stopped a hint shy of her knees. Andrea owned so many St. Pierre designs that he dared not balk at her choice of designer tonight. She couldn't possibly stomach the fact that almost all of the guests would probably be wearing one of his designs. Andrea, could never abide being one of the crowd. No one, however, could question her impeccable taste or the elegance of her attire. The long, shapely legs caressed by silken stockings were a showstopper, and even if they were more seasoned than her daughter's, they were just as fetching. The satin cape trimmed in black and white organza swished against the floor as she glided over to meet Jacques. Helen, being used to her own accolades, was slightly annoyed. She moved over to Scott and draped an arm though his.

"From the stares and whispers, I would say you are the envy of the men here tonight," Helen whispered to Scott.

"Mmmm, for more than one reason, I might add. You look wonderful tonight," he replied.

"Probably, but I defer to Mom's sense of absolute charm, grace, and style."

"Oh, it's more than that. It's her aura."

"Meaning?" she wanted to ask, but decided against it. Andrea, who was about to hold court, had a way of including anyone within ear shot into her dynamics.

"Good evening *dahling*," Jacques pecked Andrea on both cheeks.

"Scott," Jacques said offering a hand, "so good to see you, though I must admit, it's a little bothersome that you have the best-looking women on your arm."

"Well, I'm the one who should be jealous. My wife never makes appearances such as this. You are the only person who could get her here, and that, my friend, is clout."

They both shook hands, laughing haughtily. Over the years, once Jacques had accepted Andrea's decision to marry Scott, not that he could have done more than brood, they became friends. Now that he saw how happy she was, he acquiesced completely to Scott. Not that he stopped loving her—far from it. As long as he lived, he would always think of Andrea as the one who got away. To show his sportsmanship, on occasions he had brought a date or two to the yearly summer gathering. And he had to admit that in a quirky sort of way, Scott was a great guy.

A group gathered around as Madame Andrea held court. Helen, bored, scanned the crowd for an interesting diversion. Hey eyes came to rest on a dark-haired Adonis engaging a lively group. Just as she strained forward to peer closer, he looked up and for a full minute kept her gaze. Helen turned nonchalantly back to the conversation at hand but not before she noted every detail of the charming man. He was leaning casually against the staircase, a silk scarf still hanging loosely around his black Armani tuxedo, his hands gesticulating for emphasis. Even though his stance was casual, his persona was intense, maybe even a little cavalier—too much so, she felt.

"*Mademoiselle?*" the French waiter held the tray of exquisite libations, ready to be instructed. "Rouge, blanc or champagne.?"

"Merlot, *S'il vous plaît.*"

"*Voilà.*"

"*Merci. Execusez-moi, qui est l'homme la-bas?*" she inquired.

"Pardon me, but I am not really French. You've caught me, trying to perfect my accent among these French natives—so I guess the accent is good,eh?" he whispered, a mischievous grin on his face.

"Quite. Keep it up. Now, do you know that man over by the staircase?"

"*Oui*, couldn't resist," he grinned again. "That's Mr. Victor Innes Palmer. One of the heirs to Catillion Publishing. His mother was the Catillion."

"Thanks." How interesting. The family owned the *International Moderne*. Her brows pulled together as she realized it was the magazine she had graced as a teenager. Regardless, the publication was one she needed to embrace. In the near future, the Helen Stern fashion empire would depend on every favor.

Just then an unknown woman came out of nowhere and joined the man by the stairs. She casually touched Adonis' shoulder in a way that seemed familiar. The woman whispered something and waved in the direction of Andrea's party. Helen did not take her eyes off the even though she was looking at him through the mirror. They were, it appeared, about to head in her direction. She was more than a little curious by the interaction between the two seemingly familiar people. She moved closer to Andrea's side.

Adonis, as she had named him, rose from the banister, and she realized he was quite tall. In fact, he was very tall, but his muscular, athletic build brought his height into proportion. His stride was purposeful but slightly disappointing, she noticed; although full of confidence, it was a little lazy. Maybe she should excuse him as his unsteady gait could have been from too many glasses of Cristal. As he came closer, she could see a sort of carelessness in his perfectly chiseled face. The eyes were an unusual green-brown, hooded by full, but tamed brows. The day-old-stubble on his face suggested nonconformity and a rebel spirit. It made him rather more attractive. The glint in the roaming eyes and the hint of the upturned lips suggested a mischievous Romeo.

"Jacques," the woman approached, her hand extended before her body caught up. It was clear, up close, that she was quite a bit older than the man with her. Maybe he was a gigolo. The thought struck Helen like a bolt of lightning, and then she was convinced of it. Why else would a handsome man go tagging after an old bag, even if she looked great.

"Olivia, I am so happy you could make it. After our conversation, I was sure you would be delayed in England."

"So did I, but here I am. I must say your story in the *London Times* was very nicely done indeed. Remind me to chat with you about a wonderful idea for an ad that I think would be perfect when the piece is run again."

Jacques nodded. "Please, let me introduce you. Mr. & Mrs. Scott Preston and their beautiful daughter, Helen."

"Wonderful to make your acquaintance. My, you are such a beautiful child," she spoke directly to Helen. "And that dress, I have never quite seen anything like it. If you don't mind, who is the designer?"

Although Helen took offense to the child remark, she savored the compliment, which was usually given to her mother out of deference, she was sure.

"Thank you on both accounts. Wakefield designed the dress."

"Yes! Yes, I have been following that company. Impressive things are happening there." *I have seen this face before. Where...Ah I can't remember.* "Anyway I'm interested in this designer, maybe I can make an appointment," she said before again turning to the man at her side. "Please, allow me to introduce my friend, Victor. We call him VIP."

"My pleasure," he bowed. American, Helen noted. Thank goodness. She could now more easily dismiss him.

"Well I hope you are all enjoying this wonderful party," Olivia interrupted. "Jacques sure knows how to throw a soirée. Just look at some of these fashions! I am taking notes for my column." She smiled sweetly, her dancing eyes alighting on the man standing beside her. "Well, see you soon," she strode erectly to the next group of patrons.

Victor? A name like Victor seemed much more royal than its owner! Helen studied him.

Victor, as they strolled away, purposefully hooked his finger through Olivia's shoulder bag, bringing it to rest ever so lightly on her hip. Teasing. Who was he trying to tease? Quite a flirt! Well, if he expected a rise from her, he would be disappointed. He had hardly said a word, but instantly she knew there had to be more to him than being a gigolo. After all, if his mother was a Catillion, he had to be heir to the fortune. He was definitely not the type to take money from women for favors. He was born to wealth, at least as far as she could see.

Helen's voice was controlled and calm as she queried Jacques inconspicuously.

"What an unusual couple. A very handsome one. I bet she was gorgeous at twenty."

"If Olivia has anything to do with it she will forever look like twenty-five or as we would say of that uncertain age. She is part owner and fashion editor for International Moderne, the magazine on which you appeared as a teenager. After Victor's mother died, his father married Olivia. Victor is actually her stepson. The children were bitter about the marriage at first because it was VIP's mother's family who passed on the family business; they resented Olivia stepping in and taking over. It seems they have come around, though. Olivia spends a lot of time in Europe; that's probably why you haven't met yet. The magazine is a bit stuffy for your taste, although as a teen model you graced the cover."

"I did, didn't I?"

"Yes, and caused quite a stir. Then you…"

"What does VIP stand for?" She cut him off. She didn't care to hear about her vanishing act after he had helped her so much. She was surprised he had even forgiven her.

"VIP are Victor's initials. Funny eh? His initials actually convince him he is a Very Important Person."

How charming and appropriate. "Clever. I wonder if it was a coincidence?" Helen's tone was light and inquisitive.

"I'm sure." Jacques nodded to a woman making her way over to him.

Helen turned her attention to VIP. *He is a teaser. Definitely! He'd touched his stepmother for her benefit, she was sure.* The song *Teaser* came to mind immediately and reminded her of the many nights at Nuts, her favorite nightclub in Switzerland, where she had swayed to the catchy

Soca tune from Trinidad. Watching him a bit more, she edged closer so she could remain within earshot of the deep baritone voice. The deepness of the voice had a soothing, almost theatrical quality to it. Yet, there was something about Victor Innes Palmer that was bothering her. Something not quite right. If indeed there was anything clandestine, he would fit right into her plans.

Victor, too, was thinking of Helen. The masked look that he had perfected over time gave an air of mystery. He could just see her mind churning trying to fit him into a category. Women like Helen Stern always needed categories. He was betting, though, that even she could not resist his allure or his charm. No one had to tell him that mystery and intrigue were very attractive to women—he had proven that theory. His hooded eyes that were cloaked under thick eyebrows had missed nothing about her. The erectness of her spine, the toned body sheathed in scarlet taffeta in a room full of women all wearing black, showed the danger and individuality of her personality. The dress that was mid thigh exposed long shapely legs that were gloved in a midheight pump. Siren? Vixen? Not a chance in the world.

Her lack of jewelry, except for a butterfly broach, again showed her spunk in a room of bejeweled women. There was only one other woman in the room that exuded the kind of style this Helen did. The woman in the black satin and velvet. Had Jacques not introduced them as a family? Realizing he was instantly attracted to the women with the deep jet eyes that complemented his own green-brown ones, he decided that he would be a gentleman tonight, even if just in the company of *these* ladies. And now that he could see their glasses were empty, it was an opportune time to leave the old bag Olivia and offer his assistance.

"May I get you both refills?" he indicated the empty glass in Helen's hand. He also took the opportunity to offer Andrea Jacobson-Preston a delightful compliment on her appearance. Helen stiffened. *Why was it that her mother always stole her thunder?*

"Charming young man," Andrea offered before turning back to her conversation.

Before Victor returned from his gentlemanly errand, Helen excused herself, whispered something to Jacques and her mother, then she was out of there. Outside the entrance of the building her waiting car was in sight. She heaved a great sigh of remorse. What a pity. She couldn't stand anyone who sucked up to her mother, and VIP had made a fatal error. No need to play where one had to work anyway. And there was no doubt that with what she had in mind she needed *International Moderne* on her side. Ah well, she sighed again, he sure was refreshing. If only he had been a foreigner.

"Hello. Pardon me, *Mademoiselle*. Do I know you?"

"Me?" Helen looked around to see who the man was talking to. She wouldn't mind if it was she, because for some unexplainable reason the charm of VIP had made her feel rather enticed.

"Aren't you Helen Stern?"

"Surely. And you…Geraud. Geraud…oh my God. It's really you?"

"Yes. Oh Helen," he embraced her, kissing both cheeks. "What a wonderful surprise. I would never have expected to see you in America."

"I live here now. In fact, I have lived here practically since high school. And you?"

"No, no, no. I am here to debut at Carnegie Hall. I will be here for a month. I can't believe it's you."

"Nor I you," she said quietly, for her heart had not forgotten the love she'd felt for this man as a young girl.

"Do you have a moment?" Geraud didn't want to say good-bye just yet. "I'm just on my way to a friend's party. Would you like to join me?"

"Where is the party?"

"Just inside the building behind us. It's an old friend from Paris. I promised him I would stop by after rehearsal."

"If you are talking about Jacques St. Pierre, I'm just leaving the party."

"Ah, you know him, too? That man sure gets around. How do you know Jacques?"

"I'm in the fashion world."

"So, why are you leaving so soon?"

"Claustrophobia. But we have time to see each other if you'll be here a month. How about lunch sometime tomorrow?"

"No, I want to see you now. We'll go for *café*. Wait here for me. I will just go in and make my excuses. Do not leave," he begged.

"Sure, Geraud. Just don't make me turn into a pumpkin."

"Wouldn't dream of it," he pinched her nose playfully.

What a pity. He was the man who could have saved her. Who could have restored her faith in love and her trust in humanity. With a renewed flood of emotion, she remembered his repudiation and was angry enough to get into her car and leave him waiting on the sidewalk all night. She deliberated too long, for it seemed to Helen that Geraud could not possibly have made it all the way upstairs before he came striding back.

"Now," he said, "where would you like to go? It's so good to see you," he embraced her again.

"Actually, I was on my way home when you caught me. We could have coffee there."

"That would be lovely. No let me say it in American. That's swell." His eyes crinkled and the dazzling smile erased all Helen's resolve to leave him on the sidewalk.

Helen instructed her driver to take them back to her *pied-à-terre* on Seventy-Ninth and Park.

Geraud, the consummate gentleman, navigated her by the elbow in and out of the elevator. When she found her keys he took them and let them into the apartment, flipping the light switch by the door as though he belonged there.

"Ah, my dear. This is *magnifigue*. What a wonderful apartment! I see you have not forgotten your European roots." He indicated his approval of her furnishings.

"I loved it the moment I saw it. I swear to you, Geraud, I had looked for over a year with zippo luck. My poor realtor was so exasperated with me she almost gave up. 'You want a *find*,' she often exclaimed when I kept vetoing everything she found."

"And so how did this 'find' come about?" Geraud's genuine curiosity gave her a comforting feeling of sharing.

"Apparently this place was occupied by two sisters for almost a half-century. When the first sister died, the second went only a month after. The grandchildren didn't want the place. Too many memories for them."

"Well it was worth the wait, wasn't it?"

"Yes, it was. I think my realtor thought that, too, for she must have charged me twice as much to make up for all the time she spent looking. The day after she found it she called me at 6:00 a.m.! 'This is it, Miss Stern. Nothing better exists. This place is exquisite. You should see it now. Each room is completely different from the other, they are large, airy, and the East River is directly outside your bedroom window. It's even immersed in light when it's dismal outside.'"

"'I'll be there right away,' I shrieked, but I had done that so many times that I don't think she was convinced. "Go and sit by the door so no other agent can get in,' I ordered, and *Voilà*, here I am."

The mahogany-stained wooden floors of the entranceway gleamed under the recessed lighting, glittering in spots as the street lights bounced off them. The hallway dramatically dipped down with three semicircular stairs to a glass-enclosed living room. The plush ivory carpet was strewn atop with silk Indian rugs on which sat the most exquisite furnishings.

The steps came up again on the other side of the sunken living room to end in a dramatic platform. Dead center and surrounded by soft silken chairs was a Steinway Grand Piano. It was elevated above the eclectic array of splendidly chosen furnishings and just to the right was a marble fireplace. The thirty-foot ceiling added a grandeur to the room that could only be described as a rare vision. Outside, the skyline of Manhattan twinkled.

"That's a magnificent instrument." Geraud moved, entranced, toward the piano.

"Thank you. I couldn't agree with you more. May I offer you a drink?"

Dragging himself away from the piano, he followed her to the warm, brightly colored kitchen that was as large as a comfortable living room. Helen had purposefully decorated it like the one at Rollan Hills. Overstuffed chairs surrounded the wooden fireplace and welcomed the weary body.

"Do you spend a lot of time in here?"

"How I wish." Helen shook her head ruefully. "If I had time to spend this is where I would spend it, though, but I'm afraid, as it is, I hardly ever get to use this kitchen." Helen snuck a peek at the handsome face. Too cultured to look like a typical artist, she thought. The angular jawline and grayish-brown eyes caught the softness of the recessed lighting in the kitchen rendering him, in her mind, a work of art. Only the shoulder length dread-locked hair gave away his radical bent. Otherwise, Geraud was conservatively dressed in a smartly cut tuxedo.

"So what do you think?" he said, obviously noticing her stare. "How have I grown?" Geraud's face relaxed into a smile.

"Very handsomely," she led the way back to the living room a little self-conscious of her attraction for a man who had rejected her innocent love.

"And how do you feel about that?" his smile broadened.

"Oh please," her eyebrows raised as she tried to make light of the moment. "What would you like me to feel?"

"Ah, who knows. Do you still play?" He gestured at the piano, changing the subject abruptly.

"Every opportunity I get. It keeps me company." Helen felt rejected—again. She should have left his ass on the pavement!

"Play for me." His voice was excited.

"All right," she consented, "but I'm not nearly as good as you think." Helen stood by the piano and lifted the shiny lid. The ivory keys sparkled in the dimly lit room. She ran her fingers lightly over the keys, almost caressing them, but still only silence. No sound yielded under the soft touch. Momentarily, she was entranced, as though she had been remembering all their times together at *La Briton*. Quickly she sat on the stool, trying to get her emotions under control by focusing on being perfectly aligned before the instrument. Slowly her fingers curled over the keys, and as she adjusted her position her short red dress slipped up her thighs. Expertly, Helen ran her fingers across the keys, this time warming up with an F Minor scale. Moments later, the beautiful melody of the *Dance of the Flowers* from the "Nutcracker" filled the air.

Geraud stood mesmerized, for he had no idea she had gotten so good at the instrument. He was deeply touched that she chose to play the melody they often shared together at school. Carefully, so as not to disturb her, he sat beside her, picking up the tune of the song an octave higher. Together they made the most incredible music, each carried by the passion of their nostalgia. When the song ended they were breathless and sad.

"That was wonderful." His voice reflected the sadness. "That was wonderful." He was facing her now, his chest heaving slightly from the intoxication of the music. "Oh Helen, I've made a terrible mistake. We should have stayed together. I was a fool not to see how right we were for each other. We would have been incredible as a duet, *Ma Belle*," he reached out, allowing his index finger to trace the curve of her chin as he turned her face toward him and looked deep into her eyes. "We would have been good together." he repeated.

"Yes, Geraud. We would have made beautiful music together," she breathed softly against his temple.

"We still can." His lips brushed hers. "We still can."

"Maybe," Helen sighed, allowing herself to be swept into a lingering kiss. Quickly the music started again, only this time his hands were caressing her soft skin instead of the ivory keys. Each stroke nuzzling farther down her dress, fondling, stroking, and kissing, until her nipples ached through the silk organza. As the music escalated, his hand unbuttoned her dress, releasing the pointed dots while gently massaging the chestnut mountains heaving with desire. Waves of lust washed over her. Viscous liquid flowed. The rhythm was beating steadily now. With each beat Helen drifted further and further into the abyss of passion. Suddenly the rising vibrato of the violin increased her urgency. And as the harp's melody washed over her, and as the music got louder and louder, working its way to a fever pitch, Geraud delicately found her nexus of desire. Helen's arms twitched, her legs quivered, and as her entire body reached its ultimate pleasure, small sounds escaped her lips. There was no question that she wanted the overture to continue.

Soon their half-clothed flesh was intertwined. Geraud's lips demanded her hungrily, and she responded with complete abandon. Obeying the demand of raw animal passion, she arched her back to receive Geraud's gift, her hands pressing deep and deeper into the taut flesh with each thrust.

The maestro was conducting his orchestra, each instrument in perfect harmony. Her emotions were fast approaching the point of ecstasy. The tiny bud of her womanhood throbbed as the incoming tide of wild spasms washed over her. Urgently she ripped at his clothes, freeing him to participate fully in their sensuous indulgence. There was no turning back now.

They were beyond the waves now. The music and the waves engulfed them, delivering them to the point of absolute content. Languishingly, the tempo subsided. They laid, satiated and exhausted on the carpet just to the left of the piano. The beautiful music lingered. It had been a long time for Helen.

Monday found Helen at her desk by 6:00 a.m. It was cluttered with messages. She was sifting through the pile, an appreciative smile on her face, when Chance poked her head around the half-open door at six-thirty.

"How was the party? The fashions that were unveiled?"

"I left early, even before the preview. Arrange to have the video sent over will you, Chance? We'll watch it together. Now, how was your vacation? Nevermind, nevermind, don't tell me. Since you're here this early I take it you are eager to come back to work. Good, we need you."

A look of suspended animation and softness crept over Chance's face. "I didn't want to go at first, but this was a lesson in the when-you-least-expect-it theory. I'm glad I did go even though I didn't feel like it. It was wonderful experience and now I'm really feeling great! Ready to work to death."

"My, we're really in a good mood. The last time I saw you, you were dragging out of this building. Was it only the vacation that caused this drastic change of energy?" Helen smiled.

"Actually, I met this wonderful, really swell guy, and can you believe he lives right here in New York?"

"You don't say! Is he in the fashion world?"

"Funny, come to think of it I don't know. He seemed important, though." Chance suddenly realized that throughout their time together Victor hardly spoke a word about himself. He'd been so interested in her. "To tell the truth," she continued, "I was more interested in his personality than his fame. He's kinda special and terribly romantic. When I came home on Saturday night a FEDEX was on my doorsteps. He sent me two lemons with a note that said, since life gave me to him I don't have to make lemonade anymore unless I am thirsty. Now is that cute or what?"

"Cute, definitely cute."

"I'll bring…"

Chance's conversation was interrupted by the ringing phone, none too soon for Helen. She hated idle and personal chatter. But more than that, she was a little jealous. Her passionate evening with Geraud had only served to remind her how lonely she was, and considering her true intentions, she was very surprised how often her mind drifted back to the intoxicating, unexpected, and spontaneous journey. Even more orgasmic than her physical climax was that she had finally won. Now she would reject him as he had done her. For her there could never be any forgiveness for disloyalty. No second chance for those who crossed her—for Helen Stern lived only for her moments of retribution. When Geraud had called the following day, despite the glorious symphony their bodies had made, she refused the call. And each day for the month he remained in the States, all his calls went unanswered.

"Just a moment, please." Helen grabbed the phone, as Mrs. Walters was not due for another hour or so. The call came in on her private line.

Helen lowered her eyes to the report on her desk, signaling the end of the conversation for now.

Chance left the room, closed the door behind her and went skipping a little down the hallway.

"Yes, Hello."

"Miss Stern, this is Victor Innes Palmer. VIP, you know?"

"How could I forget, and how did you get this number?"

"From Jacques, of course. How else?"

Now he was being exasperating. "It's a little early. What can I do for you, Mr. Palmer?"

"I'm usually up and jogged by now. Glad to see you are an early riser too."

"Uh huh." Helen was monotone. "And what did you say I could do for you?"

"I am calling to find out how I offended you on Friday night. I returned with your drink and you were gone. Your Mother said you had gone to the powder room, but you never came back. Now that is rather naughty."

"Really? I thought it was rather wise myself. Actually, I was feeling a little sick. Too much champagne. Thought it best to get some fresh air and one thing led to another. Out in the night air I could hear my bed calling very clearly. Sorry I offended you, but somehow I get the feeling you can take it."

"I should say you guessed right, but I now hold a trump card that I might decide to use in the near future. Would you consider lunch?"

"In a few weeks. Call me, ah," she pretended to check her date book. "June 21st."

"That's eight weeks!"

"I know, but until then I am afraid it's high gear around here. If you take me to lunch then, I can tell you all about it."

"You're sure there is no earlier…"

"Positive. Until June then." She hung up the phone and laughed aloud.

Helen got up to stand by the window. The rising sun was creeping into her half-darkened office, its rays creating the curvaceous silhouette of the woman gazing out the window. The early morn was peaceful and rejuvenating. It was indeed sad to realize that in less than an hour Manhattan would be a hubbub of activities, both good and bad. Suddenly, despite her anger at Geraud, Helen again felt the urge to be nuzzled in his strong, protective arms. Glorious was the Sunday morning they'd spent lazing around in bed. Later, they had had breakfast on the balcony outside her bedroom. How she loved the way each balcony of the high-rise apartment was made private by the bunches of potted flowers plants with their profusion of color.

Against the bright flowers, and in contrast to her deep skin tone, her white silk robe was stark. Her enticing body beneath the thin sheath had again stirred Geraud's desire. After breakfast they had returned to bed, making love over and over until he was forced to abandon her for rehearsals. Oh she wished she could have rested in those arms forever; instead she had settled for coffee. Besides, no matter what she felt, there was no place in her heart ever for forgiveness.

Moments later Helen was engrossed in her work, Geraud's memory encased in ice, never to surface again. Truly Helen Stern qualified as the new artistic rich, for everything in her life took a back seat to her work.

Today, she'd talk with her financial people before completing the final proposal for Andrea. The documents, as well as the numbers, had to be done in the most creative way, for she needed this win.

"Mrs. Walters," she buzzed the intercom. "Get Chance on the line would you, also Charles Dunham. I need them both to come to my office."

"Certainly," Miss Stern, "right away."

"Come in," she beckoned to the knock on the door some ten minutes later.

"Morning again." Chance entered the room, still beaming.

"Oh Chance, come in. Coffee? I made it myself."

"I'm laying off the stuff, but thanks anyway."

A few minutes later Charles Durham entered the room.

"Let me get to the point as we have a mountain of work to do. I wanted to remind you both that on Thursday we are presenting the idea for our expansion of Wakefield, and for the official name change. I met with Ms. Preston last Friday. She seems quite impressed with our performance. I asked you here, Charles, so we can go over the numbers.

"Chance, I need you to oversee the project, and please be sure that everything is ready by Wednesday. I know it's short notice, but you can do it. Authorize overtime if necessary. I would aim for early Wednesday for its completion just in case we have to make changes. Charles, can you be ready with your figures by then?"

"No problem at all," he answered

"This is really great news," Chance offered, "I guess one can't fight excellence, eh? Congrats, Helen."

"Well you have as big a role as I do."

"So much for margaritas or lemonade. I'll pull all the information together." Chance said like a trouper.

"I'm okay with this," Charles said. He was used to the demands of Helen Stern. Anyway, he would do anything to prolong their contact, for he had a severe schoolboy crush on his boss.

Helen couldn't say she felt sorry to have interrupted Chance's cozy evening. She had no appreciation for gooey romance, for she was not a woman who would let anything stand in her way, especially love affairs that always seemed to end the same way anyhow. For a woman who was abandoned by her own mother, she made no apologies for her lack of undying love for another human being. Carnality and satisfaction, as she had experienced with Geraud, were good enough for her. For an entire month she could actually play house if she wanted, but she didn't want to. Her loneliness would just have to be her company for a little longer.

"That's all until later."

Alone, Helen clasped her hands together in a gesture that indicated a prayer. A triumphant look was on her face. The sixty-fifth floor. That was where she was heading, and nothing or no one would stand in her way. Yes, Indeed! This was the beginning of her ascent. Helen poured herself another cup of coffee, adding a bit of Kahlùa to calm her excited state. Her bitterness ran deep at times. Finally, everything was within reach. She was tired of playing the loving daughter, sister, and beloved stepchild role in her make-believe family. It had been hard to conceal her true feelings. Each time she looked at Andrea she always remembered the lonely nights in boarding school and the taunting she had endured for being an orphan witch. The chime of the Tiffany clock on her desk signaled noon.

"Mrs. Walters. I'm taking lunch now. Do the same, will you? We have a bit of work this afternoon, so be back sharply at one."

"Have I ever been late, Miss Stern?" Mrs. Walters said indignantly.

"Not ever. Sorry."

Locking her door, Helen pushed the concealed button under her desk and a wall slid back to reveal a beautifully appointed apartment. Her "Gestapo" office she called it. Changing into black leggings and a T-shirt, she straddled her exercise bike, reached for her cellular phone, and dialed the office of Brandon Snowden.

"I'm afraid Mr. Snowden has left for today, Madame. Would you like to leave a message?"

"No, Helen rang off." She needed Brandon's cellular phone number.

"Now, Andrea Jacobson," Helen snarled to herself, "I'm ready to go to war." And each time she thought of her pitiful childhood, her anger deepened. She could still hear the taunts of her classmates.

"Witchy, witch. Witchy, witch. You have no mommie. You have no mommie."

Chanting and "extraordinary" behavior from all those around her seemed so normal to Helen. But when she started chanting openly at school, it wasn't long before she suspected that something was wrong. No one else in her class it seemed, found chants and mumbo-jumbo popular. She was ridiculed and teased mercilessly and told that her parents had left her because she was a witch. Soon her hopes of being a normal kid with friends and sleep-over party invitations vanished. That had hurt her tremendously.

But now, all that crazy fortune-telling and mystic nonsense was just a dream. A dream she hardly recalled. Her "gift" was now closeted where it belonged, unless, of course, it became absolutely necessary to use it. Like when she used it on that poor slop at Columbia. He deserved it. And, if she must, she would use it with Andrea Jacobson.

The only gift Helen was interested in now, though, was the one she would take from her mother, fair and square—the ability to trust one's own flesh and blood. And in the process she, Helen Evelyn Stern, would become greater than the legendary Andrea Jacobson.

Back at her desk, with a wilting Caesar Salad, Helen wondered what would have happened if things had turned out differently when she first met Andrea Jacobson at her fourteenth birthday party. Their bond was instant, and for the first time in a long time she had wanted to have a mother all her own. It had been so easy to express her deepest longing to Andrea in the garden only to have the entire and moving conversation turn out to be a farce. Andrea Jacobson had only pretended to be empathetic towards the distressed young girl. An impatient knock jolted her back from her reverie.

"Enter," she instructed, and her assistant hurried in. Mrs. Walters was no spring chicken, but she was impeccably beautiful at fifty and moved with lightening speed. And she knew how to be an indispensable assistant. Anticipating Helen's every move, solving problems even before they arose had earned her a prestigious and coveted position and a hefty paycheck. Today however, she was flustered.

"We have problems with the Paris show. The model that was booked never showed up for her fitting, and I'm afraid the dress was cut just to her size. There is no time to re-cut the dress and Madame Duvelleroy is furious. Her search so far for a replacement has not been successful. She is threatening to pull the line unless we come up with a replacement model the exact size of Franchesca."

"How the hell does she expect us to do that? We are not a modeling agency of wax replicas. What time is the damn show?"

"Six o'clock Paris time Friday. That's in two days."

"Have you checked with every agency here in the city?"

"Yes, but on such short notice, everyone is booked and those who are available are not appropriate in size or character."

"What are they saying about the disappearance of…what's her name again?"

"Franchesca. You know. The girl you hand-picked yourself. Chance recommended."

"Yes, yes, yes, of course I know." Helen was furious.

"They have checked everywhere and there's no sign of her. What are we going to do?" Mrs. Walters' anxious voice continued. She knew how hard Helen's team had worked on this show and how much rested on its success.

"When was she last seen?"

"Madam Duvelleroy said she last saw her at rehearsals a day ago, but some of the models apparently had seen her that night with an American guy. What do you think could have happened?"

"Frankly, Mrs. Walters I don't have a clue. And at this moment I can assure you I don't give a damn. My only concern is that we find a new model. I can promise you one thing, though, if the explanation of Franchesca's disappearance isn't iron-clad and verifiable, that little addict will never make another dime from this company. We did send her to detox to take care of her drug habit, didn't we?"

"Yes, I'm sure Mr. Evans took care of it. She was, it appeared, doing very well until this."

"When they find her, if she's back into drugs, fire her, but only after the show. And let me know immediately if any other news comes in. What size is this diva?"

"Oh, I would say about your sizeish. A four or six, I imagine. I can get the details."

"See if you can reschedule the board meeting. Book Chance and me on the concord to Paris tomorrow. And get Jacques on the phone. I think he left for Paris on Sunday. If you can't find him at his studio, call him at home and then every one of his haunts until you reach him. Are you sure there are no Wakefield models that could stand in, even a novice one?"

"The new girl we got in just a week ago might work. She is three inches shorter than Franchesca, but she hasn't even been trained on the runway. It could be a disaster." With that Mrs. Walters hurried off to place the call to Paris.

In a few minutes, the buzzer signaled a call.

"Yes, Mrs. Walters."

"I have Mr. St. Pierre on the line. I just caught him walking out the door."

"Thanks." She clicked the flashing line. "Jacques, so glad I caught you. I have a bit of a problem. The model, Franchesca who was supposed to show our new line of clothing has disappeared. Everything was fitted exactly to her body and there is no time to do many alterations and have the same effect. Everyone, her body type anyway, appears to have been booked here, in England, and over there. Any ideas? I really need your help! This show is very important to me."

"Ah, *Chèrie*. What a dilemma. Most of my girls are already over booked for the show. *Aye ya ya*. I am eh…at a loss. This is a very sad situation. You have tried Italy, Germany?"

"Everywhere in Europe. This is so complicated and to say the least, distressing. I can't lose this opportunity especially since it is the anchor of the new look of the Company. If it's a success it will cut our name recognition and PR budget by 60%. I was really counting on this. Ah well, I am flying in tomorrow on the Concorde. I'll be staying at the Bristol. If you think of anything, *anything*, please call me immediately. Oh Jacques," she sounded heavy, "what a mess. Anyway thanks, love, and see you tomorrow. Sorry for delaying you."

"Helen," he caught her just before she hung up. "Franchesca, she is about your size. With a slight alteration here and there, things could work just fine. I'll do the alterations myself. If this means so much to you, why not consider doing the runway yourself? It could add a wonderful intrigue to the line. After all, it's not every day that a business woman models her own fashions. It would be intoxicating to the audience, and it will certainly break the stereotype that models are airheads. Let me take that back, they are airheads."

"Impossible. I have never been on a runway."

"But my dear you are a natural. You would have been the greatest supermodel from here to Nairobi if you had stayed. Remember?"

"Well, I'm glad I didn't stay if you think they are all air heads." She tried to sound light, although the weight of the situation was pressing down on her.

"Listen, I think you robbed your audience so many years ago. Do you realize that many still ask me whatever happened to that fresh model I once used. This will finally put your audience's curiosity to rest. You know your face and spread sold more magazines for International Moderna than ever before. They begged me for months to try and find you. That woman you met at the party, Olivia, is from International Moderna. Even today, your face is plastered around the lobby of their British office. I think it was the uncaptured mystery, that sinister intrigue, and that haunted sexuality that caught people off guard. Your exotic look was more than just your color; it was what the camera could not quite capture yet was obvious to the soul. I think it would be marvelous! Say the word, and I will have every magazine reprint your unforgettable picture with a story to match in tomorrow's paper. We can also have it inserted into the evening's program with the caption: Is she back? The Sultress of Nairobi. What do you think?"

Helen let out a pearl of a laugh. "Surely you jest not to talk about exaggerate." But as she was laughing, ideas were forming in her head of how this might just help her future plans. If the show was a success, there was no way Andrea could deny her anything! If it failed, she would be dead meat, humiliated. She really should consider this option as a last resort.

"Jacques, I think you may be right. I'll think about it. Give me a couple of hours and I will call to tell you if we need to do alterations. Thanks, luv. You are a snookums."

"A what?"

"Oh, never mind. It's a private colloquial term of endearment. Learned it here in Yankie town. *Adieu*, Jacques and thanks."

"*Attends*. You should take my cellular number."

Helen was elated and depressed at the same time. All was not lost. If she had to do the show she would, and frankly it was beginning to sound like a swell idea.

The Wakefield Crisis.
"Chance, it's Mrs. Walters. I have booked you on the Concorde to Paris as Miss Stern requested. I'm sorry I couldn't get you an aisle seat. There was only one left for Miss Stern. Anyway, you both need to be seated together, so that's that. Lot's of work to do, I'm told. I'll have your secretary cancel everything for the next few days, and in a minute I'll FAX over the itinerary."

"What the heck happened all of a sudden? Why are we going to Paris?"

"Franchesca has disappeared. You both have to go and out some fires, I imagine. The woman in charge of the show is furious, so be prepared."

"Oh, shit." Chance was taken aback. Franchesca! Disappeared! Damn it, she should have taken her call last night, but she had been in the throes of passion with VIP. She had actually wanted to call her back but didn't know the hotel she was staying. Damn, what the hell could have happened? She'd stayed clean after rehab, she was sure of that. They had actually celebrated her eight months of sobriety. Why on earth had she called? Chance felt a rising panic.

It was Chance who had been instrumental in getting Franchesca the job at Wakefield. She had to help her long-time buddy out for the many years she had protected her from the perils on the streets. They had agreed that no one could know of their friendship, for it was too risky for either of them to chance any exposure of their past lives. Now, however, that help could come back to haunt her. And God forbid! Now that Helen was involved who knows what would happen.

"Damn the girl," she repeated loudly this time. "That's what I get for trying to make a silk purse out of a sow's ear." What then did that say about her and Christy? They were definitely from sow's ear country.

Nevertheless, Chance was less than pleased at the turn of events. She had been ecstatic that her calendar was free of all travel for the next six weeks, thus allowing her the opportunity to see about a relationship with VIP before she had to wonder off again. "Damn! Shit," she said aloud, banging the desk drawer shut. At the rate she was going, she was destined to be an old maid. She was probably going to pass her eligible bachelor and last chance on different planes in the sky! Nonetheless, she dialed VIP's private line to break the bad news. He would probably be off again on another trip before she returned.

It was only 2:00 p.m. and already Victor had downed three glasses of Courvoisier Napoleon. He couldn't believe Helen Stern. Eight weeks. He had never been so snubbed. The ring of the phone interrupted his swig. He bet that would be her calling to change her mind. He let the phone ring three times before he picked it up. But how did she get his private line. He imagined the same way he got hers.

"Palmer."

"Hi." So much for apologies, he thought.

"Chance, how nice to hear from you. I was waiting until after the morning rush before calling you. I had a wonderful time last evening."

"So did I." He could tell she was blushing. "So what are you up to?"

"Having a late lunch in the office and a bit of cognac."

"Cognac? This early?" she said incredulously. She had seen this habit before. As a child of alcoholics she knew very well that she would probably find the traits of an alcoholic attractive. She had to be careful.

Why was she so shocked? Victor was irritated. Hadn't she heard of the idle wealthy? Hell, what else was there to do with his days? If she knew his employment at the firm was nothing but a sham and that he was nothing but a wall painting in the dynastic Catillion family, even she might not be enamored. And to make matters worse he might even be losing his charm with the women, if one could classify Helen Stern as a woman.

Hal, his older brother, had been running the business ever since his old man decided to retire. Because there was really no functional place for VIP, Hal had given him a token office with a skyline view so he could be ready at a moment's notice for a photo op. His assignment was to be a handsome face behind Catillion publicity. Unquestionably, he was the best-looking of the family, and it was his handsome face that kept the pretty women coming back to buy more space in their publications.

And yes, he had fulfilled his role as the eternal Adonis. Yes, he had done the posing thing with the Jag and Mercedes in front of the family home that had appeared on the cover of *Town & Country* and as the Sailor on Kashoggi's Yacht in the Greek Islands. On the inside pages of the articles, however, were usually pictures of his father and Hal. Even his sister Kathy, who wanted no part of the business, was often featured in magazine articles in a more meaningful way than he was. She benefited from the name as she was constantly ready to avail herself to any Catillion perks that offered her art exposure. Kathy had left the fold and the Catillion business behind six years earlier to marry a prominent socialite, Winston Therm. Not only had she married into old money, much older than her mother's, but also she managed to build a fabulous career as an artist. Her prominent Manhattan gallery was another place he was often required to play the pretty boy show piece.

This morning there were no boats or crowds; there was only him. He and his fancy, important initials and nothing else. Since his unfortunate, fatal teenage drunk-driving accident where his date had died, no one had taken him seriously except perhaps Olivia. His father, to make sure he toed the line, had put her in charge of him. Olivia took her job to convert the straying Palmer into a respectable gentleman very seriously, but she hadn't been aware of his debonair charm, or the fact that his success did not lie in the boardroom but in the bedroom. If the old fool of a father knew that his son was banging his old lady, he wouldn't have been so eager to make him her charge. Victor owed Olivia a lot, though, for it was at her insistence that he was included in the company at all.

At fifty-five, Olivia was well preserved. Not even the soft skin of her abdomen showed excessive signs of aging. He was sure all the youthful skin was due to many tucks and clips, but what the hell did he care? Yet, she was not just an aging woman trying to preserve her beauty as her only asset, Olivia was good at what she did. His father had made a good choice, and even he had to acknowledge her contribution to the Catillion business as important. Growth had been steady both in income and prestige. And likewise, she could boast success with Victor who she had taken under her wings.

He could still hear her pleading voice. "Matthew," she had said to his father and her husband, twenty years her senior, "all the boy needs is a little help. Don't be so hard on him. The past is the past! I will personally be his mentor, and I promise you in a few years this young man will be a source of pride for this family. Matthew, kids really suffer when they lose a parent so young. Think of what you went through when you lost Charlene. Please darling, let me try." Olivia had to do very little to win battles with Matthew Palmer. Any resistance would dissolve with a trip to their bed. It had been a wonderful win for her. Now, she could have her lover nearby without anyone suspecting while keeping up the charade of a respectable marriage between two of the oldest families.

But Victor no longer wanted to be her approved window dressing, required to show up at every society party. Now that the thrill for her was gone, her body was no longer enough of a reason to keep him interested in being her walker. He was ready to audition for a different role. Olivia would be furious, for the present arrangement gave her free rein to be with him and do with him whatever she wanted without causing any suspicions. Too bad. He was getting exceedingly tired of Olivia

"So, Chance, are you out of lemons already?" His voice sounded mellow and sexy. No need to be professional or businesslike on the phone, for the only people who called him day in and day out were his paramours. He always played a game with himself of trying to guess which one it was before he answered. If the Stern girl hadn't thrown him off, he would have been right on the money, he would have guessed the eager one. The one who is desperate to make him lemonade. Ha! He had done that with all his girls. They thought it was so very cute.

"I'm sorry," he heard her saying, her sweet voice mixing with the little battalion marching around in his head beating their drums to the cognac. The alcohol gave him a good feeling.

"I have to go to Paris tomorrow. I am truly sorry that I have to cancel our date."

"*Mon amour.* Paris. What for?"

"Well, we have a crisis brewing over there. Helen and I have to fly there to try and do something about it. I am not sure what, but I guess it's best for us to be there."

"Oh, a little separation. I cannot stand it."

She was really feeling bad now.

"I won't be too long," Chance emphasized and was glad Victor seemed disappointed she was leaving. She too was irritated that she couldn't be with him.

"I'll come with you. Is it something our magazine should be covering? I'll check to see, but either way I'll be there. That's it," he repeated, with resolve. "I will come with you."

"But I might be awfully busy and…"

"Never mind what Helen will say. I'll be there on official business. Why can't we just bump into each other there?" he chuckled. "Where are you staying?"

"The Bristol."

"Great. Catillion has a suite there. See you tomorrow night," his tone was suggestive and rather pleasing to Chance's ear. Eight weeks, huh! That Stern girl would see.

Victor was laughing softly when he hung up the phone, but there was a nagging feeling in his body. Christ, he envied Chance's challenging work and her commitment to it. Admittedly he liked her, but she was far too normal for him. He had to confess that he had renewed respect for her, because most silly women would have canceled their lives to be with him. His mind shifted to Helen Stern. Now there was a woman with fire in her eyes, and frankly he was far more interested in igniting the fire in his belly that was burning him up than pretending with Miss Lemonade. He must play his cards right and make sure Helen didn't see him with Chance.

What a coincidence that he picked up a woman in Italy who works for a woman who had his jockeys in a twist. Somehow he had to keep Chance and Olivia happy until he could ease out of the relationships with them. He wasn't sure what he was going to do yet, but he would think of something. Helen Stern would soon be in his possession. Never had he failed to charm a woman. Helen Stern, who piqued his interest in a new and exciting way, would be no different. Once he got her in the sack she would fall apart like the rest of them, just like broken cement.

Back in his Manhattan flat, VIP locked the liquor cabinet. The phone was ringing but he had no desire to answer it. He dropped his silk robe to the carpet, switched on the stereo and sashayed towards the bathroom. Ironically, the song playing on the radio was *Sixty Ways To Leave Your Lover.* Victor's laughter rang out loudly as he swayed his hips to the music, doing a rumba on his way to the bathtub.

"Where the hell are you," Olivia roared into the answering device. "We have to go to Paris tomorrow. I know it's short notice, but call me the moment you get in so I can tell you about the travel arrangements."

Victor had been out a lot lately. Lately he seemed somewhat distant. Maybe since Italy but more so since Jacques' party. The thought that the Stern girl, who he had been jabbering about a lot might have something to do with his distant and pensive mood had crossed Olivia's mind numerous times. Christ! How she hated those PYT's. The vixen sure was pretty and young, Certainly she could understand Victor's attraction to the exotic, wealthy daughter of one of the richest women in the world. Damn him and damn her. Olivia had been fooling herself ever since they were introduced to the Stern/Preston clan, that the look on Victor's face, that rapturous, forlorn look, was nothing but an appreciation of delicate beauty. In fact, she'd convinced herself, she had been overreacting. Victor was a gentleman. What they shared together was not some common, trashy affair. It would last a lifetime. Hell, she wouldn't give him up ever, not after all the planning, cajoling, and begging she'd done. Not a chance in hell! Now that they had a great sex life, she was absolutely convinced he was her perfect mate. But it hadn't always been so easy to get him into her bed. In fact, it had taken some time to convince him that their liaison would be good for everyone concerned. Now he really *was* her significant other, at least in the bedroom.

Olivia sank back into the plush, white silk sofa, her body enveloped into its softness. A smile crept onto her lips as she remembered their first time together. It had been six months after she'd volunteered to be his champion in Catillion. Yet, she remembered it as though it was yesterday. They had gone to a God-awful fund-raiser in midtown, a frequent event in her job. After a perfectly boring evening they decided that for the night not to be a complete bust a little excitement was necessary before heading home. Painting a bit of the town was the only ending to a pretentious, boooring evening. By the time they left TriBeca, they'd both had too much to drink.

On the way home, sitting on her hands was the only way Olivia could find to keep them off Victor. Sneaking frequent peeks at the handsome man at the wheel of the black Mercedes, she'd blushed like a schoolgirl every time he caught her stare. But a schoolgirl she was not. It was tonight or never that she had to make her move. Her constant, laser-focused attention on what it would be like to be in bed with him was killing her. In a moment of bravery, her hand crept over to encircle his crotch.

"Olivia!" He was startled, abruptly pushing her hand away. "What are you doing?" In spite of himself, he felt a familiar rise.

"What does it feel like? And if you don't like it, what ever is that snake doing in your pants? Come on Victor, what harm can it do? You find me attractive, don't you?"

"Yes I do, Olivia. You are as gorgeous a woman as you are intelligent. But this is incest!"

"Well if I'm going to be unfaithful, it might as well be in the family," she smiled. "Listen to me, Victor. I need a man in my bed. Better you than some Joe. Let's face it, your father is an old man, though thank God, he is still interested in sex. I would love it if only his body was not betraying him. We do what we can, but I need a man. Come now, sweetie. I am only your stepmother." Her hand again crept to his crotch. This time he didn't move it.

"Listen. We are both a little drunk and this lack of control is making us do things we wouldn't normally do. Let's wait until tomorrow and see if you feel the same."

"Victor, don't be naive. Why do you think I volunteered to take you under my wings?"

"I didn't know that meant under your covers as well?" he replied sarcastically.

"I am not an under-the-cover type of girl. Victor! Listen to me. I can get you what you want most. I know how you feel about being left out of your family's business, really I do. I can see the look of pain on your face when Matthew speaks to Hal about some business problem as though you weren't even in the room. All that will change, I promise. Look at the headway we have made in only six months, but darling you must take care of me, too." She ran a finger along his angular jawbone. "I promise it will just be you and me all the way to the top. You'll see. What do you say?" She squeezed harder.

There was no denying that he was turned on. Hell, he could have pulled over the car and banged her right there, but even in his inebriated state, he still felt a twinge of conscience about fucking his father's wife. But as she unzipped his trousers, his mind screamed, *why the hell not*. God had given him ultra good looks, and he was not afraid to use them to his advantage. They owed him that much.

Olivia felt the hot surge rise up her toes, creeping along her inner thighs until the hot spring had her gushing. She moved a hand over her firm, silicon breast, pretending it was Victor's and closed her eyes. Such sweet memories.

Dear, dear VIP, she mused. The only important thing about him in the Catillion Family were those initials. The third child, and it seems the forgotten son, he was trying desperately to win his father's respect. Ten years younger than Kathy and twelve years younger than Hal, at twenty-eight, Victor seemed to have been left to fend for himself emotionally since birth. Being the last child, there was no sibling to bond with. Even his nannies were mean to him. Maybe they were only acting toward him in the same mean-spirited way that his father had.

Matthew Palmer had gone into a severe depression when his wife died during childbirth with Victor. His despair had been pervasive. For five years he hardly spoke, and the melancholy got so bad that he had to be hospitalized. After that, even upon his return to the family, he barely participated in life. Miraculously one spring Hal got him to go on a publishing retreat in St. Barts. That was where he met Olivia and suddenly the sparks returned to his eyes.

Unfortunately, Matthew's recovery was too late to offer the love that could have saved his last child from emotional instability. Victor, armed with his developing good looks, charm, bawdy friends, and survival skills of a child forced to raise himself, was already on the path to self-destruction. At sixteen, he found his place in life. Women and booze became his addiction. They had been good to him. With them, he could forget the pain, loss, and his lonely life. Throughout his adolescence, Victor had perfected the art of being the ultimate charmer, a charmer who would make every one of his seven girlfriends feel special. He often joked to Olivia that he should have been born in China where concubines were an acknowledged and expected part of a man's life. Now, with their covert relationship, he realized the full power of his charm. Olivia didn't fool herself that it was exotic love that made him bite; she knew very well his motive. The fact that he could take something of his father even if it was his wife was a justifiable payback for Victor's unbearable life. Olivia shifted her position as her mind relived their first night.

"Do me right here," she had begged in the elevator on the way up to her New York apartment. "Now," she cooed, and flipped the red button to stop. Trapped in the elevator, they tore passionately into each other. He had done her, all right, rough and frantic, just the way she liked it. Half-an-hour later, stark naked, laughing and tugging at each other, they let themselves into the apartment. On the soft white carpet they fell for another round of lustful forays. The dramatics were, of course, for sexual excitement rather than for risks, because the elevator opened right into the spacious apartment.

If Victor felt entirely disgusted the morning after, it did not stop him from being in her bed the following night and many nights thereafter. Her risqué behavior kept him coming back, and she was fun, spontaneous, and certainly not a bimbo who had married an older man for his money. In fact Olivia was rather a well-bred girl, who thought she could help Matthew and in the process expand her publishing company. Another thing Victor confessed that he liked about her, paradoxical as it might seem, was that he felt she genuinely loved his father and was severely protective of him.

The daughter of a Greek dignitary, Olivia went to boarding school in England. There, she discovered her body under the covers with Sara Dumfield. The two girls innocently explored their sexuality, but when Sarah moved on to other things Olivia was still stuck in carnality. From the tender age when she had first discovered her sexuality she had never stopped having sex. But despite all the time spent in bed, she had managed to attack her career with the same energy she put into getting laid. Soon she rose to the top of the English publishing industry. With her father's inheritance she purchased a small magazine and turned it into a respected empire. Her first husband, who died shortly after their marriage, left her childless. She had never seen fit to remarry until she met

Matthew. A year later they merged the two companies and Matthew went back to work one day a week. Olivia had confided in Victor, as she had not done with her husband, that by some quirk of nature or genetics she was the way she was—she couldn't help it if she qualified as a nymphomaniac—she just simply loved sex. As much as she loved sex, however, she could separate the act of lust and love. She was falling in love with Victor.

Chapter Ten

Andrea looked over the preliminary proposal Helen had submitted for her review. It really made a whole lot of sense. Her daughter was definitely a critical thinker, but more than that she was a visionary. She was proud of her. Very, very proud. There was just one little part of this whole expansion plan that bothered her: Jacques. Even after his disappointment in their love affair, he had remained her true and most treasured friend. One day when Jacques was tired of the mountain top and ready to descend, she could think about Helen's proposal for true couture, but not now. At sixty-three, Jacques seemed just in his prime.

What her daughter proposed, although it made good economic sense and was the logical sequence of events, could threaten Jacques' empire. How could she approve an idea that would compete with her favorite friend and designer? And just how was she to choose whose clothes she would wear? Although JI desperately needed the burgeoning growth of Wakefield for its continued financial solvency, she had to try to convince Helen to look at an alternate game plan.

Maybe accepting and sanctioning the name change might appease Helen somewhat, but if she knew her daughter, it wouldn't be enough. Although Andrea wanted to make Helen privy to the true financial picture of Jacobson Industries, the new developments at Bingham, Lewis, Viking & Gould prevented her from doing so. They couldn't risk a company leak. And frankly there was something more intangible that was stopping her.

Andrea removed her peepers and rested them on the table. Closing her eyes to focus her thoughts, she thought back to Helen's arrival in New York. It was never a matter of if she would arrive but when. Andrea had waited every day for four years for her daughter to come home. The dark, fiery eyes had warned of disaster, but it had come as a pleasant surprise that the road to trust and loyalty between them had been smooth. Having been acutely aware of betraying her own flesh and blood, Andrea had gone out of her way to accommodate the child and vowed upon her arrival to make up for their years of separation. Today, Andrea could say without reservation that she was truly impressed, not only with their relationship that she valued above most things, but with Helen's aptitude, business ability, and her passion to succeed. It was a compliment to Andrea that the child tried hard to emulate her and to make her proud. No doubt that had been a strong driver for Helen's outstanding performance. Whatever the reason, Andrea was quite proud. And that made it even more difficult to upset the apple cart. Still, there was no way she was going to approve Helen's plans for couture.

"Yes, Janice," she answered the intercom.

"Helen's assistant is on the line for you, Ms. Jacobson." Talk about telepathy.

"Janice, whenever are you going to call me by my name?"

"Never."

Janice had never gotten used to calling her Preston. And frankly, Andrea never minded. "Can't teach an old dog…" she had never quite finished the sentence before Janice would respond.

"Old or aged to perfection. What would you do without your old dog here, missy?"

They had become friends, confidants, and spiritual sisters. There was no way Andrea would do without Janice. She had been the source of her strength when Johnathan Buckley, the former Vice-President of Jacobson's Industries, had betrayed her trust and when, because of her shattered nerves, her world had seemed to come apart at the seams. Both

Janice and Melissa had taken turns nursing her back to health when her deep, dark depression threatened to consume her entire life. Dear Melissa, now almost eighty, still ran the Jacobson-Preston household including Reginald, Andrea, and Scott, if necessary, with an iron hand.

"You have a child who depends on you for his life, Andrea," Melissa had said in disgust at Andrea's pervasive withdrawal. "If you have no life left in you neither will he. If you don't carry the torch to the end of the tunnel, he will forever be in darkness. Andrea, you are not a quitter. Never have been, never will be, and I believe your heart knows what's right." It was in this period that she had grown in spiritual appreciation, accepted her special "gift" and moved on with her life. In her year absence from Jacobson Industries it was Janice who ran the company and continued to do so for months after she'd first returned to work.

Her journey had been arduous and painful. She would never have made it without them. As for her husband, Scott (a smile lightened her lips), she couldn't love or trust him more. It would be obscene. She would call him right after her chat with Mrs. Walters and remind him of how much she loved him.

"Mrs. Walters, how are you today?" Andrea said cheerfully as the thought of her husband continued to linger. "Who has died down there on the fiftieth floor?"

Mrs. Walters laughed. She adored Andrea Jacobson-Preston. She could never get over the fact that the CEO of JI Industries always called her Mrs. Walters.

"Good afternoon, Mrs. Preston." She smiled into the phone. "No one yet, Madam, but if things keep up at this pace I will certainly be the one to kick the bucket."

"Don't you actually mean if things didn't keep up at that pace, Mrs. Walters?"

"You're right, I honestly don't know what I would do with my time if I ever had a minute to think about it."

"That's good to know, Mrs. Walters. Now, to what do I owe this pleasure?"

"Miss Stern wants me to verify that you've received the preliminary proposal she sent through company mail. She would also like to reschedule the board meeting for next week to a different time, if possible. She has to fly to France early tomorrow and has left the office in a hurry. She told me to inform you that her trip will definitely strengthen her position in the Industry, and that she will call you from Paris. She is booked into the Bristol if you need to reach her. She couldn't call herself because of the urgency of the situation and the last-minute things only she could handle."

"Why is she staying at the Bristol? Isn't the company flat available? Come to think of it, you probably don't even know about it, do you?"

"I didn't, Ms. Preston. Shall I change plans? I'll try her cell now and see what happens."

"I wouldn't change anything right now. I'll let her know about the flat when she calls. If she decides to change locale, I'll let you know what to do, Mrs. Walters. By the way, did she give an inkling of what's going on?"

There was a hesitation. Mrs. Walters might have loved Andrea dearly, but there was no question her loyalties were with *her* boss. She had learned from experiencing the wrath of Helen to give no information to anyone unless she was specifically told to do so.

Andrea, recognizing the hesitation, silently applauded the devotion of Ms. Waters. She would certainly mention it to Helen.

"Thank you, Mrs. Walters." She rung off the line. For a moment, Andrea mused over the possible reason Helen would leave for Paris in the wake of a board meeting that meant everything to her. Funny, Andrea had no idea what went on on the fiftieth floor. Her rule to inspect what she expected was somehow put on the back burner for Helen. For everyone else in JI, Andrea knew their jobs intimately. Having entrusted Wakefield entirely to Helen, she had forced herself to butt out, and so far the results were excellent. Resolved she'd find out nothing further about her daughter's sudden departure to France, she dialed from her private line.

"Hey baby," she whispered into the phone. "Wanna play hide and seek."

"Who is this?"

"The cream in your coffee, the T in your thrill the S in your…"

"Smut. S for what? Let me hear you say it over a public line. You know these lines could be bugged."

"I wouldn't care. I am willing to go public with our affair. But all I was going to say was S in your smile. If you want me to say something else though, I will." Andrea was laughing loudly now.

"I take it this is my S as in Sunday Girl, wife." Scott was also laughing. Andrea remembered what a big issue being considered a Sunday girl had been-the type of woman who only gets attention from her lover on Sundays, *after* she cooked dinner.

"No honey, I graduated a long time ago from that role, remember? I, my sweet man, am now your very heart, your very soul, and naturally your inspiration."

"What's gotten into you?"

"Do you mean what could get into me?" She was taunting him, and shamelessly his zipper was bulging. "Meet me now," her voice was rasping. "Now my sweet, sweet man. I can't wait another minute."

Scott pushed the button on his desk, and a sound-proof wall slid silently back. He looked at his wife, now clad in only her knickers, and felt for her deep, deep passion. Even today, Andrea always solved everything with seduction or denial. Now happily married, he had to admit he liked it that way. It was indeed convenient and satisfying to have an afternoon tumble with his beloved, but today he wasn't going to fall for Andrea's ploy. There was something he had to discuss.

"You're still dressed!" Andrea was surprised.

"Hi honey." Scott got up from behind his desk. "I've been meaning to talk with you and I think it's a good idea to do it now. Your timing is perfect." Scott eased on one elbow.

"Who want's to talk when....What about?" Curiosity got the best of Andrea.

"Helen. Melissa seems to think...."

"I know what Melissa thinks. She's told me at least a thousand times."

"So what are you going to do?"

"I don't think it's a good idea to bring up the past. Helen is doing so well and maybe the past no longer matters. I don't feel we should throw her back into the pain when the present is so bright."

"Her or you?" Scott was insistent. "I think you are wrong. The past never goes away without explanation. Melissa feels the girl wishes you no good. Maybe because she doesn't understand"

"Poppycock. I can understand her distrust even now. It has been hard for her Scott. If I ever feel there is a time to chat with her I will. Melissa is a bit overprotective. Helen loves her."

"Her concern didn't translate into her visiting Melissa when she was in the hospital though, did it? Well I suppose you are going to treat this like everything else you don't want to deal with?"

"Today, Scott. I'm not in the mood." Andrea grabbed her clothes and headed to the bathroom.

Chapter Eleven

France

"*Rue du Faubourg St. Honoré, Le Bristol S'il vous plait.*" The taxi driver turned to look at the women entering his car. The tall dark one was French, he concluded, but the other one was definitely American. Her wan complexion could have made her British, but the clothes were a dead giveaway.

Realizing he was not taking tourists, the cabbie kept to the normal route. It wasn't uncommon for them to take foreigners on an all-expense, unauthorized tour of Paris, and frankly he felt no remorse about the deceitful practices levied against rich American tourists flaunting their haughty manner. Just his luck to get an expatriate. Paris rose in all its glory, dignified and sophisticated. As the cabbie sped through the Arc de Triomphe, down the Champs Elysées, and made the left on Avenue Montagne, one of the world's grandest squares welcomed them. The Musée d' Orsay and the Louvre loomed beyond.

"As soon as we get to the hotel, I want to check with every agency again to make sure they don't have a model that will fit our needs. Helen said to Chance, flipping through the list on her lap.

"Sure," Chance answered.

"Has anyone tried Rebecca? She has the look we are after. That sultry, feisty look. I've heard her parents are from the Islands; maybe we have enough in common to get a favor."

"I can't imagine she wasn't one of the first to be booked, but I'm not sure if we have spoken to her. Of course, when we checked before, many of the top models were already booked by competing designers for this very show," Chance offered.

"I suppose part of our problem, and why no one will give us the time of day, might very well be that we're not yet super players in International Fashion. I swear to you, Chance, it won't be long before those snobs will be eating crow. We are going to make a sensation tomorrow. That, my friend, I promise you," Helen seethed. "Do you have the second list that was faxed from Jacques? He felt it would be useless, but you never know what could turn up at the last minute."

"Got it right here," Chance said, pulling out a folder from her briefcase. Right now, though, she really wanted to just look out the window and catch the sites. She had glimpsed famous landmarks on the ride through town, but she couldn't remember which and would never ask. Later she would look in her *Fodder's* travel guide. Chance doubted they would have much time for site-seeing, but she was excited to be in Paris for the first time and wanted to take in as much as possible.

"*Cinq cent franc.*"

"*Merci.*" Helen handed him the oversize five hundred francs as two red-jacketed doormen in matching pillbox hats rushed to help. Helen walked into the hotel that seemed more like a palace, as though it was home. The large foyer, decorated with ornate brass and French furnishings, glowed under the period lighting of the sconces. Chance could actually imagine early nineteenth-century well-dressed women descending the stairs. This was exactly how she imagined the Belle Epoch period. Down the steps to the right, Chance noticed a bank of elevators and farther forward an antique, mahogany hand-operated elevator attended by another man in a red outfit. It would appear that only special dignitaries were transported in those elevators, and she guessed they went to private floors.

Chance moved quickly behind Helen, who stopped briefly by the desk to get her suite number. Apparently all other details were taken care of before their arrival. They, of course, took the mahogany and brass elevators. As she imagined, they opened directly onto a private floor. Chance mused momentarily what ordinary person would pay seven hundred dollars and upward per night for a mere room. Nonetheless, she acted entitled. Of course, their adjoining suites were four times the cost per night. Who would ever believe a girl from the wrong side of Boston would end up in such a world.

With not much time to find a model, the women delved into work. They split the list and worked relentlessly to cover all their calls in the remaining two hours of the work day. Helen was moving faster through her list because her French was impeccable. Chance, on the other hand, had to wait for an English translator.

"Yes," Helen was saying excitedly on the other line. "Is she really? Do you think she might chat with me for a minute?"

"I'll check," the person on the other line replied. Moments later.

"Rebecca."

"Hello, Ms. Collins. This is Helen Stern from Wakefield Company."

"Yes. You're the one making waves in America, aren't you? But I had no idea you were British? Jacques hadn't mentioned it. Jolly good for us."

"I suppose I am," Helen replied. "My parents are really from the Islands, though."

"Naah, really? So are mine. Geez, we have so much in common."

Helen took exception.

"So you're calling about the show, eh?" Rebecca continued jovially, "Jacques already rang this morning. I'm sorry luv that I can't do this show for you, especially now that I know you're a home girl, but I have to be on a flight to NYC tomorrow for the opening of our new diner. I've tuned down this very job seven times already. I'd done it for you though if I could. Believe me, everyone was furious with Arlene and me. Shoot, who cares. No pun intended," she giggled. "We don't care a bit 'cause when we're old and decrepit with no place to go, our fancy designers will have replaced us long before we've finished our last walk down the runway. Designers can continue till they die and those too old to continue can afford to retire to their chateauxs in Monaco. Enjoying a spot of tea with Prince Albert, no doubt. We have to take care of ourselves, too, don't you think? I'm sorry, luv, that it's such bad timing. I would love to have done this for you," she repeated. "Hope you can come to the opening of The Runway Café."

"Manhattan, right?" Helen interrupted, trying to terminate the conversation.

"Yes, Manhattan," the 'Barbie' answered. "Silly of me, but I can't remember the exact address. Our business manager is the organized one," she giggled, "but give me a ring when you're back. Would love to do lunch and chat about the struggles of being the product of a hybrid culture. Let me give you my number in the Apple."

"Shoot," Helen mimicked, "No pun intended. I've got pen and paper." Helen scrawled the number on the back of her list.

"Sorry we couldn't work together. I'm sure it would have been wonderful. Of course one never knows about the future." Helen could barely get a word in. Rebecca chatted nonstop like she imagined an excited, speech-enabled Barbie doll would. And if that girl knew what was good for her, she'd learn what her business manager knew.

"I'll call," she said, needing to get off the phone and on to the next possibility. One thing about Helen, even when things seemed bleak, she never gave up. Of course, she could…No, that was not yet an option.

The next hour proved just as fruitless, and she finally gave up.

"Why don't you call in for room service if you're hungry," Helen signaled to Chance to stop for the evening. "No point continuing. I can feel that we'll have no success. Can't say we didn't give it a good try though, eh?"

"What will we do now?"

"I haven't a clue. But by tomorrow I will have a solution." Helen pulled off her earring and rested it on the table.

"That's real close," Chance said nervously. "If we have to cancel they won't be able to reprint the program. It'll look really bad if we reneged with such short notice and that would devastate the new company image."

Helen knew all Chance said was true, but she needed some time to think, and she didn't want to listen to Chance's yapping.

"Well if you really think there is nothing I can do I'd love to go and look around the city." Chance glanced at her watch.

"Haven't you been to Paris before?" Helen was startled. She was aware that although most Europeans traveled extensively, Americans seldom did. Of course, America itself was as big, if not bigger than all of Europe, and evidently Americans felt they had enough land to cover in their own country. "If all goes well this will be your home away from home. Let me rephrase that. This will be your home away from home."

Chance made her way back to her room, making sure she bolted the adjoining door. She doubted however, that any sound would escape the solid walls of the room. Not only because Helen's suite was as big as a generous size ranch house, but because the walls were solid plaster. Her suite, more modest than her boss's, was just as luxurious. She poked around, peering out windows and examining the bathroom with the funny un-lidded toilet. Had she ever seen one? She almost wanted to have a dip in the Jacuzzi, but was too excited about the call she was about to make to Victor. He was to have arrived at the hotel an hour ago.

"Jacques," Helen was jabbering at the phone, "I had no luck whatsoever. I can't imagine that not one model is available who can handle our show. It seems entirely impossible. Do you think they might be trying to sabotage the line?"

"Hardly. I know you'll find this hard to believe, but I actually think this is a blessing in disguise. I think this might be very lucky for you, *ma belle*. The obvious choice is for you to do the show. I will make myself available to do the alterations personally. A fitting with me tomorrow will prove me right. But now, let me take you to The Bistro.

A wonderful French meal is necessary before such a major decision. Helen, believe me. Your doing the show will do wonders for the line. It's perfect. *No?*"

Helen thought of the great repercussions for her emerging company. If the owner models her own line, it would be a terrific vote of confidence, quite different from what would be expected and may enhance her breaking into the European market-the crux of her future plans.

"I think you are right, Jacques, and after all what choice do I have?"

Friday morning started out frantically, remained frantic and ended leaving Helen completely frazzled. Never did she believe she'd survive the hoopla that surrounded a catwalk. But she had. And probably in the process of putting on and taking off twenty outfits in fifteen minutes with as many hair changes, she'd lost a few pounds. Through it all, her greatest fear had been that she'd suavely pull off the gold cape, and the zipper on her dress would be open! But none of that happened, thanks to Jake.

Jake, a tall, muscular Frenchman, was the most organized, determined, and confident person she had ever met. A hard taskmaster, he insisted that firm management made people achieve more than they ever thought they could. Though they hated him initially, at the moment of their glory he was thanked profusely. Jake wasn't as brutal as he wanted others to believe. He smiled as quickly as he barked. Nevertheless his orders would set a whirlwind of activity in motion, and by the end, everything would be accomplished.

"You were superb," Helen said as he helped her out of her final outfit.

"And so vere you," Jake replied "I felt really committed to making zis happen for you after all you have put into it. Especially taking such a grueling session after so many years of not modeling. I live for ze commitment to excellence."

"May I buy dinner as a thank you?" She stood before him in her skivvies hauling on her black leggings. If he'd noticed her nakedness, he answered her without an ounce of self-consciousness, continuing without hesitation to hang the dress she had just abandoned.

"I vish I could, but I have some plans for ze evening. I'll take a…how do zey say it in America?"

"Rain check."

"Yes, yes, zat's it. I sink you did very vell tonight," he beckoned her to come to the mirror. She moved over to peer out the secret one-way mirror onto the floor that was still in a frenzy. Chance was frantically answering questions, writing orders and deflecting the media all at the same time. Helen's proximity to Jake was disturbing her sense of orderliness. While he chatted, moving around to restore order, she took a moment to study him. Handsome beyond words in a natural sort of way, he was no Adonis like Victor Innes Palmer whose initials might well have been TFB—Trained For Bullshit. Jake's naturally thick brown hair hung shoulder length, was brushed straight back, curling a little at the end. He wore a black tee shirt, black jeans and a checkered jacket that hung to perfection on his broad shoulders. His eyes were an unusual brown with flecks of green. A tiny diamond stud gleamed from his left ear, and his lean body stood she would guess a good six-feet-two. His walk was strong and purposeful as he managed to make his tasks effortless.

"Why a name like Jake? It's not very French!"

"My father vas a service man. Left my mother pregnant when he vent back to the States. She named me Jake after him, and hoped if he ever came back to town he vould be proud of his namesake. Needless to say he never came back."

Helen put a hand on the strong arm. "I know exactly that kind of pain," she said softly. "Have you thought of going to the States to find him?"

"I do not vish to find him," he turned to look at her, and for a moment their eyes locked before he allowed them to travel over her body. Helen's heart did little cartwheels as she hastened to pull a sweater over her head.

"Ah there you are," Jacques entered the room. *Ma belle Superb. Superb,* he put his hands together in an applause. Truly, you were *magnifique.*"

"Indeed she was," Jake said as he left the room.

The show was a raving success, and the orders poured in. She could see the bespeckled buyers riveted to their chairs as she sauntered, strutted, and careened down the freeway of success for Wakefield. The idea of dressing up a day outfit to the ultimate chic eveningwear proved popular. As Jacques had watched his protégée breathe new life into supermodeldom, a smile lingered on his lips. With the combination of supreme confidence, class and mystery, Helen was unquestionably the star of the evening. Not only had the orders poured in, but the modeling offers from powerful agencies created a bidding war for this unforgotten teen model.

"You could command upwards of one hundred thousand per show. Ten shows a year Helen, that's all. And consider the millions in endorsements and ads."

"Ouch, aah," Helen was barely listening. Her feet were now vibrating in the footbath brought in at Jake's command. She poured more Epsom salt into the bubbling water. "If you had my feet now, Jacques, twenty million dollars would not be enough. Thank you, though, for encouraging me to do this show. It was a phenomenal move for our new focus at the company. Mother will be proud." *And maybe she was right about not competing with Jacques. He was an ally.*

Their conversation was interrupted by Chance's entry.

"Hey, great work," Chance said as Helen waved her to the chair next to her.

"What'd ya think?"

"Fab. Awesome and fat!"

"Fat? Whatever do you mean?" Helen eyebrows went up.

"Fat. As in much mula, dinero, cash. We took in over five million in orders, and I anticipate we'll get a lot more by the time word gets around.

There were some powerful tastemakers out there tonight. I wouldn't be surprised if we have a huge spread in *Vogue* and *Mademoiselle*

"Make sure we pay our respects." Helen intimated the expected protocol of fashion editors to Chance. It was widely known that although no money ever exchanged hands in the fashion world, editors *expected* their gratuities. And gratuities they would get from Wakefield if it meant more press and better rates for their ads.

"If I wasn't so tired, we would have to celebrate," Chance halfheartedly said, hoping Helen would veto the thought. "Kir Samba. I hear it's the hot spot for exotic foreigners."

"Dancing? Oh God no. I'm bushed, and my feet are completely dead. Thanks for the offer though and for being here," Helen touched Chance's shoulder lightly. "I really needed you."

"I wouldn't have missed it for the world." Chance smiled warmly. "See you tomorrow and congratulations."

"To you too," Helen answered.

"Jacques," Chance turned to him. "You are a genius. Goodnight."

"Shall I drive you home?"

"No thanks, I'll catch a cab"

"Well, I must be on my way too, *Cherie*," he pecked Helen's cheek. "We'll see each other before you leave eh?"

"A promise," Helen returned his kiss, rising from her warm footbath.

"No, no please don't get up. I'll escort Chance to a cab."

Helen was still soaking her feet, which were turning to prunes, when Jake came back into the room.

"Still here?" she asked

"For awhile yet, I'm afraid. Only the models get to go home now. Ve have to take inventory of the pieces."

"May I reach you before I leave for New York?"

"Sure." He gave her a card.

"How about cashing in your raincheck for lunch tomorrow?"

"Consider it done."

Back at the hotel, Helen stripped down to her knickers. Even raising her arm to put on her nightdress was painful. Were there really that many muscles that didn't get a workout in her daily exercise routine! Looking closely at her body, Helen appreciated her physical assets. She could've used them to her advantage but her looks had never been what she counted on to sway decisions. All her life she'd relied solely on her brains, her business savvy, style, and indeed, her anger to fuel her success. Her anger with Andrea, Maya, and even her dead father was enough impetus to reach the summit where she could exact her ultimate revenge. Glancing at her watch, Helen noted it was already eleven o'clock. She really should call her mother. At that very moment she dialed the phone.

"Hello Mother, it's Helen. Sorry I didn't call before, but you wouldn't guess what I did today."

"I bet I would. I've already heard," Andrea announced

That woman had ears and eyes everywhere. I should remember that more often.

"It was really heady," Helen filled her in on the details of her runway jaunt, making sure she emphasized the economic gain for Wakefield.

"I am truly impressed, Sweetie. I can't wait until the board meeting to show you off. We must celebrate when you get back. Sorry you had to stay in a hotel. I should've given you keys to the flat. Go over and tell the doorman you are my daughter. It's in the 8th Arrondissement close to George V. Palace de International Concord. You know the…"

"Mom, I know exactly where." She realized how little her mother really knew about her. "Just give me the address."

Andrea felt chilled. Helen's tone was sharp and impatient. She supposed she deserved that. It was times like this that Andrea wondered if she had really been forgiven for the past. Such little hostilities were understandable, but maybe she should listen to Scott and stop trying so hard to please Helen. "When you get home I'll give you a key," she informed Helen.

"That's fine. I really must go now, Mom. I am exhausted. Just wanted to keep you up-to-date before the news hit the morning papers. I'll be catching the late flight out tomorrow, so I'll see you soon. I'll fill you in then on anything I've forgotten now."

The next morning the ache in Helen's body had grown to titanic proportions. Groaning loudly she tried to get out of bed. "Ouch," a spontaneous groan left Helen's lips as she tried to place one foot gingerly in front of the other. Although they felt like puff balls, she was not discouraged enough to cancel her luncheon. Wow! Prancing around must really keep models fit.

Jake answered the phone on the third ring.
"*Allo. Bonjour mademoiselle* Stern."
"How did you know it was me?"
"No one calls me, unless of course zere is a show. Zere is no show today so I could tell who it vas."
"Sounds lonesome."
"No, it is just the vay I like it."
"So is the *Café de Paris* a good place for lunch?"
"*C'est un bon* restaurant. I'll meet you zere at noon, or vould you rather me pick you up?"
"I'll meet you there." She hung up the phone. Although she found Jake attractive, it was almost in a brotherly way. She had felt an immediate kinship when he told her about his father's abandonment. After the excitement of the evening and the sobering morning, she felt somewhat foolish about her initial attraction to him. Still she was impressed with his obviously well respected position in the Paris fashion circles. Immediately, she saw his value to Wakefield.

Casually dressed, Helen left the Bristol early to visit her mother's flat. What she found was not just a flat but a penthouse apartment some ten thousand square feet in size. The sloping cathedral ceilings added an openness to the place. Impeccably outfitted with the most exquisite furnishings, it could have been an *Architectural Digest* masterpiece. She toured every room with renewed energy, for she took great delight in discovering more and more of her soon-to-be assets.

Victor Innes Palmer rubbed the Gillette shaver over his three-day stubble. Today, the feeling of emptiness was pervasive, and he was clearly depressed, for his desire had not been fulfilled. In the not-so-distant past, he would have been satisfied to have a skillful lover like Chance in his bed anytime, but not today. Examining his feelings, he realized his disappointment was not with Chance, but with not seeing Helen Stern. After all, he had flown to Paris hoping to force the hand of coincidence. It would have been a personal triumph for him to change the eight-week appointment she had given him by "planning" an accidental meeting. Unfortunately, all he saw of her was what everyone else did as she effortlessly glided down the runway. By God, the woman was magnificent!

"Hi, who are you again?" the sleep-drenched voice purred.

He looked over at Chance, her svelte body wrapped in the lightweight down comforter.

"Can't remember my name," he played along, switching off the razor.

Damn! She was a very pretty girl. A little too pale for his liking, but pretty nonetheless. The fact that they had had delightful sex and expensive champagne the entire night didn't do much to shake his depression. Even as he sat beside her and pulled back the covers he was finding it difficult to pretend. Frankly he was tired of these fun and games. He wanted more. He wanted Helen Stern.

As Chance's electric hands brought him to life, his mind, if not his body, was consumed with the wooing of Helen Stern. With Helen Stern at his side, he would be envied. His days as an entertainment gigolo would end, and he would take his rightful place as a Catillion heir. He needed Helen to fall in love with him.

Acutely aware that Helen would be unimpressed with the mere son of a dynastic family whose only fame was as a brainless icon, he began formulating his plans to transform himself into a real businessman. Like her, he would not rest on his family's fortune. He would make his own mark on the world. For his plan to work, he had to give up booze and women. That very moment Victor decided to make an enormous change in his life. He would take a discreet vacation and check into an alcohol rehab center. Not that he was an alcoholic, but he'd heard that the program at *Aix en Pravance* was good for anyone trying to change bad habits. No one had to know his whereabouts, for his trust fund provided enough money to pay the bill with ease. If Helen cooperated with his plans, he would dump Olivia, and he would make it worth Helen's while. *International Moderna* was very well positioned to take her over the top with a few well-placed articles.

After her runway performance last night there was little he had to do to make his brother Hal bite. Knowing Olivia, she was already sewing up a deal anyway. Talking about Olivia, he'd better get this romance shit over with and scadoodle.

"Uuummm," Chance purred beneath him. "Come back to bed."

"Sure," he kissed the nape of her neck. "Sure." With his new resolve, Chance was going to be as crucial as Olivia is in his game plan. Damn! He smiled. He had wasted his brilliance all these years.

"Ohh," he groaned. It was so very natural.

He had not been standing there for more than a second before she arrived in a taxi.

"I'm late. I really wanted to be on time. Sorry."

"Hardly, I only arrived a second ago. I vould say you are very much on time. Shall ve?" He opened the door.

The waiter seated them immediately as the lunch crowd was not yet at its peak.

"I've always loved this city." Helen sat by the window, her gaze fixed on the women, clad in black from head to toe, passing by. It seemed no one rushed in Paris like they do in New York.

"It's so refreshing to be back on the continent."

"How long have you been in New York?"

"Almost sixteen years. It was such a strange place when I got there, but I have to admit it has its intrigue."

"Yes, I have been zere several times on ze set of Lagerfeld. Sought one day I might move zere for awhile, but as you see, it hasn't happened yet. Frankly, I doubt that it vill."

"Actually, destiny may be approaching faster than you think." Helen was glad for the opening into her topic. "Jake, I was really impressed with what you did for me and the show yesterday. I have never quite seen anyone so, how do you say...eh, *complet*. I could really use someone like you at Wakefield. Good things are happening for the company, but it needs another leader. I am committed to making the transition of Wakefield to an international Company painless, exciting, and as successful as possible. When I saw you at work yesterday, I knew you were the person I needed.

"Jake, I would like to offer you a position with my company. The project I have in mind in the near future is bigger than anything I've ever tackled. I need the right person beside me to execute, and I'm convinced it's you. The offer can't be official until I see the outcome of my proposal to my mother. If things go as I predict, there will be no hitch. Her decision *will* determine the speed with which I can forge forward with my plans, but I feel confident it will be positive. What can I offer for you to consider this proposition?"

"I am flattered. Truly I am, but I am not sure zat I am ready to relocate."

"How about a flat here in Paris, one on the Park, company cars, the unlimited expense account, free creative range, and a salary of two

hundred and fifty thousand. If we meet our goals as set forth in our plan, you get 3% of growth," she continued.
"Just like zat? Vhy all the confidence in me?"
"Just a feeling, Jake. Just a feeling."

Chapter Twelve

KLM touched down precisely at 6 a.m. New York time. Chance was still basking in her weekend escape with VIP. She had no idea how she got off the plane and ended up on the curbside of JFK. Reminiscing was all she could do. She wished she could have bubbled over to Helen, but not only did they not have that kind of relationship, Victor had insisted on privacy. She wouldn't have dreamed of detailing her private life before, mostly because there was none, but she couldn't help her excitement and her need to blabber like a teenager in love. Chance couldn't wait to get to her condo so she could spill her guts to Christy. At the thought of VIP, a smile graced her lips. *The smile factor.* That was always a good sign in relationships. Her theory was that if you were driving along and thought of your lover, and he brought a smile to your lips then it was a good relationship. Not that she had much experience with real relationships. VIP. Wow! She had never met anyone like him before. Spontaneous, rich, educated, well traveled, and gorgeous. She was floating.

"Our car is waiting, Chance. Chance!" Helen was shaking her by the arm.

"Oh, right. Sorry."

"I understand, I am exhausted too, but we have a bit of work to do before we can call it quits."

Chance heaved a big sigh. There goes her chat with Christy.

Closing the confidential report once again, Helen was satisfied. It was a remarkable show and a coup for her company. The sky was the limit for her now. The financial report in her hand was living proof. The Helen Companies. That was the name she wanted *her* establishment to have, no matter what Andrea said.

Helen was on the phone the moment she set foot into the car.

"Larry Hortenski?"

"Speaking," he bellowed into the phone, none too pleased to be awakened.

Larry Hortenski was from the CPA firm of Stephens and Hortenski, P.C. Now senior partner of the two hundred-person firm, it was a far cry from his humble, poor beginnings in the Bronx. The son of Polish immigrants, he was the one who managed to feed four siblings on the measly salary his father brought home from the textile factory. His mother had not survived the trip across the Atlantic. But long gone were those days. His company was now the CPA firm to the fashion industry, and he himself had been instrumental in most of the Initial public offerings that came to market. Nowadays he hardly participated in a deal directly unless it was over the top.

"This is Helen Stern. Wakefield Company. I sent over our financial records before I left for Paris and I want to know what you think. I'd like to FAX over some additional info from our show in Paris. What number shall I send them to? I hope you have a FAX at home."

"Yes, of course, and good morning to you, Miss Stern."

"Well?"

"Send them to 555-9455."

"And what do you think of the current statement?"

"They are great, great."

"What does that mean?" Helen was annoyed.

"I mean you can go public anytime you wish. Listen Helen, may I call you that?" He didn't wait for an answer. "I'll be in your office in one hour. I'll explain everything then. It's pointless doing this on the phone. I'll just wait to get the FAX and run a few numbers before I come over. Everything will be up-to-date when we meet."

"Good. We'll see you then."

Larry was still not quite awake. He glanced ruefully at the bedside clock as his wife covered her head with the pillow. Six-thirty. Normally he would get up at eight, frolic with his beautiful, young wife, and then have breakfast. He had earned the rights to leisurely mornings, beautiful wives, and great sex. In the past sixteen years, he had had four wives. Four years was his limit on any marriage. The broads bored him after that. All they wanted anyway was his money, and if the firm continued its growth, doubling its earnings yearly, he could easily afford his dispensable pleasure toys—wives.

His wife, stirring as though on call, reached under the sheets for her morning candy. He pushed her away. Not this morning, baby. No matter how early it was, he was going to be in Helen's office within the hour. It was that flexible service and kiss-ass attitude that made him king of the fashion financial empire. Anyway, he was dying to meet the lass in person. Who knows, maybe she would become wife number five, although that would be quite a departure from his blond cookie cutters.

If that Helen babe was anything like her mother, most people who crossed her would never survive the deep freeze. After seeing what happened to Johnathan Buckely and his lovely wife, Larry was sure he was not up to playing in that ferocious pen. Hell, he wanted nothing to do with those African women who probably used voodoo to kill their victims.

But alas, times were a-changing. In his forty-five years, he had never met any black women who were not cleaning his office. Not that he was racist, but he hadn't ever met any. Frankly, since he was from the wrong side of the tracks anyway, all he was interested in was the color green. Didn't bother him a bit that these women were voodoo queens. Green Money. Green, Green, Green, that he would take even from the Japs.

"No hanky panky this morning, sweetie?" wife number four purred.

"No baby. Not today." He replaced the receiver, flipped off the sheet, tweaked his wife's nipples and hurried to the bathroom. His mind was quickly calculating the dollars associated with the deal he was about to perform. Well worth it, he reminded himself.

Next Helen called Anton DePaul, the uptown young Harvard lawyer who was making big waves on Wall Street. He was known as the token boy wonder at the prestigious firm of Bingham, Lewis, Viking & Gould, at least by reputation. Jane Kreiza, whose company's stocks had soared beyond expectation, referred him to her. DePaul had been the lead council on the team that had taken the company public two years before, and she was told he was a tough negotiator. When she finally called him about the Wakefield transition and the possibility of going public, she had to wait two weeks for an appointment. That annoyed the crap out of her, but she definitely wanted only the *crème de la crème* on her team. Anton DePaul was the best, and that meant she had to cool her jets.

But just to pay him back she never showed up for the appointment. She had sent Chance with the laundry list of introductory paper work he had requested, and they had since communicated by fax and e-mail.

"It's early," he said as he answered the phone.

"Sure it is, but isn't that why you are a star?"

"Who is this?"

"Helen Stern. I want to know, what's your opinion about Wakefield? The JI board meets soon, and I would like to present the feasibility of my plans to take the company public. Sorry for such short notice, it couldn't be helped. I want to make sure everything is in order and that there are no last-minute surprises or reasons why I might want to avoid bringing up the topic. What would be great is if you can meet with me this morning."

"I sent you an e-mail, but I see you were away. That, of course, is why you didn't respond."

"How did you know I was away?"

"Front page news this morning. Don't tell me you haven't seen the paper." His tone was slightly amused. Not only had he been up since

5:00 a.m. but he'd already retrieved the morning's headline news from his internet.

"No, I haven't seen the paper yet." She felt teed off by his matter-of-fact attitude. "Can you meet this morning?" She brought the conversation back to business.

"I can meet at 9:00 a.m. sharp. Is that good for you?"

"We're on our way to meet with the accountant, and I imagine that meeting will last until nine o'clock. It might be a good idea for you both to meet anyway. Nine is fine. And I trust you will be ready?"

"Am I to assume you have little faith in my abilities?"

"Yes, Mr. DePaul. I have faith in no one but myself. I am just making sure I'll get what I pay for. I do believe at the high prices your firm charges that the customer must always be right."

"Not always, Miss Stern. That's why we are who we are. We help them to become right. You can't imagine how many need us to do that and *do* pay for it."

DePaul was not sure how he felt about Helen Stern, but he wanted to meet her face to face. It was too bad he had to break the news to her. From the picture in the paper he wouldn't have minded working close to her. She was a pushy broad. There was no mistaking the acrid tone of her voice from the phone conversation. A bit too aggressive for his liking, but he would reserve judgment until 9 a.m. Anton hung up the phone, poured a cup of coffee and studied the beauty with the long legs that graced the Paris runway. Humm, he glided his tongue over his lips.

The beautiful glass building pierced the Manhattan skyline, crowding out the pale sun that was just barely rising from its night's slumber. The JI building was only another tall building in the concrete jungle, Helen thought, pausing momentarily to cast her eyes upwards. No matter, Manhattan was a place so comforting that even in its steel encased walls, it created an illusion of the ultimate endurance, chic, and class. JI Industries' brass letters gleamed even in the early dawn, and frankly, the building actually fit in perfectly with her description of Manhattan as durable; only she knew, however, that JI's durability would be over soon. A feeling of satisfaction came over her as she realized that every day Jacobson Industries came closer and closer to being hers.

"Good morning." Helen spoke to the security guard as she passed through the entrance to the elevators.

"You're early this morning, Miss Stern."

She had never noticed the accent before, but he suddenly reminded her of Cecil, her guide while she was in Jamaica.

"Good morning," she replied pleasantly. "Nice to see you again."

A couple of hours later there was a light knock on the door. Larry Hortenski pushed his head around the door as she beckoned him through the glass wall of her office.

"Come in." Helen rose from behind her desk.

"Miss Stern." Larry extended his hand and then likewise to Chance.

Helen motioned him to an empty seat by the coffee table.

"How do you take it?" she asked, holding up the coffeepot. She assumed every accountant drank coffee.

"Black, one sugar."

"Good. Now, what do you have to tell us, Mr. Hortenski?" Helen inquired, her back still to him.

"I've run all the numbers." Larry's voice was excited. "If the growth of Wakefield continues the way it has been, the company will gross over $500 million by the next fiscal year. That number could go up or down depending on tight managing of the PR budget. We have slated $15 million for advertising and promotion, and although that sounds high, we want to leave nothing to chance." He smiled at Chance as he realized the pun. "I mean fate. With the success of your show in Paris and the free publicity," he pointed to the paper still folded on the coffee table, "you'll probably come in under $5 million for advertising and marketing. And that much you've just made in one night, Miss Stern.

"We can take you public right now. Thousands will be scrambling to buy stocks in such a lucrative company with such impressive earnings. The only problem I see is if your mother's approval is not forthcoming. Since Wakefield is still privately held and she is the majority share holder, this discussion could be moot without her."

Helen's eyes flashed murder. It did not go unnoticed.

"Why discuss the obvious, Mr. Hortenski? I assume you are asking that my mother be present at the next meeting."

"It's the only way to make sure we are not wasting time. Just six months ago my firm was handling a deal. The entire thing went bust because everyone felt they could convince the 90-year-old majority stockholder of anything they wanted. The plans didn't go as they had expected, and they had to pay me a half a million dollars for nothing."

"I'll call a meeting with you after the board meets," Helen informed him curtly.

"Good. It sounds to me that anything else we could discuss would only be academic. So," he smiled broadly, showing capped teeth, "until then we can wrap up. I look forward to hearing from you." He drained his coffee cup and began packing his briefcase. "It's really a simple thing to do. Either way, to go public or to transfer stocks, my firm can help you.

"If your mother wants to keep the company's earnings separate from JI, she can simply transfer the company stocks to you or she may, for procedural reasons, ask you for a buy-out option. My guess is that it will be strictly business. From what I hear, your mother does not go in for this nepotism stuff. I understand that even her husband pays rent for his space in the building." He wouldn't let on what else was being rumored around Wall Street.

The man was crass. Snubbing him would be a waste of time if he didn't realize that discussing her mother's husband was socially unacceptable.

"And if she asks for a buyout?"

"You'll have to come up with the value of her stocks. Of course, all this could be just on paper."

A trilling phone interrupted the conversation and Chance got up to answer the buzzer.

"Good Morning, Ms. Livingston. Mr. DePaul is here," Mrs. Walters announced over the intercom.

"Mr. DePaul," Chance informed Helen.

"Show him in."

Anton DePaul's entrance was dramatic, maybe to no one else other than Helen Stern. As he crossed the room, she felt the air catch in her lungs, her knees buckling, her head woozy and her heart galloping past its usual point of caution. She held her breath for what seemed like eternity until she was forced to gasp for air. Christ! What was happening to her? Some kind of adrenaline reaction. For chrissake, she might just be allergic to his good looks. Helen poured a glass of water and forced herself to regain control. She had not envisioned him this way. Not by any stretch of the imagination.

"Good morning." He extended his hand to Hortenski and then to Chance and finally to Helen. Hortenski! That was bad business. The news on the street was that the guy would sell his mama for a dollar.

It's a good thing Helen was concentrating on not hyperventilating, as she would have blasted him for his chauvinistic attitude in greeting her last. Who the hell did he think was paying for his service!?

"Sit down, Mr. DePaul," she ordered, her voice more unfriendly than she had intended, waving him casually to an empty seat.

"I am fine, thank you," he said, reminding her that good manners were usual in his circles.

Helen glared at him. Chance stifled a smile. *Oh Oh. Two bulls in a pen.*

Anton rested his briefcase on the side table. While he was removing his folders and other pertinent information, Helen studied him intensely. So, this was Anton DePaul. Cute. Definitely cute. Maybe thirty-six years of age, God handsome, and six feet two inches tall with an athletic body built to suit. The deep, black eyes were penetrating and his ample mouth seemed always in a cocked smile. He looked aristocratic, or was it just distinguished. Either way, with the patch of gray at his temples—too early for such a young man—he was striking. The slightly down pointing nose and strong jawline were commanding. His expensive Italian navy suit, which fit to perfection, was tailor made and of exquisite fabric. A crisply starched, white oxford shirt was accented by the navy and maroon Brooks Brothers tie of the best quality silk. Black wing-tipped shoes matched the expensive, black leather briefcase and the black and gold Waterman pen he removed from it.

Conservative, handsome, and successful, confidence exuded from Anton DePaul's every pore. Helen was silently delighted that he oozed such, *ahh* she couldn't think of a suitable word-pizzaz maybe. Privy to true wealth, Helen surmised DePaul was not from *significant* money, but he was well enough bred to be haughty.

At the very moment she was studying him, Anton looked up from his briefcase and caught her staring. Quickly averting her eyes from the jet black ones unnerving her very core, she'd already observed all there was to note about Anton. His deep pecan skin, was naturally silken. He was clean shaven and truly attractive. When listening, he had, it seemed, a habit of cradling his jawbone between his thumb and index finger, as he was now doing in response to something Chance was saying. Anton DePaul seemed much too mature and calm for his age.

Resting his folders on the table, Anton rose as Helen approached.

"Would you like coffee, Anton?" Chance offered. First-name basis, Helen noticed.

"Yes, thank you. I take it black." He raised his eyes to meet Helen's, who casually looked away.

"I'll get it, Chance. Why don't you brief Mr. DePaul on our discussions while I freshen the coffee." She made sure she emphasized the appropriate way to address an associate. He had better not call her

Helen. She wouldn't care just how much of a star he was. She would fire him before she hired him if he got too familiar.

"Your coffee," she brought over a mahogany tray with a fresh china coffeepot, cups, saucers and sterling spoons.

"I must say your picture doesn't do you justice. You are far prettier in person."

Helen blushed visibly. How dare he embarrass her with his unprofessional comment.

"That's certainly true," Larry echoed. "You were quite a splash according to the fashion editor of the *Times*. Have you seen the paper?"

"No, I haven't, but I was there," she said sarcastically. That's exactly why I am so exhausted now. *Too exhausted for trivia and small talk.* "Now," she said, "let's continue."

"Helen, may I speak with you alone?" Anton interrupted. "I have something you need to know before the meeting continues."

"Chance, Larry," Helen indicated. "If there is nothing else, I think Mr. DePaul and I can take this from here. I know you are exhausted, so go on home."

Chance was relieved to have been dismissed. As much as she tried, she could never be as driven as Helen. In fact, she was not sure she wanted to be. And now that she had met Victor, she was seriously considering an alternate life-style to super-womanhood. She wanted to settle down and have children. In two weeks she would turn thirty, and her pendulum was swinging a little to the left.

"Looking forward to hearing from you," Larry replaced the remaining contents of his briefcase, nodded to Anton and ambled out of the office behind Chance. He always felt like a clod compared to suave fellas like that DePaul character. Folks like Anton DePaul and Helen Stern usually made him remember his humble beginnings. In him was still the shy, insecure Bronx boy from Polish parents. "Confidence, my boy," he could hear his father's voice, and his shoulders automatically straightened. Of course, that was his father, but now he was feeling inferior to black folks! Damn, what planet did these people come from anyway? He was going to work hard at being as cocky as this DePaul guy. Yeah, he'd be there soon. Power-ties, power-lunches, power vacations, and a new power-fuckin' wife would soon be his. A deal such as this could take him from just being rich, rich, rich to looking and feeling rich as though he had been born to it. And then he'd want a more respectable woman on his arm, someone like Helen Stern; the thought caught him by surprise. This was the second time he'd met Anton DePaul on a deal, and Larry knew if he was involved this was going to be big. He was definitely getting involved in this deal! Even if he had to jump ship and give JB the kiss of death.

"What was so important?" Helen spun around to face DePaul, conscious that her hands were getting moist. Alone with just him in the office, she felt exposed, and the look in his eyes made her feel as though he could read her mind.

"Sorry, but I couldn't talk in front of the others. I just found out at our meeting a day ago that my firm has accepted an offer that would make my representing Wakefield a conflict of interest. I could have told you on the telephone, but I wanted to come down in person."

"What! I just can't believe this," Helen was furious. "Why did you waste my time?"

"I thought it was courteous. I am not a senior partner in the firm, and I'm not immediately privy to every deal. I hadn't brought your offer to the partners yet because I received it only a week ago. We didn't have a meeting until yesterday. I am truly sorry. Your trip to Paris delayed our meeting, and by then they had already accepted the other offer." His revelation seemed to have taken her off guard, and she looked at him wide-eyed.

"What offer is this?" Helen demanded.

"I am sorry. I am not at liberty to discuss that at this time. It would be a breech of company confidentiality."

"Hell, what difference does that make, we'll find out soon enough anyway. It is something to do with JI, then?"

"Sorry, I can't comment."

"In that case then, Mr. DePaul, our meeting is over isn't it?"

"I can refer you to someone who is not quite as good as I am, but will do a marvelous job for you."

"I just love your modesty," she said sarcastically. "Won't it make your people nervous to know that you are recommending a competitor, or are you expecting a kickback? And for your information, Mr. DePaul, if I chose to work with anyone other than yourself, they wouldn't *just* be as good as you, they would be better. Why would I trust your recommendation anyway if you are going to take on JI?"

"Did I say that?"

"You don't have to. The only thing that could make representing me a conflict of interest has to be something to do with JI."

"I see," was his answer. "I see you have a problem with trust."

Helen's lips stretched in anger.

"In my experience," she spat, "only a fool trusts the enemy." With that she dismissed him.

Helen was speechless. To be so fucking stupid. Stymied by her own lack of knowledge. She'd dropped the ball, all right, for she had no idea what was going on in the rest of JI. Being consumed with making Wakefield a juggernaut in the fashion world had left her open to oversights. For a moment she wondered if DePaul was really working under disguise for her mother. No doubt this could have been a plant. How fuckin' ballsy that would be of them both. Once a sly fox always a sly deceiving fox, she thought, but if they dared, this would be all-out war. Helen sat quietly for several more minutes. If there was any truth to what Anton said, a bid for JI could speed up her plans.

After Paris and the raving news article in *Fortune*, Helen was less than concerned about *her* financial future. Firing up her spreadsheet on the laptop, she tapped out a potential earning of at least $3 million a year in modeling alone. But being a model was not why she came to the United States, and she was not leaving until her job was completed. Something big was going down, or a firm the caliber of Bingham, Lewis, Viking & Gould would not be asked to shake down JI. She would beat them at their own game, she vowed. There was nothing that could compete with her formidable force when passion, talent and her "gift", if necessary, intersected.

Helen suddenly felt very tired. The long and exhausting trip was taking its toll. This news about JI was staggering, but she had little energy left to formulate any new plans. At that moment, she had to give into the overwhelming tiredness. She buzzed Mrs. Walters in.

"Miss Stern, you look awful!"

"You're right. I feel awful. I'm going to call it a day. See you tomorrow, for I will probably sleep the rest of the day."

"Shall I call your driver?"

"No, I'm going to take a nap right here."

When Mrs. Walters left, Helen pressed a button under her desk, and one panel slid back to reveal her cozy studio apartment. She flopped across the bed and was out like a light. Not even the thought of the perfect opportunity for destroying her mother's empire could keep her awake.

There was no question in Anton's mind that something strange had happened to him in Helen Stern's office. As discreet as he had been, he could hardly take his eyes off her *very* shapely legs, and when their eyes had met, tiny shock waves went through him. They were the most curious eyes he had ever seen. Jet-black, they were mysterious and penetrating with a brightness and darkness at the same time. A contradiction of light, creating an illusion so peculiar that they looked through him, piercing his very soul as if there was something they were looking for. And for that instant, he'd become absorbed in them, moving deeper and deeper as he became completely engulfed in their watery abyss. Although it was only seconds, he was completely and totally enraptured with Helen Stern.

Anton's mind continued its scrutiny of the beautiful face. Sharply arched eyebrows added a sense of drama to the dark eyes. The high cheekbones twitched with control and suggested determination and a need for power. The hard set of the full lips and strong jawline indicated a deep anger or maybe a discontentment, yet the blood red color of those lips was inviting and alluring. Those very tempting lips, he was convinced, were used to entice unsuspecting men into her web, challenging them to find the fascination that lay behind their pouty entrance. And as her silken voice lilted along in the most educated British accent, he never for a moment doubted that her will was as strong as the lines of her jaw. There was no question that this woman was a rare beauty, an indescribable work of art; a seductress extraordinaire who used the art of withholding her love as an ace against her suitors.

He noted with interest that her hair was very short and brushed back off her face, though in no way austerely. The pouty lips were quick to cut one down to size, as he had just learned. Yet, as much as he found himself enamored by her perfect physical being, it was her confidence that piqued his interest. He felt disappointed that he would not be able to help her. What a team they would have made. Talk about a power couple. He couldn't believe his trend of thought. Not him, Mr. calm, cool and collected himself. He hailed a cab.

This was the woman for him. Anton dabbed his brow with the monogram hankie as he got into the air-conditioned car, relieved that the stifling heat was momentarily abated. He wanted to marry this girl. The thought suddenly dawned on him. Christ, he mopped his brow again, this time from excitement. At the thought of marriage before, he would have had the world's worst reaction; a sudden tightening of his chest followed by an urgent need to get out of the presence of his pursuer. Now here he was calmly contemplating marriage to a woman he had only just met and who gave him quite a piece of her mind. Not only didn't he feel the familiar chest constriction with Helen, but in fact he wished he was still in her presence. A blaring horn forced the cab to ride the embankment and Anton was thrown forward. "Oh shit!" He reached for the seatbelt. He couldn't die now! Not when he had just met his princess-maybe a dragon princess was more like it. Heck, he wasn't even perturbed by her fire breathing, and he was convinced he would make her not just a good husband but a wonderful husband. He had a lot to offer a girl like Helen Stern. He was successful, a no-nonsense kind of guy, had a sense of humor, and was quite fun-loving. Yes, yes, yes. He was the sculptor that would sculpt the ice queen into an angel.

Anton DePaul had been born thirty-nine years earlier at Harper Hospital in Detroit. As the story goes, he was always very eager and was forever too prompt. Anton arrived early for everything. Even his birth was early, for he was born a month premature weighing in at only four pounds. The trauma of the pregnancy so frightened his mother that she never became pregnant again, but she swore her first-born was destined for greatness. Gabrielle DePaul was a beautiful mulatto woman from Haiti whose family had fled the declining country in fear for their lives. From a fairly affluent upbringing, she had descended into a meager lifestyle in East Detroit. Still, she was an independent and high-minded wench. Within weeks of arriving in the United States, she found a secretarial job that helped to provide for herself and her family. Not that she knew how to type, but she was a quick learner. Her organizational and take-charge attitude won her boss over, and he gave her the time to learn to type.

Life had changed for her when she married Winston DePaul. They had met when he stopped by the office hoping to pay a sales call to her boss. She was so taken by his good looks and the smooth brown skin several shades darker than her own that she spilled the coffee she was offering him all over his suit.

"Oh dear. I am most sorry." Gabrielle grabbed the hankie from his pocket and proceeded to mop up the suit.

"It's quite all right." His English was more perfect than usual. He loved her accent and somehow wanted to impress her. As a kid, Winston was always great at mimicking various ethnic accents. "I'll come back tomorrow. I didn't have an appointment today anyway, so let me make one now for tomorrow." His lingo now had a French accent.

"Surely." She stuffed the wet handkerchief in his hand and tried rather hurriedly to flip though the pages of her appointment book, more amenable than she would have been to an uninvited caller.

Winston was smiling broadly, for what she could not understand. He seemed to like her scatterbrain. She hadn't even realized she'd used his own handkerchief to mop him up and then handed it back to him soaking wet.

After a few minutes, Gabrielle finally offered him an appointment for the following afternoon at two o'clock.

The next day Winston brought Gabrielle a rose in a bud vase, and within six months they were married. For several years they tried to have a baby and finally, when Gabrielle did conceive, she stopped working. By then, they had saved a little nest egg, and Anton's father opened his first little retail grocery store.

Gabrielle still clung to her privileged Caribbean upbringing and passed on her well-bred mannerisms to her only son. She spent her life protecting him against the harshness of the American reality. Anton DePaul became a cultural hybrid. This cultural gerri rigging became a source of contention for his parents. His father felt he should know all the perils that lay before him in a land quite different from the one his mother grew up in, and his mother insisted on cultural universality. The combination of the diverse values gave him quite an edge and an appreciation for things he would never have learned as a child of Detroit. He spoke fluent French, knew all about operas, appreciated classical music, art, and enjoyed the *Campas* music of his mom's native land.

His grandfather, a doctor by profession, had been one of Haiti's leading political agitators against totalitarianism. Anton often traveled with him on occasions when he was invited to give lectures on Haitian oppression. Sometimes in the summer he even went overseas. Anton's only regret was that he had never been able to visit Haiti, for his mother's family was in exile. Yet, he could see the country vividly as though he had been there, for his mother and grandmother had told him many stories and had painted a vivid picture in his imagination. Stories about the *Tap Tap, Papa Doc, the Ton Ton Macoute* and the unique spiritual culture. His mother was always sad when she told him about the hardship, the fear of her people and the perils of talking out against the Government. Greed and power, she reminded him, were the hands of the devil. But she also told him all about the good times. He felt very much the child of a Haitian.

Yet, it was the tenacity of his mother and her need to return to a quasi privileged life-style that encouraged his father to surpass the limits of his own society. By the time Anton was twelve, his parents owned and operated a five-chain grocery store and had several real estate properties in the neighborhood. This afforded him an existence somewhat different from his classmates. Though he could afford more than a middle-class black child, his father insisted on sending him to the neighborhood public school.

"I don't care what you say, Gabrielle. The child has got to learn to be street smart. This is not Haiti."

His mother would rant and rave in a Creole dialect she knew her husband couldn't understand. After much debate, however, his father always won.

The fall after eighth grade, Anton left St. Andrew's school for boys and went to the neighborhood public school. Frankly, he loved it. The best thing about the school was the girls. For the first semester of high school, Anton was completely taken with Blane Ferris and spent every minute chatting with her on the phone. When his grades plummeted, his mother raised holy hell, and he immediately straightened up to the task at hand. With his mother's constant reminders, nagging, and inspection, he really had no choice but to commit himself to academic excellence.

"Remember, my son," she would often repeat a favorite rhyme: "Silver and gold will vanish away, but a good education will never decay."

At his mother's insistence, however, he did not become a typical bookworm. She took care to school him in social behaviors befitting a king. As a result, Anton had a healthy respect for money, but he did not worship it. He had discipline, social skills, academic commendations, cultural knowledge, and even acting abilities. If his memory served him right, he got a standing ovation in his first-grade play, "*Jack and the Bean Stalk.*" Confident and secure, he never felt as though he had anything to prove. The one thing he was sure of was that he knew how to love, for he had been very loved his entire life. No one had come along until now to bring his desire to love to the forefront.

At the University of Michigan, to which he had been admitted at age seventeen, he was one of three hundred entering minority students. He felt proud that his status there was not because of affirmative action, but because he was a straight 4.0 student. As his Caribbean mother always told him, "No one owes you anything. It's out there, and it belongs to you as much as it belongs to anyone else. Just take it, my boy. Just take it." Growing up with that kind of attitude, he was able to give himself the necessary strokes he needed. Approval from his peers or being in a popularity contest was not his thing. His steady girlfriend, Celine, was a foreign student from Belgium whose parents were from Martinique. Together they conquered U of M. Later, Anton went on to law school at Harvard and she to the medical campus. His outstanding performance in law school earned him interviews at every major Wall Street law firm. His offer from Bingham, Lewis, Viking & Gould was the most outstanding and prestigious of them all.

Twelve years later he was king of the mountain with an impressive portfolio and a first-class reputation. He was up for partnership. His only black mark was that he and Celine had drifted apart. She had later married the head of her residency program at UCLA Medical Center and was now a well-respected cardiologist with one child and one on the way. She had been hurt when he didn't want to marry her, but he was just starting his career and his classic anxiety attack at her proposal was acute. He hadn't regretted saying no to marriage, although from time to time he thought of her fondly.

Now suddenly and without warning, he wanted to be part of the DePaul-Stern power couple. As he stepped out of the taxi, he vowed to find out everything there was to know about this woman who had his jockeys in a twist. Suddenly an odd thought came to him. Helen Stern reminded him of Hierra, the exotic sorceress in the eerie stories his mother often told. She had surely casted a spell on him.

Chapter Thirteen

Helen woke with a start, incredulous that the Manhattan lights were glistening on her window panes. How tired she must have been. Switching on the bedside lamp, she ruminated over the ridiculous dream she'd had about Anton DePaul. Shaking her head vehemently, she went to the bathroom to wash her face, laughing and murmuring softly, "What a silly dream!"

It was dark but not really late. Only eight o'clock. She'd been asleep since 11:00 a.m., and dear Mrs. Walters had protected her from the multitude of messages now piled atop the desk outside her office. She skimmed through them, noting calls from several major retailers, a copy of the messages no doubt on Chance's desk. Mrs. Walters knew that anything to do with business transactions were to be *cced* to her. Repairing her makeup, Helen rang for her driver.

"Peter, sorry, I fell asleep. Bring the car around. I am ready to go home." Home, she thought nostalgically. It was time to return to England. Not much longer now, she consoled herself, for immediately after her plan was executed, she would leave America. Now with this new wrinkle from Anton, she had to work faster, so home was closer and closer to reality.

On the ride to her flat, Helen's mind kept revisiting Anton DePaul. Wasn't he a little young to be wearing wing-tipped shoes? She supposed not. Closing her eyes, she envisioned all six-feet-two of the stallion in her office. His sex appeal was electric, and though she had to admit he was dashing and dangerously handsome, he was far more appealing because of his quick mind. For the first time in what seemed like forever, Helen felt her sexuality. Not just in a lascivious way, but in a falling in love way. Taking stock, she realized she had not had an overly intimate feeling since her night with Geraud, but even their exquisite night of sex by the piano did not compare to the tender and confusing feeling she was having for this Anton character. What on earth was wrong with her? Most young girls had lived through the ravages of several failed love affairs, and by now would have been used to the tumultuous nature of love. Yet she, who had only one experience in romantic love, found these feelings unwelcome. Maybe an icy heart was lucky after all if this was what people felt like when they were in love. Ah, she smirked, I have a greater mission in my life. My obsession and my desires to destroy my mother rival the throes of passion any day.

What was it about Anton that intrigued her anyway? He was different. Yes, she affirmed, nodding her head. He was handsome. Yes. He was obviously not bound by the limitations of his ethnicity. Yes. He was successful, cultured and sexy. Yes, her mind answered. He was everything she wanted in a man. Yes, yes, yes, her mind screamed. She should see him again. No! Instantly her kharmic, kill-joy self piped up. No. Absolutely not, it said resoundingly. Absolutely not!

Her lack of interest in the male species in New York, Helen felt, was simply a cultural barrier. She missed the cosmopolitan European mind, even if she didn't trust it. Americans, she found after one or two dates, were somewhat provincial and insular. But this man, with his cocoa complexion, wide grin and peculiar sensibilities, cupping his jawbone when he was in deep thought, seemed almost aristocratic. Even the way he walked, tall, erect, confident, and purposeful intrigued her. He was driving her insane, but she had to remember he was the enemy.

Chapter Fourteen

By seven-thirty Thursday morning Helen and Chance were again hunched over the conference table poring over the last details of the proposal. They role-played every imaginable scenario that they could possibly face in less than an hour-and-a-half. Helen was surprisingly calm. By the time they walked into the board room everyone was there except Andrea. Mahogany doors to the projection screen were open, the erasable blackboard was wiped clean, and fresh markers were in the cradle. Helen looked around the room with interest. She had never seen anything like this. The maroon and gray carpet with the familiar JI logo was almost ankle deep. The highly polished mahogany table was flanked by maroon and mahogany chairs. At the head of the table was a deep charcoal, high-back leather swivel chair, Andrea's. The solid walls were covered in muted gray silk wallpaper accented by mahogany chair rails and opened into an expanse of windows boasting the magnificent Manhattan skyline. Chance walked over to the visual panel and switched on the projector screen light. A few keystrokes and she loaded the frames of the slide presentation onto her laptop computer and the Wakefield logo filled the screen. Helen went around the room greeting the board members and introducing herself. She noted with interest that most people already seemed to know who she was.

In deference to the fact that she was the CEO's daughter, she was treated with the utmost respect. As soon as the introductions were completed, Andrea, followed by her right arm, Janice, entered the room. Most of the men in the room stood, an obvious male rhetoric to a female CEO. Helen had never been in a board meeting. In fact, she was more used to seeing Andrea in her role at home than at the office. To Andrea, her daughter was just another employee at work, and there was little interface between them. It was all business.

"Good morning, and thank you for being here." Andrea beamed a radiant smile. "Janice has placed the agenda before you. I do have a favor to ask. We must move to end the meeting by two-thirty. Any items not covered will be tabled. I'm sorry to rush you, but I have to be in Asia and I have a five-forty-five flight. Shall we begin?"

A senior or executive vice president presented each item and all engaged in a healthy discussion. Helen impatiently watched the clock while listening for any clue as to why Anton's firm would have been retained. Nine forty-five. Already her presentation was cut by fifteen minutes. She had to rethink her strategy. She scribbled something on the pad provided and discreetly pushed it over to Chance seated next to her. Another fifteen minutes went by before her agenda item was up.

Helen nodded to Chance, and the video of her runway performance in Paris replaced the Wakefield logo on the screen. Everyone watched in silence, almost mesmerized. As she studied their faces she realized she was having the same effect she had had on her audience at the show. They were leaning forward as though they wanted to touch the screen. Her strategy was working. As the screen went dark Helen began speaking.

"This is what the Wakefield Company has become. A practical fashion industry for women on the move all over the world. Women who do not have the time to visit a spa and hairdresser or take five hours to dress before their evening engagement. As women become more prominent in the workplace, they are required to be tough and do what men did, but unfortunately they can't just show up in their office attire to a six o'clock event that requires more than work clothes. So like the busy male executive who can just simply change his shirt and put on a dinner jacket, the female executive can now put the chic in her day wear. It's the wave of the future, and as you can see from the report in front of you, this Paris show, as of today, has netted $20 million. One show, one day. We all have to agree that the runway elites are struggling to bring fresh ideas to the marketplace.

"Even Italy is finding it hard to maintain its Machiavellian life-styles with the declining interest in their product. The world of fashion has changed, and the audience of the nineties wants value as much as they want style and pizzazz. As you can see, the name Wakefield sounds much like it belongs to a funeral home rather than a chic fashion enterprise. We will have a harder time attracting the couture audience we are after with a name like Wakefield. I am proposing we use a name that not only trendy kids can relate to, but also our new world audience and wealthy matrons. Our future plans for the company include a full line of designer fashion. We will compete directly with the elite market such as Lagerfeld, Valentino, St. Pierre. Although there will be a tremendous cost for retooling and marketing, I believe we can bring freshness to a staggeringly boring industry. The projections and costs associated with this shift are before you. All the financial papers are with JI's CFO and the requirements of the name change with the legal department. They will answer any issues concerning the proposed transition.

The room bustled with laughter at her reference to the name Wakefield as better suited to a funeral parlor. And Helen smiled with relief. She hadn't realized how nervous she was. Her argument and presentation were good, though, and she knew it. She glanced at her mother whose hand was cocked against her jaw. A look of admiration was on her face along with something else that was not discernible. Maybe annoyance at bringing up the couture market. She hadn't quite planned to be so explicit but rather to plant a little seed.

"I know we are almost out of time, and therefore I would like to entertain any questions you might have."

"I have quite a few." It was the first time Andrea spoke, a leveling look in her eyes. "But I am afraid we don't have time for them. I would like all the board members to consider the report you have heard. Should you, as JI stockholders, choose to participate in the initial public offering, we want you to be happy with the name that is chosen. It would be helpful if you would send in a preferred choice of name from the short list in front of you. I will return in five days and be available to answer any questions. We are adjourned unless anyone has anything to say."

There was silence. Janice, who knew Andrea like a well-read book, suspected something had displeased her a great deal. She gathered the minutes of the meeting and hurried to catch Andrea, already half way down the hall.

"I think it was a very good presentation. Helen sure has keen observations about the market. And that runway impromptu was quite a success, so what exactly are you displeased about?"

"Since when do you read minds?"

"Since I have trooped all over the celestial globe with you."

Andrea laughed, pushed the button to her office and entered. Janice realized she was not going to get an answer to her question.

After a brief congratulation, everyone filed out of the room except Helen. She slumped in the charcoal chair feeling betrayed again. Her mother could at least have congratulated her publicly. She had done well. It didn't take a rocket scientist to see that, yet she felt unfulfilled. She finally picked up her papers and left the room. At the elevator, she looked back at the glass enclosed conference room with its incredible view of Manhattan. The embers of her anger, fanned by Andrea's indifference, made her sure she would stop at nothing until she sat rightfully in the charcoal leather chair—the seat that would indicate her final triumph. The seat of power and glory.

When she got back to her suite, Mrs. Walters was nowhere in sight. She left a pile of papers on her desk and entered her office. She was startled to see Anton DePaul sitting on the sofa.

"Thought you could do with some lunch. Figured you'd like to chew on something about now if things didn't go as you wanted. And if they did, then we could celebrate."

"What the hell are you doing in here?" Helen snapped, clearly surprised. No one *ever* entered her fiefdom without her being there. Not even Mrs. Walters. Where the hell was Mrs. Walters anyway?

"As I said, I figured you would like to chew on something so…"

"*And*, I said, how did you get into this office?"

"I walked in, of course. No one was at the outer desk and the door was open. So are you interested in lunch?"

"Oh just shut up with the jabbering and get out."

"I know you don't really mean that." Anton's demeanor was unwavering, a silly grin on his face. Helen wanted to slap it off.

"Now why do you say that?" Her voice was retiring rather than sarcastic, as she intended.

"Your eyes of course. They may be dark and mysterious, my dear, but they don't hide everything."

"I suppose you are interested in the mystery behind them as well as in lunch and in annoying me?"

"Look, I know you were disappointed about our meeting on Monday, but frankly, I think it's best that we are not working together; otherwise I wouldn't be able to take you to lunch. Company policy, can't lunch with the clients. I could still get in trouble for fraternizing with the enemy, but I'm willing to take that chance if you are."

"Really? So why aren't you scared of showing your face in JI's building and clearly fraternizing with the enemy?"

"As I said, I'm willing to take that chance."

"I think, Mr. DePaul, you are very mistaken about my being the enemy. Maybe you ought to take a closer look at who that might be. And next time don't be so certain that you can invite me to lunch without first checking with me." There was bitterness in her voice.

"What do you think I'm doing now? I'm checking with you, Miss Stern."

"And I'm declining, Mr. DePaul. I'm far too busy. Let's get one thing straight right now in case you feel inclined to ask me again. If you plan to take on JI, I will have nothing to do with you, ever."

"Really? That's too bad. It will definitely make things rather difficult. I never believed those dream books anyway."

"What dream? What are you talking about?"

"My dream that I had married you. Believe me, though, I understand what you mean. To be honest, since we met I've been contemplating leaving my job if it means I don't have to fight you."

Now she was getting somewhere. He had at least admitted to a fight with JI, the enemy.

"A-huh." She ignored all references to marriage. "And what would you do?"

"Come to work for you, of course. I don't mean literally. I mean I would hang out my own shingle and consult with your company. That should keep me eating for awhile."

"Funny, Anton." He was acutely aware she'd used his first name. "So exactly why do you feel *so* inclined to help me? Do I look like a damsel in distress?"

"No, but you sure do look hungry."

Helen stifled a grin that was beginning at the corner of her lips.

"Try again when you've hung out your shingle." Her brows creased. *Did he say marriage?*

"And how am I to know if I can afford to do that if you don't tell me how much work there is from you?"

"Listen...okay, okay. But never ask me again and never, ever come to my office without making an appointment. Now where did you want to go for lunch?" she asked wearily. *Why the heck not? She might as well find out what she could about JI's problems.*

"I am going to take you to the Harvard Club."

"My. Can't we go somewhere less, ahh, formal?"

"Okay then, your call."

"Good. I would like to go to *Le Grenioulle*. Madison and Fifty-Fifth, I believe."

"Fifty-Second," he offered in correction.

God she hated him, almost.

As they walked the eleven blocks, she noted that Anton always moved to the outside of her, guiding her with a light touch to her elbows as they crossed the street. *Now who said chivalry was dead!* she thought irritably.

"How long have you been in New York?" Helen asked

"I came right out of law school. About fifteen years. And you?"

"I have been here too many years to count." Helen did a quick calculation of his age. He had to be thirty-eight or nine. "I guess every Harvard attorney wants to work on Wall Street?"

"I suppose so. Wall Street is as legendary for paying a lot of money to hot-shot attorneys, as is Harvard for educating them. There are many attorneys, very good ones, who never get a chance at the brass ring because they didn't go to Harvard. Wall Street is for the best and the brightest, maybe even the *real* good ones of the best of the best. I suppose you know that though, eh? I am sure you wouldn't have wanted to hire me if you didn't."

"Well, I have to say blowing your own trumpet becomes you. But yes, Mr. DePaul, you came highly recommended. Now though I'm not sure if it's because you are good or because you say very loudly that you are good."

"Ouch. That hurts. I suppose you find something wrong with my knowing my own capabilities. I am not bragging. I am simply stating a fact. I have the portfolio to prove it, and by the way you didn't go to Harvard."

How arrogant this man was.

There was an uncomfortable silence as Helen waited for her warm bacon and spinach salad and Anton for his chicken livers and onions. Over lunch Helen steered the conversation in a less personal direction. She talked superficially about the new direction for Wakefield, leaving wide cracks for him to fill with any information he might volunteer about JI after a glass or two of wine. He didn't take the bait, however, and by the end of lunch she had no new information about his involvement against JI.

Anton DePaul did not talk glibly. Every word he said was chosen carefully. He talked about his work and his love of solitude. He talked about his zest for travel and his love of teaching. It seemed he volunteered at local public schools where he tutored disadvantaged children.

After an hour, Helen was ready to leave the presence of Anton DePaul. Not that it was unpleasant, but she couldn't hide her feelings too much longer. During lunch she found herself fixated on some part of his face as he talked. Her mind was way past the dining table, ambling gleefully along to a more private setting. She wondered what his house looked like, his bedroom. What kind of car he drove and where he had traveled. She wondered where he had learned to speak French with such an authentic accent, and she wondered when her heart would stop fluttering.

"Oh," she looked at her watch. "I am so sorry, Anton, but I have an appointment in fifteen minutes. I do have to run. Thanks for lunch." Helen offered her half of the tab as he spoke to the waiter in French.

"Thank you, but no thanks." He was clearly insulted. "Don't ever do that again," he reprimanded her when the waiter was out of earshot. "Not ever," he emphasized.

Helen was quite taken aback by the sternness of Anton's voice. He had his limits, she noted. "Thank you," she was gracious.

"By the way, Helen said, before getting into a cab, "How did you know about my presentation today?"

"Let's just say it's my job to know everything. Harvard, remember." Anton said walking in the direction of Avenue of the Americas and

Forty-Ninth where the plush offices of his client, Johnathan Buckley was his next appointment.

"Mrs. Walters, I was just forced to have lunch with someone sitting in my office when I returned from the meeting. How the hell did that happen?"

"I…I must have gone to the bathroom, Miss Stern and…"

"Left my office open."

"Hardly anyone comes up here without calling first. I'm sorry. It won't happen again. I was careless."

Back at his office, Anton rang his mother and father. The answering machine clicked on before his mother, slightly out of breath, answered the phone.

"Hello," she rasped, the mouthpiece resting on her shoulder.

"*Mama, tu vas bien.*" He always spoke to her in French. He knew how much she missed speaking her native language, plus it gave him a degree of privacy from nosy secretaries.

"I am fine," she forever answered him in English. "I was riding my new exerciser. Your father bought it for me. I guess he thinks I'm getting copious."

Anton chuckled at her choice of words. "Corpulent, Mama, not copious."

"They mean the same thing, no? Anyway why are you calling in the middle of the day?"

"Can't I just call to say hello?"

"Hello then, but call back after I get finished, eh pourpee?" she said to him affectionately.

"Okay, I met this girl."

"Aha, Anton, this is wonderful. When can I meet her?"

"Mom, calm down. I only just met her myself."

"Well it's time to have babies, you are already too old. How old is she? I hope she likes babies."

He couldn't tell his mother who it was just yet or it would be all over the news by morning. In fact, it might sound as though marriage was imminent.

"It's nothing like that yet, Mom, but this is the woman I want to marry."

A tap on his window caused him to look up.

"Got to go, Mom. Briefing time."

"Bring her home soon, Son. Your Papa and I will be happy to meet her and for grand-babies."

Chapter Fifteen

Aix en Pravance, Victor Innes Palmer's Recovery.

Victor was having a hard time. Every day was a struggle. He tried desperately to appreciate the efforts of the country club rehab center and to remain clean, but it was hard. It never dawned on him that he was an alcoholic. How did he get this way in the first place? Why hadn't he appreciated the advantage of being well-born rather than blame everything and everyone to whom he could assign some guilt? Had he not met Helen Stern, he would never have understood how much of a loser he had become. Funny how a woman can make a man want to do his best.

Looking around the center, he saw all the casualties: the children of the rich and unconcerned abandoned to the perils of excess. Everyone in the center was filthy rich and worse, they were like him, trying to get clean alone and in secret.

Nursing his sixth cup of black coffee, desperately trying to get a caffeine buzz, he suddenly had, as addicts close to their true spiritual enlightenment would say, a moment of awakening, or was it clarity? It was no one's fault but his own that he used his privileged life as a stepping stone to failure. He was an alcoholic by his own choice. Blaming and denial, as he was learning in therapy, were the best friends of addicts. Well, he was no longer going to lean on the crutches of blame and denial. He was going to earn his rights in the family.

By the time Victor Innes Palmer left the *Aix en Pravance* Institute, he was ready to take his rightful place in the Catillion Family. He made three calls upon his arrival to his midtown flat.

"Why should I help you?" Olivia was unusually calm. "You have not so much as called me in four months. What's her name, Victor?"

"Olivia, my sweet," his voice caressed. "What are you talking about? I told you I was going away to think of my future. Here I am, humbly sharing it with you as the very first person, and you're accusing me of philandering. Shame on you. I thought you would be happy for me."

"Why didn't you call?"

"Because I had to see just what I was made of. Not only that, I couldn't. You promised father you'd make something of me. Now take the credit for what your love has done for me. Without you I would never have come this far. You have given me back my pride," he said earnestly and then on a lighter note, "Anyway, why are you acting like a love-sick brat?"

"I don't know." She was telling the truth. "I never had reason to miss you before. I guess you have grown on me."

"Well, be a good girl and come over. Show me just how much you missed me. It's time we talked about the future. What do you say?" He hadn't learned how to give up his women in therapy, just booze.

Chance could not concentrate. Everything she did was thrown back at her. Her work was suffering. Her lack of concentration since Victor had been gone was more than obvious. She didn't know how much longer Helen would put up with her. Already she was sensing a growing impatience in her voice. It had been almost six months since the wonderful Paris jaunt with Victor and four months since his disappearance. To top it all, Andrea had finally sung on Wakefield's future. Chance was too depressed and on edge to respond vehemently to the summons to Helen's office. She knew what it meant. More and more hard work.

Furthermore, the news of Franchesca's death was now all over the papers. Apparently her name and number were found in Franchesca's phone book, and the police were asking questions. It seemed she'd gone off with an unknown American who turned out to be a sadomasochist. Their night of play and frolic had turned fatal, and she had been found nude and dead in an apartment in Italy. Her body had been bruised all over, and her stomach contents showed traces of amphetamines and alcohol. The cause of death was a possibly suicide or murder. Six months later, this new evidence had surfaced. Someone had tipped off the police about her death.

The phone was ringing as she let herself into her brownstone. The beautiful home she had loved on sight that used to give her so much pleasure did not salve her feelings of desperation.

"Yes," her voice was almost inaudible.

"Don't say a word, just tell me I can be with you tonight. I will explain everything, and I will beg for your forgiveness in a most delightful way. My darling, I have missed you so."

"Victor, oh Victor, is it really you?" Tears of relief, joy and more relief flowed down her face.

"Please don't cry, my darling. It is really me. Home and promising never to leave you ever again. Well, may I come to you tonight?"

"Yes, oh yes my darling. Please come to me."

He simply hoped his manhood would not let him down. After an evening with Olivia, he sure needed help. He would stop at the health food store and purchase some ginseng and Chinese brush! When Victor arrived at the door of the brownstone, he was carrying a dozen red roses, a bottle of apple cider, and a bag of scrumptious smelling food.

"Dinner. Chinese," he pointed to the bag as Chance threw herself into his arms. He kissed her, moving her backwards towards the table so he could deposit his peace offering.

"I've missed you, oh how I've missed you," she kept kissing him hungrily.

"Oh and how I've missed you too. You look ravishing."

"So do you." She was peeling off her clothes.

"Hey, wait a minute. Sit down, honey." He led her to the couch. "We have to talk. I know it was terribly unfair to disappear without letting you know what was going on. For that I can only ask forgiveness, but Chance, I had to. As a child, I lost my mother at an early age. My father went into a deep depression, leaving me to grow up on my own. Since then I have been drifting without a real cause or purpose. When I met you, I was so proud of what you had done with your life that it forced me to take a look at my own. I decided it was time to do something about it, so I went to Europe for a while to figure out how to make you proud of me. I didn't stay in one place, just traveled around until my ideas crystallized. I know what I want to do now, my sweets, thanks to you."

"Victor, I didn't know you were feeling eh…inadequate. If I made you that way I didn't mean to. You are the best thing that has ever happened to me, and really darling, you are wonderful the way you are, but thank you for sharing your feelings with me. So what have you decided to do?"

"I am going to enter the world of fashion."

"What! The fash…as what?"

"Don't sound so surprised. I studied design and art in school; it came easy for me. My father thought I was a sissy. Eventually I may want to do some design work, but for now I am going to take my rightful place at *International Moderna*. I want to start out in marketing with a few accounts. Now that I see a way to translate my studies into practice, I'm excited. I have a good eye, really."

"Victor, there is so much I don't know about you. I think it's a wonderful idea."

"And what do you think of forming a company that compliments Helen Stern's? There are young men who are successful beyond their wildest dreams and who are resisting tradition. Look at Ralph Lauren. His camp is made up of the rebel spirits. For now, though, I will settle for helping your company with some great press. This could be a wonderful project that will benefit us both. I personally want to handle the advertisement for Wakefield. What do you think that will take?"

"By the way, the company name has been changed to the Helen Companies. They announced it while you were gone. As far as marketing is concerned, there's quite a budget to drive home this new name. It's a great time to approach PR. This account alone could give you clout at *International Moderna*. A complimentary company sounds wonderful, too, but a company of the magnitude that Helen has created will require a tremendous amount of capital and some true business savvy. Just to attract the 'right' Industry experts would cost a bundle. As you know the fashion Industry is fickle, so who knows what will happen by the time this project gets off the ground."

"Well, let's just say I could get a monetary kick. I'm sure my father would help financially, especially if I did anything remotely constructive rather than what he calls bounce around. After all, that's why he entrusted me to Olivia—to make something of me. Right now I will concentrate on getting approval to handle Wake...err, The Helen Companies' account and then move on from there."

"I'll give you some names in PR and put in a word or two. Do you think you might have any objections from *International Moderna?*"

"I've already checked into that. This afternoon I got Olivia to agree, in principle, to let me handle the account. She wanted to check with Hal. They have nothing to lose as we don't handle your account at this time anyway, but after that show in Paris, I'm sure the account has been noticed. I know we can get some free publicity with paid ads. Gratuitous publicity in other publications could also be arranged. A lot of people owe Olivia favors. In fact, I have a meeting with the fashion editor from *Glamour* next week. Funny how people think this is a cut-throat Industry, yet there is so much cooperation among editors. Quite a start, eh? I hope when the time comes you might offer me some suggestions on approaching Helen."

The look on Chance's face told him he was forgiven. Nothing like adding a bit of personal drama to get sympathy from a woman.

"I hope so." Chance was massaging her temples. This news was too much. Too sudden. It was not a particularly good time to ask special favors from Helen, especially when her work was not up to snuff. But of course, now that she thought of it, this could be the way to redeem herself. Especially if she brought something to the table that offered priceless publicity for free!

"You seem worried. Do you think I should go to plan B? It seems the account is more difficult than I am imagining. I can look at plan B. I think it's viable. I have a sizable trust fund and several lucrative investments that I might also be able to tap as a last resort should I have to start from scratch, but frankly I'm not concerned. My father's word is as good as gold, especially when Olivia is finished with him."

"No, No, I am just err…taken aback by all this. This is truly a surprise. First let's talk about the account. I know a few things, trade secrets so to speak that might help when positioning your pitch to Helen. As for your own company, it will be seen as a competitor to Wakefield, I mean the Helen Companies. How do you know they don't already have the male market slated for the future? If you did decide to pursue this, there will be a major conflict of interest for me to help organize any competitor. Helen would have my liver if she got wind of this conversation," Chance emphasized, making sure Victor understood her loyalties.

"Now don't get me wrong. I would never compromise your position with Helen. The most I would ask in the way of help would be for you to recommend a few good people in the business, if it should get to that. First, I would like to approach Helen about the account, and after that, we shall see. Anyway, we've talked enough about this," he reached for her hands. Kissing the tips of her fingers tenderly, his eyes conveying a deep sincerity, he cooed, "Take me to bed."

"Mmmmm, just what I wanted to hear."

Eight months later, Victor Innes Palmer was on the cover of every important magazine as a wunderkind. The new *International Moderna*, with its successfully updated look, rivaled *Elle and* was in every household in America. Even the children of the moral majority were buying the magazine, or so it seemed from the loud screams that came from the group. The controversy was an ad Victor had designed that was considered risqué. Ads of teenagers buying condoms and slipping them into their Fromberg jeans. Nonetheless, the honesty of the commercials struck a chord, enough of a chord to transform the stodgy magazine into a real fashion rag. In the past eight months Catillion revenues had grown more than they had in ten years. Now, and rightly so, all the news articles were about Victor Innes Palmer.

Everyone was elated, including Matthew Palmer. All of a sudden Victor could do no wrong. With the notoriety, however, came many problems, especially in the world of romance. He was America's new toy boy and most eligible bachelor.

This, of course, infuriated Olivia who was seeing less and less of Victor since he was no longer dependent on her generosity to keep him in good favor with his father. Likewise, his success had created a rift between him and his brother, Hal. No one had expected Victor to maximize the Helen account, much less to be responsible for the creation of the Catillion boom. With such success, VIP's own importance mushroomed. At last his name had real meaning.

Victor received many offers to handle gigantic accounts. From the new scent by Jean Paul Gaultier to Hanes underwear, he was sought after, with fervor, to manage each campaign. The new boy wonder who broke all the rules of advertising was a maverick in the world of fashion. VIP was really meaningful now, and the hip executive even had fan mail.

Launching a career had been much easier than Victor thought. But more than that, he'd finally found a way to get paid legitimately and handsomely for his art, charm. The grapevine was buzzing with good news for Victor, and as he became more and more successful, so did his host company, The Helen Companies.

Chapter Sixteen

Helen's Windfall

The Friday morning call summoning her to the sixty-fifth floor was a rarity. It had come only months after the name change, and Helen was concerned.

"Mother, this is quite an honor to be invited into your domain."

"What on earth do you mean?"

"You probably don't realize, but *you* have always come down to me for meetings."

"Only because you were so needed on the floor every minute of the day. It was more convenient, I thought."

Things are never as they seem, Helen reflected. All the time she thought her Mother was pulling rank.

"Let's get right to the point. The success of your company is staggering. We must do something to separate it from me altogether and protect its assets. I have discussed all the options for the Helen Companies with the CFO, and I believe it's best to transfer the stocks into your name. This will actually make your IPO more attractive."

Helen's eyebrows raised slightly. "This is quite a surprise. Any particular reason for this decision?"

"Yes, but nothing I can discuss at this time."

The trump card had landed right into her lap. A welcomed surprise and an awesome facilitator to her plans of destruction that had been taking shape. *YES! Home at last.*

The day after her mother transferred the stocks to her name, Helen placed a call to Basil Morgenson.
"Hello, Basil here."
"Helen Stern."
"Oh good evening, Miss Stern," Basil was now sitting bolt upright in his chair as though she were standing right before him. "How are…"
She cut off his incessant small talk. He hated that. That's one problem about making money, big money from people like Helen Stern was that you had to take a lot of crap.
"I want to find out what's going on inside JI. I know what the stocks are doing, and I know what things look like on the outside, so please don't tell me the obvious. Knowing you, Basil, I figure you have a mole somewhere high up in JI. I want to know what's threatening its stronghold, and who is trying to put a spoke in its wheel?"
"I'm sure something can be accomplished. How soon do you need this information?"
"As soon as possible, but as long as it takes to bring me good information."

Victor Innes Palmer was now ready to try his hand at something new. One thing he'd learned about himself was that he had a short attention span. It was time to approach Helen about a partnership. Even with his new-found success she hardly gave him the time of day, something that irked him senseless. And to think he'd orchestrated this entire charade to please her in the first place.
On Monday, a year to date after his wild success as a marketing man extraordinaire, Victor Innes Palmer privately incorporated VIP International. Finding good employees was far easier than he'd

expected. There were a myriad of designers who'd on a dime jump ship to start with a smaller firm where their ideas and talents were respected. Their argument, and Victor fostered the idea, was that a ground floor opportunity with quantum leap potential was more satisfying than being on the middle rung of a conglomerate.

The next few months Victor sculpted the company in a cloud of virtual silence. Sound ideas and viable marketing plans flowed, but more than that was the willingness of the employees to work far into the night ironing out details. Within six months, VIP International had a sound plan with which to come to market. First, however, he needed the blessing of Helen Stern. By express mail, he sent her a copy of his company's plan and a letter requesting a meeting to discuss a possible cooperative effort. The least she could do, Victor scoffed. After all, the Helen Companies' sales had soared, largely because of his efforts in the past year. Now there was a cosmetic line with an emphasis on women of color, *tres chic*, a line of beach wear, and a line of scents. Hell, she owed him more that an ear.

Helen threw the letter on her desk. She was furious.

"Mrs. Walters, did you say something to me this morning about an article on VIP? Could you get me a copy? I have a feeling I know what it's about."

"Right away, Miss Stern."

With magazine in hand, Helen dialed VIP International at the number listed on her letter.

"VIP International. The company that puts you first. How may I be of service?"

Shit, could this be any cornier? Helen had to admit, however, that for middle class people who had no importance to speak of, this kind of greeting made them feel, well, thought of.

"Mr. Palmer, please."

"Who's calling?"

"Helen Stern."

"One moment, please."

After a brief pause the deep baritone voice came on the line.

"Miss Stern, how good of you to call. Haven't seen you in such a long time. I hope you are pleased with the coverage our magazine is doing of your company?"

"Yes, quite. As pleased, I am sure, as you must be about what our ads have done for your publication." A bit of sarcasm, she knew, but it was better than saying dowdy magazine.

"Seems we've both made quite a success of ideas. What do you think of my correspondence?"

"I'm calling, right?"

"Yep. But one never knows what to expect from a girl who leaves a guy holding her drink all night."

"Victor! Dump useless memories." Helen snapped.

"Fine. I can move on. What about lunch to discuss my proposal? But why, Helen, with *your* schedule and mine, it could be another year." Sarcasm dripped like treacle. "I guess we should just seize the moment."

"From your letter I thought nothing was out to the press, but from the article in W it seems someone was living in your woodwork." Helen completely ignored Victor's self-pity. She hated fuckin' whining men and she definitely hated brats.

"Yes, yes. That was distressing. Everything around here gets leaked. And to think I hand-picked the people on this project myself. Always a Judas. I hope you agree that the idea could be beneficial to us both." *Of course there was a leak, I planned it that way. Does that really come as a surprise to you? This would be entirely too much if the woman actually thinks I am an absolute idiot?*

"In a way. Just how beneficial is what we'll discuss over dinner? Or would you rather play golf?" Helen quipped. God, she had to stop with the zings.

"Dinner will be just fine. Left my golf shoes at home today. Pick you up somewhere?"

"That won't be necessary. I am not available for dinner tonight. Tomorrow."

"Tomorrow will be fine."

"Great. Have you been to *Jezebels*?"

"Not much on the biblical characters, but I'm game. What time would you like me to pick you up tomorrow?" Victor, even with obvious rebuff, insisted on being gentlemanly.

"Why don't I meet you there at eight? It's at Forty-Fifth and Ninth. Make sure you leave your Judas at home."

"Eh?"

"Never mind."

"No, sorry, not that. I was asking about the place again. Never heard of it."

"It's perfectly suitable. I am sure it will be a new experience for you. Soul food."

The Friday night traffic was horrendous. Bumper to bumper all the way down Ninth Ave. Not a neighborhood he was comfortable in at eight o'clock at night, but Victor was excited about seeing Helen.

The building was gray marble with the sign *Jezebel's* discreetly gilded on a small plaque. Victor entered and was pleasantly surprised at the chic French decor. Webs of lace hung from the ceiling and the antique mementos and collector's artifacts were unique. A woman in dreadlocks sauntered towards him nonchalantly.

"Do you have reservations?" she asked without looking at him.

"Yes, the name is Victor, Victor Innes Palmer."

"A party of two?"

"Yes." He was disappointed she didn't know who he was.

"Good evening, Sir." A waitress collected him and walked towards a table. She looked around to see where the other guest might be. A familiar face, she thought, but from where she wouldn't know. Maybe a daytime soap. Since *Jezebel's* was known for attracting celebrities, she was hardly impressed with someone not immediately recognizable.

"Miss Stern has not yet arrived, I take it?"

"Not as far as I can tell, but I can seat you." *Why the hell should I know who Miss Stern is.* The waitress smiled sweetly at Victor.

"That's great."

Victor was nursing his second Evian, and still there was no sign of Helen. He looked around the room with renewed interest, noting a number of celebrities hovering over steaming plates of delicious smelling food, some nodding recognition. His cameo role in the hit movie "Rebels", which is how he was termed, The Rebel of Fashion Avenue, had created quite a stir. Not that he would ever consider becoming a movie star, but anything to create publicity and popularity at this stage of his empire building was welcomed. His gastric juices were in full force as plates and plates of scrumptious food passed his table. He sipped his Evian and looked anxiously at his watch. The thought that the wench might have stood him up was just beginning to crystallize when Helen, dressed in a most becoming emerald green silk pant suit, walked unhurriedly through the door. She glanced around the room, pointing to his table near the piano. The same dread-locked hostess escorted her to the table.

"Worried, were you?" She eased herself into a chair, gracefully. "Horrible traffic and the parking was even worse. I think I made a mistake driving myself tonight. How are you, Victor?"

"Relieved now that you are here. Thought you stood me up there for a minute."

"How silly. Who would dare stand up a celebrity? It was I who called, wasn't it? That means I wouldn't stand you up. Anyway, I'm only fifteen minutes late." Helen looked at her Cartier tank watch. Her tone was pleasant and though her lips smiled, showing even white teeth, her eyes were deadly cold. A slight shiver went through Victor.

"What are you drinking?" he beckoned to the waitress standing appropriately close by.

"Ginger tea. You should try some. It's their specialty."

"Two ginger teas," he informed the waitress turning back to Helen. He smiled broadly. "I am glad you decided to meet me."

"You have something that interests me," Helen answered, holding his gaze steadily. "Let's, as they say, cut to the chase. As I understand it, you are interested in positioning your company as the male counterpart to mine."

"Don't you think that's a marvelous idea? Came to me in a dream."

"The idea is quite good," she ignored the dream bit, "and I think I can help you one step further. If I not only agreed to your idea but also recognized your company as the official male counterpart to our fashions, the sky is the limit for your enterprise. Since you have beaten me to the punch with this marvelous idea, we should work together."

"My thoughts exactly."

She continued as though Victor had not spoken. "You have proven yourself a marketing genius. Your persona, and America's intrigue with you as the new rebel, is fertile ground for launching the idea. But when you first contacted me, what exactly did you have in mind?"

"Actually, I'm not sure. I envision the venture exactly the way you do, but I have no experience in running a business. In exchange for management advice and direction, *International Moderna* will certainly be quite generous, I'm sure.

"Mm hmm." Helen sipped her tea. An idea had begun to germinate and she could certainly see some exciting possibilities for an affiliation. "Yes, indeed, those possibilities exist. Helen continued to explain that an alliance was a possibility. "Americans in today's market are very fickle and must be handled gingerly. If they feel you are flaunting your success as an assumption that you would be good in another enterprise, they may feel you are going overboard and trailing into an area where you have no experience. Buying a four-dollar magazine is different from buying a six hundred-dollar outfit. I am prepared to acknowledge your company as an affiliate to the Helen Companies. The affiliation will only be a smoke screen for public acceptance, although you may use our human resources in terms of models. Design and creation will have to be your burden.

"I am sure you understand that this would be a major business coup if I announce my blessing of your ideas. Growth will be faster than if you try to go it alone. A joint fashion gala announcing our affiliation to the world could launch our companies into the stratosphere. Furthermore, if we come up with a unique idea that is not just a fashion show or another benefit, but rather a combination of both, I really think we could get a bang for the buck and an immediate return on investment. What do you think?" She looked at him through guarded eyes, trying to estimate his reaction.

"Clever. That is a remarkably clever idea."

Only to a fool, Helen thought, smiling demurely while sipping the sweet, tangy tea.

"Well?" Helen prompted for more of what he was feeling.

"Hmmm, a cause that's not a cause. Now let's see." There was a perceptible pause as Victor mulled over the idea. "Hmmm," he repeated several times and Helen offered no coaxing. *Let's see how bright you really are, my boy, or if your parents' money bought you your education.*

"What'd you say we pitch the idea as a premier to the new Scorsese movie about the fashion industry?" Victor quickly offered in explanation to the quizzical look on her face. "If we can get the all cast celebs in the movie to endorse the idea and pledge a percent of the proceeds to underwrite up and coming American designers, I think this would be the arena. You know there has always been a rivalry between Paris, Italy, and New York and now even Germany is in the fashion industry, but no one really recognizes the American designer. Who better to help us lay claim than Hollywood?

"What if we made this merger of events a sort of declaration of the American fashion savvy, challenging our European counterparts? Let's face it, Paris has lost its stronghold on the industry. Why shouldn't we capitalize on the opportunity to show what American fashion is all about: updated, daring, and new. If we are not the best, we can at least be the most innovative and creative for this changing world. We have always been innovators."

"That's a wonderful idea," Helen was impressed with Victor's well-thought-out monologue. "We'd need at least two years to plan it, though."

"Not if we use every connection we have. We may be able to pull it off next spring. A huge media blitz and celebrity endorsement will bring out the A list in droves. The fall will be fine. That will give us a year and enough time to have the fashions ready."

"You're right. I think it can be accomplished if we mobilize all the power houses." Helen was excited. "You have complete access to the print media and to Hollywood, and I know just the guy who can handle this job in terms of management and organization. Shall we order?"

Victor felt triumphant. He was not only excited by the deal and the alliance but by the idea that he would be working closely with Helen. Little did he know that Helen had already chosen the henchmen for the job, and he would be lucky if he saw her before the night of the event.

"I think we have something to celebrate." He would break his no drinking rule just for tonight. "Champagne," he told the waitress. "Cristal."

Two hours and two bottles of bubbly later, although he felt a closeness to his companion, Victor knew nothing more about Helen Stern's public or private life than before. Regrettably, he also drank most of the champagne.

"One more thing, Victor." Helen spooned another bite of the delicious crème brûlée into her mouth. "For my endorsement and involvement I want 35% preferred stock ownership."

"Thirty-five?"

"What do you think I'm worth?" Eyebrows arched as Helen rose to her feet.

"A great deal more. It's a deal, Miss Stern, and a pleasure." Victor stood and shook Helen's hand. "You drive quite a bargain, Miss Stern."

"Well, Victor. Business is business. Will you walk me to my car?"

Victor bolted down Ninth Avenue. He had to get to Chance. His desire for Helen Stern was so urgent that he had to relieve his unfulfilled sexual urgency anywhere he could. Chance or Olivia, it made no difference. Chance was closer.

Victor was as handsome as Helen remembered when they'd first met at Jacques' party. And, to her surprise, quite intelligent, certainly not a trait she'd have bestowed on him. Still there was a nagging feeling that there was something she couldn't quite figure out about him. A recklessness, maybe even something clandestine. Nonetheless, there was no harm in strengthening her company. As Helen's thoughts crystallized, she was incredulous that here before her, in all its magnificence and simplicity was the missing key to her plans. Her redemption! The gods did indeed love her. As much as she detested whistling and could clearly hear Nan's scolding, "Don't dear, whistling is for the laborers at the seaside," Helen nonetheless whistled the happy tune, "*Good things come to those who wait.*"

As she navigated the black 540I through Manhattan traffic, Helen was excited. Tonight was ingenuous. Not only would the deal leverage the Helen Companies to greater heights and get a lot of free publicity in the process, she could use VIP International, if necessary, as a cover for her carefully constructed plans that were desperately in need of some help. There was no risk for her in the deal. If Victor's company was a success, she would own 35% of a successful company, and if it was not she would own 35% of a bust. Either way it had not cost her a dime.

And her advertising budget for the new line! Immediately cut in half. She was a genius. Not to mention the fact that she could take over the company if it proved successful or expedient.

Chapter Seventeen

Helen watched the handsome, athletically built man saunter toward her. Dressed in white slacks and navy nautical shirt, he looked ready for the water. His gait was confident and decisive.

"Hey cutie, want to join us today? We're headed to the island for a bit of boating. Father insists he needs to go fishing. Not that he wants to go fishing mind you, he needs to. I think he's a little stressed." The young man kissed Helen and flopped down on the lawn next to her chair.

"Heck no! You know how Scott is when he goes fishing. He'll be out there for hours. You are brave to accompany him."

Next to each other, Reginald looked nothing at all like his sister. He was excruciatingly handsome, but unlike most handsome men, he had a generous heart. He, it was obvious, took his looks from his father as she had from hers.

"You're looking very smart today, young man. Taking a date on this fishing expedition?"

Silently Helen envied Reginald, his big heart, warm smile, and ready offer to help. She had watched him cross the lawn and remembered how cautious he'd been of her when they first met. Every night Reginald would creep past her room, peeking in before dashing past.

"Hey," she'd said to him one night as he rushed past her door, "come in and chat for awhile."

"I can't. Melissa said I shouldn't."

"And why is that?"

"She says you are the devil. But if you are, why don't you carry a fork? When I go trick or treating I always carry a fork if I'm the devil."

Helen laughed. "And what do you think? Do you think I'm the devil, Reginald?" He had hopped on her bed now and was looking quizzically at her.

"No, I believe you are my sister, but why don't you call Daddy, daddy?" he questioned.

"Because I am your half-sister. I have a different daddy from you."

"Oh. Well that's ok with me. I like having a sister."

"And I a brother," she pecked his cheek, unable to deny the inevitable feeling of love that was blossoming. The warmth she felt for this innocent child with his untempered curiosity was refreshing.

"Now you had better scoot along before Melissa gets angry with you. But you can stop by every night. It will be our secret."

"Will you tell me all about your life?"

"Yes. Tomorrow night." She helped him off the bed and watched as he scampered away down the hall. The devil! Maybe she was.

As they grew older, his constant show of affection to her, even when she was unable to return it, warmed her heart, and try as she did, she couldn't help loving him back. When as a teenager his heart was broken for the first time, it was to Helen's room that he had gone for comfort. Reginald, in all her years in the United States, was the only meaningful person in her life.

"I've been meaning to talk with you, but gosh, you get in so late. I'd have to wake up at 1:00 a.m. just to call you. And you leave your flat so early. What are you building there, Sis? A new world!"

"Something like that," she grinned.

"Maybe now is as good a time as any to chat. I should take this opportunity so perfectly presented," he proposed. "Dad's out trying to buy a couple of fins to use as bait so we have a few minutes. Is it okay?"

"Okay. Shoot. But you know, Reggie, it's not that difficult to pick up the phone and call the office," Helen noted in a rebuffed way. "Whatever are you doing in the daytime?"

"Usually going to class, and the time difference in England makes it hard to catch up with you. You're right that I could've made a greater effort. Anyway, now is perfect. Can you believe I'm graduating next year, and I have no idea what I'm going to do with my life? I don't want to go to grad school without some real world experience. I've been thinking about an MBA, but as you know they require at least two years' business experience before one can apply. I swear I don't want to work with Mom, but I wouldn't mind working for you. If not I'll go to some other corporation, but not JI."

"Uh-huh. Let me tell you one thing, my *freire*. The experience you'd gain at JI would be top drawer…get you into any school in the country."

"I've got Mom's money for that."

"I know what you mean. Let me tell you, Reg, working for me will be no better, but it sounds like a great idea if you are serious. You'll have to interview with personnel, though you can rest assured I'll pull some strings for you." She ruffled his hair as though he was still five. Helen could hardly believe Reginald was twenty-four! She'd come home for the weekend just to see her young brother who, for the past year, had been a scholar at Cambridge and before that had spent four years at Princeton.

"Hi, kids." Andrea waved from the patio. "Seen Scott anywhere?"

"He went to get some bait, Mom. Come and join us for a glass of lemonade. I'm just trying to convince Helen to join us on the Island."

"Great idea. While they are out fishing, we can stay behind and make dinner. There are a few things about JI I need to discuss with you."

"Oh, Mother, I'd would love to, but I made arrangements to meet a realtor in midtown."

"Oh! I didn't know you were planning to move from your place."

"I'm not. She is bringing along a few architects to make some changes."

"You didn't have to leave home."

"Sure, Mummy. You'd love to have me here another seventeen years, but Mother I'm almost thirty-eight! You couldn't expect me to live here all my life, could you?"

Andrea sighed. "You're right. It seems only yesterday that you came. Time passes too soon. By God! Even Reginald will be moving out soon. Dear, dear."

"It won't be so bad to have an empty nest. It's been practically empty with Reggie gone anyway."

"That's why I've been thinking about spending more time in the city. Scott is so opposed to living there I haven't pushed the envelope. But I will now that you're all on your own. Do you want David to drive you back…Reggie can bring your car tomorrow."

"Naah. Actually, I'm meeting someone. I wouldn't want David to have to wait."

"Anyone, I know?"

"Yep. VIP." Helen laughed and turned to her brother. "Monday morning. Nine sharp. I'll personally give you a tour."

"Sure Sis, I'll be there."

"V…who?" Andrea pressed.

"Oh Mom, you do remember. Victor Innes Palmer. V.I.P. We met him at Jacques' soirée."

"Ah, yes, yes. I do remember. Been in all the papers lately. America's new rebel."

"A-huh. I am thinking of forming an alliance with his new company, that will give the Helen Companies even more visibility. We talked about it over dinner a few nights ago. He wants to position his company as the male complement to ours. The chic male for the thirty-something female. You must agree that it will be tremendous for us to have this additional unexpected publicity, and it does have marketing appeal."

"Is this guy stable? I hear he has a bit of a drinking problem."

"How do you know that?"

"How do you not? Just let's say I'm connected. I'm telling you this because I want you to be sure you know what you are getting into."

Helen logged the information. Even she hadn't heard of Victor's debauchery. It explained, however, why he drank two bottles of Cristal and the uncomfortable feeling she had about him. She had no problems with Victor's concealment. In fact, she rarely felt discomfort because people kept secrets. Not even with them lying if they had to. With Victor, however, she had to be careful about their association. Someone in her position needed to be concerned about public humiliation from being with uncensored, unruly drunks. "Thanks for the info, Mom, and have fun fishing. "Reggie," she called to her brother again, "see you tomorrow, right?"

"Bright and early."

In the car, Helen forced herself to revisit an earlier conversation with Andrea. One that was intended to seal her fate in the couture market place. It was the kind of stuff she willed into her mind when Andrea turned on the honey. She had to remember that at all cost Andrea was the enemy.

Too bad, Mother, that your loyalty to your own blood is not that deep. Even after abandoning me you feel more loyalty to a complete stranger.

"There are other more lucrative opportunities that can be pursued other than couture. What about a children's line?" Now there was a thought. Dressing the children of the thirty-something's. What about dressing her own children? Helen thought scornfully. Children she would never have because of her inability to sustain a relationship with a man. She was thirty-eight, for God's sake, and her biological clock was tic tocking away. Not only had Andrea robbed her of her childhood, now she was destined to be childless. This time Andrea would not win. She wanted fuckin' couture and fuckin' couture she'd get.

Chapter Eighteen

The VIP Company

Helen could not have asked for a better PR campaign. Merging the identity of The Helen Companies with Victor's toy company, as she'd termed it, was the thing to do. By the evening of Friday, April 13th, the day of the gala event, not even the superstition of the date deterred patrons. The ticket committee was still turning away hopeful attendees three hours before show time. There was not even standing room in the house.

"We need to make space for Mr. & Mrs. Ferris. They have been traveling for a year and only returned for this event. They are personal friends with one of the stars here tonight." Chance was pleading with Jake who had agreed to manage the benefit as a favor to Helen. He was still very much undecided about accepting an offer to work for her company.

"Vhat vould you like me to do, Chance? There is no room. Even the pre-dinner and afterglow function are completely sold out," Jake responded in frustration. "Vell let's see. Ve could have eleven people at two of the tables, but unless someone at table six is kind enough, Mr. & Mrs. Ferris vill not be seated together. The thought of eleven people at a table and doing table switches so late is God-awful at functions like this. And vhat about the name cards? Vho vill print them this late?"

"We can come close with the font on the computer. If you think it can be done, I'll get marketing on the stick, and I will notify the Plaza's staff. Thank you, darling." She kissed Jake and was off out the door.

Only in America, Jake thought, and turned his mind to yet another budding catastrophe.

Helen looked over the final plans and was very pleased. Victor Innes Palmer had outdone himself, for all of Hollywood had turned out to play. There were so many celebs that security numbered as many as the guests. Scorsese was ecstatic. Just that morning he'd sent her the most beautiful orchids and roses in appreciation, and shortly after he'd called to reiterate his gratitude.

"You are incredible, Helen. I love you, love you, love you. I couldn't have planned a better PR campaign for the movie if I had tried."

"Thank Victor. It was his idea."

"Oh, I have. I have. But it wouldn't have happened without you, too."

Of course, Scorsese did his part by making sure the evening was a star-studded fiesta and a paparazzi's's heaven. New York would be at the Plaza in droves.

Two hours before curtain, Helen was exasperated. She had not left the rehearsal room.

"Tell me, Victor what is so difficult about walking to the end of the runway and then turning to wait for me?"

"Nothing, except I can't seem to get the timing right. It seems I am more scared of marriage than I thought." He laughed.

"Try it again." She ignored his attempt at humor. "And this time, for God's sake listen to the music, make an association and walk! Do any damn thing, but get it right! We can't afford to bungle the final catwalk of the night, especially with the owners of two great fashion empires doing it. They would laugh us to scorn!"

"Actually, I think it's you who's making me nervous."

"Then forget that I'm here and just pretend it's someone you really want to marry. Your girlfriend, perhaps."

"That will make matters worse." He paused and looked directly at Helen, thinking *it is you that I want*. Instead he said, "I told you I have marriage phobia."

Chance was in full gear making sure the last-minute needs of the stars, models, and guests were taken care of by Jandel Entertainment, the organization engaged to handle the evening. They had done a wonderful job. The entire room was one big, glowing extravaganza. Purple, yellow, and orange balloons accented the decor. On white-draped tables, votive candles surrounded a unique centerpiece made up of "Yellow", the new scent from The Helen Companies. Each patron was allowed to take a bottle of the perfume along with exquisitely wrapped boxes of silk scarves or ties. Seating assignments and names embossed in sterling silver also served as souvenirs for attendees. Rosenthal crystal bowls filled with Swiss chocolates were available to nibble throughout the night. Indeed it was one night where even the anorexic forgot about dieting—a superb evening of elegance and excitement. The crowds were packed like sardines as Helen peered into the ballroom from behind the curtains.

To a flurry of lights and music the first model, adorned in discreetly placed purple and yellow flowers, sashayed down the runway throwing bags of scented yellow and purple potpourri into the audience. The MC invited the patrons to throw handfuls of potpourri on stage as designs moved them. The hum again became a buzz and then a frenzy as the evening flowed towards a crescendo.

Suddenly the lights dimmed, the music slowed to Yanni's, *"Standing In Motion"* and a single spotlight danced towards the left of the stage. By the time it illuminated Helen and Victor, the entire room was at a fever pitch, not only from the chocolates and free flowing champagne, but also from the energy that flowed from the stage where Helen Stern and Victor Innes Palmer stood silhouetted.

And when the King and Queen of Rebel fashion were finally illuminated, the entire room stood in applause. Victor confidently moved toward center stage and to Helen's surprise, he didn't falter once. When the bride crossed the room to meet her groom the din in the room drowned out the music. As she reached Victor, Helen turned slowly to look at her groom. To conjure up the emotions she needed, Helen tried to muster all the years of passionate anger, forcing it to course through her veins and translate itself into the deepest look of love she could ever imagine. To her surprise, it was not the revenge that brought out the naturalness of her feeling, but the sudden realization that it would have been wonderful to be marrying Anton DePaul.

Victor was sure she loved him. No one could look at another that way without loving them. In turn he smiled at his *faux* bride, looped her arm through his and walked into the sunset as the spotlight faded.

From the audience there were gales of laughter, sniffles of deep emotions, and much cheering. To Helen's surprise, Victor, on the walk of the King and Queen of young fashion, got his steps right! And she had to admit he was dashing in his checked silk tuxedo. That they were showing off their thirty-something bridal fashion did not escape Victor, and he couldn't wait until the story line was a reality. What he was feeling for Helen Stern at that moment was beyond words. As they turned to make their last bow, the entire room was on their feet and the applause raged. Helen could not remember when she had seen such display of excitement in a fashion crowd.

For the after party, Victor changed into a black silk shirt, black slacks, and a black and white plaid jacket. He couldn't wait to join Helen in the ballroom to continue the pretense. When he saw her across the room, she was deeply engaged in conversation with a group of patrons. She was more beautiful than ever, but tonight it was more than her beauty that made him want to lay claim to her—it was her unaffected sensuality and the mystery that always lay behind the black eyes. Her yellow empireline dress of the sixties flavor, brought entirely up to date for the nineties, was very becoming. By tomorrow, he was sure, the entire thirty-something crowd and even those perpetual, youthful older kinds would be wearing yellow empirelines.

Across the room Chance waved at him. He acknowledged her and proceeded to join his bride of the evening. Chance, who had worked on the project for over eight months, was feeling left out. It seems that everyone was congratulating Helen and Victor, and no one bothered to notice her or Jake. Even Victor could only manage a wave. On the occasions when she'd tried to congratulate him, he seemed rather distant.

"Magnificent!" Olivia, whose control of the media mill had made the night a major success, approached Victor. She leaned in closely to him and, if Chance was seeing right, she stuck her tongue in his ear. "This was a wonderful show. Never seen anything like it. Victor, it seemed so real!" Turning to Helen, Olivia said. "When I saw you up on the runway, I vividly recalled your first foray into fashion. You picture is still on the wall of our London office. Your face sold more magazines than any other for our company. Maybe you missed your calling, my dear." Helen didn't miss the sarcasm.

"Victor," she was tugging at his arm, "I would like to introduce you to Lucia Venuchi of *Town and Country*. They want to do a piece on tonight's event in next month's issue." Deliberately ignoring Helen, Olivia grabbed Victor's hand and pulled him away before he could say a word. The bridal walk down the runway had been too real to her, and now that she had gotten Victor in an enviable position, she was damned if she would share him. It was time for Victor to dump the association and increase his merger with her. She would ask Malcolm for a divorce.

Chance watched as Victor walked past her without an acknowledgment. She smarted badly. Angrily she spun on her heels, making her way to the coatroom. It was time for her to leave.

"Darling," Andrea beamed at her daughter. "You are a genius. I am so extraordinarily proud of you. Congratulations."

Helen was engaged in conversation with her mother and hadn't noticed Victor's absence. She was, however, quite aware of Anton DePaul walking towards her, smiling broadly.

"Good-evening, Mrs. Preston, Helen."

Andrea, Helen noticed, stiffened a bit.

"Mr. DePaul." She nodded and moved off to join Scott and Reginald.

"Well kiddo, what do you know? You have just cut your PR budget to zero." He noted her most talked-about concern. "Tonight was wonderful. I believe you have put your company in the realm of Fortune 1000 status. Impressive."

"Thank you, Anton. I am glad you enjoyed it."

"You know, now that you own the Helen Companies, there is no longer a conflict of interest in my representing you. Why don't we plan to meet on Monday to discuss a possible alliance. You'll need a good lawyer if you decide to go public. I must say, after tonight you'd sell a heck of a lot of stocks."

"You really do know everything, don't you. That's all well and good I suppose, but tonight I feel more like celebrating than discussing business. Would you join me for a late night Cappuccino, or will it keep you up?"

"Not a chance. I have a special relationship with sleep, one that even caffeine can't interfere with. I would love to."

"Meet you outside in fifteen minutes. Have to get out of this party gracefully and give a few quick interviews."

Victor was only half listening to Madam *Town & Country*. His eyes were scanning the room for Helen. He wanted desperately to chat with her and maybe offer to take her out for a nightcap to celebrate their success.

"Marvelous. Simply marvelous and original. You have certainly set a fashion trend tonight. What's next? This will be a hard event to top,

Victor. I especially loved the evening attire, so simple and yet so elegant. Is there a possible merger between the companies? They work so well together," whatever the hell her name was cooing.

If Victor wasn't being gracious he would have pulled back from the aging queen's too familiar touch and socked her in her gibbering mouth.

"I'm hoping to see Victor do a line of fashions for men, independent of the female pairing. No need to lose one's identity before it can completely stand on its own," Olivia was purring, a gleaming look pierced her eyes as the thought of the evening she would spend with Victor popped into her mind. She had to be careful because the entire family had shown up for the gala event. As she scanned the room, she saw Malcolm, looking dashing in his evening attire engrossed in conversation with Jenette Cochrel from *W* magazine. The other siblings were, likewise, chatting with some belle or gent. Just then she saw Helen tuck her arm through that of a handsome black man as they walked towards the door, pausing momentarily to chat with a woman from *Essence* Magazine. She was glad to see her leave.

"What do you say we give Victor a chance to enjoy his triumph," Olivia said to *Elle's* editor, trying to pry her hands away from Victor's. "We'll see you Monday in your office. Ten sharp."

"Monday," Victor repeated, moving in the direction of the crowd. "Olivia," he untangled himself from her, "please excuse me; there is someone I wish to speak with."

"Right, darling," she whispered. "I must talk with Malcolm to make sure we can spend the evening together."

Victor inwardly winced. He had no intention of spending the night with her.

Chance was walking toward the door when the deep baritone voice stopped her. She was close to tears.

"Chance, my darling, forgive me. I feel as though I have neglected you all night."

"You have, Victor."

"But not for long. I will make it up to you tonight," he winked. "You'll see. Have you seen Helen? I must say my congratulations."

"She left a few moments ago with Anton DePaul. Said she had enough of the show. She told me to express her congratulations and that she'll ring you on Monday."

Victor was crushed. No, he was devastated.

"Great, now we too can leave the party. I'm afraid you'll need to go before me, and I'll meet you at the apartment. No need to have tongues wagging."

"What time will you be there?"

"As soon as I wrap up here, an hour or so. Keep the cider warm. We have a lot to celebrate."

"And the bed?" she purred, already forgetting her slight.

"Need I say?" He flashed pearly whites.

Chance was relieved. She had to stop feeling so persecuted. Hell, as a child of alcoholic parents, she was entitled to a few insecurities. Slipping into her coat, she retrieved her bag from the sofa as Victor's stepmother approached.

Olivia had orchestrated her deed. Having ducked into the rest room to freshen up, she was ready for a night of celebration with her paramour and protégé. Her pulse quickened at the decadent thoughts, and immediately her knickers were damp. Victor was getting to be more than a habit. She didn't know when she started needing him like an addict needed their drugs, but she did. And now that he was America's darling, she reveled in the fact that he was hers. When she reentered the room Victor was talking with Helen's hench-woman, Chastity…no Chole…ah well something. She wasted no time in careening over. Had to protect her territory now even more than ever.

"All is well now," she informed him, knowing he'd get the message. "Hello…eh…"

"Chance," Victor offered.

"Good evening, Mrs. Palmer. Congratulations on your choice of supporting Victor. I am sure you are pleased."

"Quite," she said, half turning to look at the woman beside her. "Your company did a wonderful showing, as well. I think congratulations is in order for you, too."

"Thank you," Chance said, gathering up her shawl. "I must excuse myself as I have an engagement after this," she glanced briefly at Victor. "Mrs. Palmer. Good-evening."

"An attractive woman. I hear she was a top dog at DKNY. How did Helen get her?"

"I'm not sure."

"You might want to consider her for the VIP companies. She must have a lot of experience in the industry and must be rather solid. From what I hear, Helen Stern is a bear to work for. Exacting and precise. Let's talk about it on the way to your place, shall we?" She glided her tongue over her lips, flicked her cape to half cover Victor, and gave his crotch a quick squeeze.

"Olivia, I am so sorry, but I've accepted an invitation to join Miss Stern in an hour. We'll have to rendezvous later."

"Victor! How could you? You know I would be looking forward to tonight. Please darling, I am burning up with desire for you. And with all this power surging in me, I can't stand to burn alone tonight!"

"I'm truly sorry, Olivia, I will make it up to you, I promise." He used the cloak opportunity to squeeze her breast. No need offending a woman's sexuality. Frankly, he was beginning to despise Olivia.

"Why not drive me to my place? I'll wait there until you come home. I have the whole night. I've cleared it with Malcolm."

"If you insist, Olivia, but I can't say when I'll be back."

"Okay darling. I promise to be patient if you have just one quick drink with me before you leave. I took the liberty of having our favorite toy."

"Sounds delightful," he informed her. The least he could do was give her a lift to her place. Of all the people who wanted him to themselves tonight, he would have given his life to be with Helen Stern.

On the way to her Manhattan apartment, Olivia could hardly keep her hands off Victor. She pleaded and cajoled, but he was firm. Victor pulled the car to the curb and jumped out to open the door for her.

"Joseph, would you watch the car for me? I am just escorting my stepmother upstairs. Won't be a minute."

"No problem, Mr. Palmer. No problem at all." Joseph knew everything. He could write the biography of the wealthy people that lived in the building. Good thing doormen were a part of the scenery. But who knows, one day he might just write a book. After thirty-eight years opening and closing doors for the rich and evil, why shouldn't he make some money off cheap gossip.

Victor gave him a twenty-dollar bill. Joseph also knew why he hadn't yet written the book. He made at least five hundred dollars a night for his discretion. He really was a wealthy man.

Inside the lavish apartment, the lights were soft and already dimmed. It was the kind of lighting that would flatter any flaws of nature, including Olivia's contrived youthfulness. Soft music was playing in the background, and the distinct smell of freshly baked cinnamon rolls permeated the air. Olivia had surely gone through some trouble to set the stage.

"Are you sure you can't have a teensy weensy drink with me?" Her hands were stroking his chest. "Just a little glass?" They were moving down to his hips. "I promise to be patient." They were unbuckling his belt, "and to be a good girl." They were in his jockey shorts.

"Olivia," Victor grabbed her hand, "it would be very rude to keep my business partner waiting. We both need her to be on our side for awhile. No need pissing her off, now is there?" He placed her hands gently at her sides. Firmly he took her face in his hands and kissed her without feeling an ounce of passion. "Be patient, I'll be back."

Outside, Victor wiped his mouth thoroughly on his handkerchief and sprayed two squirts of his breath refresher in his mouth. He opened his glove compartment and removed the baby-fresh wipes he always kept there. He wiped his face and neck clean and splashed Calvin Klein's men's aftershave over his day-old stubble. After shave! Eureka. He would add it to his line. Now he was ready for an evening of fun. He was disappointed that he was not meeting Helen Stern, but he could still get it up for Chance. She had a beautiful body and an equally beautiful face. Damn, he felt like a drink. Anything to get through the night.

"This is a wonderful place, Anton. How did you find it?" Helen inquired.

"As a man about town, I know everything. It's a bit noisy, though, hardly a place I should have taken you to tonight, but you have to admit it's festive and the story behind its success is also a financial role model for entrepreneurs."

The Shark Bar was wall to wall with people. The energy and buzz in the place was high. Good-looking men and women lined the standing room only walls whispering and cuddling. Lovers seemed oblivious to the sweat running down their partner's faces and dripping onto their clothes. These were the women Helen wanted to dress. Just her crowd. She had never been to what appeared to be an ethnic black American bar before. What a difference from an English pub! The music was hot. The men were hot, and the energy was contagious.

"What will you drink?"

"Beer. Any kind. No. Make that Redstripe," Helen said excitedly, tapping her feet to the lively music.

"Like in Jamaican Red Stripe?"

"Wonderful," she shouted over the din.

As Anton weaved his way to the bar, Helen felt elated, alive and ready to let go. She felt carefree and happy. She eavesdropped as men tried to pick up women and vice versa, and listened to lovers cooing at each other. She loved this place, and she wanted to be in love tonight.

"Listen, Ms. Thing," a guy with dreadlocks and a gold hoop in his right ear was saying to a beautiful girl whom Helen noticed earlier had eyes only for someone else. "I was just asking you for a dance."

"The answer is NO, Mr. Thing," she retorted.

"No sweat. Maybe next time." He turned and saw Helen. She admired his spunk and the ease with which he took rejection.

"How about you, pretty thang?" He out-stretched his hand to Helen.

"You mean me?" Helen was looking around hoping to espy his next victim.

"Yes, Queen Elizabeth, you. Do you want to dance? They do dance in the mother-country, don't they?"

Obviously he was making fun of her accent.

"The lady is with me, man. She's not able to dance right now. Got to drink the beer, see, *I* just bought it." Anton pointed to the glass.

"Everything is *Ire,* man." The guy moved on down the wall of gyrating women. *Ire,* Helen smiled at the word, for Cecil had always used it. It was the Jamaican way of saying okay.

She had never heard Anton speak this way before, but she liked it. It gave him a whole new dimension.

"I'm afraid you're going to get hit-on all night, so drink up and let's get out of here."

"Why would anyone want to hit…oh crikie, I got it?" Helen reddened at her own stupidity. "Ah, I think I've got it."

Anton laughed. "Can you blame a guy for trying? So, how would you say it in England?"

"Trying to court me."

"Boooooring." Anton rolled his eyes. "What'd you say we walk part the way back. It's a great night, and I could use the fresh air. When you get tired we'll catch a cab."

"Walk in these heels?"

"Oh, sorry. I didn't think of that."

"Well, I'll just take them off."

They left the bar shortly after 1:00 a.m. and as promised, Helen yanked off her shoes and began walking in her stocking feet.

"I have a better idea. Let's go to the all-night drug store over there," he was pointing across the street, "and buy some Dr. Scholls."

"You solve all my problems, Anton. Let's."

And so they did. "Looks good with this outfit, doesn't it." Helen slipped on the sandals.

"Now I know why you are the fashion queen of New York." Anton slid her arm through his. Being dressed to the *minus* nines did not deter Helen, for they stopped in every reasonable hip spot and had another beer to quench their thirst from walking. By the time they reached Central Park West, Helen was quite tipsy. It wasn't Anton's intention, but he decided they should lie in the park for awhile before going home. No telling what he would do if he had to undress her and put her to bed. Better not tempt fate.

"Did you know I could sing?" Helen said to Anton out of the blue. She noticed what a gentleman he was, always walking on her outside, opening cab doors and front doors and so on. She felt relatively safe to share her frivolity with him.

"Let's hear it."

"Right here?"

"Why not. This is Central Park, New York, anything goes."

"Okay, Helen cleared her throat. Ready?" He nodded.

"I feel pretty, oh so pretty, I feel pretty and witty and wise and I pity any girl who isn't me tonight."

"Fantastic, Fantastic." Anton clapped enthusiastically. Taking Helen by the hand he joined in with the next stanza of the song. He wondered how many people would believe any black man and woman would be out in public singing a song from *West Side Story*! Good thing it was one of his mother's favorites, and tonight he didn't give a damn who heard him sing.

"*I feel charming, oh so charming, I feel,*" Anton belted out into the night air.

Olivia looked at the clock. With each passing moment her libido was doing greater somersaults. Where the hell was Victor? She watched the hand tick from one to two. Finally, at three she heard the door open. She jumped out of bed ready to fly into his arms and seduce him on the spot, but ran into the arms of her husband.

"Malcolm, darling! What happened?"

"It got too late to drive back to the island so I thought I would just spend the night here. You look ravishing dear, I'm glad I came. No need to be alone tonight, eh."

"Just what the doctor ordered." She guessed coaxing his limp phallus into action was better than no play at all. But what the hell would she do when Victor arrived?

Victor climbed out of bed feeling content but not fulfilled. What on earth was he going to tell Olivia? Maybe he could make up something about a fender bender and that he went straight home. Of course, she would have called all night. Ah, he could have taken a sleeping pill and turned off the ringer on the phone. He showered quickly and kissed Chance on the lips. Her arms, stretched across her chest, moved instinctively to embrace him.

"Don't leave, darling," she stirred, "I'll make breakfast."

"How sweet," he kissed her again, "but I have to run through some numbers before tomorrow morning. Give me a few hours and then join me. I'll make dinner for two."

"And you cook, too." She rolled over and was fast asleep.

He walked towards the door, still thinking of what to do about Olivia and Chance. He needed them both right now. Once his company was strong enough however, he would not need any of them. Tonight he might ask Chance to work for him, off the record as Olivia suggested. He turned the car in the direction of his home.

Monday morning the phones never stopped ringing. Several of the calls were from Victor who insisted on meeting Helen.

"Today is an awfully busy day, Victor. Why not FAX me the info, and we can communicate by e-mail. I promise to make some time tomorrow, but today I have several meetings scheduled that I really must attend." Helen apologized.

"I suppose you have the preliminary numbers already. Can't imagine you wouldn't."

"I do, indeed, and they were wonderful. I look forward to a long and mutually beneficial alliance."

"What time tomorrow would you like to meet?" His voice weighed heavily with disappointment.

"Dinner time. My treat. Sorry, Victor, I have to run. Someone is at my door."

Chapter Nineteen

The Demarche

Helen nodded at James Sheridan who was being ushered in by Mrs. Walters, waving him to a chair in front of her desk. "Be with you in a moment," she mouthed, covering the mouthpiece of the phone. James watched her intensely as she wrapped up her phone conversation. She was looking particularly chic, yet classic, in an olive suit accented with a white satin collar. He hadn't noticed until now the little mole on the right side of her upper lip or the long fingers that could belong to a musician.

"Good to see you," Helen smiled, placing the phone on its cradle, extending a hand. Her tone was formal yet friendly.

"I suppose this will take awhile. Can we talk preliminary stuff anyway?" Helen handed James a stack of paperwork for review.

"Theory mostly since I haven't seen these yet. What would you like to know?"

"How much will a company our size be able to raise on our initial offering?"

"I really can't answer that accurately. There are so many variables. What I garnered, from my cursory overview, is that you could go out for $30.00 to $40.00 per share. Other things considered, maybe even more. As for the VIP Companies, I really couldn't say off the top of my head."

"Isn't there a magic formula you put numbers into and come up with some ratio on this stuff?"

"I wish." James chuckled. "The valuation of the company and the selling job is far more complex than that. Give me a few days, and I'll have an accurate recommendation for you on both companies."

"When I hear the number I want to sell stocks for, I'll know whether it's right or wrong. So far I haven't heard it." Helen smiled, a smile that indicated she was no fool. "Thank you for your time, Mr. Sheridan. I look forward to hearing from you."

"Again, Miss. Stern, we thank you for the business. Talk with you soon."

As soon as James left, Helen put in a call to Basil about his mole activities at JI. Basil, an employee of JI had a very, very bad habit with drugs. He was one of those functional addicts who darted off to the bathroom to get his fix. His nasal passages were probably wafer thin. Hell if she cared. All she cared about was that she could blackmail him into spying for her.

"What did you find out?"

"It seems JI is in a lot of trouble. The union is putting pressure on them and accusing them of taking jobs out of the U.S. It's all very hush-hush at this time, but I bet everything is set to blow. The financial condition of the company has been weakened from having to fight a number of lawsuits. The Board has sent a strident letter to Mrs. Preston about their concerns over the drastic reduction in stock prices. The stocks are extremely volatile. But worse, the law firm of your friend, Mr. DePaul has been retained to act as legal counsel in a hostile takeover attempt."

"Really," was all Helen said, but inside her head fireworks were exploding.

"That's probably why your mother transferred the stocks of the Helen Companies into your name."

"Yes. That seems logical. Do you know who the company is that's bidding for JI?"

"I couldn't find out. It's top secret."

"Well keep on the story and keep me posted."

Immediately Helen pressed the button on her desk and disappeared into the sound-proof apartment. She put a call through to Higgins of London on her cellular phone.

"Brandon Snowden, please. Brandon. Marilyn."

"How are you?" came the answer. Brandon immediately recognized the code name of his client, a necessity in his business to protect his clients' anonymity—a crucial part of his job. There was no room for slipping up in Brandon's world, for he dealt with powerful men who didn't understand fuck ups and who would kill a traitor by proxy. Helen Stern was the first woman client he'd accepted, but she was as ruthless as the shark-eaters he was used to. "What's on the agenda?" He fretted at her displeasure.

"Two things. If things hold up the way they are going you can make a bid for the VIP companies. When the stocks are ready for an Initial Public Offering, I will let you know. Buy at least 16% of the stocks. Since I already own 35% that will make me majority stockholder. Use many aliases not just one name to be sure we avoid SEC regulations and eradicate all trails. I'm not sure we'll need the company, but since this opportunity has fallen into my lap might as well use it as insurance."

"I understand."

"Secondly, JI is in trouble. I don't know who's trying to take over the company but the stocks are quite depressed right now. People are trying to unload them left, right, and center. Buy everything that becomes available. I have set up an account in Switzerland and one in the Grand Cayman. Funds can be transferred instantly to make the transaction. In fact, I can do it right from my laptop, but I want no trace to me. When the time is right and I own enough stocks I will go for a takeover myself."

"What help is out there?"

"I know a guy at the law firm representing the take over. I'll find out what I can from him, by any means necessary, and keep you posted. That's all for now. By the way, Brandon, I need your cellular number. At a time like this I hate having to talk with anyone there but you. No secretaries, okay?"

With the turn of events, Helen was convinced that destiny was responsible for the ease of her plans falling into place. The fact that VIP International better facilitated her strategic plan to take over JI was immensely appreciated, and there was none better to execute her plans than Brandon. Helen never fathomed what made Brandon want to roll the high dice, but she didn't care. What she did know was that he didn't have to. Born the son of a Member of Parliament, he could have chosen any life he wanted to live. Maybe it was that privileged life that taught him how to use his position, power and influence to control people and their lives. In exchange he got to live on the edge of the precipice of excitement, excitement that sex, money, even delectable food no longer afforded him. Brandon Snowden had floated enough stocks to launch a ship and leaked enough information to sink it. He was a maverick or rather a barbarian of trade. In respectable terms, Brandon Snowden was an ingenious financier. Nothing could go wrong because the accountability was too obvious. Only Helen Stern and Brandon Snowden knew of her agenda. And if he screwed up, she had him by the balls with enough dirt to bury him for several lifetimes. Indeed, Brandon Snowden, with his twinkling, trusting blue eyes, would help get her there. Help her deliver the final blow to Jacobson's Industries. Revenge, at last.

Chapter Twenty

Tuesday morning Helen returned a call from Anton. Gone was the tipsy school girl, today was a woman of all business.

"Helen Stern," she snapped, embarrassed about her silly behavior the weekend before in the Park.

"Goodmorning."

"Yes, for me it is." She didn't want to engage in cordial behavior.

"It's Tuesday."

"What?"

"It's Tuesday. I called you last Friday."

"I was very…"

"Just a moment," he interrupted. "I need to get this foam off my face. I'm shaving."

Christ, this guy never quit. She was still trying to comprehend that he had actually put down the phone without her agreeing to hold!

Tapping her finger restlessly, she waited. Helen could hear the water running. Idly her mind was envisioning the strong thoroughbred body of Anton DePaul in a Zest commercial. Carefully she was examining every crevice of his wonderful physique. Of course she didn't have to admit that she'd privately dreamed of it since the day they met. If the truth be told, every night as she'd wrap herself in her down comforter, her mind would undress him piece by piece. Often, too, her mind wandered back to the night in Central Park. How clearly she remembered his soft skin as they had walked hand in hand till dawn. Even now her body tingled from the spicy smell of his aftershave. It was at that moment in her fantasy that she would close her eyes, eagerly awaiting the lingering kiss and the pressure of his strong muscular legs…

"It seems to me," his voice jolted her back to the present, "that you should be more prompt in returning calls. You're a business woman after all."

"Was your call for business, Mr. DePaul?"

"Maybe? I think I can find a way to work with you if you're still interested in retaining my company."

"Your company or Viking & Gould?"

"Viking & Goul…"

"Anton," there it was again, his first name. "Please don't insult me."

"I wasn't trying. Really I just wanted to help." *Help. That was a good sign. It meant, that he was losing his rationale in the face of love. She ought to turn up the heat. Play, baby, play, right into my hand. Now she could really get some scoop.* "What do you have in mind?"

"Well, since the Helen Companies are theoretically separate from JI, and you now own all the stocks, I can help you with your IPO. There's nothing to stop you from doing the deal now, is there?"

"No, but I must plan well."

"Why? That's what you'd have us for," Anton reassured her.

"Send me a proposal. I'll look it over."

"May I bring it?"

"When? All I have to say is that you'd better hurry up. I certainly don't want to be walking down runways with Victor for too long."

"Frankly, I thought you made a wonderful bride and groom."

"Chuckle, chuckle." She was not even smiling.

Helen became quiet and pensive for a moment. She knew there was no one as competent and with whom she felt more comfortable than Anton DePaul, but what were the implications of his representing another firm against JI? Technically, since JI and the Helen Companies were separate there was no conflict of interest, although morally, it was questionable. Of course, since she was not privy to the dealings of JI, she could simply plead ignorance to the information should Andrea find out about the alliance. Like herself, Andrea would want only the best person in the industry to do a job, and there was no question that Anton DePaul was the best.

There was another reason, though, why Anton was best in Helen's book. There had never been a man that had made her feel so…well so female, so pliable, so in love. At the thought she almost jumped out of her seat.

What she wanted to say was, "Dear, dear Anton, I wish I could share my dark secret with you. I wish you would ease my pain and take me off into the sunset. I hope, when you find out that I am illegitimate and 'gifted', you won't reject me. I wish I could be the mother of your children. I wish I could tell you exactly what's going on, for somehow I trust you and I hope you'll realize after all is done, that I love you." Instead she said,

"I'll wait to hear from you, then."

"Good. Now that that's settled, I would like to invite you out."

"Where to?"

"Camping."

"Camping? Like outdoors, no water, no hotel camping?"

"Yeah. That's what I mean."

"You sure know how to give a girl a new experience."

"Is that a yes or no?"

"A maybe if I can get over the idea by Friday. Call me."

"Okay." Anton retied his towel that had slipped from around his waist. To his surprise, he had an erection that was pulsing uncontrollably. "Oh, I will," he replied forcing his mind off his lower body. "I think we will do great things together in more ways than you can appreciate right now."

"Smashing. I can't wait. Anyway, just for decision-making purposes," she continued, "how far is the closest hotel to the camp site?"

If Helen could have seen the look of triumph and laughter that danced in Anton's eyes, she might have changed her mind.

"Three hours. Do you have fishing gear?"

"Oh, God," Helen covered her mouth. "What! Fishing? What other activity could you plan at a camping site?"

"Fishing," he repeated and laughed heartily as he hung up the phone.

What a nut from hell that one was. She grimaced at the thought of wiggly little creatures hanging off her fishing rod. "Aarrgh, yuck," she said, but he had already hung up the phone. Aghast as she was, she found herself smiling.

"Mrs. Walters," she buzzed. "I would like you to purchase the best fishing gear money can buy and some of those extra long rubber boots. You know like the ones the guys wore in *The River Runs Through It*. Oh there is a store on 57th Street…ahh what's the name?"

"Wathne. Ms Stern, is there any particular type of attire you would prefer? Any particular brand?'

"Please! Just make sure I am covered from head to toe so fish smell does not permeate my skin."

Mrs. Walters chuckled but wasted no time. She dialed every sports store in the phone book. Not only did she get the best deal in town, it was delivered by closing that day.

Chance was crazy in love with Victor, and each day she wanted to be closer and closer to him. At dinner that night when he'd asked her to join his staff, it was a dream come true. Clearly she was flattered and although she felt a great deal of loyalty to Helen, Victor was offering her a chance of a lifetime. The advantages of a partnership were staggering- her ideas would be implemented, she would be a stock holder and she would be at the helm of the company. Such a prestigious position would catapult her into the midst of the power brokers. The best benefit, however, was that she would work closely with Victor and at last have an opportunity to develop their relationship. Once Victor realized how indispensable she was he would surely ask her to marry him. After weighing the laundry list of positives, Chance could find no reason to say no.

The jubilant feeling dissipated quickly. How would she ever be able to hand Helen her letter of resignation? For six hours after Victor had asked her to jump ship, Chance practiced writing her resignation. Each time she'd ended up tossing the crumpled linen paper into the wastebasket. The words were just not right. Maybe her hesitation was from a nagging feeling that kept telling her she might be making a mistake. Anything too good to be true usually is, her fearful mind kept repeating. Shrugging, she dipped the old-fashioned fountain pen into the inkwell and started again.

Dear Helen:

The thought of resigning from The Helen Companies is one that leaves a huge gap in my brain and in my heart. Not only have I learned so much from working with you, but it's like giving up my baby for adoption. Together we have nurtured, through gestation and birth, a wonderfully successful company. I want nothing more than its continued success. So this is really not a resignation letter as much as it is an informative one that outlines the offer that has been made to me by the VIP companies and the advantages it offers me in my career path. If after reading this you feel it is an unwise decision, I will remain with The Helen Companies.

Respectfully yours,
Chance.

Victor sulked all morning after Helen again turned him down for a date. It seemed there was nothing he could do to please the wench. Even their success as the Bride and Groom of the century didn't soften her feelings toward him. Though Chance had offered him sexual healing and he'd survived Olivia's wrath, simply because she believed their failed planned rendezvous was divinely ordained, Victor was unfulfilled and restless. He really had to do something about Olivia, too. Her saccharine voice still echoed in his ear.

"Oh Victor, thank goodness you called. No, no…" she interrupted him as he was going to offer one of his charming excuses, "I forgive you. Malcolm came by last night at nearly three in the morning. God knows where he was until then. What about tonight, darling? I'm still panting."

"Sorry, Olivia, I have some work to do. I'm meeting with Helen. Stern to talk about a new direction for our companies and the IPO. I need your advice, though," he smoothed his way." Just let a woman feel you need their advice and you are as good as gold. "I liked what you said about that Chance woman. I offered her at job with VIP. It will probably make my position with Helen Stern less than honorable. What do you think?"

"I think it's a marvelous idea to bring on the girl. She would lend a wealth of experience we don't quite have in the staff now. But what exactly do you intend to propose to Helen Stern?"

We! He didn't miss the inclusion of herself in the deal. She was such a…oh, he forgot the expression. Olivia really felt responsible for the success of his company and in a way she was right, but he had been careful not to reflect that on paper.

"I'm not the one doing the proposing," Victor continued. "As I told you before, Helen has suggested that while the iron is hot we should think about an IPO. I need the cash to develop some ideas that are brewing in my head. With Chance aboard I will be afforded her expertise, and especially important are the stockholders who'll insist the company is run by people in the know. Chance's record is exemplary. Since Helen already owns a percent of the company, it's not as though Chance would be a competitor. I think she might buy the idea, and Chance will leave all her bridges intact. I've asked Chance about her thoughts on the matter. She is very loyal to Helen. I was trying to get a read on Helen at dinner the other night," he lied, "but she is one hard person to fathom. I suspect she was still too tired from the event to think about business."

"You know I have been thinking. Something isn't quite right about that Stern girl. Sometimes I get this eerie feeling when I look into her eyes. A feeling that she just looks right through you as though she really doesn't even see you. Strange girl, isn't she. Do you suppose she has a heart?" Olivia's dig was far too obvious.

"Heart? Olivia! Isn't that a joke coming from you? Why would you bring this up to me? You know how I hate idle gossip."

"Don't be such a bore, Victor. Idle gossip has its place. Smoke, fire sorta thing. Plus I trust my instincts. Anyway, just you be careful. Now," Olivia was unflustered, "as I was saying, I think it depends on how you present the deal. Make sure this Cherry girl…"

"Chance," Victor corrected.

"Right, Chance. Before she gives her notice, make sure you've spoken with Helen Stern, which by the way, you should do right away. Unless you can get a buy-in for your proposal, she'll kill the deal. The woman is no fool. She realizes how invaluable Chance's expertise and skills would be to the transition of your company. Stern is a bottom line kind of woman, and I am sure this is the line of argument that'll score points. The fact is, Victor, Helen is completely driven by power. This would definitely be a power move on your part. Don't forget to reiterate what the magazine can do for you both!"

"Olivia, Olivia, Olivia. Whatever would I do without you. You are the brightest woman I know. Are you sure you don't want to leave Catillion Publishing and come work with me?" Victor chuckled.

"For a price." She gurgled at him, happy for the compliment. "I'm really glad you see things the way I do."

As much as Olivia's ideas had cheered him up, and in fact were a good strategy, he was still smarting from the Ice Queen's canstance dismissal. Such cavalier treatment was not good for his fragile ego, especially since he had built his self-worth and self-esteem on the availability of women. Deep down Victor Innes Palmer was a sensitive, insecure and self-destructive man.

But Victor would do anything to make Helen take a more active interest in him, even under the disguise of business. Still he was acutely aware that he needed to be circumspect, for he needed Chance to run his operations and Olivia to boost his limping self-esteem. Having failed to be invited to compete in the fast track at his family's own successful company, Victor had a lot to prove in making his business successful.

If things worked as planned, he could retain his profile, image and carefree lifestyle while Helen and Chance's business savvy catapulted his company to unheralded fame and fortune. He would show that old geyser he called father just what power he was able to align himself with even if it was not his own. It took brawn, if not brains, to convince the right people to invest their time, energy, and money in his project. As far as Victor was concerned, that was winning. Energized, he prepared himself for his meeting with Helen Stern. He had to practice his candor because he had a feeling she chewed up sensitive people and spat them out.

"I have to admit I'm more into creating than maintaining," Victor glanced at the masked face of Helen Stern. "VIP really needs a powerhouse like you to maintain its upward trajectory. I've been giving some thought to who might be the ideal person for the job." Now that he was before the ice queen, Victor sounded unsure of his strategy

"Have you come up with anyone in particular?" Helen responded.

"I know this might sound crazy, but I have been thinking Chance would be the right person for the job. She wouldn't be you by any means, but she has learned from the best." He tried flattery.

Helen cocked her head to the side and her eyes turned upwards as one deep in thought. The room was silent, and Victor felt the urge to continue. A raised hand silenced him.

"Yes, I can see that. I can definitely see the possibilities of what Chance could contribute. Frankly, I owe her that much for she has reached her pinnacle here at the Helen Companies. The only job left for her would be mine," she smiled coyly at Victor.

"We wouldn't want that now," Victor smiled back, knowing how lame he sounded.

"No. Well now that that's settled, the sooner she gets started with you the faster we can get things rolling," was Helen's reply, while flipping through her appointment book. "My 35% stake in the company, with Chance at the helm, will be quite lucrative. We'll tell her together next week after the papers are drawn up. It's really a transfer anyway, isn't it? I think she will be delighted. Have your attorney call mine. They can hash out the deal. If the price is right for Chance, I'll sign it." She handed him a note card with the attorney's name. This is the guy that's looking over the possible IPO proposal. We are scheduled to meet him next week. Mrs. Walters will give you the date and time. Chance should be there too."

Helen rose from her chair before finishing breakfast, signaling the end of the meeting. "I'm sorry, Victor, but I have another appointment. Is there anything else we need to discuss?"

As always, his meetings with Helen were to the point. They never chit-chatted or tried to get to know each other better. Strictly business as far as she was concerned. Didn't she find him the least bit attractive? Hadn't she eyed him favorably at Jacques' party? What had he done to discourage her? She was one difficult woman to read. Even in discussing the possibility of Chance's employment with VIP, Helen gave no inkling of what she was thinking, much less how she felt about him.

"Discuss. Aaah…nothing in terms of business." Victor took the opportunity to move the relationship in another direction.

"What then?" Helen's eyebrow shot up

"Would you consider joining me at the opera on Saturday night?"

"Oh golly Victor, I wish I could, but I am going fishing."

"Fishing?"

"Can you believe it?"

"Not in the slightest. Another night then?" He tried hard to be nonchalant.

"Sure, call me." Helen flashed a plastic grin, already on to a new task.

At the doorway, Victor turned back to look at Helen. As if sensing his stare, she met his eyes without hesitation.

"What now, Victor?"

"Why don't you like me?" His question took her of guard. "And what can I do to change that?"

Helen stared at the pathetic man in front of her. She opened her mouth and then shut it again. Finally, she said, "Victor, you are presumptuous. I haven't thought about you enough to assess whether I like you or not. But now that you've asked and I have given it a thought, It's not that I don't like you, Victor. It's that we are too much alike. Like you, I have never been kind. We are both damaged in that way, and damaged people should only love healthy people. And I'm afraid we are both very, very damaged."

Victor left the office without another word.

Chance walked into the foyer as Victor came out of Helen's office.

"Victor, what are you doing here?"

"Oh hi, Chance. Just talking over some strategy with Helen for the next showing of our wears." Victor was noticeably detached.

"I see." Her tone was nonplus. *And why was I not included in the meeting?*

"Gotta run. See you later."

Helen watched the exchange with curiosity. Was something personal going on between the two? *Huh. She wondered why Victor was so eager to go out with her then? Could they be plotting against me? Something was fishy.* At the thought of the word fish, she gagged.

"Have a moment?" Chance asked poking her head through the door still ajar from Victor's departure.

"Come in. Oh, for Christ's sake don't look so nervous. Victor already told me of his intent to ask you to work for the VIP Companies."

Chance held the envelope firmly behind her.

"From the way he explained it, it would be beneficial for both companies, that's why I want to consider his proposal. I'm not sure that you know I own a sizable amount of stocks in the VIP company so this is not a resignation, just a shift to the weaker arm. So, Madam Chance, give me the note behind your back." Helen placed her hand on Chance's shoulder.

"*Phew*." Chance let out an audible sigh. How like Victor to pave the way for a hard decision. "Thank you, Helen. I really appreciate this. This company is so well-run that it can truly do without me. After all, it has you, so there is no way the vision for the future could be bettered. If you intend to continue your alliance with the VIP companies, my move there will help to bring them on par. As you said, I would bring all the valuable assets I've learned from you to that company."

"I actually think it's a swell idea. Don't know why I didn't think of it first. That man is very bright, very bright indeed. You have acquired great skills here at the Helen Companies that are needed at Victor's company. A company can only grow as big as the vision of its management."

Now it was Chance's face that was bright, beaming with pride at Helen's assessment of Victor.

"You will be missed around here, Chance, but what the devil, life must go on. And because I have a vested interest in the company I would much rather know that it'll be well run. Not that Victor isn't capable, but with you I am assured success. Don't think I would have let you go so easily if I didn't have a vested interest. Shall we have a drink to our new relationship, and would you give me the damn envelope behind your back. I'll call Victor and tell him of our decision. He will be very pleased."

"Thank you, Helen. This was not easy for me."

And it won't be for me if it suits my purpose to take over your company in eight months, she thought as she poured them each a snifter of brandy. What Chance didn't realize was that she had just been drafted into Helen's games of ruthlessness and revenge. Revenge! This was a game to which Helen knew all the moves. What did it matter who the pawns in the game were? If they were strategically placed to help her win, she would play them. Helen watched Chance retreat, oblivious to the perils that could lay ahead. At that very moment, Helen's mind was repeating a line she had read in a novel by Josephine Hart. So ironic, too, that the author's name was Hart, for there was no heart in this story. Yes, indeed, she repeated from the infamous line of the book, "Damaged people are dangerous, for they know they can survive."

On Friday morning Helen deliberately wore trousers to work in anticipation of her—she couldn't believe it—fishing trip!

"My, I have never seen you wear slacks to work before," Andrea said as they helped themselves to breakfast before their hour-long ride into the city.

"That's because I haven't before, Mother, but today I'm going fishing. I leave directly from work. Can you imagine spending the weekend throwing bait?"

Helen was spending a week with her family in the Hamptons while her apartment was being renovated. In a moment of utter craziness, she'd had the entire place redecorated to be less somber. The beige carpet in the living room was now gleaming oak, the white kitchen canary yellow, and the bedroom, hunter's green. No more just barely living colors. She would have a vibrant, dramatic style to match the drama she was soon to create. Refurnished in its entirety, Helen was actually looking forward to moving back the very weekend she'd accepted Anton's invitation to go fishing. Now, reorganizing her life would have to wait. Coming back from the weekend to a place crammed with unpacked boxes was not something she looked forward to, but that's what had to be done. The movers were arriving later that day, thanks to Mrs. Walters, who had agreed to receive the deliveries. She'd have asked Melissa, but for some reason that woman had never taken to her. The matriarch of the Preston household, her face wrinkled like well-worn leather, was forever watching her cautiously, peering deep into her eyes as though she was looking for something in particular.

Bait was about right. Melissa sighed at the girl's comment about fishing. This girl was preparing a bait for something and it wasn't a fish. If only Andrea would listen to her.

Melissa distrusted Helen Stern, and for some reason she suspected the girl's presence in America was more than just returning home to a long-lost mother. From the moment she arrived at 666 Baldwin, the air in the house had changed. After all these years, with nothing to substantiate her distrust, Melissa still had misgivings about Helen. Maybe it was the eyes. The big, black sinister eyes that turned blacker and narrower at times when she looked at her mother. The eyes that seemed like a whirlpool of hate and anger; the eyes that showed, even in their apparent calm, a level of rage that was extraordinary.

Melissa had often hinted her discontent about the child, but Andrea either intentionally ignored it or missed the subtle hints she tried to give her. Like the night when she had found Helen in Scott's study snooping around, and the times she had tried to question Melissa about Andrea. Finally Melissa confronted Andrea.

"I never said she wasn't nice, Andrea. You have to understand, these people are nice, charismatic, and apparently sincere, but that doesn't mean they are not dangerous. I have no proof, but I would watch my back if I were you. Why not call on your powers to see if anything is unsettling? It is so easy to love people like Helen for they are the success stories we all love to tell, but that doesn't mean they are not manipulators of emotions or that they are decent. Do you remember the story

"What About Eve? Don't forget, Andy," as only Melissa was allowed to call Andrea, "the girl has powers too, you know."

"Come now, Melissa. You're being hard on the child. If Helen did have something up her sleeve, don't you think she would actively block her psyche from being penetrated anyway? Just how do you propose that I break through her barrier?"

"I don't know. But just you be careful."

"I love you, Mel, for always protecting me, but I think you are wrong this time." She kissed the wizened cheek of her long-time guardian.

As always, Melissa was disappointed, for her comments fell on deaf ears, and Andrea, she knew, probably chalked her fears up to overprotection and senility. Granted she was old, but she was not dead yet!

"So, who is this person you are going fishing with? Surely not Harrington. I had no idea you were seeing someone."

"I am not seeing anyone, I'm simply going fishing."

Her mother raised her eyebrows. "Um hmm. Come on, Helen, do tell, with whom?"

"With Anton DePaul. You met him at the benefit."

"You mean the attorney from Viking & Gould? I wouldn't get too attached." Andrea was obviously perturbed. "I don't like him a bit." The voice was cautionary.

"Would you like him better if you knew his mother is West Indian? From Haiti, I believe." Andrea was quite partial to West Indians. She always commented how keen and talented they seemed to be. "Even the Jamaican Posse are terribly formidable." She would defend the notorious group of rebels, but not even that affiliation could make her like Anton DePaul.

"It figures. Haiti is the one Island that's so very different. Noted for its Voodoo and Charlatans."

"Uh-huh. So that puts us in good company now doesn't it, mother?"

"I am sure I don't know what you mean. Is it serious?" Andrea was prying.

"Oh Mother, bugger off, will you! He is just a friend."

"Uh-huh. Well just you be careful." She walked towards the breakfast table. "He may be using you to get information. Just be very careful, Helen."

So indeed there was truth to the rumors of JI. Maybe soon enough her mother would tell her everything she needed to know. For now, however, Helen let the subject drop.

"You got a ladder in your stockings." Helen eyes narrowed, obviously delighted to find an imperfection with her mother's otherwise impeccable dress.

There was that gleam again. Melissa was observing Helen as she always did. It was not a kind look. Melissa began spooning eggs onto Reginald's platter as she saw him bouncing down the stairs. Even at twenty-four, she still fixed his plate. *Andrea is wrong. That girl is dangerous and something is definitely wrong*, Melissa reaffirmed. *Definitely wrong. Why would she take so much delight in finding such a trivial flaw with her mother?*

"Is that true, Scott? I have a feeling Helen is just trying to get me out of the room so she doesn't have to answer any more questions about her fishing trip."

"Fishing? I was planning to stop by the office today." Reginald reached for a roll. "Did Helen tell you, Mom, I'll be working for her this summer? Can you believe I had to interview? So much for blood ties." He kissed Melissa's wrinkled cheek.

"As it should be," his mother responded as she lovingly slapped Scott's hand that was reaching up her leg to feel the run in her stockings. After all these years he had the ability to turn her resolve to putty.

"What are you going to be doing for Helen, son?" Scott asked.

"I'm not sure yet, but I bet I'll be starting in the mail room or something menial." He looked pleadingly at his sister.

"That's possible," Helen smiled, "but we'll try for something more interesting, like Marketing. It's okay to come in this morning, Reggie. I won't be leaving until noon or so. I'll take you down to personnel myself to make sure you get a fitting job for a family member."

Chapter Twenty-One

It was a beautiful day to travel. The sun, bright overhead, filtered its rays through the fluffy cumulus clouds. With the sun-roof of the Range Rover open, the wind was blowing just enough to offer a layer of coolness to the skin as it whipped through Helen's short mane. It was not a day to talk business, but Anton felt obliged to put Helen at ease. It seemed, when she was talking about work, she was more relaxed.

"Aren't you going to ask me about the proposal? For some reason I thought it would be the first words out of your mouth instead of hello."

"What makes you think that?"

"Pavlov's training. Do you realize you never say good-morning, hello, or any such salutation when we meet? You always say 'Helen Stern', or 'That will be all', or 'Let's get right to the point'. Do you know you do that?"

"I do not. Didn't I say hello when you picked me up outside the office?"

"No, you said. 'How far is this place?'"

"Anton DePaul, you lie."

"Fine. Next time I'm bringing a tape recorder."

"Defended Nixon, did you?"

Bantering came easily for them. Anton was the only person who could point out Helen's shortcomings without throwing her into a fit.

"Touchdown."

"What?"

"Touchdown, as in you scored, as in football as in Touché? Helen, you must acquaint yourself more with American ways and culture."

"I knew that. I just didn't hear you," she said simply.

"Anyway," Anton informed, "I do have a bit of business to talk about. I think you should make an offer to buy out VIP. I hear he is back to his old ways again."

"How'd you know that?"

"Let's just say I'm well-connected, and it's a small world in high finance."

"I'm listening. What are you offering in the way of free advice?" Helen pumped for information.

"If you intend to buy out VIP, make him an offer with a two, maybe three-year payout of profits, a paid position to stay *away* from the company and a few perks such as use of the jet, etc."

"Aaahaugh. Why do you suppose I would want to buy him out?"

"A hunch. It would be good for your opening bid price."

"Or a rumor?" Helen fixed her eyes on Anton, daring him to lie. "VIP has been drinking all his life. I suspect he operates best that way. Just a week ago I okayed a deal for Chance to head the company. The place will not be run by him but by Chance, though I imagine you already know that."

Anton implored innocence. "That changes the picture somewhat. You do, of course, know that he sees Chance?"

"I suspected. But there is another reason I am not interested in buying him out completely. Not that it's any of your business, but I plan to go back to England soon. I'm getting tired of life in the United States. The rat race wears me out. Let's just say I want a more quiet, boring life. Delayed culture shock, you know. I'm getting out of the business world for a quiet life in the country. She was intentionally misleading him. The IPO for both the Helen Companies and VIP was simply waiting on her signature and the right time to launch.

"And your mother, how does she feel about that?"

"She doesn't know. I have no idea how soon this could be, so why talk about it till I'm sure. But," she continued nonchalantly, "I'm sure she will understand."

All is not well, but Anton left the subject alone.

"If you should choose to work with my company on the IPO deal, it'll be imperative, when the time comes, that I know everything that could possibly affect the outcome. And Helen, I mean everything. One scandal could kill the deal before it gets off the ground."

"Hey, what are you talking about, and why does it sound as though you think there will be a scandal?"

"Look, I don't have much to lose as you can see. My time costs three hundred dollars an hour no matter what the outcome. But I have a reputation that must not be tarnished."

"What exactly is it you want to tell me, Anton?" Helen turned, unnerving him with her alluring eyes. Deeper and deeper he was falling into the black pool. What he felt for this woman was confusing, exciting, and exposed. He was not in the least bit intimidated by her, but he found himself crumbling in her presence.

"I just sense that something is amiss. My Haitian roots, you know. I'm just making sure we understand each other."

Phew. Was that all. Listen, my friend, this IPO will be over before your firm ever hears of it.

Anton was disappointed to hear that Helen wanted to leave the U.S. How was he ever going to let her go? He'd just have to relocate to England, he mused, yet he couldn't imagine being a barrister in England walking around the courtroom with white curly wigs on his head. But who knows. People had done worse for love, and he might just do it for the woman at his side.

Helen smiled to herself as she remembered Anton's early Friday morning call to her office making sure all the plans were set for their trip. Still perturbed by his sport of choice she had said, "Anton, I have to ask you, is fishing the only thing you could have thought to do on this lovely Friday?"

He'd laughed. "I think you are going to love it. I'm taking bets that you're going to enjoy this camping trip so much you'll want to come back next weekend. Fishing is a very good way of communing with nature, with oneself, and to relax. But if you really think you are going to hate it, I can fly us down to the Cayman for a weekend of scuba diving instead."

"Scuba? Now that sounds like fun. Oh no, I've changed my mind. Getting to the airport on a Friday at this hour will be horrendous…and knowing the airlines, there will be delays."

"I said I would fly you down. That means me. *Moi*. I have a pilot's license."

"Holy cow. Are you crazy? I'm not getting into a prop plane with you. Fishing is fantastic. Did I say it wasn't?" Helen back-pedaled from her complaint. "OK, here is my offer, take it or leave it. I will spend all day Saturday fishing, but by Saturday night I must find a hotel where I can take a shower. I have no intentions of going to bed smelling like fish, especially in the wild where it's a mating call!"

"This will be difficult. But I'll see what I can do. Now let's see, I'll wake you up at five-thirty a.m. on Saturday…"

"Five-thirty! You didn't say anything about having to slave at fishing. Slaving is still in your blood, I see."

"I didn't say anything about five-thirty? Shucks. Is it a problem? Six then. I'm a good Massa."

"Now you hold on a minute, I'm not going anywhere until I wake up naturally. That's usually about eleven on Saturdays."

"We'll see about that. But let's not go too far into the weekend before making plans to leave. What time shall I pick you up?"

Helen flipped through her appointment book. "I had a staff meeting scheduled for 2 p.m., but I suppose I could move it to 10 a.m. And don't bother to come up to the office. I'll meet you downstairs at noon. If I get out before then, Roger will give me a lift to your place, but I'd call first."

"Give you a lift as in give you a ride?"

"What's wrong with giving me a lift?" Helen asked defensively. "It's British and so am I. Anyway, what makes you think giving you a ride is more correct?"

"I didn't. I was just translating so I could comprehend."

`Helen felt stupid to have overreacted. Serves him right. He was always yakety yaking.

They had been traveling for three hours, singing, whistling, and bopping to the music. Helen was having the time of her life. From behind her sunglasses, she snuck quick peeks at Anton. He was such a man.

Suddenly, the car made a sharp turn off the narrow winding road to an even narrower, unpaved trail. She grabbed the dashboard and quickly buckled her seat belt to keep from flying forward as the car jerked and bumped along. Helen's heart dropped to her stomach as she envisioned a whole weekend in the bushes of the Catskills mountains.

"Nice ride," she said, swallowing hard as the Range Rover blazed along.

"I have a feeling you are just being kind."

"What makes you say that?"

"I'm an attorney, Helen. I am paid to watch the nonverbal communication of my clients. Travel bag in the glove compartment."

"Oh, shut up. You don't have to observe me. I'm not on trial, am I?."

"Don't worry, my skills at criminal trials are limited. At one point I was going to become a criminal lawyer. I had the feeling that I would never lose a case. I was so sure I could set up the conditions to control the jury's reactions that I would feel powerful. And then I saw my hero, Christopher Lockheed, shredded to pieces in the courtroom, and I decided against it."

"What made you so sure you could control a jury?"

"You have to understand that most people are followers, and if you convince them you are a leader they will gladly follow the Pied Piper. Unfortunately, there is always a rebel for the cause."

"That's a rather arrogant way to look at life. Yet, you may have a point. I was always the rebel."

"Yep, that I am sure about, but it's the way you look at it, too, right? Right now, technically, you are following me on an expedition."

Helen thought for a moment. How far off he was from the truth. Frankly, she had calculated every move of their encounter. It was she who was setting up *her* victim to give the response she wanted.

"Maybe," was all she said to his insinuation.

Soon the car pulled up to what appeared to be a log cabin. From the look of things, someone was there as a light was burning in the house. Anton put the gearshift in reverse and backed the car into the covered carport. He pulled up the emergency break to prevent it from rolling back down the small incline.

"Why are we stopping, and how can you just pull into someone's carport?"

"Got to check for directions. I'm afraid we may be lost. Folks in this part are very kind. They won't mind about the driveway."

"Oh, Christ. I thought you knew where the hell we were going." Helen was up in arms. "Serves me right. Should have known we'd be wandering around. Just peachy. Hell, we may be out here in this wilderness wandering for forty days and nights," she lamented.

"What religion?"

"What?" She had no idea what the hell he was talking about.

"Forty days and forty nights. Isn't that biblical? What religion do you observe?"

"Damn you," she snapped. "Just shut up and go get the directions. Fishing! Camping! I should have been shot! Where are we supposed to be going camping anyway?" She opened a map she found in the glove compartment.

"You could check the map for me if you turn it the right side up." Anton was clearly amused.

"Fishing!" she snorted. "I should be shot." She repeated.

"Yes, that's what we're going to do. Fishing and camping, but since you were so very concerned about our accommodations I was trying to go someplace near where you could at least have running water. Don't worry, though. I'll haul iron so we can be there before long."

"Charming. Thanks for the thought," she shooed him along. "Now just you hurry in there and get the right directions so we won't be stuck out here when it's pitch black trying to find somewhere that does not exist," she said sarcastically.

"Actually," he was laughing heartily, "this is my little cabin where I come for respite when the city gets to be too much. I called the caretaker and had him spruce things up a bit just for you. However, I have every intention of pitching a tent right back there near the lake. Come," he took her hand, "let me show you the water. It's beautiful when the moonlight glitters and dances on it. One of my favorite things to do is to fish at night."

Helen followed him silently, too annoyed with his little practical joke to join in the laughter. She didn't know how to be light, funny, or spontaneous. It was a fault. Trying to see the humor, she walked a step or two behind Anton. The paradox of this heavy-hitting New York attorney fascinated her.

"Where do you think? Over here?"

"I'm no expert on camping spots, but I would say here is fine," Helen replied.

"Good. Now that's settled, would you like to go inside and check out the establishment?"

Again, she trailed after him and hoped this would be the last time she ever followed anyone. Leading was something she was far better at or at minimum falling in line beside her partner. The glow inside the cabin was welcoming, and Helen wanted to stay in the midst of its open arms, take a shower, and ensconce herself under the comforter. "Thank God," she breathed silently, "I have somewhere to change." After all, she had to get donned in her fashionable sporting clothes, for even such mundane adventures had a fashion statement of their own.

The rugged cabin was what Helen would describe as the perfect Ralph Lauren setting. Very masculine and comfortable, it welcomed its visitors with open arms. Its brightly covered chairs, open fireplace, and pine smell were bewitching. Scottish flannel throw blankets in hues of blues and reds were casually strewn over chairs. Although expensively appointed, nothing was pretentious, and Helen felt very much at home. Before heading into the shower she jumped up on the king size log bed, bouncing twice before resting peacefully on top of it. She felt as though she belonged there. Hearing Anton's footsteps, she quickly escaped to the bathroom, lingering as long as she could. But as soon as she had finished showering, he was ushering her back out into the darkening night to the lake where they would settle for the night.

"Please Anton, just a teensy weensy bit longer. I have to adjust to this," Helen begged.

The large, wooded grounds were all theirs. Helen stopped to listen to the loons chirping, the soft serenade of the gentle waves crashing against the embankment, and the rustle of the breeze as it whispered through the waving branches. It was quite dark now, but she felt safe in Anton's presence. She stole a look at the silhouette of the man unloading gadgets from the truck. He was powerful. She could feel his power filling the distance between them. Today, he looked magnificent, his potent body hardened with sinuous muscles that rippled through the black t-shirt. He stirred in her an intoxicating emotion. As it often did, Helen's mind glided easily into the familiar scene where she imagined vividly this agile man commanding every fiber of her body to obey his will. The narrow hips, clad in Levi jeans, had moved with authority as she yielded to their demands. Anton DePaul, even though he was built like a warrior, exuded a peace that seemed to emanate from every pore of his body. And there in the storm-lit night, he glowed with an inner light that seemed beyond the body—a hypnotic and calming light. She envied him—envied that feeling of contentment that she had not achieved in far too many years.

Helen was still staring transfixed in his direction. Without warning, the storm light cast a glow on her, and as though Anton knew what she was thinking, his eyes conveyed her thoughts. He approached her, coming within inches of her face. She could feel her heart racing and her cheeks glowing. Something magical was happening to her, and as her own heart took flight she vowed to keep Anton DePaul at arm's length. There was nothing she could do about their distance now, and to be frank she didn't know if she wanted to. "It's a beautiful night," was all she could manage to whisper in the inflamed moment and as foolish as she felt, she could not make herself look away.

"Over there," his voice broke the spell. "That's where we'll set up the cooking fire. Will you help me?" he invited. There was a look of uncertainty on Helen's face. "Don't worry," he smiled, "I'll instruct you every step of the way."

When the tents were erected, they lit a fire and placed a kettle on top of it. "Hot cocoa," he indicated, "what one needs at bedtime. If you want, you can go inside and wash up from the mess of digging, but if you *really* want to be authentic you can use the thermos and basin. That's your tent over there." He handed her a lighted storm lamp. It was pitch black by now, and the woods were silent and haunting. The wind had died down a bit, and the birds had gone to sleep for the night. It was now the crickets' turn to do their ballet. And as they danced, the fireflies lit their way into the dark night. Only the crackling fire under the kettle punctuated the silence.

"Right." Helen took the challenge, hoisted her duffel bag, and headed for her tent. Inside, Anton had inflated the sleeping bag and placed a make shift cardboard bedside table next to it. A down comforter covered the narrow bed. Helen placed the lamp on the table and proceeded to pour water into the basin. She washed her face and brushed her teeth, inhaling the cool air against her fresh mouth. She breathed deeply and realized how unpolluted the air felt in her lungs. This commune with nature wasn't so bad after all. Abandoning her clothes, she pulled on the pecan cotton pantsuit pajama and covered it with a lined damask peach robe.

Anton could see the shadow of the fantastic figure through the tent. He felt shoddy looking, but he wasn't able to take his eyes off the contour of the slender body as she disrobed. She was a Herculean woman, he knew, but tonight he almost forgot that she could be contemptuous and ruthless. It was not just her beauty that made him crazy, it was her…words failed him. He had slept with a good number of New York's bewitching beauties, but their hold over him barely lasted past one night. And although he could not ignore the ebony eyes, the inviting, pouty lips, or the exquisitely sculptured face, it was the mysterious effect of Helen Stern that had him intrigued. She was like a woman possessed. Yet, in his heart he knew this was the only woman he *would* marry. This was the woman who would bear his heirs and this was the woman he would hold in his heart for eternity. Abruptly Anton turned towards his cabin, chiding himself for engaging in idle fantasy. When he returned to the fire he was wearing cotton pants and moccasins.

Helen rejoined Anton by the fire. "You're dressed for bedtime at the Plaza," he chuckled, handing her a hot cup of cocoa. "This will make you sleep."

"It's the worst I could find," she retorted. "Next time I promise to go to Walmarts."

"I'm sure you'd look as swell."

Helen rolled her eyes. "I hope you've drugged this cocoa with sleeping pills. I'm going to need drugs to get through the night." She took the cup of cocoa he was holding out to her.

"As a matter of fact, I did, but only because I was thinking it would help you sleep through the bear's nightly prowls. They roam at night hunting for food. Usually about three or four in the morning. Didn't want them disturbing your sleep."

This time she was not incensed, for a lovely smile lighted her face; a rare and ravishing smile. Although Anton had seen her laugh and sing, he had never seen her smile. That dazzling smile transformed her face completely, and it was at that very moment that Anton DePaul knew his heart would no longer beat without her.

Anton's eyes burned through the fancy night-robe, examining every inch of the sleek, curvaceous body. He needed Helen like he'd never needed a woman before and tonight, he was committed to go wherever the furious waves of her love took him—into the abyss of its darkness, its passion, or its rage.

The seduction of the golden moon above made Anton feel bold and presumptuous. In an instant he was touching her face. His voice was huskier than he expected. "You are beautiful, Helen. So very, very beautiful."

"Thank you," she said softly. "Thank you."

It had been a long time since a man had touched her so tenderly. Helen sighed sadly as she rested her face in the warm palm of Anton's touch. Her sigh was a deep expiration of distress that caused Anton to look at her more closely.

"Does this bother you?" He eased the pressure of his hand.

"No," she said genuinely. "It's really very nice, Anton." Her gaze was childlike. "Why did you invite me camping?"

"Because from what I hear you need to learn to enjoy life a bit more. Rumor has it you work too hard."

"And what rumors are those?"

"They say you are a slave driver that cares about nothing but the win."

"Yes sir, they are right. I learned well from the Massa. But tell me, what else is there to do in life but work?"

"How about roasting marshmallows," he handed her the fluffy candy on the end of a stick. "Go on, put it in the fire."

"There's a lot you don't know about me," Helen said, thrusting the marshmallow into the fire and twirling the stick. "Why are you so sure you want to teach me about living?"

"Everybody has to have a teacher, and I can teach you how to be free."

"Free? Ah, no, my dear," she looked sadly at him. "I will never be free, for you see I have made a bargain with the devil."

"Then I'll be your devil, and I will set you free."

Helen's body responded to Anton's touch with uncontrollable desire. Her upturned face was flushed with excitement and involuntarily her lips parted with longing.

"*Mademoiselle*," he whispered, "I want your soul."

"*Monsieur*." She was breathless. "Oh yes, but only for tonight."

As Anton covered her lips with a burning and longing kiss, a deep moan escaped Helen like a wounded animal offered relief. She had been ready every night in her dreams for Anton's gentle kisses to cover her face, neck, lids and finally again her waiting mouth.

Helen felt her feet growing wings, and she was floating into the warmth of the deepest hunger and passion she had ever experienced. For the first time in her life she did not want to return to her house of ice. But just before the point of no return, she abruptly turned on her heels and said good night. Anton was stunned, disappointed, and erect. How would he be able to stand the unfulfilled aroused passion that she left within him? "Helen," he said softly, but she did not stop. He looked up at the sky offering a silent prayer. It looked like rain—a sure sign his prayer would be answered.

In their tents both Helen and Anton tossed and turned for awhile before falling asleep. Helen awoke with a start. Outside, the rain bashed against the side of her tent as lightning lit up the sky. The quiet wind was now howling, and she was scared. She pulled the covers over her head and closed her eyes tightly. A loud clap sounded near her tent and she scampered out of the bed and ran the short distance to Anton's tent.

Although it was only a few feet away, she was soaked. Anton was wide-awake and, it seemed, waiting for her.

"Is it safe to be out here among the trees in all this lightening?" Helen asked, trying to sound unconcerned, but the look on her face was an obvious telltale sign. She was genuinely scared.

"Goodness, you are soaked. Better take off that robe and dry off a bit." Under the robe, the cotton pajamas were soaked against her body, outlining the curve of her full breasts and hips. Anton wrapped her in a towel he'd retrieved from the foot of his bed. "Take those off too," he said, handing her the black T-shirt he had worn earlier. It smelled of Aramis.

"Where?"

"Come on. Don't tell me a man has never seen you naked?"

"Maybe, but you won't. Turn around," she ordered.

"O.K. Now to answer your question, it's fine to be out here in the lightening and thunder for the tents are fire proof."

"Well, I might as well just go back to mine. No need to change."

"I think you'd better spend the night in here. You can sleep on the bed. I happen to have an extra sleeping bag. Brought it because the forecast said rain was possible, and I kinda imagined this was going to happen."

"Anton! You are so damn cocky. Have I ever told you you make me sick?'

"You just did, but I know you don't mean it. Drink this," he ordered. "It's just some Remy."

Helen gratefully swallowed a full glass of cognac. Not a minute later she was feeling light-headed and was forced to sit on the makeshift bed. She was one stupid woman for being out in the middle of nowhere with Anton DePaul.

A bolt of lightning lit up the tent and Helen flew beneath the covers and pulled them over her head.

"It's just a little lightning," he reassured her, coming to sit beside her. "If you want I'll massage your shoulders until you fall asleep. Slowly Anton's hand moved up and down the side of her neck. A soothing touch. With each stroke Helen felt her tensed muscles relax and she allowed herself to give in to the sensual feelings creeping up from her toes.

"Thank you," Helen said, closing her eyes as her body responded to the soft touch of Anton's gentle hands. When she opened her eyes again Anton was staring at her, transfixed, with a look of extreme yearning that cast a potent spell on her. She smiled at him, gently and invitingly, bringing her finger up to trace his smooth skin.

"Do you want me?" she whispered against his cheek, feeling the full effects of the cognac.

Anton didn't answer. Instead he let his hand glide down her supple body until it was under the loose T-shirt-pulling, stroking and caressing the rising buds of her desire. Helen's nipples hardened even more as Anton lips covered her parted lips, his hand slid downwards, inch by inch, by inch until it was resting on her flat, taunt stomach.

"Do you want me, Anton?" Helen forced him to speak his desire.

"Yes..." Anton murmured as little sounds of pleasure escaped his lips.

She was beyond words now, her mind totally focused on the pleasure in her body. With a mind of its own Helen's hand reached down for the throbbing member in Anton's pajamas, pulsing hard against her stomach. With haste she undressed him and within moments, Anton lay naked and ready beside her.

Above them the dark sky twinkled with stars that refused to be dulled by the roaring thunder or the deluge from the clouds. Like the heavens, lightening and thunder raged in Helen as Anton's fingers electrified her burning skin. Little groans were escaping his lips as his mouth formed a suction over her breast. Helen's body contorted, her breath gasped and she abandoned herself to the pleasure as Anton's hand gently stroked the inside of her thighs, feeling their smoothness and their quiver.

Suddenly he was climbing farther and farther until his hand finally reached her triangular spot. Helen sinking deeper and deeper into the passion felt the dampness of her delicate honey trace her inner thigh. The fiery eruption of her desire inflamed their passions and drugged their inhibitions. She was drowning in him and he in her and neither of them could stop.

And as their bodies mingled, she rose to meet him with matched passion: violent, giving, and dark—her years of loneliness, resentment and fear melting under the inferno. Their bodies united again and again, expanding the contradiction of the lightness and the darkness of ecstasy, and every fiber, every muscle, every nerve of their being was consumed with lust. Helen abandoned herself to Anton, responding to the uncontrollable, unbearable desire. And as they filled each other with exquisite pleasure, she felt the tears of loneliness kiss her cheeks but she felt safe and loved, and was wishing beyond reality that this night would never end.…Exhausted, they fell asleep wrapped in each other arms.

When Helen awoke, Anton's hand was covering her left breast, and she was snuggled up, fitting perfectly into his embrace. But Helen knew within days or weeks of this most memorable night, Anton, like all the rest, would no longer feel so tenderly towards her. She was prepared for the escape lines, for she had heard them so many times before. "You! How could anyone love you? The only better name they could have chosen for you other than Stern would have been ice. Black Ice." So, with her limited but shattered experience with love, Helen had learned to enjoy only the moment, wishing for nothing more. One moment was all she could have before they would shrink from her power, slip into the realm of uncertainty, lose their erection and soon after, disappear. Miss Sub Zero would have struck again. Helen Stern's heart had no need for the love of a man. Perhaps her heart was no longer beating but for the one passion left, to sit on the sixty-fifth floor in Andrea Jacobson Preston's CEO chair.

Still, glorious could hardly describe the two days they spent together. Incredibly, Helen actually enjoyed having the smell of trout under her fingers and in her hair. She had spent hours sitting by the water throwing her line, anchored with wiggling worms, into the deep lake. While waiting for her fish to bite, her mind kept replaying their first night in the tent. It was bliss. Magical. Powerful. She shuddered with excitement as she remembered the fingers burning desire into her flesh, and she was eager to return to the arms that had promised safety and love. And again and again they had fulfilled each other's desires with a knowingness that they would never again be apart. It was with regret that she left the haven of the watery bliss to return to the concrete jungle of New York.

Chapter Twenty-Two

Chance's contract was in place, and Helen wasted no time in bringing Jake to America permanently. After months of Helen's badgering, Jake finally gave in. Chance's departure was the key card in sealing the whole deal with Jake. It hadn't taken more than three hundred thousand dollars, a lucrative stock option, an apartment on the Avenue, and a chauffeur-driven limo to have all his doubts evaporate. Jake was well worth it, for he had taken the company by storm. The Helen Companies turned into a ball of energy. With his French savvy, he infused into American designers a quasi European style and chic with practicality. Every woman loved him and if not him, his accent. They were willing to work long and hard just to be in his presence. He always had a friendly but challenging air. Jake challenged the good to be better and the better to be best, and before long they had a lean mean working machine in the Helen Companies that was ready to soar to even greater heights. Even Helen, believe it or not, had renewed energy for work.

Chance assumed her position as President of the VIP companies to less than a welcoming bandwagon. Most of the people at VIP realized that Victor was no great leader, and they were not sure if he could actually pick someone who could be. But even though Chance's reputation preceded her, there was still the transition period where she had to prove herself. Elizabeth Star, the operations manager who had assumed most of the responsibilities Victor ignored, was quite annoyed that she was not at least offered the position. She made Chance's first few weeks uncomfortable to say the least. And she had many opportunities to rib her, as poor Chance was pretty much left alone after the first week. Victor, who was playing the CEO's role to a hilt, came into the office no earlier than 1:00 p.m., and therefore Chance was forced to rely on Elizabeth for routines and procedures. On the days when Victor did come in, he was usually gone by 3 or 4 p.m.

"Victor," Chance accosted him a month after she'd assumed her role. "You have to be in the office more often or you have to relinquish full control of the business to me. How am I to proceed if I am not allowed to make certain decisions without you?"

"Chance, I'm sorry. I should have done that a long time ago. As you can see, this is really not my forte. I just wanted to prove to myself that I was not completely useless. Now that I have, I would rather go back to being a man of leisure. Of course, with you at the helm I can relax. Listen, darling," he came to stand in front of her, his warm breath caressing her face. *Did she smell alcohol!* "I am not cut out for this day to day business but what difference does it make, a Palmer will always run the place." He could sense that she was getting tired of him. He had to clench her loyalty.

"What exactly do you mean?"

"It means that I would like you to marry me. I will be the man behind the most brilliant woman in fashion."

"Oh, Oh, Oh, Victor," Chance flew into his embrace. "Oh Victor." She kissed him passionately.

"Well? Is that a yes or a no?"

Neither of them heard the door. Olivia stood speechless and motionless as she watched the embrace. What the fuck!

"Ahem," she cleared her throat to announce her presence.

"Olivia," Victor moved quickly to stand beside Chance. "Come in."

"I hope I'm not interrupting anything important." Her voice was icy cold.

"Only my proposal to Chance. I would say that was pretty important wouldn't you, darling?" He turned to Chance, who was beaming.

"Congratulations, then." Olivia's voice was controlled. "I'm so very happy for you both."

"Thank you." Chance blushed, too happy to notice the edge of disdain in Olivia's voice.

"Which of us would you like to see?" Victor asked, unconcerned with Olivia's displeasure.

"You." Her eyes glared at Chance, but her comment was directed at Victor. "Do you have a moment?"

"Excuse me, will you, darling?" He leaned over to kiss Chance, infuriating Olivia even more. A few doors down from Chance's office, Olivia yanked him into an empty room, ready to run perfect red fingernails across his face.

"What the fuck are you doing?" She was throwing wild punches.

"Hold it, hold it." He grabbed her hands. "I can explain."

"You'd better or else I am going to take you and your fucking company into the pits."

"Come now, Olivia, no threats. I did this for us. You know I hate running this damn company. I've had it. This day to day shit gives me no fucking pleasure. I need Chance's loyalty and that means I have to marry her. If Chance marries me, I will not have to work day in and day out in that damn office. You know how I hate to be cooped up. And how has your marriage interfered with us all these years? It's just a piece of paper, baby, as you well know." He squeezed her tit for effect. "How do you think we can spend our days while my dear wife is working to make us richer than rich? Don't forget that we are a team. Now," he grabbed her by the waist, "do you have a better plan?"

"Humm," her voice was gravel. "You did that for us? Oh darling," she was unzipping her dress, her tongue running excitedly over her lower lip. "Oh darling, you make me crazy."

"Come on, Olivia, not now. I just proposed to my bride and left her. I will come to you tonight."

"Just a quickie," she was running her hand across her belly. He reached for her bag and pulled out the vibrator he knew she always carried. "Take care of yourself until tonight." By the time he left the room she was panting. Stupid horny bitch, he thought to himself. What the hell was he getting himself into. He should have dumped her years ago, but there had never been a good time that wouldn't have backfired.

The entire fashion industry turned out to the nuptials of VIP and Chance, including Bryan Benson. He didn't have an invitation, neither did he need one. His look of entitlement and cavalier charm usually got him wherever he wanted to go. He entered the church and seated himself in the last pew. Chance had never looked prettier, he thought except perhaps…. Oh he shouldn't spoil the evening with his sordid thoughts.

"We are here today to join this man and woman in holy matrimony. If anyone has a reason for this marriage not to take place, speak now or forever hold your peace." There was a pregnant pause.

"I now pronounce you husband and wife. You may kiss the bride." Victor kissed his wife passionately and there was no pretense.

Chance was radiant in a white satin gown with an exaggerated portrait neckline caught in front with a white satin rosebud. The handsewn pearl bodice hugged her slender body, flaring out around her hips in a cascade of starched satin. The swirl of satin opened at the front where more pearls and lace were anchored over her left hip with yet another rosebud, it's stamen of glistening diamonds. In her hand she carried a bouquet of white roses and around her long neck she wore a single strand of Mikimoto pearls. The glamorous dress was a Helen Companies exclusive design. As the organ piped out the marriage waltz, Chance looked up at her husband, a broad smile on her face. She clasped his hand in hers and vowed silently to walk beside him forever.

Thank you, God, she silently prayed. She had never, ever, envisioned so much happiness.

Victor was looking especially dapper in his Christian Dior Parisian black tuxedo. The satin bowtie heightened the crisp white shirt and the gold and black studded buttons. On his lapel he wore a white rose bud.

"I love you," Chance whispered to Victor who smiled lovingly at his wife before his eyes scanned the room for Olivia. Even though Olivia was smiling beguilingly, he could tell she was quite emotional. They exchanged knowing glances as he escorted his bride to the limousine, waiting to take them to the Four Seasons for the wedding reception.

Olivia sat erectly beside Matthew Palmer as Victor kissed his bride. Her soul was boiling with anger, for the kiss was no pretense. It should have been her. After all, she made the son-of-a-bitch.

Bryan fished through his pockets for his gold fountain pen and scribbled a note. Leaving the church, he handed the note to the door attendant and asked that it be given to Chance sometime after the service. In the cool evening of this perfect September dusk, Bryan had finally found a way to continue his abundant life-style. Too bad Franchesca had such an untimely death.

"Congratulations, Mrs. Palmer," the doorman said before handing her the note from the stranger in the church. "Someone left this for you. He said he couldn't stay for the entire ceremony but he wishes you the best life."

"Thank you." Chance stashed the note, pushing it up the sleeve of her gown.

"An admirer already, eh?" Victor smiled as they sped off to the reception. In a fervent embrace, they had both already forgotten about the note.

Hours later they left the reception for their penthouse suite in the Four Seasons. Tomorrow they would fly off to St. Barts for a week's honeymoon.

Inside the room Victor gathered his bride and kissed her intimately as though it was the very first time he had laid hands on her.

"Ummm," Chance cooed. "I love that, and I love you, Victor."

"I love you too, sweetheart."

"I'll be right back," she bustled to the dressing room to rid herself of her elegant but most uncomfortable wedding frock. As she slipped the contraption over her shoulders and slid it down her shapely legs, the crumbled piece of paper from the doorman fell out. She retrieved and opened the note.

Next week, September 15, meet me at the Chinois. Don't be late. You know just how much I hate waiting.—Bryan.

Chance let the paper drop from her hand as though it had acid on it that burned right through her skin. How did he find her? How did he know to turn up at her wedding? Oh God! What was she going to do now?

Victor Innes Palmer could not believe he was betrothed. Never in his wildest dreams had he ever thought this day would arrive. He found solace in the thought that it was more of a business deal than a foolhardy decision such as love. He needed Chance for many reasons: to get rid of Olivia, to stay closer to Helen, and to run his budding empire before his incompetence became too evident. Well, he consoled himself, it was not really incompetence but rather a short attention span. Yet, in his own way he did very much like Chance. She was beautiful, passionate, ambitious, and really quite expert in the bedroom. He licked his lips in anticipation of the evening to come. To look at his wife no one would guess that she was actually kinky.

Chance fumbled with her hair, her nightgown and finally with trembling hands sprayed on her perfume. Why did Bryan have to spoil her evening? She had to do her best to appear normal, for such disclosures on her wedding night could end the marriage before it started.

Calmly she walked into the room where her husband was already waiting for her in bed. She felt disconnected as her mind traveled down memory lane.

She was sixteen years old and already Chantel Stevenson was burdened by life. Her parents, full-fledged alcoholics, cared nothing about their two daughters. Chastity, her younger sister, was only thirteen and already she was plagued with illnesses mostly from a bad diet. Chantel, feeling completely responsible for her sister and parents, was forced to hold the family together. With no money to pay the normal bills, she worked odd jobs to help make ends meet. But the money was hard to come by because she was a minor and not legitimately able to work. At nights she was waiting tables at the Bussy Den, a strip bar. She was so made up that if the place got raided no cop would ever think she was less than thirty. That was where she met Franchesca.

At thirteen years old Franchesca was sent to America on a one-way ticket to get away from Brazil. Her parents were too poor to find passage for themselves, but scraped up enough money to send their beautiful daughter to America to make her mark in the world. Franchesca went straight to the address her parents had given. They told her it was the home of an American who they had made friends with when he was in Brazil, and that he would be glad to put her up until she could manage on her own. When she asked for Mr. Walton, no one knew of whom she spoke. Compelled to support herself, she used her only asset to find work. By the time Franchesca was sixteen she was already a budding druggie with her own pimp. As she told the story, she was the hottest hooker in town. She was always well dressed and well sought after.

"Why do you bother with this chump change?" Franchesca drawled as Chantel cleaned the table. "You're the daughter of those drunks, no? Tryin' to support them are you?"

"Sorta." Chantel was careful. No telling who was undercover.

"I can introduce you to a real gig. You'll make enough money in one night to take care of your family for three months at a time. I have saved over fifty thousand dollars. I send some back to my parents. As soon as they get their visa, they'll be here, and I will no longer have to do this shit."

"And how did you make all that money?"

"Bryan. He is wonderful to me. Gets me all kinds of gigs that pay well."

"What kinds of gigs. I really need to find a job. I had been working at the supermarket in town, but I was just fired. Missed too much time taking care of my parents and sister. This is my last resort."

"Well, this job would suit you just fine. You can pick your own hours."

"Do you think Bryan would help me get a job?"

"Of course, he'd love to. Come with me to this party tonight, and I will introduce you."

Some party it was. Chantel never realized that such subversive places existed right under the nose of the law. Sex, drugs and rock and roll was putting it mildly. By the time she left the party she had done coke, slept with men and women alike, and earned a wad of money. She was prime for her new profession as a night hooker. Not the sleazy street walking hooker, but an upscale entertainment audience that provided the best champagne, drugs and kinky sex. She ignored her nagging conscience in favor of the money, and the money kept coming. By the time she was nineteen she had had enough. She ran away from home, leaving money for her sister to take care of her parents. She just couldn't take it anymore. Chantel checked herself into a rehab center and quit drugs cold turkey. She was never going to be like her parents. Never!

She applied to New York University and was accepted. Despite her dark life she had been able to maintain her grades in school. Chantel moved to the city and two years later sent for her sister, Chastity. She couldn't afford to go anywhere too small for she needed a city in which she could get lost. With the money she had saved, she paid her tuition in cash.

"This is our only hope. I know it's going to be hard, but it's the only way we can help mama and papa," she explained to her sister. "If we make it, we can help them. If we don't try we are doomed to a life of worthlessness.

We have to change our names and our identity just to be sure no one finds us. I love you." She kissed her sister, who was still only eighteen.

Together, the girls made a pact to break the negative cycle of children of alcoholics no matter what. They changed their names from Chantel and Chastity Stevenson to Chance and Christy Livingston. They were not accidental names because a chance was exactly what they were taking and they needed Christ to protect them along their perilous way. Two teenagers in New York City were fair game for anything.

Working at menial jobs, the girls set out to conquer the world. The only thing they had in abundance was hope, although Chance still had some money she had stashed away from her years as a hooker. Every week Chance added their paychecks together and took care of their bills. Every Monday morning she also bought a money order and took the bus to New Jersey to mail it to her parents. There was never a note or a return address. As far as her parents were concerned it was money from the Almighty.

Christy went on to law school after her four years at Pratt Institute, and Chantel went into Design and Fashion at Parsons Institute for Fashion. Chance lived only for her school and her work, avoiding men like the plague. So when she met Trent, she was emotionally isolated and starved for affection. He offered a place where she could lay her burden. Unfortunately their love didn't last long, for he had been killed in a fatal accident one night after they'd had an argument. Chance had never forgiven herself. She threw herself into her work and vowed it was all she ever wanted in life.

When she returned to the present, Victor was groaning and breathing hard, his body moving up and down above her. She was repulsed. Tonight of all nights, her wedding night, she felt like a whore. Suddenly, it was as it had been with all those men she didn't even know: animal, sleazy, and unfulfilling. Damn the bastard, Bryan. How did he find her? And what the hell could he want?

"Oh, Chance, it's good. Real….oh, oh, oh, really…." Her husband was in the throes of passion. Chance couldn't even pretend to be having a good time, for instead of looking at the ceiling and making noises as she would have, she squeezed back the tears brimming in her eyes. What a disappointment she felt on her wedding night. Victor collapsed on her, spent. And the only thought in her mind was that she would get Bryan. If he ever tried to hurt her she would kill him.

Anton dialed Helen's office three times and hung up. It was months, and she had not bothered to call since their fishing trip. Of course, she was gracious; she had e-mailed him a thank-you note. How hi-tech, he thought with annoyance. As cold a thank you as anyone could get. Why not one of those sentimental Hallmark cards or a more intimate expression of thanks? Because, he answered, she didn't want to spend the time looking. How about having her secretary send flowers; she hadn't even thought of it, he figured. But she was not that cold on their night together in the tent. The fact that he had heard her purr his name over and over again in the throes of passion told him she cared somewhat. They had floated from bliss to ecstasy, their entwined bodies demanding, giving, and accepting the wondrous dance of magic. And his eyes had devoured her with ravenous desire, her own need glistening in the dark glossy eyes. And the softness of her nakedness, hazelnut in the glow of the candles, left him awakened to every sensory feeling of love.

The strident sound of the telephone jolted Anton.

"DePaul." It was his private line

"Helen Stern. Anton, must you always use your last name when you answer your private line?"

"Habit. Must you always use both your names when you call. Good afternoon, Helen. Did I miss an appointment?"

"Don't be daft. I just wanted to thank you in person for the fishing trip. I know it's been awhile but I hope you got my e-mail."

"Certainly did. I was just here ruminating about its personal touch."

"Ah, get with it. This is a hi-tech world. I hope I didn't get you at a bad time."

"No. I have twenty minutes before I have to examine the closing papers of Lorimar's deal. I don't actually have to be there, but I need to meet with my colleagues on last-minute details."

"Well, don't let me hold you up. Good to know you work on a Sunday. Just wanted to say thanks for a lovely time."

"Want to have dinner later?"

"Wish I could, but I have finally committed to finish work in my apartment today. It's been moths of living out of boxes and I can't stand another day in this chaos. Another time."

"It was a wonderful time, wasn't it. You know you've lost the bet, don't you? And by the way, I must tell you, you are a terrible fisherman."

"Fisher-person," she corrected. "You have to be politically correct." It was Helen's time to have some fun with Anton now. He always had fun at her expense.

Helen hung up the phone regretting that she had not taken him up on his dinner invitation. Reluctantly she returned to dragging furniture from one end of the room to the other. She was having a hard time arranging the room just the way she wanted it. Everything seemed to be in the wrong place. Worn out, she finally plopped down on the yellow silk couch in her sweaty jogging suit. She looked around the room and, although pleased with the new architecture of her Park Avenue *pied-à-terre*, she was entirely displeased with the progress of her organization. Boxes were still strewn everywhere, pictures were still lying against walls, and furniture was still bunched up in the center of the room. She should have taken up the interior designer's offer to whip the place into shape, but she really needed her home to have a personality that reflected her own style.

Realizing she was drenched in sweat and probably dehydrated, Helen padded into the sunny kitchen, the floor cool under her feet. She rummaged around the sparse closet to find some alcohol and then decided to have something colder. In the center of the refrigerator was the six pack of Redstripe beer she had picked up at a specialty store. She had been buying it ever since her trip to Jamaica when Cecil introduced her to its thirst-quenching ability after a hot day. Reseating herself, this time on a burgundy and yellow fatois, she stretched her feet out on the footrest. Frankly, even in her chaos she felt calm; calmed by the wonderful night she had spent in Anton DePaul's arms. But the distance she'd had put between them was necessary if she was to survive.

Around seven o'clock, the doorbell rang. Helen braced herself against the rash of reprimands she would get from her mother for taking so long to invite her over to see her new digs. She hadn't invited her because the state of the apartment was still in shambles. This was her weekend to have everything in order, so why didn't people leave her alone. She deliberated on answering the door, chiding herself for not moving into one of those security ridden places where no one could get in without being announced. Somehow, though, that seemed rather stifling. Anyway it could be her mother or Reginald, for only they had her address. She flung the door open ready with all the defenses she could muster.

"It's a mess but...Anton!"

"Hi." He handed her a dozen yellow roses. "Thought I'd bring you a house redecorating gift and dinner. Chicken salad." The irony of the yellow rose escaped them both. In Haitian culture, the yellow rose means revenge and in American culture it means coming home.

"Ahh...thanks," she took the flowers stepping aside so he could enter. "As you can see, I was not expecting company."

"If it's a bad time..."

"No, of course not. As long as you don't mind eating on the floor and having beer for desert, I can handle this. How did you know where to find me?"

He handed her the delivery paper that had fallen out in his truck. "Must have been from when you called Mrs. Walters from the truck. I've been trying to use this as an excuse to see you for months. After hearing you voice I couldn't resist.

"How controlled. Come in. As you can see, not much is done. Let me arrange the roses and I'll be with you in a minute. They are so beautiful, thank you." She inhaled the aromatic smell as she put a single rose in a crystal vase ontop of the piano.

"Do you know it is believed that the rose was created from a mixture of Aphrodite's tears and blood as she deeply mourned her wounded lover Adonis?"

"I hadn't a clue. Well, it was a noble thing for the goddess of love to do for her lover. It has made many women happy."

After they arranged the flowers and placed the vase on a make shift coffee table, Helen began her search for utensils.

"Now let's see…eh…I think the linen box is in the pantry. Wait here a minute. Don't want you suing me for workers compensation from this unsafe environment. You could very well fall flat on your face trying to navigate around these boxes," Helen said, pushing open the kitchen door. Inside were a zillion boxes! Futilely she tried to remember in which of the boxes she had packed the linen. Giving up in desperation, she returned to the living room. Anton was upon the raised platform by the piano. She noticed he had cleared a spot for them by stacking boxes. It was just enough room for the two of them. Spreading an old cloth he found on a large box, he made a makeshift table in the middle of the floor. On the monstrosity was the boxed food and plastic utensils. Helen without remark placed the pack of Red Stripe beer on the table.

"Red Stripe! That's what you had at the Shark Bar. How did you acquire that taste?"

"Like everyone else, of course, I watched *The Firm*." She smiled as he looked puzzled. Obviously he had not seen the movie. "Actually I spent some time in Jamaica many years ago and found that it was the only thing that could quench my thirst. Really got to like the stuff." She twisted off a bottle top and handed him a cold lager.

"Thanks." He twirled the bottle in his hand as though it was an expensive glass of wine before taking a generous swig. "Shall I help you move things around after dinner?"

"Yes, that would be a big help. I told the interior decorator I wanted to arrange everything myself. Big mistake since I don't have a husband. I guess that's why women get married; so their husbands can move heavy stuff." She answered the question in his eyes.

"I hope not. I hope to get married for love. What about you?"

"I don't think that's in the cards for me."

"Why not?"

"'Cause I have never given it much thought. I have always been a career woman, and men don't seem to like women like that. I have a job to do, Anton, and it comes before anything else. My work takes up just about all the energy I have, and I don't think it's fair to start something one may never be able to finish."

"Speak for yourself. I happen to know how to multi-task. And I happen to know that I care about you a lot."

Helen smiled. "Don't," she said solemnly. "I think you are better off with someone who has a heart to give and wants to give it."

"And you don't?"

"Not just yet," she answered, handing him a container of chicken salad.

"What if I say I'm prepared to wait?"

"That's your decision, Anton, but you should expect very little from me."

"What about our night together? Didn't it mean anything to you?"

"I live only in the moment."

"But you begged me not to leave you!"

"Passion has a language all its own."

"What's so terrible about your life, Helen, that you have to remain so distant? Can't you see I'm trying to make you fall in love with me?"

"It's no use. My heart is already taken with its own obsession. Don't wait for me, Anton. Find yourself someone who really appreciates you. Find yourself another girl."

Suddenly Anton ran toward the piano, his body jigging before the music started. In the fashion of Jerry Lee Lewis he belted out the song, both vocally and on the ivories, of *Find Yourself Another Girl*. Helen, helpless and reduced to fits of laughter, began her own jig as she joined the singing…*another girl, doo doo, who loves you true, true, true.* As Anton's fingers danced over the ivory keys of the Steinway, Helen felt a deep longing to be in his arms. *She loved him. She loved him very much.*

Chapter Twenty-Three

Bryan spat on his leather shoe and rubbed out the scuffmarks. The broad had better show up this time. How dare she stand him up three times? This was his last request before he applied real pressure. Had it not been for Franchesca, he would never have found the bitch. Never would he forgive her for running out on him all those years before. She was his best hooker and his best lay. Now she was an important harlot with a sordid past that could be worth millions to him. Married to the pretty-boy Palmer, she most certainly wouldn't want her past rearing its ugly head. Bryan winced as he put on the shiny shoes. Years of crappy shoes had given him awful corns. Even the podiatrist couldn't do much. A final look in the mirror, and he walked out the door to meet Mrs. Chance Palmer and a million bucks.

Chance waited until Victor had left. Feigning a headache, she told him she would go to the office a little later than usual. For a moment she thought of packing her things and flying off into the sunset as she had done years before, but she didn't want to risk all she had worked so hard for without at least trying to reason with Bryan.

When she finally left the house, no one would have known she was Chance Palmer. Dressed in a floppy brimmed hat, wide legged pants, a well-worn smock and outdated dark glasses, she looked exactly like a bag lady trying to be fashionable. Slipping though the back door into the garage, she swiftly made her way to the prearranged spot. She parked the Porsche Carrera four blocks away and walked towards Huntley Street.

Bryan looked at his watch in annoyance. He glanced around. There was no one in sight but a dowdy old bag lady. He pulled out his cellular phone and dialed the number to Chance's office.

"Looking for me?" she said right behind him

Bryan spun around to see the bag lady he had noticed coming up the street.

"My, my baby, you look very different from the other day at your wedding. Is this a disguise or has your husband found out about you and thrown you out?" He tipped the brim of her hat, allowing his hand to linger on her cheek.

"None of your damn business." She knocked his hand from her face. "What the hell do you want, Bryan? No, don't answer that. A little sleaze like you could only want one thing. I see you've still not learned the value of a hard or honest day's work."

"Don't be so on the attack, sweetie," he touched her cheek. "We used to make beautiful music together."

"Don't ever lay your filthy hands on me again," Chance angrily slapped his hand away from her. "Now you have two minutes to say what you want."

"Well I have two things. A good-bye message from Franchesca and a financial request."

"Franchesca!" Chance was taken back. "You bastard." She was trying to scratch his face. "What do you know of Franchesca's death?"

"Everything, of course. But right now I don't want to talk about it. I've been adding up the interest since your disappearance from the business. It was a terrible thing to do to your old man. I was heart broken. Mrs. Palmer, or shall I say Chantel, you owe me a lot of bread. I would say a cool million might take care of my hurt and disappointment."

"What! Where do you expect me to get that kind of money?"

"Your in-laws, of course. My dear, you just married into one of the richest families, and from what I understand your husband's company is doing marvelously, especially now that you are running it. I want a million dollars, Chantel." His voice was sinister, "or I'll ruin your life. And if you push me too hard," he slid his hand over her breast, "you'll go the way of your dear friend and traitor, Franchesca."

"I said don't fuckin' touch me, you bastard." She slapped him hard across the face. "And don't ever threaten my life." Chance was frightened, but she knew showing fear to a cockroach like Bryan would be like slitting her own wrist.

"You've gotten feisty, whore." His voice was low and menacing. "Don't you ever do that again or I will gut you right here. Now, you low-down whore, I said a million will take care of my disappointment."

"I cannot afford one million dollars. So you might as well kill me now, Bryan."

Bryan was agitated. He spat on the ground and wiggled his numb feet in the too-tight leather shoes. "Eight hundred thousand."

"Four hundred," Chance rebutted

"Half a million, and that's my final offer."

"I will have to make it in monthly installments of ten thousand a month for five years. Take it or leave it, Bryan. I am in no mood to negotiate. And just one more thing, why did you have to snuff out Franchesca?"

"She was back on the sauce, the heavy stuff too. Blew all her money up her nose as usual. Who do you think she came running to? I had her handling some deals for me to make extra bread and she fucked up. When I went to collect my money she didn't have it. Told me all kind of stories. Told me she would get the money. I suppose that's when she tried to call you but you weren't home. Too bad she was so messed up she didn't even realize I was still there. That's how I found you. When I heard your voice on the answering machine I almost flipped. Would have known your voice anywhere." He paused and looked intensely at Chance. "I was in love with you, Chantel. I was really hurt when you left."

"You pig," she spat in his face. "You've never been in love with anyone but your filthy self. Where shall I send the money?"

Bryan pulled out a pocket-handkerchief and wiped his face. He would have killed any bitch that did this to him but he needed the money. Sleaze-bag thought for a moment. There was a lot he could do with ten grand a month, and spreading it out over time was not a bad idea as he was a little irresponsible with money.

"Here," he handed her a check leaf. But I want twenty thousand immediately. And that does not count as part of the half a mil."

"Fine. But you will never see me again and you must never, do you understand never contact me. If after the five years you decide to continue to blackmail me, you should think again. Powerful families have ways of getting rid of scum. I will have twenty thousand dollars deposited into your account by tomorrow at five. Every month on the fifth you will get funds wired to that account. Now Bryan, if you ever as much as call my name again I will kill you myself, and I won't mind going to jail."

"No need to be so mad, my little Chantel, we had good times together. I was truly heartbroken when you left. Really I was. Just think of this as alimony."

"Go fuck yourself." Chance moved swiftly out of the disgusting presence of Bryan. How had she ever gotten into such a life? To think she used to hook for that nasty specimen much less sleep with him. In her car, she drove like a madwoman until she reached her home. Inside Chance jumped into the steaming shower, and stayed in the hot water until she was almost a prune. *She could go to the police. No, she couldn't. Bryan had told her about Franchesca because he knew she would do anything to avoid a scandal. She hated him.* One hour later, she was on her way to the office, her hands trembling as she careened sidewalks and corners in her Porsche. Thank God that was over. She hoped she never heard from the weasel again.

Chapter Twenty-Four

Summer

Reginald tapped on the calculator keys. Something was not quite right. This break he was working with the finance department and found the work exciting. His job was to categorize and track the spending of both the VIP and the Helen companies and see how to cut cost by 10%. Reginald sat back in the chair and looked over the records again.

"Ms. Harris." He buzzed through to his assistant. "Come in, please."

"Yes, sir." She was promptly in the office, for she could look at Reginald Palmer all day.

"Will you bring me the records for several of these cash transactions for the VIP company? I needed to examine them closer for proper categorization."

Reginald spent all afternoon crouched in his office trying to track the destination of the cash. Listed simply as cash payment for merchandise, he couldn't understand why it was from one particular account that was nowhere on his ledger. He rang the bank.

"Chembank. Mrs. Dailey speaking. How may I help you?"

"Reginald Preston from The VIP Company. I am trying to verify that a check has been cashed, and I want to know by whom."

"That account number and tax I.D. number, please?" the voice requested.

He gave her the number, and she went off the phone. Moments later: "I'm sorry, Sir. The check is not cashed, it's wired to an account in Switzerland every month on the fourth."

"By whom?"

"I'm not able to tell, Sir, from these records."

"What bank in Switzerland?"

"The Swiss Continental."

This was rather curious. Reginald hung up the phone and dialed Switzerland. In his fluent French he asked for information about the transfers.

"The funds are wired to a Bryan Benson in Long Island. It is listed as a payroll transaction," the clerk told him.

Funny. Reginald scratched his head. He had pored over all the employees at the VIP companies, for he needed to see who could be eliminated once the Initial Public Offering and possible merger took place with the Helen Companies. After examining the personnel records of each employee, he was quite familiar with the names. He didn't remember a Bryan Benson. Bryan Benson seemed to have no records at all. Of course, it was possible that he was an overseas employee on contract. But why send the funds back to the U.S.?

"Ms. Harris," he called his assistant again, "could you ask personnel to send up the records of a Bryan Benson."

"They can't find anything on a Bryan Benson." She returned after fifteen minutes empty-handed. Shall I track it down, Sir?"

"No, no. I'll take care of it. Someone must have the records out. I'll just wait until they return it. Thanks."

But Reginald did not ask anyone. He simply traced the transaction of the deposits. Every two weeks five thousand dollars was deposited into the Swiss bank account and the fourth of every month sent back to this Bryan Benson in the U.S.A. The account in Switzerland, however, was set up in Chance's name. Maybe he should just leave well enough alone. Finally he categorized the expense as miscellaneous.

Weeks later he was putting the final touch on his financial analysis when Helen shoved her head around the door.

"Want to have lunch with your big sister?"

"As long as you are buying, Sis. You are, as they would say, a magnate." He held up the almost finished report.

"So? Why do I have to buy lunch? Wealth is what I've worked for and deserve. We'll go Dutch."

"Stingy, stingy."

Lunch was at the noisy Planet Hollywood on West 57th.

"Everything looks great on paper," Reginald said. I have found a way to cut cost by 15%. The company is doing fantastically. Congrats. By the way, do you know what department a Bryan Benson belongs to, or is he a consultant?"

"Never heard of him. But then again I don't know the hundreds of employees by name."

"So now, Sis," Reggie had a gut feeling to change the subject, "how's your love life?"

"I don't have one."

"What ever happened to that Anton fellow Mom hates so much?"

"Don't ask. Who are you seeing?"

"Can you keep a secret?"

"Secret? Reginald, who could you possibly be seeing that's a secret."

"I'm not seeing her yet, but Christ I have never been so smitten."

"Do I know her?"

"Yep."

"So who is she?"

"I changed my mind I don't want to talk about it."

"C'mon," Helen prodded, but Reginald for the first time was tight-lipped.

Reginald knocked on the door and waited. It was way after the offices had closed, but he knew she was still there.

"Just a moment," the sweetest voice he had ever heard replied.

He mopped his face and paced slightly.

"Yes?" The door opened and in the dimly lit office the woman glowed like an angel.

"Reginald? Ah, come in. I was just going over some last-minute figures before leaving. What are you still doing here?"

Her perfume, *Yellow*, was a Helen Companies exclusive, and it permeated his nostrils as his eyes traveled down the perfect body to the stocking clad, shoeless feet.

"I just finished the numbers for cost cutting. Congratulations. You have done a marvelous job with the VIP companies. Could hardly find anything to cut."

"Why, how sweet of you to stop by to tell me this." She beckoned to the sofa. "Thanks. May I offer you a drink?" Chance noticed Reginald's eyes glued to her lips. Nah, she was imagining things. He was just a baby. But what a baby he was. She certainly wouldn't throw him out with the bath water.

"Cognac."

"Now that you are done with the financial work what will you be working on next?" She watched his eyes follow her everywhere. She felt a little quiver in her groin. What exactly was wrong with her? Granted, she was sick of Victor and his constant drinking, but it wasn't his fault she was icing the relationship for fear of getting too close. But Reginald? No! She would not play where she worked.

"Actually, I hope I can get to work with the IPO team."

"We can arrange that, I'm sure. But tell me, why did you come up tonight?"

"Actually, there is just one thing I need clearing up before I submit my report."

"And that is?" She smiled as she handed him the drink and sat next to him on the sofa, her eyes making four with his before she looked away.

"Do you know a Bryan Benson?"

Chance stiffened.

"Am I supposed to?"

"I'm not sure. I just wanted to know if you know about the deposit that is made to an account in Switzerland in your name and then resent to the U.S."

Oh shit. Finally. She had to think fast. Reginald was no fool and she heard he was a financial wizard. The next Wall Street wunderkind, no doubt. But how on earth did he get those books? Christ, she must have accidentally given it to Muriel with all the others. How could she have been so careless?

"What did you say the name was again?"

"Bryan Benson. He must be a consultant or something, for personnel has no record of him." He could tell she was nervous. Something was wrong here.

"Err. Bryan Benson." She was visibly twisting her hands. Not a woman used to lying.

"Is this something you want me to overlook? I can hide it better than it is right now, if that's what you want."

Chance choked back the tears. "Why would you do that for me?"

"Because," his hand rested on her soft stocking clad legs, "you seem to need me to."

"Oh God." She buried her face in her hands.

"Listen, we all know about Victor's drinking. If you're trying to build a nest egg, it's okay. I just think you should bury it deeper; it's a little exposed."

"Oh, my dear Reginald. I wouldn't want to drag you into this mess. It's a long story. You shouldn't have had that account. I gave it to Muriel by accident."

"I'm sorry. I didn't know. How can I help?"

She raised her face and looked into the kindest eyes she had seen in years. She trusted him.

"I can't...."

"What is it, Chance? I can help you."

"Oh no you can't," she was sobbing. "Nobody can help me."

"Why not try me?"

"It's so sordid and so dangerous, but I need to tell someone. Oh God, I'm so alone in this world. I don't know where to turn, Reginald, and I don't know who to turn to."

"I'm here," he said softly. "You can trust me."

When Chance had finished her story her face was contorted in pain and shame, the black mascara streaking ugly blotches under her eyes. "I didn't mean to burden you, Reginald but there is no one…no one I can turn to." He cradled her head and rested it on his shoulder. "Thank you," she looked up at him, tears still streaming down her face.

Carried away by the moment his lips were on hers, demanding, understanding and comforting, Chance did not resist, and she allowed the warm, tender kiss to momentarily allay her pain, her disappointment with life, and her fears.

"We mustn't," she pleaded, but was too in need to stop him. By the time his hand slid under her blouse, she had forgotten that he was twelve years her junior and that she was married. It wasn't anything more than emotional comfort. Their intertwined bodies slid to the floor. Reginald slowly undressed her and took complete control of the moment. She felt like a woman for the first time in a long time and not the hooker that she had been many years before. By the time they were spent in each other's arms, she was crying softly against his chest.

By morning, Reginald Preston knew all there was to know about Chance and Bryan Benson. That very morning, he erased all the files that pointed to the Swiss bank account and returned the books to her for safekeeping.

"Not in this building. A safety deposit box," he told her. Chance was lucky that he was working on the project.

Reginald had been attracted to Chance before he came to work for Helen. In fact, he wanted to work for Helen just to be near her. Having doggedly watched her when she came to the Hamptons with Helen, and often inviting himself over when he knew she would be working at Helen's place, his infatuation had deepened to an obsession. He never quite understood what it was about her that made him crazy. Maybe it was the unique blending of helplessness and strength that she exuded. Whatever it was it kept him hankering. In reality, there was nothing helpless about Chance, yet, he felt this need to protect her. When she married Victor he had been devastated. Now working in the office where he saw her daily only intensified his crush on her.

Bryan was living high off the hog. He was, in his own right, a celebrity. This morning his bed was empty, thank goodness. Springing out of bed, Bryan grabbed a glass of freshly squeezed orange juice and glided to the mailbox. It was time for his monthly Christmas present. Oh, he loved Christmas everyday! Collecting the mail, Bryan headed back up the driveway of his expensive house on Long Island. If only his neighbors knew who they were living next to. Ah, screw them, he thought. He wasn't a pimp anymore. Well, not the kind that runs women anyway. No more sleazy life for him if his luck keeps up. Now he was Mr. Suave. He had women like flies, and not the hooking kinds either. No sirree, the wealthy bored matrons and their daughters. It was great as he didn't have to spend his money on them and paying his way somehow salved their morality. How the tables had turned. Thanks to little old Chance. Sifting through the mail, he did not see the familiar envelope. He threw envelope after envelope to the ground, hoping it was stuck to another. No Envelope! He picked up the phone and dialed Chance's home number.

"I'm sorry. The number you have dialed is no longer in service. The new number is unavailable."

"Bitch."

Well maybe he was overreacting. He'd wait until Monday. But for three days no mail arrived that he wanted to see. Bryan dressed quickly in his thousand-dollar Italian suit and headed for downtown Manhattan. He was stopped by the security guard.

"Who are you here to see?' the guard asked.

"Mrs. Chance Palmer."

"And who may I say is calling?"

"Bryan. Bryan Benson."

The young man buzzed upstairs. Moments later.

"I'm sorry sir. She does not know who you are."

The downright snooty Bitch. She would know him all right. He had a good mind to blow up the bitch, but going to the press would be better. Nah, that wouldn't work. He'd never make as much money selling his story as he could get from her. Now why would she risk the exposure? Something was up. The sneaky whore. He had to try a new tactic. That night he wrote three letters. One to Victor Palmer, one to Chance and one to Helen Stern. "Aye," he touched himself, that Stern woman made him crazy. Ever since he first saw her he'd been fantasizing about doing her. He'd imagined her in the jungle, her black body…"Ah shit, enough." He removed his hand from his crotch. The bitch didn't even know he existed, but she would now. Franchesca had told him about Helen, and he'd seen her on TV the night she'd modeled in Paris while poor, poor Franchesca was rotting. He would mail Chance's letter first with an ultimatum. For the little fiasco she pulled, the price for his silence was now doubled. If she didn't respond in five days he would blackmail the others. Hell, he'd blackmail the others anyway. A scandal like this would destroy Helen's plans of going public and Helen Stern and Mr. Very Important Person, Victor, wouldn't want that. Bryan knew his silence had to be worth a pretty penny. A million here, a million there would be peanuts to the likes of the golden children. He'd heard the broad Helen Stern was rich, rich, rich. If he sent that kinky photo of Chance along that would definitely get some action.

Chance was nervous, but Reginald reassured her he knew what he was doing. That he'd stuck by her even after knowing of her sordid past showed a loyalty that was uncommon. For this, and because her marriage to Victor was falling apart, they became secret lovers.

"Listen to me." Reginald turned her to face him. "This guy is a sleaze. He gains nothing if he goes public. The benefit is to blackmail you. No one in the press would pay him more than a few hundred dollars, maybe a thousand for his story. That's not enough for Bryan. He's greedy. He'll remain quiet as long as the checks keep coming. Blackmail is what he's into. I say we visit the punk at the address you had the checks mailed. Shake him down a bit. Tell him you won't pay another dime and that you're willing to have your past touted all over the place. That he should drop dead. If that doesn't shake him up, we'll break his legs. Guys like this won't go away unless you make them."

"But I couldn't bear being exposed like that. I will…"

"What! This story is tame. Chance, this is the fashion Industry, anything goes."

"Maybe for models and designers, but not for corporate executives. And at a time like this? No, Reginald, I couldn't."

When he kissed her trembling lips reassuringly, she was impassioned but not convinced of what her future would bring. Nonetheless, she followed him. They waited until it was dark before driving by the address in Long Island. It was a sprawling house partially hidden by trees. Reginald turned off the car headlights before driving up the circular driveway. He told Chance to duck down until he found out who actually lived there. Reginald rang the doorbell.

"Who is it?"

"Reginald Preston. I have a message for you from Mrs. Palmer."

"Yeah, what did the bitch say?" Bryan opened the door, a cigar cocked between his lips. Reginald expected to see a low life, greasy, dirtball, but instead a tall, handsome, clean-cut guy, dressed in silk pajamas, answered the door. He couldn't have been more than forty.

"So, what the hell did the hussy say?"

Reginald clenched his fist trying to gain control. He was so pissed he'd gladly make this guy swallow a few teeth.

"That she is not going to pay you another dime. She's already told her husband about her past. You have no ammunition. It's over, Bryan, and if you continue, she'll go to the police about Franchesca."

Bryan was agitated. Real agitated. He'd fix the whore. "Well, Mr. Pretty boy, you give the lady of the night a message for me." With that he drew his hand across his throat. "She is a dead woman."

Helen opened the perfumed letter addressed to her in sprawling, almost illegible handwriting. A secret admirer! Maybe Anton trying to get her to see him. After their night in the apartment, when she had again fallen into his arms, again, so vulnerable and happy that she almost babbled everything and anything, she completely withdrew. She refused his calls, flowers, cards and visits and she had fired him even before she had hired him. Helen couldn't go on pretending she would allow him to handle the IPO, and this was a good way out. No way was she going to fall into his love trap, either, and become a forlorn idiot. Hurriedly she unfolded the matching paper and read the letter in disbelief. Dear God. Chance! Blackmail!

"If you don't want this all over the paper, you'll need to pay five million dollars."

"Oh for chrissake," Helen hissed, she couldn't afford a scandal like this right now. How had she missed this information. As every other core employee, she had had the girl investigated. In her portfolio of usable data, she knew that Chance's parents were alcoholics. Helen had kept the information in her safe with all the other vital facts she needed. But a prostitute! Her sources hadn't dug deep enough! Maybe the letter was a hoax. Its anonymity told her that whoever sent it was lying low. So how was she to know where to send the money? She supposed she should expect a call. But by God that was indeed Chance in the picture.

She would never have guessed. Who could have such a vendetta against Chance, she wondered. Hell. Just her bloody luck to have something this ugly rear its head at a time like this. Both stocks were due to go public in a week! She simply had to find out who sent the letter and soon. Helen examined the postmark. Manhattan. Shit, that could be several million people.

Out of a hidden compartment in her desk, Helen removed a single key. She pushed open the liquor cabinet and pressed a discrete black button. The left side of the cabinet slid back noiselessly. She inserted the key and carefully placed the letter inside the cabinet along with all the take-over papers for JI. Helen then entered the sound proof apartment attached to her office and punched out a number on the telephone keypad. She had no time to wait for phone calls.

Victor tore open the FEDEX letter addressed to him, carrying the instructions to request his signature only. What was this all about? He flipped over the envelope to look at the name of the sender. The scribble was almost illegible. As he opened the envelope a photo fell to the floor. Oh, he was disappointed; it was just one of his paramours sending a lewd photo of herself, no doubt. Those things had long ceased to entice him. Curious to find out which one it was, he turned the picture over. His mouth fell open in disbelief. Chance! His wife. He had no idea she was still interested in him. How cute she'd sent him a photo to try and make up. But who was the other woman in the picture? Christ, he knew his wife was kinky but...this! He felt a certain regret about the way things had turned out between them. But he couldn't help who he was. After all, he could keep his end of the bargain but she had insisted on not sleeping with him. Sure he was drunk most of the time when he came in from carousing, but that was life with the VIP. After his marriage to Chance he had come to the realization that he really preferred bimbo type women who were just satisfied with what he had to give. This photo could mean his wife was a bimbo after all. He opened the letter.

"This was your wife seventeen years ago. She was my whore and my girl. Wouldn't you like to have been the one being whipped and chained? If you don't want this in the papers you will have to pay five million dollars."

Blackmail! Victor turned the letter over to see if it was signed. No such luck. What the hell was going on and what the hell was he going to do? Victor looked closer at the picture and there was no doubt it was his wife, down to the heart-shaped birthmark on her ass. No wonder she was such an expert in bed. Christ, the only fuckin' luck he ever had in his life was bad luck. If any of this ever got out, his father would disown him, and he would lose the respect he had worked so hard to earn. Victor had to know who had sent the letter. Should he confront Chance? What a damn mess!

Bryan had to find a job to keep up with his mortgage payment and he was annoyed. Annoyed that both his women had finked on him. Rotten bastards. He should treat that Chance to the same send off as Franchesca. How dare she send some boy over to his house to pimp him? He of all people. Didn't she know he was master of the game? Yeah, she might as well kiss her life good-bye.

Living large, Bryan had spent every dime he got from Chance because he knew that the money would flow for five years. Now barely a year later the broad had gotten nervy, and here he was broke. Changing into his leather gear, Bryan wondered what he had done with all the money anyway? Ah yeah. The marching band: right now he actually needed a fix of the white powder before he went cruising. Shit! Now he couldn't be discriminating about his clientele. Tonight he would have to pick up quite a few rich men to keep up his life style; and he hated those rich bastards. Bored with their wives, these closeted types were the worst, but paid the best. They were so very kinky. Between his rich women, whom he would now have to charge double, and his sundry night activities, he might make out okay. Damn! He'd been on his way to giving up the life of fucking his way to success, he was thinking as he got into the black Mercedes.

"Don't turn around," was the last thing Bryan heard.

The article in the morning paper about Bryan Benson's death was so inconspicuous that only someone looking for it might have found it.

Victor rolled over and covered his head. He reached out to answer the ringing phone as Chance stirred.

"Hello," he said, but there was dial tone. Suddenly he realized it was not the phone but the doorbell that was ringing. He grabbed his robe and walked sleepily to the door.

"Who is it?" he asked.

"Mr. Palmer?"

"Yes. This is?"

"I'm Officer Keates from Homicide."

Victor looked out the peephole and saw two men holding their badges. He opened the door.

"Sorry to bother you, Sir but is your wife home? We need to talk with her for a moment."

"What for, officer, is something wrong?"

"Yes, Sir. But we can only talk to your wife."

Chance was already on the stairs when she heard the officers ask for her.

"I'm right here, officer. How may I help you?"

"We'd like to speak with you privately."

Chance shot a glance at Victor. "It's okay, my husband can remain. Now what may I do for you?"

"Do you know a man by the name of Bryan Benson?"

"I did many years ago. What about him?"

"He's dead, Ms. Palmer, and we have reason to ask you to join us downtown. We'll wait outside."

"It's okay, Victor," Chance said wearily. "I'll go alone. I'll be with you as soon as I'm dressed," she said to the officers who retreated to the unmarked car outside. In that neighborhood the police always drove unmarked cars and wore plain clothes.

In Bryan Benson's car there were more letters and pictures that he was about to mail to Helen Stern and Victor Palmer.

Immediately as Chance left, insisting that her husband remain and make sure nothing got out of hand, Victor called Helen Stern.

"Yes," he was saying, "they took her downtown. I felt you should know because it may cause a scandal we can't afford."

"Do you know why?"

"Not really. The officers said something about a Bryan Benson. I am assuming he was the person that sent me a rather disturbing letter. Well he's dead."

Bryan Benson. Bryan Benson. She knew that name. Helen's mode went immediately into damage control.

"What's in the letter," she asked, although she suspected it was similar to the one she'd received.

"Err…I'll show it to you."

"Listen, Victor, I should go down to the police station and see what can be done. I'm sure it will be all right. I'll probably bring her home."

"They allowed her to drive her car. I really should come with you."

"That's not necessary. We don't want to draw any unnecessary attention to this. Chance is right, just stay put until you hear from me, and talk to no one."

Helen was not about to allow Victor to handle anything this serious. She got into her car, called Kent Julia, the attorney for the Helen Companies and asked him to meet her at the police station. They arrived at the station practically at the same time. As an attorney, Kent was able to see Chance, and because of who Helen was, so was she.

"Listen, Chance," Helen was saying, "I know you didn't do this but we have to secure some business, as this could have damaging effects on everything we've worked for. You need to transfer all your stocks in the VIP Company and in the Helen Companies into temporary holdings. You can put VIP's in your husband's name, but The Helen Companies stocks must be in mine. Once this blows over we will relinquish control. Our Initial Public Offering cannot be jeopardized. You do understand, don't you? Right now Kent is talking to the DA. You'll probably leave with him this morning, but in the meantime, please do this for me."

"I didn't do this, Helen. You know that, don't you?"

"Of course I do. I know that," she repeated, but she just couldn't be sure. Not after Reginald's questions and the letter from this guy. "Nothing will get out to the press, but we have to do this to protect the companies we have built. I'll have Kent draw up the stock transfer papers as soon as he rejoins us. Believe me, this will be over before you know it."

Chance decided to transfer all the stocks to Helen Stern, making her temporarily the majority stockholder of the VIP company. Chance wasn't sure how her husband would feel about her after all this, but she considered Helen a friend.

That Evening.

Reginald answered the phone, hoping it was Chance. She hadn't called all weekend. Usually she would call at least once on the weekend and because of his meeting with Bryan he was on edge. He itched to call her house, but he couldn't risk Victor answering the phone. And of course he was forced to keep a low profile, for he could add no embers to the smoldering fire that was engulfing Chance.

On the spur of the moment Reginald dug out the address to the house of Bryan Benson. He had no fear of being recognized as he cruised by 675 Morton Place. To his surprise, a For Sale sign was in front of the house. Frantically, Reginald dialed the realtor listed from his car phone.

"Oh, the house at 675 Morton. Yes we just put the sign up this morning. It's priced for a quick sale."

"Just this morning. When did the owner leave? I was just there last weekend looking around the neighborhood, and my wife and I really loved it. It seemed occupied then."

"Err. It was. As I said, the bank has it priced for a quick sale because the previous owner err…died in an accident." The realtor was careful not to say murdered in the driveway and turn off a potential buyer. "The bank would love to make an attractive offer…"

"Sorry, my wife hates deaths."

"Yes! Yes! I have done it." Helen danced around the room of her office apartment, albeit she felt sorry for Chance. Well, things could have been worse. Luckily she didn't have to fight a media catastrophe, thanks to Kent. Anyway it took this emotional jerker to get both Chance and Victor on the right road. They actually made out very well, considering what she might have done to them both had she needed to use them as pawns in her scheme against Andrea.

On her fax machine in the private office was a confirmation of a successfully executed plan. The word from London was her liberation. Only five more percent. It seemed word had gotten around that Jacobson's Industry was financially at risk and was up for a hostile takeover. Tut tut. *Lo siento mucho, Lo siento mucho,*" Helen cha-cha-ed over to the phone and dialed London.

If all went well, Helen Stern would soon become majority stockholder of yet another company—Jacobson's Industries. "Checked baby," she whispered. "You are in checkmate, Andrea Jacobson-Preston and you are history. Death I say. Death to the Queen. Yippee. You go, girl!" Helen squealed.

Chapter Twenty-Five

Johnathan Buckley sat across the table from Anton DePaul, his great bulk spreading out beyond its confines. His left eye was twitching noticeably as he passed a hand impatiently over his balding head.

"You stupid asshole," he shouted. "I should have known that even a Harvard Nigg…"

"You should stop right now, John, before you say something you'll regret." Anton's eyes flashed murder.

"I'm sorry, man. I'm real sorry. It's just that I spent the last twenty years planning this."

"Planning what? This takeover?"

"Yes. The takeover of Jacobson Industries and the ice bitch of New York, Andrea Jacobson."

"Whoa. Wait a minute. You mean this takeover action is because of personal vendetta rather than business sense."

"Damn straight. That woman has cost me my wife, and a great deal of personal pride and money."

"What did your wife have to do with this? I thought…"

"Yes, Anton she is dead. But I am still living. That's the problem. We have to find a way, *man*." He tried to be as ethnic as possible. "I know you can understand. I heard the daughter is even worse than the mother is. Didn't she dump you?"

Anton's hair was on end. "Forget about me and tell me what happened, or I'll drop this case immediately."

"I used to work for Jacobson Industries thirty years ago. I was good, Anton, real good. Everyone called me a rising star, and by the time I was thirty I was senior VP of this mega company. Unlimited expense account, flew around in private jets, two thousand-dollar suits and all the trappings of success. I practically used to run the place when Andrea was not there, and I loved it. I made the fuckin' company successful. I really loved my job.

"Andrea was this reclusive billionairess. No one could put a face to her name. Thirty years ago the world was clamoring to interview Andrea Jacobson as though she was Jacqueline Kennedy or something. Well, my girl was a rising star, too, at the time. The next Barbara Walters. She woulda been bigger than life if she was the first to interview Andrea. So I convinced Andrea to do a television interview for the good of the company. I can't imagine why the bitch didn't thank me, it was how she met her husband.

"Anyway, Rachel kind of stumbled onto this Pandora's box and decided she wanted to be the one to break the story. I tried to tell her the interview was enough for her upward climb, but she was greedy. As the story goes, I provided her with Andrea's inside information and this was the result.

"Journalism was Rachel's life and Jacobson's was mine. After I got fired, I worked like a dog to get where I have and to make my wife happy, but even that was not enough for her. She kept trying and trying to rise above the blackball. But Andrea Jacobson would never let her. After several years of trying, for even the sleaziest job, Rachel finally gave up. I came home one day and found her drowned in the bathtub, two bottles of whiskey floating on top. I vowed that day to avenge her death. My wife died for this." He opened a locked drawer and threw a crumpled, yellowing paper at Anton. *The Star*. In that magazine was the article that appeared about Andrea's illegitimate child.

"When that article appeared Andrea was incensed beyond logic. Not only did she buy the magazine and its holding company, but she also trashed the entire operation and fired everyone. Likewise, she threatened to cancel any other magazine or newspaper that dared to jump on the bandwagon. When all was done, she fired me.

"Yes, I have worked hard to make Sterling the company that it is only to get Andrea Jacobson in a vice grip. I want JI, Anton. I want the company badly. It must be my final vengeance."

"Mr. Buckley, my company would never have taken this case if we knew of your intentions. We are a reputable firm and cannot, and will not, be a part of a malicious takeover. Even if the free stocks were not purchased before we got to them, at this point we would have been forced to drop the case. I'm afraid if you want to go forward, Mr. Buckley, you'll have to find a new law firm."

"If you'd done what you were supposed to do, you would never have known why I need this win. Anton, I can't start over now. Please! Find a way to get those stocks."

"Sorry, Johnathan. I can't."

Immediately after Anton left, Johnathan Buckley ordered his Jacobson stocks sold. He would get Andrea Jacobson-Preston some other way, or at least he would die trying. "Promise," he whispered to the heavens. "Rachel, I promise."

Outside Anton opened the paper still squashed in his hand. Christ! Maybe that's why Helen was so scared to love anyone. She didn't trust anyone. It stung when Johnathan called her an ice queen like her mother, but those were exactly the words he had used to describe her on their last evening together some eight months previous. She had told him she was not interested in having him represent her especially since he was with a firm that was pursuing legal actions against her mother, but he knew that was a cop-out. She'd also informed him that she had only slept with him to see if she could loosen his lips, like Rachel had loosened Johnathan. She had even commended him on his professionalism and loyalty to Viking & Gould.

But was her loyalty to her mother or somewhere else? Ah, he wouldn't think of Helen Stern. He had gone on with his life and even broke the news to his mother that he wouldn't be getting married after all. However, in his dreams not a night had passed that he hadn't relived their last night together as he held her in his arms amid the rubble of her apartment. She would come to him. In time she would come. He knew she would because no one could alter destiny. He would wait.

Chapter Twenty-Six

Five-thirty and Andrea was at her desk trying for the last time to see if she'd missed anything that could save her company. She could make it happen. After all, she'd saved her relationship with her daughter. It had taken her years, but she had done it. If she could do that, she could save Jacobson's Industry. Yet, she sensed an ending. Maybe the lawyers could not ward off the impending failure of JI but she would keep on trying. She'd refused to sit in on any negotiations while they candidly discussed the disposal of her corporation. If she could have made herself ask Helen for help, this might not be happening. Andrea closed the report and rocked back in the familiar gray leather chair. She had built this company into a mega corporation. She had everything to be proud of, but maybe, indeed, it was time to pass the baton. She was tired. Deep in her heart she knew Helen had what it took to turn the company around and as they say, everything must change. Life had been good to her and she had no regrets. Momentarily her mind flickered to Adam, Helen's father, her true, true love who'd always believed in her. She missed him terribly. Not even the years had dulled the pain of his death. But thank God that Helen, their love child had come home and proved her love had not been in vein.

To lose control of something one had built through blood, sweat, tears and hardships, pain and denial, was a big blow to take. Andrea was rather pensive and solemn when the phone rang at 7:30 a.m.

"Yes," said a weary Andrea.

"Goodmorning, Mrs. Preston. This is Anton DePaul from Viking & Gould. Sorry it's so early, but I was told I could reach you here."

"Yes, Mr. DePaul. I'm here." She paused. "I see you have finally succeeded in destroying me after all. I hope you feel good about that. I hope you feel good about taking away my dream. For thirty-five years, Mr. DePaul, this company was my life and I'm not done yet. One last battle, Sir. One last battle."

"No, ma'am. We have put away our weapons. Last evening our company turned down the offer to represent Mr. Buckley when we found out the reason he wanted to take over your company. Sterling has been buying JI stocks, but we didn't know the reason until yesterday. We were unable to secure the last stocks they needed and that's when we found out."

"Buckley? As in Johnathan?"

"The very same. We are sorry for the stress this must have caused you. Our company is reputable and cannot participate in this vile act, so we withdrew our representation. I'm sure since Mr. Buckley can't get the last of the stocks he needs, he'll back off. Good luck to you, Mrs. Preston, and please accept our apology. A formal letter will be mailed, but I wanted to tell you personally."

"Thank you, Mr. DePaul. Thank you very much."

Andrea was too tired to be excited. She dialed the CFO who was at his desk even before she was.

"Barry, I just got a call from Viking, Gould."

"I'm sorry, Andrea, I did everything."

"So you did, my friend, and maybe your prayers have called off the dogs."

"What! No takeover?"

"No, Sir. They couldn't get the stocks."

"Huh," Barry was scratching his head. *But someone did. He just couldn't tell her right then.*

The phone rang again at seven-forty-five.

"Yes?" Andrea was jovial. Janice wouldn't arrive for another half-hour or so.

"Mrs. Preston, this is Lizzy from Hampstead, Miss Maya's house help."

"Good-afternoon, Lizzy. It is afternoon isn't it?"

"Yes ma'am. I'm trying to reach Miss Helen. I tried but there was no answer from her office, the operator told me. I'm calling with very bad news, Madam. Miss Maya passed on earlier today."

"What do you mean?" Andrea was bolt upright.

"I mean, ma'am, that Miss Maya died this afternoon," Lizzy said between sobs.

"Oh my God, no!" Andrea covered her mouth. "God, no!"

Immediately she dialed Helen's apartment. It was ten minutes to eight. It rang without an answer. Why wasn't Helen in her office at this time? Maybe she should drive over to the house. Helen could be in the shower. No! Andrea looked at her watch. Helen would never be at home at eight o'clock. She tried the office again and this time Helen answered.

Chapter Twenty-Seven

Helen's Office, July 1997

"Oh no, Mother. Please don't let it be true."

July 20, London 1997

Helen walked slowly up Victoria Street, her body heavy under the weight of the moment. Clad from head to toe in black, she carried, in her hand, a bowl-shaped black hat. She was intentionally arriving early to the church, for she needed a moment alone with her grief.

"Miss Stern," a reporter pushed a microphone in her face. "What do you know of your guardian's death?" Although the service wouldn't begin for an hour, a crowd of paparazzi was already gathered outside.

"Nothing," she spat, pushing the microphone out of her face.

"Can't you see these things…can't…"

"Get out of my way." Helen's voice was low, an implicit threat conveyed in its gravel tone.

In less than an hour, the chapel would be filled with legions of people, many of whom she had met years before at Maya's infamous spiritual gatherings or some such occasion. She wondered, momentarily, what those crackpots, who always needed validations about their lives, would do now. She supposed they would have to find another mystic! It was incredible how dependent people were and how they never stop looking for answers outside of themselves.

Not her. She was a survivor. As if portending the challenges of her life, even her birth was difficult. Today, her life was proof that it was how one manages the difficulties of life that determines success or failure. There was no question that Helen Stern was successful, an experience only appreciated by those who struggle. But she would never be satisfied until final success was realized. Her mind jumped quickly to her enemies. If only the naysayers and betrayers knew of the ultimate success that awaited her in less than a week! With renewed anger, provoked by her own guilt of betraying Maya, Helen's need for vengeance translated itself into quicker steps, and she dug her hands deeper and deeper into her pockets. Even in her aggrieved state, a sardonic smile curved on her lips. *Revenge, Revenge, Revenge* were the only words in her head and their resounding conviction was the only thing that gave her any pleasure.

Casting a suspicious eye at the overcast sky, Helen noticed the sun desperately trying to break through the fluffy, gray clouds. The stir of the crisp breeze signaled rain. It was already noon. A typical English summer day, really, nothing to be alarmed about. The English, used to the unpredictability of a day, were always prepared with their rain smocks and brollies. If the sun had been glaring full blast, it wouldn't have done much to brighten her day. Frankly, Helen was glad for the coolness of the afternoon, and even if it rained all summer, she would have much preferred summers in England (at times barely distinguishable from spring) than the smoldering heat of New York City. New York's heat was unbearable and worse, a hot day wouldn't be an exception in the many days of unending, indomitable heat. Helen had termed those hateful summers the punishment of the concrete jungle, and indeed today, a hot, sticky, scalding day would have been far too jarring to her already-shattered nerves.

Coming into the final stretch, as though time had been erased, it seemed as though she had been here, on this very spot, just yesterday, heading to Sunday service with Nan—the name she always called Maya.

"Come along dear, we don't have all day!"

"Maya? Maya?" Helen spun around for she would know that voice anywhere. But it was only a memory in which every small detail was preserved, yet was so very real. In fact, memories were everywhere and though everything seemed as ordinary as it used to be, she knew it wasn't. The tremendous boom of Big Ben shattered her rumination. In a hesitant trot, she entered the gates of Westminster Chapel.

"Miss, you can't come in here this morning," a bobby informed her. Bobbies and guards were patrolling the gates, and the notability of the occasion did not escape her.

"I am Helen Stern," she whipped out her identification. "I am…"

"Sorry ma'am, you may pass."

You always had style, Maya. It is fitting that your final resting-place should be in the company of Kings and Queens. Westminster Chapel held the crypts of England's most noted statesmen, and this indeed was a great honor to Maya. Today, all of England would be coming to give their last respects and to pay tribute to one of its informal royalty—for that was how Maya was perceived in her role as spiritual leader to all of England. Helen crossed the courtyard swiftly. When she reached the entryway to the Chapel, she again identified herself, acknowledged the guard, and hurried up the steps.

The last chime of the bell tower signaled twelve. The death toll. The noise permeated the solemnity of her thoughts, reminding her of the tragic reason for her visit. The imposing portal of Westminster Chapel separated her from the grim reality that she would soon be forced to face. Helen took a deep breath, filling her lungs as if to brace herself against the gravity of the moment. Slowly she pushed on the Roman doors. They yielded easily to her touch. Standing in the entrance of the historic landmark, its dark, cold interior deepened the sadness that rose through her body. Her knuckles were taut against her skin as she held onto the door for support. As she nudged it open, a waft of stale air from the old tombs escaped, the staleness bringing with it the fresh smell of a recent death. Helen turned her head from the penetrating smell of embalming fluid and formaldehyde. It was a horrible smell, one that she never again wanted to experience. But with the splendor of the church, there was no denying the grandness of the sendoff. It was befitting, quite befitting indeed that Maya's memory was imbued in a place of historic significance. Today, no tourists were in sight and no one knelt in prayer at the altars of hope and faith.

Each side of the long, red-carpeted aisle was adorned with garlands of white flowers. The archway to the inner sanctuary had been opened, and the white, lacquered coffin directly in front of her suddenly interrupted the burst of color at the altar. A breath caught in Helen's throat as she fought to stay on her feet. Her knees were buckling. She slumped against the door, her feeling of remorse and guilt now more acute than ever. Slowly she walked across the inlaid stone floor, stepping on tombs of those brave souls who gave their lives for England, making yet another pause before stepping closer until she stood before the open coffin. Her hands flew to cover her mouth and unexpected tears wetted her cheeks.

"I'm so sorry. So very, very sorry, Maya." Tears blurred her vision. And when she realized how much this woman, lifeless and peaceful, her dark hair resting atop a satin pillow, had meant to her, the sobs racked her slender body. There was no escaping, here in front of Maya, the feeling of betrayal that enveloped her. It had been so long since she'd felt such deep emotions. "If ever I die," she pleaded to the spirits surrounding her. "Please make sure I'm cremated. I don't ever want anyone to see me like this."

Helen stumbled back from the coffin, her world now completely hazy from blurring tears. A drop of the salty tears fell upon the silk lining on which the still body laid, spreading out until a wet spot encircled the little finger on Maya's left hand. Funny it should have landed there, for it was the very finger that often signaled Helen when she was in trouble. Silently she sat looking at her former guardian. The picture left an indelible impression on her mind.

Even in death, a slight smile adorned her lips, for Maya always had a smile for everyone. Someone had made it clear just how she would have wanted to look, for her perfectly coifed hair, clasped with her favorite pave clip, lay across her shoulders in the style she most often wore. Simple diamond earrings sparkled in her bloodless ear. In this grave instant, Helen realized suddenly that everything she had experienced with Maya had ceased; all the laughter, the baking, the childhood romps, and the divine power of a wonderful and caring human being. What a waste of a vibrant human spirit. What a profound and tragic turn of fate that life could betray a being as virtuous as Maya.

"Oh, God!" she asked. "How could I have been so heartless, so unforgiving? Dear, dear, Maya, can you ever forgive me? Please," she begged. "You must forgive me." She kept speaking as though any moment now Maya would smile and stroke her hair gently. She reached out and touched her folded hands, jerking back from their coldness, staring blankly at the deceased woman. "What use were your powers," she whispered, "if you couldn't even save your own life?" Just as the bell tolled one o'clock, she reached over and pinned the butterfly broach that Andrea had given her at her fourteenth birthday onto the woman who had been her mother for countless years. The diamond and sapphire broach lightened up the yellow suit. Yellow was Maya's favorite color, and even now with the pallor in her cheeks, it suited her. "Fly away on the wings of my butterfly," Helen whispered as the door opened.

"I'm so sorry, darling," Andrea Jacobson said as she walked through the door. She was fully dressed in black up to the pillbox hat covered with lace that concealed her face. Her voice, soft and understanding, floated up the aisle and her aura exuded the assurance of entitlement and one who was powerful.

"I hope you don't mind my being here now," she said as she walked toward Helen, who was leaning heavily against the coffin. The stiletto heels of Andrea's black pumps made a loud clicking noise against the marble floor and the echo in the silent room was resounding. To Helen it seemed that each step was louder than the one before and intensified the pounding in her head. Andrea had arrived early to give what support she could to Helen, but she'd kept out of the way so the child could have some time with the woman she had known all those years as her mother.

At the sound of the voice, Helen turned to face the woman who, even at a funeral, was radiantly beautiful. Scorn contorted her face.

"What is there to be sorry about now, Mother? We cannot take back the past, can we? And now we can't even rectify it! I suppose we are damned to live with the guilt of our actions for the rest of our lives." Firmly, she put the black hat on her head, bringing the veil down to cover her eyes.

At the look on Helen's face, Andrea concluded that allowing her to come to the chapel alone might not have been a good idea. She understood Helen's pain, maybe even her momentary resentment, but why couldn't Helen understand that she, too, felt a deep sadness and loss for a woman whom she wished she'd known better, a woman, who in her daughter's life was an impostor, albeit a good one for so many years. She, too, had regrets about the past, but she had made peace with Maya. She only prayed to God that Helen, too, had made peace with her. From the look in her eyes now, however, she could be mistaken.

"Time heals," Andrea said quietly. "People make mistakes."

Still radiant at sixty, only her hair, flecked with gray, aged Andrea Jacobson at all. If Helen hadn't known better, she would have branded her mother a silicon implant type. But admiration for Andrea Jacobson did not lessen her hostility towards her. If it had not been for that black widow's lying and deceit, she would never have left Maya. There was no question that Helen despised the woman walking toward her. From a distance, Andrea saw the look of disdain on Helen's face. She was taken aback, for she thought that through the years they had succeeded at repairing their damaged relationship. Things had been wonderful, or so she thought.

It was obvious from the cars arriving, the myriad of flowers in the church, and the minutest detail of the final sendoff that many people cared deeply for Maya. Andrea had not known the woman intimately, yet their meeting had drastically altered her life. What, she wondered, would her life have been like had she never met Maya? Would she have been Andrea Jacobson, tycoon businesswoman of the eighties and at sixty still a formidable competitor in the nineties? As much as she had despised Maya in the beginning, she had come to respect and trust her as a friend.

Since Helen's arrival on Andrea's doorsteps some nineteen years before, not a week had gone by that Maya had not called to inquire of Helen's progress. And not a day had gone by that Andrea hadn't thanked her guide for delivering her child back to her.

"I am grateful to you for taking her in, Andrea." Maya often said. "After all I have put you through, I appreciate your kindness toward Helen. I do miss her an awful lot, but I'm glad she is happy with you."

"I love her dearly, Maya. And it's I who should thank you. Why don't you hold a minute. I'll get her," Andrea responded every time. "Maybe she'll talk with you now. It's been a long time, and I'm sure she has put the past behind her. Let me get her."

"No. No. Don't do that," Maya had pleaded. "Let her have you now. I've had my turn. There is no need for her to be torn between us," Maya insisted, making Andrea promise never to inform the child of the calls. Maya lived in fear of the eruption of Helen's anger. Indeed for many years, Maya had taken good care of Helen as though she had been her own. The love she had given her had, no doubt, helped her survive the traumas of life, but there was no question Maya had been deeply hurt by the child's rejection, and she only hoped that pain and rejection had not put Helen's heart beyond human reach.

As Andrea shifted her gaze from the casket to Helen, she was even more saddened by the look of fear and loss on her daughter's tear-streaked face. Realizing Helen's anguish must have been so much greater than her own could ever be, she reached out, taking the trembling hand of her grief-stricken child. To her surprise, Helen did not recoil from her touch.

"I'm so sorry, Helen. I only wish there was something I could say to make you understand. Please believe me, neither of us ever wanted to hurt you."

At those words, Helen burst into a full wail, the moment of finality too much for her usual control. Andrea gathered her up and the two women embraced. A look of fright and helplessness had replaced the icy-shadowed eyes of the girl she held in her arms. Andrea Jacobson-Preston suddenly realized that the unusual mysterious eyes with their dark, hooded look could have been the plea of a scared and frightened child.

Within minutes, the entire church was filled with mourners. The most distinguished of British society had turned out to bid farewell to Maya. It was a traditional farewell, presided over by the Archbishop. Following the service, a few dignitaries were invited to speak. Most recalled Maya's friendship, kindness, inspiration, and insights. And when they were all done, although entranced, Helen rose to deliver the eulogy for *her* Mother. In the manner that Maya had taught her—books on the head and all—she walked with dignity to the podium. Pausing slightly to look at the hundreds of people who had come to pay their final respects, a deserved and reverend farewell, Helen adjusted the microphone, lifted the black veil that covered her face and said:

"It is believed that many lifetimes are required to reach perfection, at which time we become an angel in the heavens. If such is the belief, then we are here to say good-bye to Maya as we have known her as a mortal here on earth. Whether her loss is because her life had reached its pinnacle or an oversight of the gods, I know that as we say good-bye today, Maya is saying hello to the angels in the heavens.

"Maya's life represented what each of us strive for in our short time here—to be a light-bearer whose love changes lives forever. But even though she is gone, I know her love will shine as brightly in the heavens as it did here on earth. And for me, it doesn't matter where it shines, because I have lived in the glory of her love, been embraced by her light, and will forever be blessed by its warmth, for there is nothing that can alter the effects of true love.

"I, for one, will never stop counting my blessings, for it is not often that a child, an orphan, really, has the opportunity to be so loved. Like you, I will miss Nan dearly, but when I am feeling lost or lonely I know I only have to look up at the sky. When I find the brightest star in the heavens I will know that it's Maya's love shining just for me. Beginning now, I pledge to do justice to her memory. I also hope I have been articulate enough to capture for you just a fraction of the goodness of my friend and guardian, Maya. But there is another reason to be articulate; and that is because I know Nan is listening carefully, and should I use improper speech, she might just sit up and say, 'Young lady, bite your tongue.'"

Between the sniffles and the hankies, a welcomed laughter echoed.

"There are so many things I have learned from Maya, and there was so much more to learn. And as I grieve the loss of Nan, I do so selfishly because I was the one who didn't stay to learn all that she had to teach.

"Today, the community loses a great spiritual leader and a friend whose function it was to unite the human spirit. But from her I am born, so on behalf of my *mother*, Maya," Helen deliberately sought Andrea's eyes, "I thank you all for your kindness and your presence, and I promise I will continue in the path that she has taught me so well. Don't worry about me, dear Mom, just you fly away on the wings of my butterfly."

There was a perceptible pause while people dried teary eyes, blew noses, and recomposed themselves. The entire room lifted their voices in a final tribute to Maya as they sang, *You'll Never Walk Alone*. Immediately after, the pallbearers hoisted the casket and the procession began. Helen walked in front of the casket to the entrance of the church to thank each guest as they left. Andrea stood close behind.

"My dear," Eleanor, Maya's dearest friend said. "You were very eloquent. Maya would have been as proud of you today as she has always been."

"Accept our condolences...."

"We are sorry...." Helen heard those words at least a thousand times and shook as many hands before the procession was over.

Finally, after the last mourner had left, Andrea turned to her daughter and said, "Will you come back to Claridges with me after the gathering? I have booked you a suite."

Helen wanted to be alone. She couldn't possibly be in a room of people all eating and drinking as though this terrible tragedy had not happened. For most of the mourners, tonight would mark the finality of their grief. For Helen, there was never going to be peace, for by her own doing, she was left holding the guilt. At this moment, she couldn't even envision how she would manage the guilt, much less forgive herself for punishing the very woman who gave her life meaning.

"If it's all right with you," she said formally to her biological mother, "I would like to go home."

"You want the jet to take you back to New York?"

"No, Mother, I mean my real home in Hampstead. I have only had one home."

Andrea did not respond immediately, for she knew her daughter was in great pain, and the cruelty of her words had to be magnified by this pain.

"I understand your need to be alone, Helen, but Hampstead? It may be too much for you right now."

"Look, mother. Don't use me anymore to salve your guilt. Haven't I played the prodigal's daughter long enough? I was not the one who abandoned me. You were. Just like me, mother, you will have to live with that. The kindest thing you can do now, mother, is to allow me to grieve in my own way about the only mother I have ever known."

"Helen. That's not true. What you say is not true at all."

"All these years. All these years, hoping you'd at least try to explain what happened and not a word. Not a single word. I don't want to hear now, mother. I have no need to love you."

"You are just upset." Andrea squeezed back the pain. Come with me. Don't go to Hampstead tonight."

"I will have to go sometime. It might as well be tonight."

"Very well." Andrea slid into the back of the black Daimler, her shoulders slumping. For the first time since her severe depression she felt old. As their eyes met, Andrea shivered. The look was back! The cold, vacant stare that she'd observed when Helen first came back to her. Yet, she could tell from the narrowing of the eyes and the deep fire that burned behind them that there was nothing cold about that stare. Nothing cold at all. Had she misinterpreted the look of hatred as helplessness? The look in her daughter's eyes as the car pulled away from the curb was one of pure loathing. Andrea pulled herself up to height, poured herself a brandy from the hidden bar and dialed the phone to her husband Scott.

"Hey, good-looking." He was cheerful.

"Hey, honey," she said sadly. "I'm coming home tonight. Please tell David to pick me up."

"Is everything okay there?"

"As much as it will ever be," she said, choking back the tears. "I should have told her the truth a long time ago."

Helen waited until the hearse had left for the burial ground. She wouldn't reconsider her decision of not going to the cemetery. That, she just could not do. Instead, she got into her rented car and headed in the opposite direction, circling London before she drove the distance to Rollan Hills.

Chapter Twenty-Eight

The imposing house covered in lush, green ivy stood clearly visible against the blue-gray sky. Helen pulled up to the guard-gate, noticing it had been freshly painted.

"Yes," the guard said. He was dressed in black and somewhat solemn.

Helen clicked the window control, and the tinted glass slid slowly down.

"Miss Helen! Oh Miss Helen! I'm so glad you came. What a blessed day. Miss Maya will be right pleased," he said sadly before realizing Maya was never again coming back. "I'm sorry, Miss. Truly sorry." He lowered his gaze.

"I'm the one who is sorry, Patrick. But why are you guarding this gate tonight? Surely that's not necessary, and why weren't you at the funeral?"

"Ah couldn't, ma'am. Ah just couldn't."

"Lock the gates and come up to the house with me," she offered. "We'll have a spot of tea like old times."

"Yes Ma'am, I'd like that." Patrick pulled the door behind him, fishing for a key on a bundle attached to his belt.

"Get in then," she unlocked the door of the passenger's side.

"I just couldn't go, Miss Helen. You understand don't you, Miss? Lizzy and I just couldn't," Patrick's head fell to his chest.

"I understand, Patrick. I couldn't go to the burial site, either. It's a sad day for all of us."

At the front door, Helen took out her house key, which had remained on her key chain since the night she left Hampstead, and slipped it into the door. Hearing the door open, Elizabeth came scurrying.

"Who is there?" she asked, the look of panic turning to relief when she recognized Helen.

"Good evening, Miss Helen." She bowed graciously, her face lit with surprise and deep satisfaction. "Welcome home. The Missus would be right pleased that you came home. It's so sad, Miss Helen." Tears welled in Elizabeth's eyes.

"That it is, Lizzy. Dear, dear Lizzy." Helen lifted her head. "Never bow to me. I am but Helen, the little one whose diapers you changed." She put an arm around her shoulder. The British were so very respectful. Their boundaries never overstepped. It used to pain her to see the homage they paid, but after living in America where social order and status were nonexistent, Helen was convinced that America should institute a social class structure.

"What'd you say we all go to the kitchen and have a cup of good old tea? It will cure the blahs," she heard herself say, just the way Nan used to. And at that memory, as much as she wanted to be strong, the tears fell. In the center of the massive old hallway of Rollan Hills, Helen, Patrick, and Lizzy sobbed.

"A fine bunch we are," Patrick was blowing his nose. "Come on, let's have that cup of tea."

As Lizzy and Patrick made their way to the kitchen, Helen remained in the antique-filled entranceway a moment longer. She ran her hands along the banister vividly remembering the night she had walked down the very stairs, vowing never to return. In her pain and anger, she had hated the place, but as she stood there now, surrounded by all her childhood things, she realized how many wonderful memories this house held for her. In fact, she was sure her Nan would be coming around the stairs any moment, holding her hot chocolate.

The sweeping staircase rose from each side of the room, converging dramatically into a huge landing at the top of the stairs. Cut into the walls of the stairs were semicircular glass-enclosed top-lighted bays. Inside was Maya's collection of priceless sculptures and porcelain statues. It was a grand old English mansion that seemed more like a renovated castle. It had hosted the most distinguished of English society.

Although it was thought that even Nan had great powers, they were never ever reduced to common witches. In fact, they had been very highly regarded, not just as society women, but as gifted women. This had earned them a unique position in society. As magnificent as the house was, it was drafty. Even in the summer months the draft was noticeable, and in the winter, though they had put in central heating long before she left, they would all have to sit around in woolly blankets. Their favorite place was the kitchen. Many of her childhood memories were in front of the fire wrapped in thick, Scottish blankets.

"Well, you couldn't very well change the entire ambiance of the place now, could you, dear," Nan used to say. "After all, who ever heard of an English castle with central heating. Don't be so daft about a slight draft. It adds character."

Only moments after starting up the stairs, Helen suddenly stopped. She couldn't just yet. She wanted to walk upstairs to her bedroom and sit there and weep, but she was too frightened by the memories. With a sudden pang, Helen missed Maya dearly. Turning around, she headed for the kitchen. Too many memories, both good and bad.

They were seated at the table in the kitchen now, the old wooden table that still had the burned circle from one of Helen's cooking accidents. The fireplace no longer looked inuse, but her overstuffed chair was as it had always been. Even the cookbook that Maya had used to teach her from was still opened to their favorite recipe, plum pudding. Nan knew the recipe by heart, but she always left it open to that page so Helen could peek at it if she forgot what to do next. Plum pudding! Christmas Time! Huge parties! There were happy times at Rollan Hills.

"What happened?" Helen finally asked. "Until now, I really don't know the whole story."

"It was ever so ridiculous," Patrick began. "Ah told the Missus not to drive herself into town that morning. Ah told her ah would cancel my doctor's appointment to take her, or that ah would take her right after ah returned. It would only 'ave delayed her two hours. Me old ticker has been acting up, you know." He diverted from the story, pointing to his chest. "Anyway, she insisted that she could drive herself. Well, the Missus was not a bad driver, as you know, but ever since you left she had been kind of funny. She hadn't driven since. For some reason she was excited that morning to go somewhere. She couldn't wait. I should never 'ave let her go."

"Oh come on now, Patrick," Elizabeth was saying. "It could hardly be your fault. The Missus does as the Missus pleases."

"Ah don't exactly know where she was going," Patrick continued, "but as I said, she was very excited. It wasn't forty minutes later that the bobbies came to the house. Some tourist was driving on the wrong side of the road and slammed into her car. She was, it seems, going pretty fast. Neither of them survived. I'm just glad she didn't suffer."

Helen didn't share her thoughts with them, but as clairvoyant as Nan was, she would have felt an accident, unless of course, she had intended it—or was completely distracted.

"Was there anything noticeably unusual about her that morning?"

"Just her excitement, as I said."

"She had been talking about visiting the States for the past year," Elizabeth offered. "Each time she decided, she would put it off. She waited for years for a letter from you, Miss Helen. At first she tried to find out where you had gone. She even used her powers of vision. She figured you were blocking your mind. When your pictures came out in the glossy magazine, she feared you had run off to some sleazy place with people who used runaway young girls as bait. Once she found out that you had gone to America, she stopped worrying so much but stayed much to herself. There has been no plum pudding since you left. Can you believe we never had another party?"

"Hardly," Helen said sadly. "I am sorry, Lizzy. I wish I could alter things. Anyway," she changed the subject abruptly, "there is a lot to do, I'm sure. I will plan to be here for as long as it takes to sort out Mummy's affair." Both Patrick and Lizzy looked up, for they had never heard her call the Misses Mummy.

"This may be a bad time, Miss Helen, but there is a letter that she left if you ever came back. When you are ready I'll give it to you. Do you want me to go and get your room ready?"

"Please Lizzy, and leave the letter on my dresser. I'll take a bath now and retire to bed."

"Good night then, Miss Helen," Patrick said, walking toward the door. He and Lizzy lived on the premises in the coach house. "If there is anything you need Miss, just call. And you don't have to go driving yourself around in that little old car. Tomorrow we'll take it back."

It was hardly an old car but Helen smiled, for pomp and circumstance was never a part of her household in Rollan Hills.

"'Night, Patrick." She hugged him. Although he was trying hard to be cavalier, she was sure he missed his Mistress of nearly thirty years.

"Oh, I left my luggage in the car. I'll just follow you out, Patrick. It's not much. I can manage."

"Don't worry about it tonight, Miss. From the looks of things you haven't grown very much and everything is as you left it."

They parted ways as Lizzy collected the cups and saucers and Helen climbed the stairs, walking hesitantly down the familiar hallway. She paused at Maya's room for a moment before she turned the handle. She stepped into the spacious room and sat on the canopied bed where Nan had always read her stories, often times weaving in tales about Helen's special powers. Powers! Even the thought of the word made her shiver. Immediately she wanted to be out of the room. She got up abruptly from the bed, for the first time noticing the numerous pictures of herself on Maya's dresser. A framed picture of the magazine cover, *International Moderna* was there. Hastily she left the room, vowing to be braver tomorrow as she gathered Nan's personal belongings.

Her own room was three doors down on the right. A feeling of *déjà vu* overcame her as she twisted the handle of the door. The four-poster bed with its pineapple carvings stood gracefully in the center of the room and above it was the picture of the Man on the Horse. Only now did the tropical motif of her room suggest that maybe Maya had been trying to tell her something all along about her heritage. Slowly she raised her eyes to the picture. Nan had obviously re-hung it in its original position. Staring into the deep, black eyes, a replica of her own, she felt a sense of disappointment.

What would life have been like with real parents? Impatiently, she turned towards the bathroom, catching a glimpse of herself in the mirror. No need getting emotional about such a fantasy. She was alone in the world now, in an every-man-for-himself world. The matching dressing table, which now had the broken glass replaced, looked back at her questioningly, as it always had before she'd broken it in anger. The only trace of the damage she had done the night she left home was the faint smell of Joy perfume. She had smashed the bottle violently against the dresser's glass, splintering both on impact. The concentrated liquid had obviously seeped into the pale blue, ankle-deep rug and remained there. It was the night she found out about her real mother and father. Since then she had never again worn Joy, preferring instead to dab herself with Yellow, her own scent. Andrea, she knew, still wore Joy. She walked around touching things, running a bath, playing her music box, and looking for her love letters to Geraud that were never posted but rather hid in secret places. Funny, but it appeared as though no one had entered her room for a long time. She jumped at the sudden tap on the door, immediately realizing it was Elizabeth.

"Come in, Lizzy."

"Here you go, Miss." She handed her a yellowing envelope with 'Helen' written on it in Nan's handwriting and proceeded to turn down the bed. Helen turned over the envelope. It was sealed. It was very old. She placed the envelope on the table with trembling fingers.

"Anything else I can get for you, Miss Helen?"

"No. I'm going to clean up now. 'Night, Lizzy." She hugged her old caretaker. "And thank you."

Helen stepped into the hot bath water, hoping the heat would somehow warm her cold heart and salve her guilt. She stole a peek at her face in the glass behind the door. She never made a habit of studying her features, so it was a startling surprise to see the face that looked back at her in the mirror. All the innocence of youth and frivolity on her face had been replaced with skepticism and hatred. The face looking back at her was one she hardly knew. It was an attractive face nevertheless; pretty, maybe, but a more confident beauty than that of the beautiful waif on the cover of a fashion magazine. She leaned closer to the mirror. Experienced and dangerous eyes glared back, narrowing with examination as though they knew what lay ahead was not much different than what rested behind. It was reassuring, the face, for she had half expected to see the face of a heartless demon looking back. Something like what had happened in Wilde's *The Picture of Dorian Gray*. Instead she saw the vacant look of her eyes reflecting the barrenness of her soul; the haunted mask of guilt was the only indication that she still had emotions.

Yet, the creases beginning on her forehead told her the emotions she stifled went deep. Even if she had not buried her heart, she supposed it was time to show slight lines of aging. She was thirty-eight. Whenever had she reached that age! Time, she reflected, waits for no one. What could Anton really have felt for this icy heart? Why would he try to woo someone whose hatred had rendered her a caricature of a human and her heart a block of ice? She no longer lived, she just merely existed; existed to execute her final plan that had been smoldering for years; a smoldering that would explode soon into a volcanic eruption of unheard-of proportion. The hot water stung her skin as she imagined the hot, molten lava would melt away the life of Andrea Jacobson-Preston.

It wasn't much longer to wait now. If it hadn't been for Maya's death she would only have been a week away from her final triumph. Tomorrow they would read the will. Tomorrow, she could go back to New York. Tomorrow, everything would be as it was before. She didn't have a worry in the world about Maya's estate. Knowing Maya as she did, she bet everything would be in order. Tomorrow, after the will was read, she would read the letter. Yes, she decided with some urgency. Tomorrow, she would go back to New York and finish what she had started. It was time.

The next morning, Helen awoke to the smell of bacon and freshly brewed tea. She was delighted, for she knew that on the table would be scones, tea biscuits, marmalade, kippers, eggs and anything else Lizzy was able to find in the larder. She hesitated for a minute before the yellow envelope, deciding not to read its contents just yet. That evening, after the will was read, she would open the letter.

"Hmmm, something smells scrumptious." She pecked Lizzy on the cheek, grabbing a Peekfreen biscuit and a cup of tea. "Where's Patrick?"

"Out gathering logs for the fire."

"In the middle of summer?"

"The weather man says it will cool down considerably, in the high fifties, that's all. Nothing like the English weather, but I really think he just wants some memories for old time sake."

"I'll go find him." She headed in the direction of the door.

"Not before you eat. Anyway, he'll be here shortly. He has never been able to resist my breakfast in forty years. As soon as he smells the bacon, he'll come right inside."

So said, so done.

Atop the yellow damask table cloth, as Helen suspected, was a feast. After a hearty breakfast, Helen and Patrick walked around the premises of Rollan Hills. She had forgotten just how big the place was. This magnificent garden, with its lush shrubbery housed, as far as the eyes could see, bluebells, heather and garlands of roses that blossomed in pinks, vibrant reds, white and pale yellows. She used to know all the roses by name: *Douchesse D'Angoulême, Duc De Guiche,* for she had been right beside Patrick and Maya as they planted them and discussed the importance of the Austin roses. This garden was where she had spilled her guts to Andrea, only to have been humiliated years later. Looking for a distraction to her unsettling thoughts, together with Patrick, she picked wild flowers for the vases. The house, when she was a child, was filled with laughter, flowers, and song. This new Rollan Hills needed some life.

"How many acres are there, Patrick?' she asked.

"I don't rightly know, but I tell you it's a bear to keep this place in shape. I think Miss Maya once told me it stretched for about a hundred acres. I don't do much beyond the trees. Would have to build another premise for respite while I worked the whole land if I did."

"It's a beautiful home. I don't know what will become of it now. I can't ever imagine selling it, but I have to go back to the States. I hope you and Lizzy will stay on and take care of it."

"Wouldn't think of anything else, Miss Helen."

By the time they got back to the house Mr. Prowling, the barrister whom Helen had known from childhood, was chatting in the hallway with Lizzy.

"Good day, Helen. It's so very good to see you again. Sorry it is under these circumstances."

"Thank you, Mr. Prowling. May I offer you some tea?"

"I would love that."

"Lizzy, would you bring some tea into the drawing room, please."

"Right away, Miss Helen."

Mr. Prowling fell into step beside Helen.

"There are a few things we have to talk about if this is an appropriate time." He held her elbow, stepping back to allow her to enter the room first. "I took the liberty of bringing the will with me. No need to wait until four o'clock unless, of course, you so desire."

"Not at all. Let's wait for the tea and scones to arrive. So, Mr. Prowling, how is your family? And do tell me all about the England of the nineties. I have a bit of catching up to do, and there's a lot I don't know anymore."

"Ah, nothing ever changes in England. The Queen's gotten a bit poorer but one couldn't tell. From what I hear, she actually has to pay taxes now, Camilla and Charles broke up, I suppose, but frankly, my dear I think it's just a plot to keep the press out of their business. I think they have just gone further underground. But who wants to talk about England! Tell me about America. We'll get there one day before I die, but I haven't been able to get the Missus to budge. 'Why do you want to go to that country?' she always says. 'I'll never understand a word they say anyway!' That woman talks too much, I tell you. Now," he twinkled, patting her fatherly on the knee, "you tell me about America. It seems you have held up well there and that it's done you some good. But why, not even an accent!"

"Gosh no! Have you ever heard them speak? Poor Eliza Doolittle would have many friends there. The Americans, Mr. Prowling, speak as they wish. They add new words to their vocabulary daily. What they need is a good Henry Higgins," Helen chuckled.

"Of course you don't say that there, do you, Helen?"

"No, no of course not. I am what they call quite politically correct."

"Here we go," Lizzy rested the tray on the cocktail table. "Sugar in your tea, Mr. Prowlings?"

"No my dear, just a spot of milk. Have to watch the waistline you know." He patted his rotund belly.

What for, Helen wondered. No diet in the world could help that generous midsection from years of roast beef and Yorkshire pudding. Mr. Prowling looked at the watch hanging from the chain on his waistcoat. What a throwback he was, really. To Helen, he looked a lot like she pictured Mr. Pierot's character in Agatha Christi books. She was disappointed when she finally saw the movies. They should have cast Mr. Prowling!

"I've got the car ready, Miss Helen," Patrick pushed his head around the door. "We could take care of that business anytime you're ready, Miss."

"Talking about business, why don't we get down to it?" Prowling said between sips of tea.

Lizzy and Patrick moved to leave the room.

"Wouldn't do that. This concerns you as much as it does Miss Helen."

For the next hour, Mr. Prowling read the details of Maya's will. By the time he was through, Helen Stern was an exceedingly wealthy woman. She hadn't given much thought to Maya's financial position before, and were it not for her upbringing, she'd have dropped her spoon when Prowling read the extent of her holdings. Dear, dear, sweet Maya; Helen felt deep regret for abandoning her. And even so, she'd left everything to her.

"It seems to me you are all going to need a barrister," Mr. Prowling said, rising from his seat. "Let this sink in for a bit, and then we should talk. Good afternoon, then," he said, "I must get back to the office. Helen, it was so good to see you again. I am sorry it had to be an occasion like this, but of all the people who understood that to be born is to die, it was Maya. I'm glad we had the time, though. I am sure we will talk soon. Please, join the Missus and me for afternoon tea one day, will you? Miss Lizzy, Patrick," he tipped his hat. Helen nodded her acceptance of his invitation, and after a few more words he ambled out of the room.

"I suppose if you and Lizzy don't want to stay at Rollan Hills, Patrick, you don't have to. You are both very wealthy now."

"We don't care too much about wealth at our age." Lizzy spoke for her husband as well. "We are going to give a lot of this money to our grandchildren. They are the ones who should have it."

Maya's generosity had indeed left them wealthy. And even though they were married, she'd left each the same amount. Such a feminist that Maya was. Equal rights indeed. Each, now 100,000 pounds richer, could live quite well for the years they had left. Combined, they had more than enough for a lovely home of their own, and they would continue to draw their monthly salary as long as they both lived. They chose to remain at Rollan Hills.

That night, matters concluded and as she expected without complication, Helen decided to remain in England an additional week. As she lay in bed, still unable to open the letter from Maya and feeling quite like an impostor and a fraud in accepting her fortune, she was torn between her need for a simple life and her desire for revenge. What would she do with all that money? One thing she did know was that tonight she would neither think of the money nor the letter. Climbing into bed, she paused before the picture of her father. "Why did you not claim me?" she asked, teary eyed. "Why didn't you love me?"

A week later, Helen Stern boarded a plane back to New York. It was quite a different trip from the first time she'd arrived in New York, but no less emotionally charged. She pulled out the faded yellow envelope and with trembling hands tore it open.

My Dearest Helen,

If you are reading this letter it's because my end has come. I wrote it the night you left England hoping to send it to you, but I could never find you. When Andrea finally called to tell me of your arrival in New York, I felt it was too late. But sometimes life cannot be complete until all the pieces of the puzzle are in place. I hope this letter....

The plane suddenly jerked forward and the seat belt lights came on. Helen stopped reading for a moment to obey the warning.

Chapter Twenty-Nine

In Flight: London to New York

The turbulence was severe, and Helen felt nauseous. She beckoned the flight attendant and asked for some dramamine.

"We don't…Right away, madam." She recognized Helen Stern. When settled, Helen again took out the letter from Maya.

Who knows why life sometimes gets so complicated. In its simplicity it often turns to chaos. Maybe that's what life is all about: chaos and peace. For years I have trained you to be a teacher. A master teacher-—a conduit for spiritual wisdom to help bring peace to those around you. Yet, I know that for years you have thought you were adopted by me because of your mother's abandonment. But that is not true. I adopted you so you could be trained.

You see, Helen, we are all special beings. Your Mother, her Mother before her and now you. So was I and my Mother before me. I don't know why we were given this gift but we were. We are the chosen maidens that posses the great power of life. When a woman's power is exercised and transcends the individual need, it can reshape the direction of the world. So maybe we were chosen to save the world, maybe to destroy it, or maybe just because we need a better understanding of self.

But we are not the only ones. Many people are given the gift of divination. As you can see, some use it to seek power, some to seek harmony and yet others deny that they have it at all. Even when life forces them to take notice, and even in the face of that enlightenment, they flee from their own self-knowledge. No matter what the reason, all of us are given a choice. The decision as to how to use our gift is ours. My mother in particular was given the responsibility of securing the next Messiah, so to speak. As you can tell, the world is moving towards a rapid decline and only we, the light-bearers, hold the key to raise the collective consciousness. Those of us with the 'gift' have to be secured, nurtured, and trained to do the job for which we were born. Your Grandmother refused to become a part of the 'gifted' circle, and so when she had Andrea she denied her the right to understand and to use her gift. Like my mother, I was sent to help Andrea, and although aware, she was clearly unfamiliar with the meaning of her 'gift.' She too resisted my help.

When your mother got pregnant with you it was clear to me that she hadn't developed her master ability enough to be able to teach you your destined duty. When she was six months pregnant I exercised my powers of mind control and put her in a state of obedience. I took her away until she gave birth. We didn't even allow her to see you, for we knew after your birth our hypnotic hold on her would diminish. She cried and cried and begged and pleaded with us to let her take care of you. She promised to do whatever we said, but we knew it was too late. We couldn't risk another generation just to save one person's pain—not when the whole world could be in jeopardy. I know this will be hard for you to understand, but it had to be done and this is as it was. The way of the teacher is one of sacrifice.

For years she tried to see you, but I would never let her until I was sure your training was complete and your powers were fully developed. Most of the money that I have left for you is money your mother sent to take care of you. Even when she could only afford five or ten dollars she never missed paying a single month. When you were fourteen I felt it was time to let her know you. I wanted to see if your powers could pick up the forever-unbroken bond of mother and child. I told her it was her decision if she wanted you to know who she really was. But she said you were so happy that to cause you pain was more than she could bear. She was going to tell you when you had a chance to get to know her better, the summer you were to visit her in New York. But, alas, fate took its turn. That's the thing, Helen, even the best-laid plans go awry.

I'm truly sorry, my darling, for I meant you no harm. I have loved you more than you will ever know, and so has your real mother. You see, Helen, things aren't always as they seem to be, for in life you had two mothers who really, really loved you. You have a gift, my child, that is powerful and honed. Someone of such great powers has within them the instrument of good and evil. I have taught you only the ways of good. Bide your anger, for uncontrolled anger can bring out your dark side. I trust in the light and will forever watch out for you. I love you always.

Forever yours,

Nan

Helen wiped the back of her hand across her eyes. Her mother had not abandoned her by choice.

P.S. I have enclosed a letter your mother sent for me after she visited you at Rollan Hills

> Dear Maya:
>
> For years I have tried to forget that horrible night when I lost my baby. That night, unbeknownst to me, I unwillingly gave up the rite of passage into womanhood. You see, when a woman's life hangs between life and death, as it does in childbirth, she is prepared, if she lives, to learn the discipline of sacrifice. For she then becomes a Master Teacher. I was robbed of my rightful place as a mother and in so doing retained all the selfish ways of a barren woman. I had no need to give up my body, my time, my knowledge, or experience, any spiritual sacrifice necessary to raise a healthy offspring. When I saw Helen, I did not know how to be a mother to my child. Nonetheless I would never have

been at peace until she was with me. After seeing her, I am glad, glad that a lifetime awaits us, and I thank you for that. For even though I have traveled the path of the selfish, I have in fact experienced, in reality, the most precious gift of all: to give life. The truth is, I did have a child and although the loss of that child has suspended me between the worlds of the living and the dead, I am hopeful that in time I will come to learn the ways of a mother.

I just wanted to share with you that that night in Surrey I wanted to die. I wanted to float away into the bright beckoning light and never return. The only reason I came back when my heart started beating again was because my child needed me and because she was all I would ever have of the greatest love of my life. As I write this letter I am trying to find my own purpose in life and to understand the gift that means so much to us all. I thank you for the opportunity to know Helen and hope she will come to love me even after these years of separation. I look forward to her visit next summer.

Regards,
Andrea Jacobson-Preston.

Helen was sobbing quietly. She had a mother after all. Oh God, what had she done?

"Don't cry, my dear." A bony, fragile, outstretched hand gave her a Kleenex. Helen had hardly noticed the old, wizened woman sitting next to her on the plane.

"Believe me, at my age I now know there is nothing that's ever worth crying about. If you live long enough you'll find that out, too."

Helen stared at the woman in disbelief. "Err, thank you…"

"Maya," she offered.

"Maya!"

"Yes. It's a beautiful and unusual name, isn't it? It is Indian. The root *ma* means magic, and is the embodiment of the female power. My name means the Goddess of Goodness. Like *Aphrodite, Isis, Ishtar* and the most renowned *Mary*—mother of Jesus. As women, we are the givers of life and the keepers of power. One woman should never harm another woman for she harms a whole civilization. My mother named me after her mother, who was named by an Indian nanny.

Helen looked at the fragile woman with the crackled face in amazement. She was a messenger. In her heart she knew that.

New York

Victor realized how much he really loved his wife when confronted with the fact that she could have gone to jail. Frightened that she would see him for what he really was, he had started drinking again. When drinking, he could act braver than he was and he could always blame the alcohol for his irresponsible behavior. He wasn't ever going to see Olivia any more. Anyway, Olivia was furious with him, for he had curtailed their rendezvous to once every three months or so. Now she had begun to snub him as though he never existed. Only last week he saw her with a new young stud on her arm, her new toy boy no doubt. Thank God. Resolved, Victor punched out the numbers to *Aix en Provance.*

"*Allo. Bonjour.*"

"Hello, this is Victor Innes Palmer. I would like to check into the hospital next week."

"Just a moment, Mr. Palmer, while I check our availability," the woman on the line answered. Victor was glad he had made the decision to take care of his problem. He knew every day would be a struggle, but with Chance's help and love, he would make it. Poor Chance was in pain, too. Luckily she'd keep busy while he was away looking for a house by the lake for them to move into. Now that the company had gone public and they had sold their stocks to Helen, they had more money than they would ever need, and for a while there was no reason to work. Thank God, Victor sighed, he was out of that stifling business.

Reginald went to Helen's office at midday. He was even going to offer to pay for her lunch, for he had to talk with her urgently.

"Good morning, Mrs. Walters. Is my big Sis in?"

"Oh no, Mr. Preston. She left last Thursday for London. An emergency."

Ah, damn! Now who was there to talk to? No one knew of his relationship with Chance, but he felt comfortable talking with Helen. She had always kept his secrets and he felt she was level-headed enough to offer him good advice. Chance had told him about her arrest and her quick release after Helen and Kent, the company lawyer, contributed a few well-placed dollars to the Precinct. Now she was insisting that he should get on with his life without her. What life was there without her? He had to talk to Helen. She would know what to do.

"I'm going to try to make my marriage work, Reginald," Chance's lips had quivered. "Victor and I need each other now; we both have a lot of pain to deal with and a lot of work ahead of us. He's checking into a rehab center, and I am going into therapy. We are going to help each other. Please believe me," Chance pleaded. "I didn't mean to hurt you."

"Stop, my darling," he reached for her. "You are just upset. Everything is confusing right now, but it will be all right soon."

"It's all right now!" She eased out of his grip. "I'm not saying this out of anguish. You see, Reggie, I have never stopped loving my husband. I was just too ashamed to tell him about my past. I would have died with the secret had you and Bryan not come along. When you reached out to me that night, I was so alone in the world. I am so very, very sorry, but I thought I loved you. I suppose need and desire are not love, though, are they Reginald? Love knows no fear or shame. I am fearful that you will give up your youth for me and ashamed that I used you for my own selfish need."

"But I love you, Chance. I really love you."

"You only think you do, Reggie. You don't love me. You feel sorry for me and you want to protect me. That's not love. Love is what I feel for Victor and what he feels for me. You are young, Reggie, and you deserve someone whole and new and fresh. Leave my burdens and me and find the woman of your true dreams. The one who will make you smile rather than cry; make you laugh and sing and dance."

"So it's over then. What now?" His lips stretched in concealed anger.

"Now that the companies have gone public and it was such a success, we are checking out. We have sold our stocks to Helen and are planning to move some place by the lake for awhile. Both Victor and I need a rest and some time to really get to know each other. I'm sorry, Reggie." She kissed him on the cheek. "And I thank you for everything."

As Reginald watched Chance walk out the door of his office, he could still feel her kiss lingering, the smell of her fresh hair and intoxicating perfume. "I love you," he'd whispered. "I really do." Agitated, he slammed the desk drawer and kicked the chair. Suddenly he dashed out the door, pushed the elevator button and headed to the fiftieth floor.

"I have a number where you can reach her if it's an emergency, Mr. Preston." Mrs. Walters' voice interrupted his thoughts.

"No, no, no. It can wait. But, Mrs. Walters, I have to make a call or two. Is it okay to use Helen's office? "

"Of course, Mr. Preston. Is there anything I can get for you, some coffee?"

"No. Thanks."

"Then I'll just go to lunch. I'll lock the elevator on my way out. It'll be okay for going down, but no one can come up. Please pull the door of the office when you leave."

"No problem. Have a lovely lunch."

"Will do."

Reginald sat at the desk and dialed his school chum, Robert. No answer. He tried Jason. No answer. He flipped through his phone book to see who else might ease his emotional burden. Sally. She was a good listener. As he turned the pages of his address book, his elbow knocked the crystal paperweight off the corner of the desk. It rolled under it.

"Shucks!" He crawled under the desk to retrieve it. "Ouch," Reginald shrieked moments later as his jacket caught on a protruding part of the table. Suddenly a noise started and he scampered out to see what the hell was going on. To his surprise the mirrored wall in Helen's office had slid back revealing a wonderfully decorated one-bedroom efficiency.

"What the dickens?" He moved toward the room. He looked around the apartment and found the liquor cabinet. He poured himself a whiskey and stretched out on the bed. What he needed was some quiet time. Reggie hit the button on the wall and locked himself off from the world, but he was awakened by the noise of a FAX machine that was spitting out a note. Huh. A private den for lovers, eh. He bet that was a love note from her boyfriend whoever it was. Reggie lifted the paper without tearing it off.

The deal is done. You are now majority owner of Jacobson's Industries. Go in for the kill. AJP is checkmated and you, my friend, have succeeded in the greatest coup of all times. Look forward to the press. Awaiting your instructions for final blow to be struck.

Sincerely, You know who?

What? What on earth was going on? Reginald read the note again. Helen. Checkmate. AJP. Andrea Jacobson-Preston. Holy shit! What the fuck...Shit. What was he going to do? If this note meant what he thought it did, Helen Stern had double crossed his mother and betrayed his trust. She would be the devil after all. Now she not only owned VIP International and The Helen Companies but JI, too! But why? Why would she do that? Reggie looked nervously at his watch. It was only three o'clock. Mrs. Walters would still be at her desk and he couldn't let her know he was still in Helen's office. He had to wait until closing hours. Holy cow. What now. World War III. This really put him in a tight spot. It was testing his loyalty. Of course, it had to be to his mother, but how would he break this story? Maybe he should call his father. No, Melissa. Yes that was it. She would know what to do, for Melissa knew everything. Hadn't she warned him that Helen was the devil?!!

Chapter Thirty

Helen felt a pressing need to call Brandon Snowden from the airplane. But there was no way she would risk being overheard. Helen consoled herself that there was little need to worry as Brandon would do nothing further until he'd heard from her. Nonetheless, as soon as the plane landed, Helen dashed full speed for the door. Within seconds, minus her luggage, she was in a yellow cab. At six-o-five, Helen bustled through the door of Jacobson Industries. If her office wasn't on the fiftieth floor, she'd have run the entire way. Impatiently she waited on the elevator. At six ten, she entered her office, hurriedly pushed the button under her desk and entered the glass-enclosed sanctuary. "Thank God," she breathed a sigh of relief. Nothing was on the FAX. She was about to dial Brandon Snowden as the phone on her desk rang. Uncharacteristically, she didn't jump to answer it. She glanced at her watch. Eleven-twenty in London. She'd have to call Snowden at home. The phone stopped.

At six o'clock Reginald left Helen's office. He took the elevator to the sixty-fifth floor. The outer office was locked but he saw lights under the door of his mother's office. He turned to leave. He should give Helen the benefit of the doubt. She had always been true blue in his eyes, and he owed her at least the opportunity of an explanation.

"Reggie," the door opened and his mother stood, larger than life in the doorway. "Is something wrong, honey?" she was reacting to his sudden jump and the look of terror on his face.

"Mom. I....I...was just going to see if I could get a ride home," he lied.

"Really?" Andrea was not biting. "Come in, Son. I can tell something is bothering you. Girl troubles?"

"No mom," he reached in his jacket pocket and pulled out the folded paper. "I think you ought to see this." Facing his mom, he was unable to conceal what he knew.

"What is it?" Andrea unfolded the paper. She reached for her glasses. "Can't see a damn thing these days. I'm getting old, Reggie." She placed the peepers on the bridge of her nose, unfolded the paper…

Helen dialed Snowden's home. No answer. She dialed his office. No answer. She had to wait till morning. There was nothing that could happen anyway tonight and if he hadn't sent her a FAX, the deed was not yet complete. By tomorrow, she could cancel the entire ordeal as though it had never started.

The phone rang on her desk.

"Helen Stern."

"Helen. *Bonjour*. It's Geraud. I have been trying for months to get in touch with you. Why have you never returned my calls?"

"Oh, Geraud. I never got them," she lied. "I was away for quite some time. Out of the country. Just got back fifteen minutes ago." *Well two weeks was a long time!*

"I'm in town for a week. I'd love to see you. Want to go to the opera tonight? I have two tickets and just on the spur of the moment I tried to call you. Please?" Geraud begged.

"I'm very tired. I won't be good company, and I may even fall asleep…"

"I'll keep you awake," he persisted.

"In that case, I'd love to. What time does it start?" Anything was better than spending a long, sleepless night alone.

"Seven."

"Seven! It's six-thirty now."

"I'll hop in a cab and be there in a minute," he promised.

"Oh, don't do that. You'll never make it through the traffic. I'll meet you there."

Helen took a cape from her closet, threw it over her shoulders and instantly her ordinary attire was transformed to a chic evening outfit. She hurried to the elevator.

Andrea was shaking with anger. No. I don't believe this, Reginald," she grabbed her son by the shoulder." Where did you get this?"

"In Helen's office."

"On the FAX! In plain view?"

"No, mom. She has a private apartment behind the glass wall. I accidentally found it when I dropped something under the desk and was trying to retrieve it. My coat collar snagged on it and the door slid open. It's an apartment, and I fell asleep in it. I was awakened by the FAX machine going."

Andrea looked at her son's still disheveled hair. He had been sleeping, all right.

"Show me," she said.

"I'm not sure we can get back up there. Mrs. Walters locks it every night when she leaves. Once you're up you can go down, but when you're down you can't go up."

"Never mind that. I am the owner of this establishment. I always have ways of getting what I want." Andrea removed a picture from the wall and revealed a wall safe. She spun the combination lock and the safe flew open. "Keys," she said, "to the entire building."

Everyone, Reginald noticed, had a secret hiding place.

Geraud was waiting in front of the theater as Helen arrived. He leaned over and gave her a lingering peck, hoping her beguiling smile portended a promise of the night. Hope was written all over his face as Helen looked up at Geraud, and the implied request in his eyes was clearly understood. She broadened her smile for she, too, could stand a night of…suddenly she grimaced.

"Miss Stern?" The voice was music to her ear. "Good evening."

"Mr. DePaul," she stammered. "Errr…, meet Mr. Geraud Manbusa."

"How do you do, Sir? May I introduce Erica Peoples?"

Like a well-bred Frenchman, Geraud lifted Erica's hand to his lips while Anton's intense, unsettling stare melted a hole through Helen's ice tower. Her carefully guarded tower was liquefying in the heat.

"What a gentleman," Erica said smiling sweetly. "So good to meet you." She was glad for the attention, for Anton was not what she had hoped. He was, it seemed, still recovering from a broken heart. Geraud and Erica seemed absorbed with each other. Oh Christ, Helen thought, not another Simone Alexis. Helen allowed her gaze to fall to the ground, for Anton was not backing down from his confrontational stare. It was evident that he was still angry at her mistreatment of him.

"Where are your seats?" Geraud was obviously interested in prolonging his contact with Erica.

"Row six, three and four," Anton answered, not taking his eyes off Helen.

"How coincidental. We're in row six, one and two. Lovely. Lovely."

Helen wanted to slap Geraud senseless for being so enthusiastic. She should excuse herself, dash into a taxi and retreat to her home from all her emotional baggage of the day. She shouldn't have accepted Geraud's invitation, but didn't want to spend the night alone. A convenient night of passion would allow her to displace fearful emotions into something far more pleasant—wanton passion. In fact, the embers of disquietude would surely make the night more intensely lustful. For one night, as long as it suited her purpose, she could do the unthinkable and forgive Geraud.

"Shall we?" Anton finally spoke, opening the door for the women.

Unfortunately after the theater, Helen was in no mood to frolic with Geraud. Every time her leg accidentally touched Anton's seated next to her, she could feel the beat of her own heart pounding in her chest. In the dark theater they knew they both had to make closure.

"How about a drink?" Geraud asked as they stopped outside the theater, trying to decide on a course of action.

"Not tonight," Helen interjected. "I've only just returned today from London. I'm jet-lagged and need to go home."

"Another time," Erica said regretfully, extending her hand to each of them. "It was nice to make your acquaintance."

"Good night, Geraud, Miss Stern." The icy look froze Helen in her tracks. Taking Erica's hand, Anton DePaul crossed Broadway without looking back. She watched him go, wishing she could run after him. In all honesty, Helen was distressed at seeing Anton with another woman.

Bidding Geraud goodnight, she hopped in a cab.

"Seventy-Ninth and Park," Helen instructed. The cab was not two blocks away when she noticed Anton putting Erica into a cab, before getting into one himself. It seemed they were going their separate ways. She was elated. Maybe Anton was angry that Erica had made her attraction to Geraud so obvious.

Anton picked up the paper lying at his door. He could hear Springer, his old German shepherd, yapping. As he opened the door, his faithful companion jumped on him, wagging his tail gleefully.

"What'd you know, boy." Anton bent down and scratched the pet's fur. Yelping, the dog bounced around before settling down.

"I saw her tonight, Springer. She is so beautiful. I am in love with her, but she hates me. I can't beg, Springer; I'm a man."

"Yap, yap", the dog answered as though he understood.

Throwing his coat over the sofa, Anton switched on the answering machine. It was then that he heard the soft knock at his door. He looked at his watch: ten-fifteen. Christ, he hoped it was not Erica!! He couldn't possibly be with her tonight, not after seeing Helen Stern. He waited for a full minute before deciding whether or not to answer the door. It was times like this that a doorman was useful.

"Shush," he pushed Springer into the kitchen, locking the door.

The rapping continued. Anton walked to the door and pulled it open, ready to send Erica back out into the night.

"Helen!"

"Good evening again, Anton."

"Lost your way or feeling bad about the way you've treated me all these months?"

"Don't make this hard for me."

"Why not? You've made my life miserable, dismissing me for no reason at all as though I was some servant. I can't imagine it's conscience that brings you here, so you must want something. Now what could that possibly be...?"

"Shut up, for God's sake. You sound like an Ever-Ready Battery commercial."

"And you have the nerve to continue to insult me."

"Are you going to invite me in, or am I to stand here while you berate me?"

Anton stepped aside and waved her into his apartment. Springer was scratching against the kitchen door, whimpering for his release.

"So, congratulations on going public. Something isn't wrong already, is there?" His tone was sarcastic.

"Don't...oh don't," Helen's lower lip trembled. "I just came by...." She was choking back tears.

Anton was completely taken aback. Helen Stern crying! He didn't know what to do.

"Er...Helen, what's the matt...?"

"Oh...," she lamented, "everything."

Anton opened the kitchen door, and Springer came bouncing out, stopping immediately as he saw Helen. The dog could have stopped suddenly because he sensed Helen's power.

"Drink this." He handed her a snifter of brandy, placing the bottle on the side table.

"No thanks," her head shook. She remembered the last time she drank brandy with Anton.

"Take it, Helen," he insisted. "It's 104 years old...smooth as can be. Sit down." He removed a pile of clean laundry lying on the sofa and sat down. Helen responded in kind.

Anton's apartment overlooked the East River and was anything but organized. Although expensively appointed, it was a classic candidate for A-1 Maid Service. This place would never pass the white glove test. Strewn beside the sofa were *Time*, *Money*, and *Fortune* magazines interspersed among the law journals. This was indeed a bachelor's pad. Helen pulled out a sock as she sat down, tears brimming in her eyes.

"Anton, I've been stupid."

I know that...very stupid indeed.

"Why? Helen, what's wrong?" He was quite touched by her tears, and immediately his protective instinct was at the forefront. "Have this." He gave her a hankie into which she promptly blew her nose, nonchalantly handing it back to him!

"You can keep it," he said, grimacing.

"I don't know where to begin. I'm so burdened, and I need to talk to someone. I need to get some advice, and you seem to be the only one capable of giving it."

Despite her lack of control, her words were still stinging. Helen composed herself.

"I've been a fool, and now I'm in big trouble." Anton poured more brandy as she had already emptied the one he had given her. "I've made a terrible mistake, and I don't know what to do."

"And what is tha..."

She continued as though he had not spoken. "I was born, as you know, in England. For years I thought that my guardian, Maya, adopted me because my parents didn't want me. Although I loved Maya a great deal and she was a perfect parent, I was haunted by the fact I'd been abandoned. I was obsessed about finding my real parents. When I was fourteen, I had a big birthday bash. Hundreds of people attended. It was my initiation into the world as a Master Teacher."

"A what," he interrupted.

"A Master Teacher. You see, Anton," she raised her eyes to his. "I have a 'gift.'"

"As in?"

"Psychic abilities."

Anton's jaw fell open. "What do you mean Psychic abilities? As in *Exorcist, Damian, Rosemary's Baby*, psychic abilities?"

"Something like that." Helen was unapologetic. "Anyway, at my fourteenth birthday party, I met this woman for whom I felt an instant attraction. I lamented to her the pain I felt about not knowing my parents, about my anger at having a 'gift' that made me an outcast, and my desire to do all I could to find my real parents. She was so understanding and kind. When she consoled me in the garden and told me I could pretend she was my mother, I felt grateful. She invited me to visit her here in the States but before I came, I found out she, Andrea Jacobson-Preston, one of the richest women in the world, was my real mother. I guess if she had been a pauper I could have been more understanding but *she!* Of all the people to abandoned me. I was devastated. The night I found out, I ran away from home and for months I had to support myself on the streets of London anyway I could. Almost to my last dime I got lucky through a modeling agency headed by Jacques St. Pierre. Little did I know it was because I reminded him of my mother. They, it turned out, had been lover years before. Anyway, before he could make me truly famous I took all the money I earned and went to Jamaica to follow my mother's trail like a bloodhound. I spent two years in Jamaica, which is where she was born, and found out everything I could about her. I got to know my father's family and endeared myself to them. You see, my father was the greatest love of my mother's life and he died in her arms two years before

I arrived. I vowed to hunt my mother down and destroy her as she had destroyed me with her lies and deceit. At eighteen, I came to the U.S., I endeared myself to the family and began plotting my revenge…"

"Revenge? By God, I hope you knew what you were doing. I hear your mother is a formidable woman who hates to lose."

"You see, you were no more than pawn in my scheme of things. At first, I only went out with you so I could entice you into telling me what company you were working for against JI. The night after you came to my apartment, I realized I was in love with you, and I couldn't continue with the camouflage. That's why I stopped seeing you. I couldn't let my heart get in the way of my senses. For twenty-one years I have plotted this fall of my mother, and I just couldn't give up. I, too, don't know how to lose."

Anton was staring cautiously at Helen, his brows knitted at the center of his forehead. "So your revenge is to tear down the walls of JI and destroy your mother along with hundreds of thousands of other lives?"

"Not, *is to*," Helen said regretfully. "Has been."

"By God Helen, what are you going to do?"

Perhaps that is why I'm here. I believe I can undo what I have done, but I need some legal advice."

"Well, you're a lawyer aren't you?"

"Don't patronize me, Anton. You know I haven't practiced law for years." Her voice was impatient, bordering on harshness.

"No need to get hysterical."

"I'm not getting hysterical." She poured herself another snifter. "Maybe coming here was a mistake."

"Sorry. I'll help if I can." Anton rose from the couch. "First, let me get you something to eat. From the way that brandy is going to your head, I think it's wise."

"I'm not hungry," she protested.

"Have you eaten at all today?"

Helen looked dumbfounded. Here she was at the end of her rope, and Anton was talking about food.

"Come, we can continue in the kitchen."

Helen stood up to follow him and felt the swoosh of blood flow to her head. "Kitchen," she said to no one in particular, putting one foot carefully in front of the other. She couldn't bear the thought of him seeing her drunk. The kitchen, in contrast to the living room, was spotless. Obviously Anton loved to cook. A massive oak table, from the look of things, familiar to the chops of knives and the burns of hot pots, stood in the center of the room. It added a certain lived-in quality she envied. Anton opened the refrigerator and realized that his housekeeper would not shop until tomorrow. There were hardly any ingredients to create an exotic meal. He figured however, that Helen Stern would be one to watch calories. So, pulling out some lettuce, tomatoes, a few eggs, some prosciutto, and pine nuts, he proceeded to make a salad. On the top, he sprinkled some dried cherry and poured a mixture of cherry vinegar and maple syrup. Helen looked at his profile and found herself riveted by his good looks. With his shirtsleeves rolled up to his elbows, he looked like a master chef.

"Dinner." He placed the bowl and two plates on the table. Before she could help herself, he had already dished her a plate full.

"Now," he said. "What happened next?"

"It all played into my hand," she continued. "As you know, The Helen Companies was a starship in Jacobson's fleet. When JI came under attack, Mother thought it best to transfer all the stocks from THC and the Taiwan mills into my name. Additionally, when the VIP Company also played into my hand, I was prepared to use it as a cover to purchase JI stocks as stockholders tried to get rid of them. That did not become necessary as my contacts in London were able to secure all the JI stocks I needed…Almost all, anyway."

"Almost?"

"Yes. I still need 5%. The problem is…I now want to stop what I have started. As far as I can tell it is still possible. What I need to know from you is how to dispose of the stocks quickly and untraceably. I would use my contacts in London, but that might give them too much power."

"So after all these years, why all of a sudden do you want to stop your plans at the finish line."

"Because…" Helen looked uncertain as though she had changed her mind.

"Tell me," he demanded, turning her to face him. A plea for help was clearly on her face. It was a look of apprehension and regret.

Helen opened her purse, knowing there was no one else she could trust, and pulled out the yellow envelope that contained the letter from Maya. "Because of this." She handed it to him.

Anton read the letter. He looked from the letter to Helen and back again. Hell, whatever he knew was no match for the powers that were before him.

"Wha what…would you like me to do?" He let go of the woman he had been holding by the shoulder. Pacing the length of the room, he was visibly agitated. His mother would know what to do with these…these mystical types.

"There is no need to be afraid," Helen's voice was retiring. "I only need your legal help. Tomorrow I will contact my London sources. Once I have the stock numbers I would like you to sell them for me at any price. I just want complete and absolute confidentially."

"That is not very hard to do." Helen could see the multitude of questions that lurked behind the black eyes.

"Do you understand psychic powers, Anton?"

"I've been to the fortune-teller once with my mother."

"I should have met her," she said quietly, picking up her shawl. "Thanks for your help and for dinner." She was feeling better from having eaten. "I didn't mean to hurt you, Anton, but as you can now tell,

I was carrying a lot of baggage. In another time and space I would have pledged my love for you."

No don't bother. Who wants Damians' for heirs? Instead he said simply, "I'll get you a cab."

Springer growled a low, eerie growl as Helen came back into the room. He jumped off his cot and ran protectively to the side of his master. Outside, Anton hailed a cab for Helen and watched as she left. Never again would he question life's kharmic justice. There were always reasons for events that more often than not were for one's protection. He could have married a sorceress! Too shaken to return to his apartment, Anton ran Springer around and around the block for his night walk. At the thought of Helen Stern he shuddered, forcing his feet to move faster and faster down the road. Finally exhausted, he returned to his apartment. Showering quickly, he fell into bed and was immediately in a deep sleep.

Anton was standing in the kitchen by the large window that overlooked the East River. The water was still and from the glow of the moon, it looked like a sheet of ice. That was when he saw her. Stretching her hand out to him, a pleading, frightened look in her eyes. The terror in her dark eyes was even more eerie as it picked up the light bouncing off the river. Anton gasped and lunged forward, extending his hand. She was beyond his reach. Please, her eyes pleaded as she drifted farther away. But he couldn't save her. In desperation, Anton shattered through the heavy window. Glass fragments buried deep into his flesh but he felt no physical pain. The red, hot pain that shot through his body was the sudden realization that he loved the woman drifting away from him farther and farther with each moment. He was ready to die with her if he couldn't save her. Helen had floated onto her back now, disappearing, and reappearing as the water undulated. "No!" *he screamed,* "No!"

Anton woke in a cold sweat, shaking with fright. The light of the day was brimming through his windows. Quickly he pulled on his robe and padded over to look out the kitchen window. It had been so real. "Helen," he touched the glass pane. "Don't leave me."

If Anton had been gifted, he would have known that the dream portended his destiny.

Helen sat on the yellow couch in her living room. "What have I done? What have I done?" she said to the walls. She felt a deep sob rising in her gut. I've betrayed my mother and I've lost Anton. She should never have told him about her powers. Now he was scared of her. Frightened! She could see it in his eyes. She didn't blame him for the speed with which he wanted her gone from his presence. "Oh, God," she moaned. Resigned to her predicament, Helen moved slowly to the bedroom. What use was it? She could never sleep. She knew what she had to do. As soon as she had corrected the course of her evil deed, she would do what she had to do. A collage of images flooded her head: "*All of us are given the choice of how to use our powers*," she heard Maya first. "*One woman should never harm another, for they harm a whole civilization*," the wizened woman had said to her on the plane. "*The responsibility of collective consciousness is on your shoulders.*" "*NO!*" Helen screamed. "I don't want any powers. I just wanted to have a mother, a love, and a life. Take it and take me." She fell across the bed and wept. "Oh Anton," she whispered. "Save me." Suddenly the memory of their love came back with a vengeance. The lust, the passion, the fulfillment. She remembered that night as though it was happening again at that very moment. She unplugged the phone and fell into a fitful sleep.

Chapter Thirty-One

Andrea, awake since 4:00 a.m., was unable to go back to sleep. She'd dialed Rollan Hills and had since been pacing.

"What on earth is the matter with you?" Scott asked, peeking from behind sleepy lids.

"Nothing I can't solve, darling." She looked lovingly at him. "Go back to sleep."

Andrea couldn't tell Scott what she had discovered. He would only have said he'd told her so. As for Melissa. God rest her Soul, she had been right all along. She missed Melissa terribly. She was the only person in the world she could have spoken to now, but her Melissa was gone and now she was alone with demons no one would understand. Andrea felt numb. The pain Andrea felt in her heart was beyond explanation, beyond numbing, beyond her understanding. Why? Why? She had really tried. Really tried to give Helen a home. That Helen had cared so little for her might have been understandable. But why hurt Reginald? Poor child. He so adored his sister. Thank God in a few days Reginald would be off to *Insead*. It would spare him the showdown and having to deal with the repercussions up close and personal. *Insead*, the best Business school in the world, would prepare him for the harsh, cold world of business. It would take away some of his naïveté.

Andrea, though devastated, was not about to roll over. She was at war. No way in hell did she deserve this. What she was about to do to Helen Stern would be terminal. There was no way that she could see to spare the unpleasantness of bloodshed. Helen had pushed her to a state of zero tolerance. If she could annihilate her very own child Andrea knew that inside she would die forever, but what could she do. For her no pain could have been greater. What a place to come to after all these years. Such a senseless act on both their parts, but there was no turning back. There was no more hope and no other solution. It was over now.

From her call to Rollan Hills, Andrea learned that Helen had left England the previous day. That meant she was already in New York. Suddenly anger rose again in her like putrid bile, and she kept repeating the same story to herself over and over again. She didn't deserve this. Not after everything she'd done for the girl. She'd tried. Really tried. What else could she have done? Helen would be sorry she'd crossed her. She had no idea just how ruthless she could be, if forced. Like an Animal going for its prey, Andrea felt her spurs rise. Self-preservation was an enormous impetus for ruthlessness. Andrea reached for the hanger as though it was Helen's neck.

The lying cheat. The traitor. Andrea pulled her skirt over her hips. The suit was more than twenty years old but was as classic as ever. Additionally, it still fit! The Christian Dior black suit was known to all at Jacobson's Industries as the suit of sudden death, for whenever Andrea wore it thunder and lightning struck in her wake. She had not worn it since she'd fired Jonathan Buckley. Today, she would have no mercy. When Andrea stepped onto the porch of her home at 6:30 a.m., it was chilly even though it was July 27th.

In the back of the limousine Andrea was lost in thought. Did she deserve what was happening to her now? Could she really be angry with the child for what she'd done? Shouldn't she have told Helen the real story years ago instead of sweeping things under the carpet? Scott had always chastised her for not dealing with things head on, for always pretending they would just go away. The Master of Denial, that's what he'd called her. No, Andrea admonished. I've done right by her. I've made up for everything. Not only have I made Helen among the richest women in the world, but also I have shown nothing but love and good faith since her return. Why after nineteen years would she do this?! Just a week before Andrea had decided to go into partial retirement to spend more time traveling with Scott. Never before had she considered the possibility of handing over her reins, but Helen had proven herself capable, trustworthy, and ready to be at the helm of Jacobson Industries.

Helen was in her office at 4:00 a.m.

"Where the hell are you, Snowden?" the phone rang unanswered. "Shit!" She hung up and re-dialed. This time she was switched to an operator.

"I'm afraid Mr. Snowden has left for vacation. He won't be back until next Monday."

"Vacation! Where? Did he leave a number?"

"I'm not sure. I'll have to check with his secretary. Who's calling?"

Helen never spoke to anyone but Brandon. She smashed the receiver into the cradle. "Sonofabitch," she hissed as the door opened and Andrea came storming across the room, waving a paper at her.

The paper dropped to the floor in front of the bed in Helen's secret hideaway. Bending down, she retrieved it, a stunned look spreading over her face as she read the content. Helen turned to face her mother, an apologetic mask transfixing her face. Andrea didn't give a damn about the anguish on her daughter's face.

"You little traitor." Andrea slapped Helen hard across the face. "How could you? How the hell could you do this, after everything I have done for you? Everything I have given to you!"

Helen raised a hand to her cheek. She could feel the welt from the hard blow to her face. She turned to the woman before her. "I'm....sorr...."

"*Don't be a fool,*" the demons in Helen's head were screaming. "*How do you know that Maya was telling you the truth? How could you trust either of them? They have lied to you before. They betrayed you.*"

"Do the right thing, Helen," the angels in her head warned. "*You are a Master Teacher. Sacrifice is the way of the Master Teacher, my child, so Helen, you must do what is right.*"

"*You have to save the world…A woman must never harm another…I will follow in the ways of my guide.*" Past conversations were swimming around in her head.

The devils lurking in her soul could not afford to lose. Not after all these years of nurturing hate." *You must do what's good for the world; they tell you. This is your duty, they tell you. Haven't they denied you all your rights before? And now they want you to give up your powers, too. Helen, listen to us, they want to control you. The woman before you represents anarchy. You must do what is right. Death! Death to the Queen of Jacobson's!*"

The good angels: "*The saying is Death to the King! Not death to the Queen. You would think they would know the mantra!*"

"*Death! Death to the King? It only so that you can fuck the Queen. That is the object of the game.*" The devils snarled. Where the hell had they heard that? Ah yes. In the *book Eight*. A wonderful opus. The devils won.

"And exactly what have you done for me, mother?" Helen's voice was calm, controlled, dripping with hatred. "Can you," she continued, "give me back the years you have robbed me? Did you think your money could have bought back the pain, the loss, the fear—the emptiness? Have you ever felt pain, mother? Pain like I have felt?"

"You could never imagine. You could never understand. A person like you has no heart, no soul. Maybe that's why I never felt I could tell you the truth. Maybe it was because of those looks with which you steeled me that I never mistook as pure hate. And I was right, wasn't I, Helen? But even my guilt can't save you now. I'm going to destroy you!" Andrea screamed, her own words doused with poison. "You will never, do you hear me, *never* survive my wrath!"

"We will see." Helen's eyes narrowed, her pulse quickened, and her eyes, oh God, her eyes exploded with fire. At the moment of explosion the devils that had been lurking in her soul for twenty-one years danced their waltz of death. This is what they had been nurtured for. This was their moment of glory.

"Get out, Helen. If you know what's best for you you'd get out now!" Andrea Jacobson-Preston couldn't find it in her heart to destroy her own flesh and blood. "Go back to England. Let this all die now." Andrea turned her back on her daughter and walked out of the room. Tears brimmed in her eyes. It shouldn't have been this way. Her daughter should have understood. She should have given her grand-children to carry on the legacy of Jacobson Industry

Good angels: *"Helen. You must do what is right. Don't forget good and evil share a dual purpose. Your actions today can do harm to the very world you were sent to protect. You will plant the bad seed. We beg you to think. The devils are promising you freedom but remember, my child, you already possess freedom. The devils are promising you protection, but Helen you are protected by the greatest power of all. Love."*

Helen ran from the room holding her head. A madness was descending on her. She stumbled blindly to the elevators. Overhead, through the skylight, the dawn was creeping in over the horizon. Dark and light, she thought, sharing the same space.

"Mother, Mother!" she pleaded as Andrea disappeared into the elevator. "Mother. I am sorry."

Anton had made up his mind. Helen Stern, no matter what, would be his bride. His dream had been too real and the thought of losing her forever was not one he was prepared for. The burning spear of fear that had seized him as he watched her drift out on the glassy water disappearing beneath its treacherous surface was a frightening wake-up call. He grabbed his coat, ruffled Spinger's shag and bolted out the door.

Helen was thundering down Madison Avenue, tears blurring her vision. "I'll do what's right," she kept repeating. "I'll do what's right." She welcomed the madness, the freedom to never again remember. She never heard the blaring horn of the car speeding down the avenue.

Andrea Jacobson was frantically dialing the phone. She would stop this takeover if it was the last thing she did.

"Barry, I want to know what can be done?" She covered the receiver. "I can't believe this. I just can't…."

"Shut up, Barry," Andrea bellowed, "and believe it! We are being murdered, annihilated! Stop scratching your damn head and do something…do something…" At that very moment Andrea Jacobson-Preston paused in midsentence and gasped. "Oh my God…Helen, Helen…no, Helen…Helen." She was gripped by a terrifying vision. "Please, no Helen, please…please," she screamed.

Anton paced in front of the elevator. "Come on," he said impatiently as the elevator doors silently glided open. He went to the fiftieth floor. Mrs. Walters was hanging her coat.

"You're early," she smiled, stopping at the look on his face.

"I need to see Helen. Now!"

"She's not in. It's very surprising, too. In all the years I've been here I've never arrived to work before her and…"

Anton DePaul was already gone. He couldn't wait for the elevator so he ran the fifteen flights to the sixty-fifth floor. No assistant was at the desk when he arrived so he walked right into Andrea Jacobson's massive office. She was staring into space transfixed as though she had seen a ghost.

"Helen," she kept repeating, "please don't."

"Don't what?" Anton's voice was distraught. Andrea only kept repeating the words, wilting to the floor like a rag.

"Tell me!" He was shaking her limp body. "Tell me!" He slapped her hard across the face.

Barry only stared. He had never seen anything like it.

"It's Helen," she said, her body racked with pain.

"Where is she? Where is she?" Anton pulled Andrea to her feet. "Take me to her."

The slap smarted, and immediately Andrea regained her senses. Grabbing her coat, she followed Anton, leaving Barry awed by the scene.

"Pardon me." Anton eased a lady, climbing into a cab, aside. "This is an emergency."

Chapter Thirty-Two

Mr. and Mrs. Stevenson hung up the phone. Thank goodness their daughter Chance was okay. No charges would be pressed against her for Bryan Benson's death.

"We did the right thing," Mrs. Stevenson reassured her husband. "If Chance had been convicted, we would've testified." The Stevensons couldn't change the past, but they could sure alter the future! No way would they have allowed that sleazy Bryan Benson to ruin their children's lives. They themselves had done a good enough job of trying.

"Come dear. We'll have coffee."

Mr. and Mrs. Stevenson felt absolutely no remorse from bumping off the pig, Bryan Benson. He should have known better than to threaten two ex-drunks who knew how to lie in the gutter.

"An eye for an eye." Mr. Stevenson winked at his wife. "Bryan Benson could have done nothing worse than force Franchesca to reveal where we were before he tortured her to death. His blackmail and sordid life caught up with him. Live by the sword and die by the sword; he got what was coming to him."

She was floating now. Higher and higher and higher. "Whee," she said gleefully as the bright sun beckoned her. "I'm coming," she promised, racing towards the bright light. Her father was there, his arms crossed, smiling at her. Though his mouth was moving, she couldn't hear the words. Suddenly, Maya, dressed in her beautiful yellow suit, was walking toward her signaling her to stop. "Don't come any further, my dear. It's not time. You have work to do, Helen. You know that. Take this with you, and give it to your mother when you see her. Make peace with life."

"But I want to play," Helen said, skipping through the white lilies, "I want the frivolity of my youth."

"You can have youth any time, my dear. Age is but a number. Turn back now!" Her voice was sharp.

The traffic was horrendous. The taxi moved inch by inch by inch.

"We'll never get there at this rate," Anton hastened the driver.

"Want me to fly, sir?" He glared at him through the rearview mirror.

"We'll have to walk," he said to Andrea. "It's not very far now." Anton handed the cabbie a twenty-dollar note, and pulling Andrea by the hand, bolted up Sixty-Fourth Street.

"Only three blocks," he kept reminding Andrea as she ran breathlessly behind him. When they finally reached Helen's building they hurried into the waiting elevator, quickly punching the button to the sixth floor. As the lift opened, they rushed down the hall. Anton banged fervently on the door but there was no answer. Andrea ran hurriedly to find the building superintendent.

"I can't find anyone," she said returning only moments later. "We'll have to try something else."

"I'm not from Detroit for nothing," Anton glanced at her hair, removing one of the bobby pins that held it in a French roll. From his wallet he pulled out his Mastercard and slid it between the latch of the door. *Don't let the dead bolt be on,* he said to himself. The door clicked and turned. "Helen! Helen, where are you?" He was shouting, running toward the kitchen. It was her favorite place. He bet she would be curled up on the big, comfy chair in front of the fireplace.

"Try in there," Andrea pointed, tears streaming down her face.

Abruptly Anton turned and ran toward the bedroom.

Chapter Thirty-Three

"Call an ambulance!" the scream was blood curdling.

"I've got a cell phone." An onlooker, shocked out of his wits managed to mumble. "911. 911." he kept repeating his hand shaking as he punched out the number.

"Why do I have to go back to the pain, Maya?" Helen was skipping through the garland of flowers. "Why can't I just stay here and play?"

"My sweet, it is no different here unless you master life there. Go on home, Helen. Your mother really needs you." Maya reached out a hand to her protégée.

Helen heard someone behind her. Maybe they were coming to plead for her to stay. Her father was still smiling." Go now, darling. Go now before it's too late. Please remind your mother for me, just how much I love her." Her father spoke and he had the most wonderful, soothing his voice.

Inside the bedroom Anton was staring at Andrea. Her face was masked as though she was in a hypnotic state. "What now?" He pleaded. "Where is she?"

"I'm not sure." She said hysterically.

Andrea's cell phone was ranging. She didn't move. Anton grabbed her bag and found the Ericcson slim-line. "Hello." He said excitedly into the phone.

There was a perceptible pause.

"I believe I have the wrong num...."

"Are you looking for Andrea Jacobson?"

"Yes. This is her assistant, Janice."

"This is Anton DePaul. Is there some news about Helen?"

Another pause. "It's okay. Andrea is here with me. We are at Helen's apartment."

"There's been an accident. They have taken Helen to the Emergency room of Lenox Hill Hospital."

"Oh My God! Anton said jerking Andrea and her eyes seem to flutter back in her head. She was disoriented, and the look in her eyes was hazy and frightened.

"I didn't give her away…" Andrea began. "They took her then and they are taking her now."

"Andrea," Anton kept jerking her.

"I don't know if my daughter is alive," tears streamed down her face. "My poor child. It's all my fault. How she must have suffered all those years." For the first time Andrea fully appreciated why Helen felt the deep need to destroy her. After all, she'd had played a big part in her own destruction. Had she told Helen the truth from the moment she'd arrived in New York this might not have happened. How right Scott was about her need to deny reality. This was a testament that problems must be faced head on. This could have been a most devastating and final lesson.

Anton looked at Andrea as though she had gone mad. How could she have known? My god, not two *Damians*!

The ambulance shot through the streets of New York like a bullet. The emergency room was on standby by the time Helen, in severe respiratory distress, arrived.

"It's real bad." The ambulance driver's arrival started a flurry of activities.

Anton's wasted no time, except what it took dragging a stupefied Andrea along, to jump into a taxi. "Lenox Hill Hospital and drive on the sidewalk if you have to. Keep blowing your horn." His voice was authoritative and the cabbie complied. They arrived at the hospital to a gale of frantic orders.

"Helen Stern," Anton said to an emergency room nurse.
"She's on the way to OR."
"I want to go with her?" Andrea who suddenly became lucid informed the nurse.
"I'm sorry, ma'am," there was empathy in the woman voice. "That's not possible."
"Where is the attending physician?" Andrea demanded. She knew the nurse was doing her job but she was going into the OR with her daughter—period. The ambulance was one thing, but she was going to be in OR. If traditional medicine could not bring her child back she'd do what she had to do.

Andrea silently slipped into the operating room.
"Her blood pressure is dropping." The anesthetist was shouting to the surgeon. There is no reason.
"IV lido. Stat," the surgeon ordered, all the time in control.
"Let me," Andrea said.
"I'm sorry, Madam…"
"Step aside." Andrea's voice was calm but commanding. "Step aside, the voice repeated and there was no question her command was understood. "Let me hold her hand."

The doctors unexplainably made room for Andrea, all attempts to work at break-neck speed on the patient abandoned. The OR staff had no frame of reference as to why they felt compelled to obey this woman, in Black. Worse they knew un-categorically that if what they were about to do got out, their licensees would be revoked permanently. Regardless, without logical reason, they stepped aside.

Andrea clasped her daughter's hand, closed her eyes and began mumbling. A glow was passing between the two women. Face masked as though in a hypnotic state, Andrea opened her hand an let go of Helen's. The doctors stared in disbelief. They were witnessing something otherworldly. If they hadn't seen it with their own eyes they would never have believed it, but as soon as Andrea let go of her daughter hand, the heart machine stabilized. Immediately Helen's blood pressure started rising and the OR staff would swear on the Bible that the unconscious woman on the OR table had clutched at her mother's hand. Andrea stepped aside, took off her mask and left the OR.

"How is she?" Anton, who was pacing the hallway pounced on her, his eyes desperate.

"She's fine."

In recovery, Helen eyes fluttered open for a second before she went under again. What she thought she saw in Andrea's eyes was resolute hatred. How angry her mother must have been to chase her into the realm of the unknown, even into her death dance! But Andrea had a right to be furious. Had she been a true warrior, she would have committed *hari-kari instead of get hit by a car*. She should go now. She should.

"Helen," Andrea felt her daughter's essence escaping. "Don't you dare. You are my daughter. Come back and fight. She held Helen's limp body in her arms. "Please, darling. I need you. I need your forgiveness. How do you expect me to go on with this guilt? I have always loved you, more than you will ever know. I understand. Truly I do. Just please, please don't leave me." A tear fell on Helen's cheek. If her daughter gave up on life it would be too devastating a final lesson. Let me show you what happened, my child. I never left you. I would never have abandoned you. "Let me show you how it really was…"

Helen was confused. Was she was dreaming or she was dead. She could see herself being born. The room was stark white and all the people in it wore white. He mother was screaming as Helen pushed her way into the world. She was losing a lot of blood and the doctors were working frantically to stabilize her. She saw her mother's spirit rise from the table, hovering over the birthing table by a silver string. She saw her mother struggle to stay alive and she knew she'd come back just for her.

"Let me hold her," her mother had pleaded, but the woman in white just kept walking.

Helen slipped into a deep sleep. My God, what had she done.

"Where is my mother?" she kept repeating when she awoke. The nurse tried to get her to be less agitated, but she kept demanding to see her mother. Andrea and Anton entered the recovery room. Helen stretched out her hands and reached for her mother's. They locked fingers and a very weak Helen lifted her hand to her lips and kissed it tenderly. "I understand," she said softly. Can you ever forgive me?"

"We both need to forgiven. I am so very sorry, Helen. I should have told you."

"I'm glad you showed me instead, mother. I glad we are so much alike."

"What about me?" Anton looked from one woman to the next.

Helen turned her head.

"Who are you, Anton?" She smiled feebly turning her head in the direction of the familiar voice. No matter how badly she had been somewhere, somehow she must have done something worthy to deserve the love of a man like Anton.

"Come close," she whispered.

"I will be close for the rest of your life."

"Are you sure about that, mister? You could have funny babies."

"So. Daren did it, why can't I?"

"Dare…never mind," Andrea got the drift. But I can assure you, Mr. DePaul, there will be no Tabithas until you have made an honest woman out of my daughter. Shouldn't you be asking me for her hand in marriage before talking about babies?" Andrea was delighted.

"Oh yes, ma'am. Forgive me."

"Well, what do you say, old girl?"

"Old! Old?" A smile graced Helen's lips. "I am not that old. Let me think about it. I'll get back to you."

"How can she be so intolerable even at a time like this?" Anton pleaded with Andrea who was shrugging her shoulder.

Okay I'll say yes if you promise to take me camping for our honeymoon. Heck I'd say yes no matter what. But I'm tired now so could you just simply go away."

Helen closed her eyes and was again entering the realm between life and death. Life was a good thing. *Maya she whispered inside her head. Indeed, good is far better than evil…*She was loved. How very much she was loved. And now, she was content. A peaceful sleep overcame Helen.

THE END

About the Author

C.C. Avram combines the unique aspects of her successful business career and her creative talents to delivery yet another page-turner. Avram lives in the Midwest and holds degrees from SGI, England, U.K., the University of Michigan, and the University of Detroit.

Printed in the United States
32915LVS00003B/112